I0677203

Judas of Memphis

E.N. McMahon

Copyright © 2016 E. N. McMahon
All rights reserved.
Cover Art Copyright © 2016 Matt Smith
All rights reserved.
Published by Nick de Blegny Publishing
ISBN: 0692675590
ISBN-13: 978-0692675595

DEDICATION

As ever, to Kevin. And to Brian and Martha, my favorite Elvis fans.

ACKNOWLEDGMENTS

This book could not have been written without the constant support and insight of Kevin Rattan. Special thanks to Graeme Hurry, whose proofreading abilities are outweighed only by his knowledge of *The Sprit*. And thanks again to Matt Smith for his wonderful cover art. Thanks also to Philip Spitzer for believing in this book.

Then Peter, turning about, seeth the disciple whom Jesus loved following; which also leaned on his breast at supper, and said, Lord, which is he that betrayeth thee?

Peter seeing him saith to Jesus, Lord, and what shall this man do?

Jesus saith unto him, If I will that he tarry till I come, what is that to thee? follow thou me.

Then went this saying abroad among the brethren, that that disciple should not die: yet Jesus said not unto him, He shall not die; but, If I will that he tarry till I come, what is that to thee?

John 21: 20-23

CHAPTER ONE

This land is full of folks hooting to the Lord, begging Him to reveal Himself, and praying for a personal relationship with Him, and they think God is maybe like the best buddy you ever had, only better. Somebody who might call you up on the phone one day and ask how you're doing, and you'll talk some about the wonder of life that He gave you ("Thank you Lord!"), and then you'll wind around to the disappointments you suffered in the past week ("Does that seem fair to you?") And He'll listen the way a good friend listens, and not saying much, still make you feel a whole lot better. And just as He is like your closest pal, God is also like famous people, who you love but have never met, and in that affection borne by blessed absence of actual acquaintance, you make them over in your image and likeness. You can pour out your heart to them, and they take it all in perfectly, because the hole where their heart would be is cast the very same shape and size as your own.

I'm here to tell you, God ain't any kind of buddy material. I know because I got stuck with Him on a one-on-one kind of basis, that only me and my twin brother can boast of having. One-on-one with God is no bit of basketball out in the driveway. I wish I could have known Him another way entirely, the way you look up at the sky some night as you're coming home, wonder a moment at its color and scope and height, then set your chin back to horizontal, and keep on moving. But I guess He needed somebody to chase around after His chosen son, make sure that he tied his shoes, and got to where he was supposed to on time.

I saw to all that for a stretch. Then for a stretch a mite longer, I've carried a satchel full of silver coins. Yes ma'am, yes ma'am, three bags full - I'm a black sheep too, you understand. The brother conceived not as the son of God, but the son of God's shadow: the first Christian schism, you'd have to say. Judas, aka Jude the Obscure, the shadow of JC, with him in the womb, but pulling away from him even there, a heresy becoming flesh as surely and steadily as the word of God.

Those coins rattle some in my pocket. If I were a running man, they'd spill out over the ground, but I have learned to walk at an even pace. The coins jingle, and announce me like a signature tune. You know what they say about money: to figure out what the Lord thinks of it, you need only look at those He sees fit to bestow it on. I'd have to say the same for eternal life, too, and I often do, after my morning head to head in the mirror. I wash my neck and clean my ears in the knowledge that I will tarry until the second coming.

Money and life everlasting on this earth are truly the least of what I carry. Those things embarrass me. They weigh so heavy, they tie my arms up and it feels like I can't never get free of them. But I am possessed as well of another capacity, as light as my breath upon the air, and as various as the shades of green in a field of moss: the gift of tongues.

I remember one night, many years ago, after another city had fallen to a vandal horde, and the days seemed to be of a piece with night, and the nights was dark and filled with smoke as if a thousand unseen candles had just gone out. I was wandering through the streets on my own. The dark was falling, and with it, a fine black rain. I heard the shuffle of footsteps catching up to me, but when I turned, I saw it weren't but a clutch of brown leaves scuttling over the stones where the fountain broke. The street was empty. My coat weighed heavy on my shoulders, and I moved on. A yellow hound turned into the road ahead of me. He was scruffy and purposeful, and knew where he was headed in life - my brother and I had a dog like that when we were kids, and it raised my spirits just to see the creature. Then he padded down a side alley, and the rain picked up and fell in a steady slanting sheet. I drew aside into the first doorway that came up.

I was huddling there, and my eyes was level with a shingle on the doorway: *Learned Translator*, it read, in wooden lettering that had seen its share of weather, *Languages Ancient and Modern*. I drew my hand over the characters. They were so solid, and books and letters and learning looked in those years to be a dying thing. I looked in through the front window. It was cracked, and the wind was whistling around the break, like it was calling for the draught inside to come on out, join hands and make for some real mischief. The candle inside had itself a fit of flickering, as if it longed to be in cahoots with the vagrant wind. A man was sitting alone at a table, his back three-quarters to the street. He had a length of dirty reddish hair. A book as big and heavy as a tombstone was open in front of him, and the page was packed tight with black lettering, infinitesimal and copious.

The man reached for a hunk of bread in front of him. His sleeve was dirty, and tattered (in all my wanderings, I never did know a scholar who was worth a damn). A bit of butter fell onto the open book. The candle sputtered. The man drew the book closer to him. He paused a moment, rubbed his eyes, and opened them. He looked the passage over, and he started off near muttering to himself. Those murmurs came together, and rose, and there emerged a creature all of a piece, which was his voice; and it was clear and strong enough for me to hear. He was telling a story, a fable, I think, about a rooster inheriting a pearl and what good did that do him, he'd be better off with a speck of grain. The man read it first in Latin, then in some other language or two I can't rightly recall.

But it don't do justice to say he read them. It was more like he moved through each language like a swimmer through deep water; he was buoyed up, defined, and sustained by it. He abided in it so fully, that when you blinked, it was as if the language was now abiding in him. And he weren't to know he had any kind of audience, and he looked to be heedless of the rest of the world anyhow. That's what seemed so near heroic to me and made me catch my breath: the way he was going to tell the story whether there was anybody to hear it or not, and tell it to whole new nations of absent anybodies.

With each language that settled on the man's tongue, it was as if his face was learning a new expression, too, and he held his whole self differently: the set of his brow; the way he clenched his fist or greeted the air with an open palm, sloped his shoulders or set them square. All alone, he told his story, and spent his breath. The set of silence descended back on him, and the words in the room were gone, and he was alone again.

In that dark and lonely night, I was jubilant, because in that man I had seen myself: a man mostly alone, and having the kind of gift with which I myself have been favored, that matter of speech and breath and the winds. You probably know about the eleven handlers, and how they got the gift of tongues, because straight away they had to tell everybody about it. That's all we need, John jawing off in multiple translation, so you can't get away from him no matter where you travel to. And that's we got, all right.

It may be news to you that I myself have a deluxe gift along these lines, because as yet in all these years, I ain't never put forth the Gospel of Judas. I've travelled wider than the eleven ever did, and been on this earth a sight of a lot longer. I have killed a person or two, but mostly in the line of duty. I marched on Rome once, to convert the Pope to Jew. Twice, and two thousand years apart, have I wandered the environs of Shiloh and Bethel and Canaan, and Memphis, a town which, whatever you slice it, Egypt-style or Tennessee, is most always a city of the dead. I have built ships, and shutters and caskets and cradles. More than once, I have waited for the world to end. I am not a regular churchgoer, neither what you would call a proper Jew, nor a Christian, but the Lord is always in my thoughts. I have been to Calvary with him, and come back without.

Matter of fact, I have rambled across this earth like a ball of tumbleweed. I got no roots in one place or the other, and I am mostly on my own. While I been sociable enough, with some of my fellows, I've never divulged my real name, nor let slip my identity. I've had my share of lover-girls; but I've never taken a wife, nor sought my share of progeny, who would but die before my undwindling eyes. For all that them eleven proclaimed a message of brotherly love, I alone have lived it, through these many years, and alone have witnessed, in a life without end, how other kinds of love, clamorous with the claims of blood and the desires of the flesh, do surely fade away. Believe me when I say to you, for I am the one who knows: of all the different kinds of love a human heart can feel, only brotherly love, whether for the holy, or the holy idiot, is truly love everlasting. Of this, I am the living proof.

And that life's been plenty long, and plenty lonely. At times, so separate and apart has my existence seemed to me that I've wondered how even a shadow gets attached to me. Exiled from the kingdom, and displaced in all eternity, I have formed a tribe of one, except for this: when the Almighty in His wisdom sees fit to catch me down somewhere for a spell, it's as if a wind from that land and time has whipped right through me, and I become like the people around me. I speak their language, and hold my face the way they do. I know to cross my arms, or not, how far away to stand from my fellows, and when a smile is called for, or is merely sly. God breathes their spirit right into me.

Maybe He thinks that way He'll have better luck - breathing His own spirit into Adam that first go-around didn't work out so hot. I can't really say. God ain't a ventriloquist, and I ain't no dummy, but He has found a way of pitching into my soul and gut the multitude's manner of speaking. I'll say that much. Not that I could accept many more gifts from Him, they're enough to kill a man: just ask my brother. God's pity is infinite, they may try and tell you, but take my word for it: that don't even begin to compare to His downright indifference to life on this earth.

CHAPTER TWO

Lately, I've been hit with a solid wave of past. It's caught me unawares, and dragged me back, sure as a rip tide, to when I first landed here. It near knocked me flat Tuesday past, the last week of August, 1977.

I was getting my hair cut. The static on the radio had finally cleared, and I sat there taking it all in: a band of devoted followers had broken into the tomb intent on proving it was empty, and the big man was still alive; and now those followers faced prosecution from the authorities, and looked forward to giving their testimony and spreading the word. I've seen this story before, the original, and close up. I knew it was my cue to steal on out of town all over again - this time the town in question being Memphis, Tennessee.

I was at the Dixie Bob barbershop on North Main Street, hunkered down in the big chair. A couple of fellows, their hair still slick with water and tracked through with comb-trails, roosted on the bar stools by the door. One was a fat man, solid and substantial. He looked as if gaining and maintaining weight was his hobby and vocation both, and you'd take one look at his belly, so imposing an achievement was it, distinctive, familiar, and a little aloof, like a local dignitary, you'd decide a separate introduction was in order before you'd feel right about looking at it so direct ever again. Next to him was a slight, stoop-shouldered man. He poked his head up every so often like he were checking to see if anybody'd made a joke at his expense, and whether they had, or whether they hadn't, he'd slink back down, dejected, vindicated, and glum.

Bob stood by the sink and slopped a comb around. The water was running, and Bob tested it every so often to get it up to the right temperature. An electric fan by the cash register pushed the heavy hot air around. Beside it, there was a radio propped up on a stack of phone books. It was on low, and when somebody moved, the reception faded in and out, and shifted around, skittish as a ghost caught in the noonday sun.

. . . *according to police, the crypt was disturbed sometime after midnight. The armed perpetrators have not yet been named but, say authorities, will definitely face charges. As fans continue to pour into the city from across the globe to pay tribute to their fallen king . . .*

"You'd think that man'd finally found peace, but it don't seem likely," Bob said. "Ain't been dead much more than a week, and nobody can just let him be." He fished the comb out of the sink, and the radio went fuzzy. Bob gave me a swipe with the comb.

"It was three men what committed the offense," the fat man said. "In ski masks and commando jumpsuits."

"There was a woman amongst them, too," Bob said.

I watched in the mirror in front of me. A pink Cadillac with a convertible top the color of key lime pie was nosing its way along the curb, slow and resolute like a catfish on the bottom of a tank.

"No, there weren't either," the little guy said. He had reddened, sorry eyes, like a defeated basset hound. He was watching the Cadillac too. "Just a diminutive sort of fella."

"You mean short as you, Eugene?" the fat man said, and chuckled.

"Unless they must have meant his sainted momma buried there beside him," Bob said. He put down the comb and snapped up the scissors. "Short back and sides," he inquired of my reflection. I watched my reflection nod yes, and the radio came back.

. . . course I had to come. To be here with him, because he was always there for me. And I'm not the only one who feels that way. You take a look in that parking lot outside - plates from almost any state you can name. I am not saying the man was a god. But he was godlike. If you . . .

Eugene turned and the sound went flat. "Fella I'm talking about was a Puerto Rican." He jerked his chin in the direction of the street. By now the Cadillac's back bumper was a metallic glint in the mirror, then it was gone. "Types that would favor an automobile like that one there. It is a fact those people abhor any color found in nature. Must have to do with all that spicy food, 'cause that ain't what nature intended neither."

"Must be how come they fart in Technicolor," the fat man said. He chortled so heartily his fleshy cheeks rose up and his eyes were barely visible. Then his face smoothed out, bland as a baby's. "But if he were a Puerto Rican, he wouldn't've needed a ski mask, would he?"

"The Spanish aren't all that swarthy," Bob said. "Take that Mario Lanza fella."

"Of course, now them perpetrators are saying they just wanted the world to know the truth," Eugene said. "That nobody but nobody is buried there. I read somewhere they were hired by the mafia."

"Now Mario was a performer," Bob said. "No disrespect to our hometown boy, but I bet he learned a thing or two listening to Mario."

"And they were planning on selling the body," Eugene said.

"Wasn't Mario Lanza Italian?" the fat man said.

"That don't mean he was a member of the mafia," Bob said. "I know many Italian Americans and some of them have been fine citizens."

"To make ElvisBurgers out of it," Eugene said.

"And peddle them at HamburgerKings across the nation," the fat man said. He chuckled.

Eugene scowled. "I heard someplace else it was the CIA." He stood up, looked out the window like he was thinking of making a break for it. The radio sputtered up.

. . . the traffic around the city hasn't gotten much better during the week. Still it's been great for business - florists can't keep up with the demand, and of course hotels and eateries . . .

Eugene faced us again, and the radio faded away. "That's why the siege went on a good half-hour, while they held the police at bay. Those men were trained in the arts of overthrowing."

"They sure weren't trained in the arts of undertaking," the fat man said.

"Those cemetery boys, skilled as you like, they just locked themselves in a crypt, soon as they heard the gunfire," Eugene said.

"So as to be in the right place if they got themselves mortally wounded," the fat man said. He grinned out of one side of his mouth.

"I imagine it was more for their own protection," Bob said. "But they sure do know how to landscape. Never seen such beautiful grounds as them they keep at Forest Hills." He looked at me in the mirror. "You know the place?"

"Yes," I said, "I am familiar with it."

"Two of the men were carrying MI carbines," Eugene said.

"I read the three of them were armed with whaling harpoons," Bob said.

"That was a joke about his weight I expect," Eugene said. He snapped his head around, and regarded the fat man. His eyes were doleful and pugnacious both. "Nothing personal there, Lavar." Then he blinked. He slumped down, and checked his watch. "Better be getting on back to the garage."

Lavar snorted. "Of course, they'll need you for the heavy lifting," he said. "And the FBI is my guess."

Eugene frowned, pushed open the door, and went out.

"I'll be moving on myself," Lavar said. He stood up. "Not that I relish going out in this heat. If I see Elvis, you got a message for him, Bob?"

That's all I need, I thought. The onset of sightings and resurrections and whatnot. His voice had been filling the land for the past week. You couldn't escape it, radios from passing cars and open windows, all down the streets.

"Tell him that black dye he's been using don't do him no favors," Bob said.

Lavar grinned, hauled his belly over to the door, gave it a final hoist, and went out.

. . . there you are. Let's close this report as the man himself would have liked - with a song. Start with a one from his early days, down in Tupelo Mississippi, 'Blue Moon of Kentu-

The sound faded out. Bob stepped up to radio, slammed the counter, and the thing went dead altogether. "How about that," Bob said. "Fixed it for good, I guess." He shrugged.

"Well, like the man says," I said. "There you are."

"What's that?" Bob said. He was rummaging around the sink for a moment, then he fished back the comb.

"You take a few guys, put them behind a barbershop window, shine some sun on them and the opportunities for the proliferation of misinformation is practically limitless. We ought to try that on our Cold War enemies."

Bob laughed. He was combing my hair back, then he stopped, the teeth still choking in my hair. I looked at him in the mirror. He was frowning. "Course, what did Elvis in weren't the FBI, nor the CIA."

"It was the man's personal habits," I said. "They'll always catch up with you."

"It weren't drugs," Bob said. "Elvis wasn't that kind."

"I was referring to the way the man ate," I said.

11

"Weren't them doughnuts neither," Bob said. He picked up the scissors, took a good-sized snip, and regarded his handiwork. "Or the burgers or the pizzas and or the peanut butter." He looked at me square in the mirror. His mouth made a flat grim line. "What done Elvis in was those jew record producers."

"You don't say," I said.

"Oh yessir, his daddy used to come in here every now and again. Vernon, I'd say, how's that boy of yours. And Vernon'd say, well, Bob, I'll tell you, if those jews in Hollywood would quit bleeding him dry, he'd be fine." Bob took another snip here and there. "They worked him to death, to fill their pockets. And vowed the whole time they were on his side, smiled like they were his best buddies - that judas touch sure don't fade."

No, I guess it don't, I thought.

"Elvis believed in Christ our Lord," Bob went on. "Nobody can take that from him."

I said, real softly like, "Well, I guess your Jesus was a much better Jew than I'll ever be. But I keep on trying, especially after sundown of a Friday."

Bob took a snip and stopped. I figured about half of what I said got through, the half closest at hand, which I was willing to bet was about as good as it got with Bob at any one time. He stood back, to get a better view. He put the scissors down. A grin spilt across his face like a jack o'lantern's. He was working overtime to make himself feel friendly.

"How 'bout that! I'd've never guessed! Don't believe I ever cut real Jew hair before," he said. "Of course, what I've been saying don't apply to a person such as yourself. I am referring to the lawyers and accountants and property agents and so on that are ruining this country."

"You say you never cut jew hair," I said, "but I am willing to bet you've got a close personal friendship with my brother." Let him figure it out, I thought. I stood up, counted out a few bills and some change, and left it on the counter. I looked at myself in the mirror. "You did fine, Bob."

Bob was folding a towel over the back of the chair. He stopped and watched me leave. "You take care now," he said.

"Okay," I said.

I had swung open the door, was fairly poleaxed by the heat that had dropped on me up close and impersonal, like a dead body from a great height, when a breezeful of high notes shimmering over a river of blue guitar jangles stopped me right in my tracks. The radio had kicked back into life all by itself. Elvis was singing. Bob and I looked at each other a moment.

Then I nodded and strode out into the high noon that lasts a good three hours in the summer hereabouts. The sun was stuck up in the sky like a nickel on a giant hot plate, with the dial set on "molten." I headed towards Forest Hills Cemetery. Burial grounds and me go back as far as I remember, which is plenty. The road ahead was getting repaired, and the drill ripped into the bleached-out concrete, and the clatter tore through the air, relentless and absolute, like the color white made not just light and heat but finally noise. A stretch of wet tar shimmered in the dead flat heat, and the smell of it rose, almost visible. I slipped onto a side street. It was shady, and the treetops above me murmured, and the shadows they cast shifted on the pavement like shadows through deep water.

I turned another corner, and walked two blocks. A late-model Plymouth passed me, trailing exhaust fumes, and a song on the radio. Elvis's voice drifted out the open windows, then the car drove on, and the song vanished. I stopped and listened to the hot, still air go empty. These past thirteen days, I felt my heart had collapsed inside of me: not failed but definitely broke, all over again. Maybe this time around, God had wanted me to endure same as JC had, long ago. I didn't know. I couldn't say. I walked on, towards a newly dug grave. But I weren't up to going

the whole way there. So I turned around, and headed on
back to where I live

CHAPTER THREE

It ain't been easy, either, tarrying until my brother's second coming. The world gets full of echoes, and they catch me unawares, string me up and tie me full of knots. You know how somebody can take a single tune and play it all kinds of ways: opera, jazz, pop, what have you. It's still the same tune but it moves different, takes you to different places somehow, and makes a different shape in the air. There's a tune I've heard a few times since I been here along the Mississippi, "Were you there when they crucified my lord," which as it happens, I was. The song moves slow and mournful, and every one of its notes sets sail with a purple ribbon trailing after it, like a funeral wreath done up, and cast upon dark and fathomless waters. I reckon I can recall most of the times that song has reached my ears; and there now it abides with me.

One spring twilight, a few years back, it was around Easter, and I was walking home to my empty house; and that song came drifting out of a little white-washed church. The sky was a bluish shadow stealing over the land, and the church glowed so white against it, and the darkness of the flat surrounding fields, it looked to be becoming its own ghost. There was an empty bottle of muscatel lying on the curb. I pocketed it for proper disposal. And all the while, that song was carried onto the wind painstakingly, a mite precariously, like a heavy coffin atop the shoulders of pallbearers mismatched in height; its procession was slow to minimize its being perilous. I had never much liked that hymn, so leaden and somber it had always seemed to me, and never getting any brighter no matter what it promised, like the light of a winter dawn. But this day I'm telling you about, that tune sounded so sad and sweet to me, I stopped walking. I weren't sure what tune I was hearing, yet. The sky went dark, and the land was cold. My heart fairly broke; for in that moment, the song had took shape in my ears, and nicked my heart, and I was reminded how the waters of redemption had passed me by again, and maybe done so forever.

Now, just the other day, I bumped into the song again. I was in the K-Mart on South Davis, stocking up on a three for two deal on the cotton-rich socks. The Muzak was set pretty loud - and there it was, as I was heading down the housewares aisle, a breezy, up-tempo, flute and vibe version of the tune. The words were absent, of course; it don't do to be looking over salad spinners and toilet brushes and solid-stick lilac-scented room deodorant and whatnot, and have words about laying Christ in the tomb spinning around you, but the tune was definitely there, all about me, bouncing off the shiny surfaces like a wonder ball. Until the cashier cut in on the intercom and requested a supervisor to go to aisle 8. And in another five minutes, I myself got into a little wrangle about the socks in question: cotton rich don't mean the 100% cotton as you might think. It means the 55% variety, and for that little more half pure, we're supposed to be grateful. Since the girl had already started ringing them up, I shrugged and bought them anyway.

As I was leaving, she broke a roll of dimes into the till, and so when I entered the street, my ears were full of the sound of money. That's the other great conversion, of course: body and blood into money and back again, and somewhere along the line, bread and wine gets mixed into the equation. Currency and exchange of all varieties is still a particular topic of interest with me. And it had seemed from the moment I transpired in this land, that every breath I spent promised me a homecoming.

Of course, that transpiring was a while ago, like everything else in my life, only not so very long as most.

Hereabouts, a lot of breath gets spent in song. You'd be surprised how far back a song can carry you. Take, say, "Blue Moon of Kentucky," tip it into the humid air that never moves hereabouts, as if time itself had just stopped and along with it, the possibility of a cooling breeze. Maybe sit me down at the bus stop at the corner and give me a bottle of lemonade to swig, beer if you can manage it.

You do that for me, and I'd be drifting right back to where this business all began. By business, I ain't talking about this here joinery shop, where I been set up over thirty years. I've lived above this shop since I came to Memphis. In the first years, I was on my lonesome, but since then, a small office park has sprung up around me, brick walls the color of a wet manila envelope, and red petunias in the single window box above the front entry. Out in what's become the parking lot, there's a single light on a tall cement pole, and it shines into my bedroom as steadfast and unrelenting as a star stuck in a prophecy.

Most days, I keep my side windows open, and sometimes the sound of somebody else's radio wafts into my workshop like a Christmas gift out of season: the folks next door, an insurance actuary and his secretary, is mostly fond of the top 40, gospel, and the big E - you couldn't get away from him these days if you tried. And other times, I can hear the man reading out rows of numbers and his assistant reading them back. I stop what I'm doing then and heed, like I was overhearing a singer practice his scales. In a way, I envy him. His only task is to keep accounts straight, and what mistakes he makes is only writ in ink, and paid over in cash. He's got a placard set up in the left-hand front window:

How Much Is Your Life Worth
To Your Loved Ones?

His business ain't so much the asking as the telling. His name is Carwitt Crusks. I reckon he's still in his twenties, but already his hair glints with steel, and is razored as short as astronaut's. If I ran a finger across the top of his head, I expect I'd go away bleeding. His eyes are some kind of blue, listing to the color of sharkskin.

Carwitt is a fine fellow. He is in the grip of statistical certainty, and that faith surrounds him like a bulletproof vest. With invincible self-confidence, he hails his fellows, and gives them praise. He's told me more than once that I have a remarkable head for figures, and just slip him the word if I ever want to retrain as a claims administrator to the insurance "industry" – that's what he always calls it, and I picture policies being churned out like pillow cases and blue jeans and lop-sided American flags from rickety sewing machines in a dingy warehouse lit by a single unshaded bulb. So far, Carwitt has remained an independent agent, but he admits he's been under some pressure to sign with "the big boys." I know what that's like, I tell him. Most of Carwitt's business is tied in with the big hospital in town, St. Jude's. The patron of lost causes, he says.

Yeah, I says, I heard of him.

Carwitt asks me now and then about myself. I ain't told him much, but mostly he nods seriously and is a well-enough bred southern boy that he's perpetually on point of calling me "sir," but is enough of a go-getter to remind himself that we are equally men of the world. Once I mentioned some construction work I'd done at a state penitentiary, and he did not blanch, or ask a question; he nodded, slowly, and said criminal justice and penal reform are matters we as a society must begin to take more seriously. (Listening to this boy jabber is like listening to a new pair of shoes squeak: predictable and giving rise, by turns, to both irritation and comfort). And he knew where I was coming from, he said (although I weren't particularly aware of being in transit at that point): he himself has a great aunt, 90 something and still going strong, a fine old lady in the grand tradition, who had the tires stolen off her 1958 Ford sedan twice; and if that weren't enough, when the garage finally got around to doing the repairs, the tires was put in loose. The mechanics don't take pride in their work, he said; but those criminals, they sure do.

I was waiting for him to launch into some such about the crisis in oil, and the imperative to break such trade unions as remained, but Carwitt took a sharp and unexpected detour, and wondered aloud about punishment as a criminal deterrent.

Such as the capital variety, I asked.

He raised his neck to its full height and drew back - that weren't the response he'd expected either. Then he shook his head at the sheer complexity of the issue, slung his stiff blue suit jacket over his shoulder, and watched a lawn mower across the highway corridor rip into high gear. For a moment, I faced into his corrugated hairline. Then he turned and asked me, above the clatter, if I was a Saints fan by any chance, they've been having one heck of a season.

Mostly, though, Carwitt is forthcoming about himself. Midway through our first encounter, out in the parking lot where I was looking over a load of two by fours, he'd announced, "Call me Carr." He beamed like a weak new sun, as if I'd been the one to share a secret with him. He pronounced the name like "care", and then reckoned further that a nickname such as his own is an unbeatable edge in his, a *service*, industry. Of course, he added, service ain't but one arm of it: the industry is built on projections backed up by the stats.

That sure is a service, I said: putting the profit back into prophecy. Carwitt smiled like his toes had been stepped on, but only lightly, and explained that his projections are *scientifically* sound.

And I'll let you in on a trade secret, Carwitt likes to say: accidents don't happen - and I know his punchline coming up because he raises a finger and it cuts through the air in a wide and rising arc - carelessness does, and thank the Lord, because that's where old Carr comes in.

Well, I guess sometimes that's where I come in too, but in a way Carwitt could never imagine.

CHAPTER FOUR

So rather than begin with the begats, the manner with which folks in my situation have long favored kicking their stories off, let's just say that this lifetime commenced, proper, December 1934.

I rode into town on a train sixteen coaches long. It made only the single stop, in an alfalfa field on the outskirts of town. I was its solitary passenger, and when it pulled away, it disappeared into the wintry mist without a sound. My ticket withered away to a handful of nothing, and the conductor, whose face I never did see proper, waved from the caboose platform with a tattered red scarf that trailed out upon the wind, and dissolved along with the rest of him.

The sky was dark, but I could see a sign that rose high upon a hill, and the sign read:

Tennessee Valley Authority
Power and Light in the Valley and Its Environs

I witnessed that very power and light. I'd been wandering about a mile or so from the field where the train stopped and vanished. The light in the sky was soft, and black, and faintly trembling against the dawn, like the wings of a bat. Somewhere in the far and purple distance, beyond the flat field going murky, a dog yelped. The yelp cut through the air like a report from a rifle, and the sound ricocheted in the hollow of my heart. I was crossing through a field of timothy grass, crushing the dry blades underfoot, when I looked up, and I saw the path of light before me.

It cut a swath that glowed through the surrounding streets of dark, and it was like a wall of starshine sunk down upon the fettered earth. The electric light shone steady and white. There was nary a flicker like you get with gas flame, or a hint of blue, and its radiance was hard as rock. Overhead, I heard the power humming, like water when it runs, as it poured into the town below and gave it light.

I walked into the town, and it was as if that power and light was a thread drawing me along. Above me, hunkered into the hills on either side, was a maze of low small houses, each one with a scrap of dirt for its front yard. I passed a farm that looked halfway to abandoned, with a row of falling down chicken coops along one side of the yard, and a bathtub laid out by the front steps.

A whistling cut through the pines, wayward as a question that ain't got no answer. I saw the hair first. It rose and drifted almost ghost-like: an old man was loping along, dark-skinned, and white-haired and wearing a cap with a shiny brim. He glimpsed my face, averted his eyes, and hotstepped it along. He whistled long and free, like it weren't no more trouble to him than breathing. His whistling was a ribbon of tune that lassoed my heart, and carried me back to a time, long ago, with JC.

It was the day he and I had first been trusted to go to market on our own. JC kept pursing up his lips the whole morning, and trying to whistle. He'd heard a fellow whistling the day before, the sound making circles in the

air like a honeysuckle coiling along a gatepost, trailing out
before him, and after - except JC's way of whistling
weren't but to tense his lips up as if for a kiss, and then
hum. He tried to look unconcerned, head to one side,
rolling his eyes the way a whistler does. Every so often,
he'd turn his face my way to see if I'd noticed, and when I
looked at him through that white-gold sunlight, his
whistling seemed a heap more wistful than the real thing
ever could.

We went by a bread stall that was crowded with
customers. Mother had given us the exact change to buy a
couple of loaves, though JC did hanker after a scoopful of
sesame seeds he saw in a sweet cart we passed by, and he
stuck his bottom lip out something fierce when I pulled
him along (for by then, I stood a half-head taller, and
weighed in a fair mite heavier, I once told JC a stranger
would've been hard put to make out we was twins, and he
took a futile swipe in the direction of my nose, and said I'd
got that right). The baker was haggling, red-faced, with
some woman, and the steam from the oven in back rose
upon the air. I heard a coin drop onto the stone floor. I
waited. No one else made a move. They had their eyes
fixed on the baker for when they could step up next and
get their loaves of bread. I scrambled underfoot, in the
direction of the glinting piece of metal. Just then I felt a
shadow standing over me. My eyes travelled upwards, over
an expanse of crimson cloth shot through with a thread of
gold.

When my chin was stretched up as far as it could go,
and my throat laid open, I was facing two rows of bared
teeth smiling down, and above them, two eyes that were
black discs floating on white. The man's face was a smooth
blue-black. It near shone, with a perfect surface, like a
baked custard or a pearl, but black. I looked into his face,
my mouth dropped open, and my breath just left me. I
ain't never seen a black person before. JC stepped forward.
He took the coin out of my hand, and he dropped it into

23

the man's open palm. The man nodded in thanks. "Looks like you got plenty already, mister," I said, near under my breath, "and we could have used that coin, my brother and me." "All are brethren in the spirit," JC said. Well, thanks a lot, I said, getting up, I guess I'll have to settle for being your brother in flesh and blood, and that dark fellow, maybe he can figure out some way to get you those sesame seeds you been whining about. And JC pursed up his lips, looked at me out of the corner of his eye, and made to whistle all over again.

The old Negro's whistling trailed out upon that Mississippi night, rising and turning like a road with no beginning and no end, long after he had vanished from my sight. I walked on, following the path of the power and the light, and in time, I reached the center of the town. The roads were deserted, and the windows glowed like still water in the light. There was a main street lined with small squat shops, and each one had a sign that marked its presence and proprietor like a holding card for the off-hour. Hettie's Dress Parlor. C&S Automotive. Charlie A's - the Cobbler's. The street was posted at regular intervals with high wooden poles, and atop each one was a globe of glass, and the glass did glow small and white and steady. I felt like I ought to look each one in the eye, and nod howdy.

By then, the night was beginning to fade. I had walked almost through to the other end of town. The shops were placed further apart, linked by a stretch of dirt road, and the lightening poles were posted but weren't lit. I was passing by a gray, shingled structure. At first I thought it was a house, on account of it had a small front porch. Then I saw the sign, Bean's Hardware. The sky glowed with half-light, neither day nor night, and as I rounded the corner, I saw a man. He weren't but a navy-blue shape of a man, as though he'd been cut from a cloth made of shadow. He was unloading a batch of wooden planks from the back of a truck, and he'd hoisted them over one shoulder. The back end of them slid down and struck the ground. He moved forward a few steps, and the back end dragged in the dirt. I stepped out of the shadows, and went forth to help him.

He scarcely nodded as I took upon my left shoulder the tail end of his burden. He headed into the shop by a back door, I followed along in step, and we laid the planks on the floor. The room smelled of paint and turpentine. There was a single window set into the back wall, and he stood there in front of it a moment, rubbing his neck.

"You got a fine lot of wood there," I said. "Lots of folks these days favor the red oak, but for my money, you can't beat a good southern pine."

The man turned and looked at me. He had a face that was pale, and like to go paler, like something washed and put out to dry. There were purplish hollows under his eyes. He raised his head an inch and looked at me down the length of his skinny nose.

"You're from out of town, boy?" he said.

Yes, sir, I said, I am.

"I thought so because I ain't seen you anywheres. You planning on staying here a spell?"

I said that I was.

He stood there, his eyes appraising my face a moment. Then he said, "My name is Mr. Orville Bean, and this here is my hardware shop. I take it you know a thing or two about carpentry. Well, it so happens I got an opening for a hired man. You interested?"

I told him I was, and I thanked him kindly. I added my name was Jud Harricut. I held out my hand but he was looking out the window again and didn't notice.

"Don't know no Harricuts," he said, shaking his head, like that was some lapse on my part I'd have to make amends for. "Course, I can tell a lot about a man just by laying eyes on him." He turned and looked at me. Then he twisted his mouth into a half-smile, medicinal-sweet like a glug of cherry cough syrup, and said, "I reckon you'll be looking for a place to stay, now won't you, son?" I could already tell he prided himself on addressing folks's unspoken demands, and leaving them to marvel at his insight.

"Why," I said, duly surprised, "as a matter of fact, I am."

He smiled, quick as a wince, at his own perspicacity. "You're in luck, boy, 'cause I got one of those too. I'll take the rent right out of your paycheck so's you won't even have to give it a second thought. How's that sound?"

Well, the long and short of it was, within an hour or two, I'd rented one of those shacks up on the hill. This one was set on a five-street lot above the highway, and I reckon it was something close to white when it was first painted, but that looked to be a while ago. Bean was unloading it at his semi-furnished rate ("three dollars extry," he said, cracking a smile, and his teeth gleamed in the dreary light) - on account of it came equipped with a low and wobbly bed, a couple of rickety chairs, and a 10-year old radio set the last tenant had left behind, a Crosley Trirydyne 3-R-3 Super Special, stashed into a pile of newspapers on the porch, and seeping black battery juice like some wounded mechanical animal. The house was wired for the light but not hooked up, just like them streets around it was posted with lampposts that had never been lit.

"Not like you could spare the cash anyhow, boy," Bean said. He'd seen to it that most of his properties were wired straight away, and so prepared for the future, for the moment it come a-knocking on his door. He raised his right fist and made a brief pounding motion against the air. His face was bloodless and grim in the lavender dawn.

The streets were lined with the promise of light not yet fulfilled, but the land was tracked, and rattled, with the reality of transport. The M&O ran along the eastern edge of the lot, and the St Louis trailed the far southern. Right as Bean was showing me the house, a train was passing by.

He was in the middle of demonstrating the proper procedure to keep the floor in order ("You're only renting the place, boy."), and rather than cause him to raise his voice, the noise made him shut up for a time. He kept his eyes on me. I listened to the train rumble by unseen.

When I first run across them, trains and trucks and all kinds of engines were like metal beasts to me, fearsome and ablaze, giving off a trail of filthy breath behind them or over them, into the vast unanswering sky. I thought their clamor was a signal that called down the Almighty's displeasure; for surely, it was unrighteous to devise a thing so devoid of life, but so full of direction and purpose. I ain't much given to dogma, however. And from a distance, I had to admit it came to comfort me to listen to a variety of larger vehicular traffic heading into the night, rolling along as if it knew where it was going, and what coming back does mean.

But trucks and trains and such weren't the only particular of the place that recalled a coming home to me. For so casually did this land chime with the land in which I was born, and stir my recollections of it as effortlessly as a breeze rustling through green and leafy treetops, that I thought I was near back at my beginning, and my wanderings approaching their end.

I'll tell you how it came to me, a glimmer at a time.

CHAPTER FIVE

First, there was the power and the light.

I saw it every day, before my eyes and above them, in the sign that spelled out the words, "Power and Light in the Valley." I could see it from my own front door, if I stood up and craned my neck a little. And so already upon my accession into it, this land was filled with the promise of the power, and the covenant of the light. The promise unfolded in the sky by day, and by night, the sky was flooded and made radiant with its fulfillment.

It was a power sustained through rushing and rising waters, and though those waters be dark, and their touch be cold, the power they imparted in turn sustained the lights and lamps and stoves of those that were connected to it. Mighty was the promise of power and light over the land; and mighty would be its delivery. For soon, the power filled the land with light, and with the voices of men, and made those voices dwell upon the air; and with the advent of radio, those men that could not be seen were still heard and heeded by the multitudes. The power and light gave such glory to the voice of men, and who could say then what it might one day see fit to take away?

Alongside the promise of the light, this land was

infused with song. Anywhere on this earth, you will find singing, and mostly it's sweet enough, and pure, just breath tipped out onto the open air. But the singing I heard here was something else again. The first time I heard it, I was sawing a load of timber over in Sunflower County, at Parchman. The oldest men of the town, who sat in the square each day collecting the sunlight like it was a pension, and casting their shadows back like the tax due on it, could remember Parchman when it had been a plantation, worked by five hundred slaves from Angola. By the time I encountered it, it was a state penitentiary, worked by three hundred convicts, "most of them niggers still," the overseer told me once, chuckling. The sun caught a point in his belt buckle and it blazed an instant like a tongue of fire, in the fields that unrolled as level and endless as the sky.

The morning I was to first hear the singing dawned cold and cheerless. The sky was the color of putty. The sun was weak and tepid, and sat there in the sky as dismal and as purposeless as the plughole of a disused sink. The light fell so flat, and so bereft of warmth, it weren't the light of day, but the light of exile. It made a body feel not just lost, like he had wandered far from home, but worse than that, like he was altogether and forever dispossessed of it.

That's when I heard the singing. It was rising off the black and clotted fields. At first I didn't know what it was. It started off unearthly, or more like, unearthed; like the dark and broken soil was yielding up its breath, and rendering over the spirits of the dead buried deep and long within it. It rolled into the rising mist, that singing, and it was as heedless of where it went as light or rain or fog.

Then one breath broke away. It rose above the others, and rolled up, and on, and picked up speed, and slowed down. It carried off everything in its path, and left nothing in its wake; and that aftermath was not a desolation, but an absolution. They were singing in the fields of toil, and the flesh was made not word, but air, and breath, and song. I was thinking that no whip could ever scar it, nor bloodhounds hunt it down and corner it with bared fangs, when the door of the workhouse swung open, and slowly whined its way shut. "You ain't here to stand around with your mouth hanging open," the boss man said. No, sir, I said, and fed another log into the mill. The wheel screeched and rattled and near fell off, but it was the rhythm of that singing that had touched my heart and stayed there to reside. It was as dark as the soil, as blue as the sky, and the longer my sojourn in this land, the more I got to thinking the singing not only rose off the earth, but tinctured the very heavens with shades of blue, from the blazing azure of mid-morning, to the cool and steady shade of midnight.

And the songs proclaimed a vision I had long carried in my soul, but never given breath to. Folks in them were always set to shout in Jerusalem, or to hear old Jordan roll, or to rise up to a city called Glory, but only when they had first quit this earth, and that quitting was an occasion of jubilation. You can say them songs were about salvation or redemption or deliverance, but those things weren't but a bunch of fish strung up on the same hook: those songs were a dream of death. And whenever I heard one, my spirit drew to a stop, as stationary as a statue, and their words drifted down on me like snow from a forgotten year, and I was still so as to let it recollect itself upon me; for in their pilgrimage, I saw my own, and in their return, I was coming home again.

This land was steeped in the Word of God, and resounded with the name of Jesus. Sunday was the most resounding day of all: the boys got buttoned into stiff white shirts, and the girls had fresh ribbons tied into their hair, and ladies in their broad-brimmed hats walked slowly down the street towards church. Their menfolk had their hair slicked back so shiny you might see yourself in it, and if you looked real close over their faces, you'd maybe catch a spot of white shaving soap that had escaped the razor. Sundays, the closed main street smelled faintly of menthol and talcum, and the smell lingered, with the afternoon light, until well after five or six o'clock.

And in those churches they went to, there was singing, and it filled the air as though it had crashed through the floor of heaven, and no building pieced together by the hand of man could hope to contain it. Then the voices rose one by one, scattered and single, and spoke in tongues, more marvelous, and heedless of grammar, than all my own excursions into the words of men rolled into one.

It was a land where the devil and the Lord scrapped on a regular basis, and their battles were no more improbable than a snake and a bird having a set-to in the reeds by the river, and no less dramatic neither. It was stalked by temptation, and raked with revival; it shone with the waters of redemption, and was lit with the hope of salvation; and witnessing happened in relation to the crimes of men, for here, too, there were thieves and banditry and paths dark and dangerous to traverse alone, but witnessing happened as well, and more, in relation to the doings of the Lord.

Here, the ways of Lord were manifest; and so too were the ways of men, and the day's doings went by so slow, as if time itself weren't but a stream of revelation unfolded at a pace that was a kindness to the lackadaisical. Nobody was ever in much of a hurry, and mostly, it was hot. Folks walked slowly, and took their time in all things. If they ducked into a shop to fetch a spool of thread, say, or a bottle of raspberry lemonade, they would likely get to talking with the shopkeeper about the weather, or the price of cotton that year, and above them, in the high shadows of the ceiling, an overhead fan revolved, the only thing in the place to be in motion, and even that was circular.

In fact, so meandering were their ways, even in the matter of stringing together a sentence and setting it onto the still and humid air, that I took to their way of saying like it was my own, because, in those very meanderings, it was. These folks took their time getting to the end of a phrase, and then they just kept on going, slowly, forwards, but in circles, till it ain't the end of the phrase any more but somewhere in the middle. I have served my life sentence in the very manner in which they pronounced their own.

And it was a land that echoed with the names of lost tribes; and then with the names of towns I'd known in childhood, flickering and glinting all over this land like God had flung His pocket change and His ticket stubs down on it all at once: Jericho, Cairo, Bethlehem, Memphis. Just glancing through the list of stops on the Mobile and Ohio timetable that first time, I knew I was in a land at once strange and familiar, and I felt like I was stuck trying to hold on to a dream that faded when I woke.

Like the land from where I came, this was a land steeped in the word of God, and stories of family. It was practiced in the arts of begetting, and untried, and uninterested, in those of forgetting. All over these parts, old men sat on benches around the courthouse square, watching their bellies and playing checkers, or folks stood on porches, taking in the shade and sipping glasses of iced tea; and they remembered this one's people, how his great-grandmother had been born in the middle of the worst thunderstorm in forty years, the sky as green and heavy as a canvas tent lowering in a high wind, and most of her long life thereafter, she spent crashing into bookcases, knocking over stacks of saucers, and generally making a ruckus she couldn't ever seem to help. Or how that one's cousin woke up one breezy spring day, to find somebody had painted his front steps a bright and unforgiving orange, visible, and near audible, for three counties; and nobody could ever quite settle on who'd done it, or why.

Now, I was an outsider myself, and nobody knew much about me, especially those first few weeks. I remember one time I walked through the town square. A half block short of it, I already felt those eyes roosting on me. As I drew closer, the shadow of the courthouse falling upon my shoulders, the men sitting there were still looking at me. Just when I thought they were about to look away, their chins gave one swift, short nod, quick as a clip to the shoulder, and they kept on looking. But after I made the acquaintance of Mrs. Greenfield, and had exchanged a few words with her - or more to the point, she had passed a few hundred of them my way, piled them onto my plate, and passed me the salt and pepper on the side - things were different. When I walked into the town square, the men sitting there nodded at me straight off, and one would call out, Howdy, and another'd say, How's that boy of yours - Jimmy, ain't he?

Yes, that's what he was called, least some of the time, and all of the time, well mostly, he was fine.

And for all of these reasons, I knew I had entered the environs of the Promised Land.

I had no wish to sully this land again, or myself in the eyes of men; and more than most any other time in my long sojourn, I had a waking terror of what would come to pass if ever I gave a hint of who I was, or where I'd been, or what I'd done. Over all these scenes, I pictured the sun coming to a stop in the sky, and specking up like an egg yolk riddled with bloodspot. And in these scenes, if I ever dipped my hand into the river, the water turned brackish, or if I patted a dog, it turned mute, or went lame. If I breathed in the direction of a fresh pail of milk, it curdled, and if my shadow passed over an azalea in bloom, it withered in that instant.

And so, to the eyes of men at least, I kept myself in perfect rectitude, my demeanor like to a shirt starched for a Sunday. I was moderate in my habits, and measured in all things. I worked a steady job, and with nails and a hammer I made my living. I saw my bills was paid, and my fingernails kept clean. I renewed my acquaintance with the business and law of death; for death did trail me in this land like the jingle of a bridle and an unseen rider through thick and flowered woods. With the hand of fate, I arm-wrestled; and I befriended the least of all brothers, three times over. To folks touched by the hand of God, I have always had a special affinity, and I buddied up accordingly. Conscious of my duties, I made to swear off the company of women.

And in short order, I had myself a love of a whole different order, color and shape; and soon enough a hate as well, which announced that love as surely as a shadow across the pathway discloses the presence of the trespasser.

CHAPTER SIX

Now the day this particular subset of the Lord's will unfolded, it was coming up on a month since I'd lurched my way through time and space to this little town, and fallen into working in Bean's hardware shop. I was learning how to watch the clock, the spectator sport hereabouts, that everybody played, but nobody ever won. It was a watery, cold, dun-colored day the first week of January. I was taking my time, sorting out the sandpaper by grade, and by the time I looked up again, a cold blue light had settled across the sky. It was fourteen minutes to quitting time. I popped a stick of Wrigley's in my mouth. The peppermint helped get rid of the taste of diesel and turpentine and paint and the lunch you had a few hours before that collects in your mouth when you stand around all day in a hardware shop, trying to earn a living. I was straightening up the shelves, when the bells on the door rattled, and I had to turn around. It was Bean.

He had a stiff felt hat on, which he wore dead level, and it cast a shadow over the top half of his face. There were those faint purplish hollows under his eyes, and they did not quite vanish when he pushed his hat back. He wore a red bow tie around his skinny gizzard like he'd had it gift-wrapped.

He was chewing the last of a peanut bar. I could see the wrapper just sticking out of his pocket. When nobody was looking, Bean indulged a taste for dime store candy bars. Mornings after Bean minded the counter on his own, I'd find a nest of crushed wrappers, stashed away in back of the wire clippers. I knew not to mention it, and that he weren't proud of the habit none, either, because the most he ever permitted himself in proper company, which mostly seemed to include even me, was a stick of chewing gum. And in my mind, the stick of gum was an icon and reminder of his very self: slim, economical, whitish-gray, and carrying the faintest hint of synthetic scent.

Bean turned his face away, and swallowed the last small mouthful. Then he swiveled his head around and smiled, kind of sickly and conspiratorial, as he spied a renegade nail on the counter, plucked it up, and stuck it in his pocket.

"How's business been today, boy?" His voice was a little rough, caught on a splinter of butter brickle.

"Okay, Mr. Bean."

He twisted his mouth up on one side and fussed at a molar with his tongue a moment. Then he went on. "Course, it ain't over yet, now is it?" He glanced at his watch, and then looked up at the clock. "That there was what you call a trick question."

I'd known what it was all right, on account of he'd been chucking a few dozen of them my way since the first day I worked there. I'd discovered right off it didn't help me none to reach up and catch them mid-air. It was better to let them hit me with a flat clang, like they was a slate of horseshoes and I was a pitch, and Bean could shake his head, confident that once again he had hit his mark.

Matter of fact, Bean's most favorite kind of conversation was to quiz me on whatever he'd been reading that week: chiefly, he favored court reports and police notes. A dairy vandalized in Jackson, the account books missing, and the hired man charged with conspiring. A gas station held up over in Enochville. A wife down in Smithfield charged with poisoning her husband on account of his insurance policy - weren't she surprised to learn he'd never signed one - or was she? And soon, I could picture Bean at home in his carpet slippers, sunk down in a comfortable armchair, and snoozily inhaling his solitary pleasures in tandem: chocolate, and the guilt of others.

I'd be teetering on the tippity-top of a stepladder, straightening out the wood stains, separating the new pine from the antique, and Bean would be tossing up queries from the sideline below. How'd they finally catch the fella in that Pied Piper larceny down in Jefferson? Heard of where a dog's wagging his tail was entered in as courtroom evidence? In legal principle, ain't embezzlement every bit as reprehensible as outright physical theft? And I'd have to say, No, sir; Yes, sir; I don't know sir. I could see his shadow as he shook his head in contented and renewed disbelief at my ignorance. Then he went and told me himself, which is what he'd wanted to do in the first place.

With Bean, I played a little slow on the uptake, as if I was a mite deaf. "Well, sir," I said, "since the day ain't over yet, as you just pointed out, I thought I'd tidy up so as to keep myself busy till such time as it is."

Bean's mouth dropped open, and he raised his forefinger in the air. I half-wondered what new miscreants were at large in the region, when the bell chimed and a fellow walked in, and stood himself at the counter.

"Need some nails," the man announced. His face was round and bland, like an empty plate at a set table, and he stuck his thumbs through the straps of his overalls like he had all the time in the world.

Bean gave me a wink. He'd been telling me from day one I ought to watch him in action with folks so I'd learn something about the business of selling. He figured this was my chance, and he was revved up with the need to impart knowledge.

I shifted the gum to the left side of my mouth, brought two cannisters down from the shelf, and set them on the counter.

Bean drew up alongside the man, and said howdy. The man nodded. "We got the two cent variety," Bean said, "and the half cent."

"Which kind is better?" the man said.

"Depends on what you got in mind to do with them."

"Join two planks of wood so as they'll stay together awhile. What you think I got a mind to do?"

Bean winced, then smiled like there was a bad taste roiling around inside his mouth but that he was too refined to spit it out. "What I was getting at, mister, was, softwood or hard? Thick plank or thin? Inside your house, where your wife'll start squalling if it don't look just right, or out in pig sty, where them hogs can squall all they like."

The man took a deep breath and held it.

"It takes time to choose the right materials," I said. "A poor workman blames his tools, but a good one, why, he'd like to thank them personal, and shake their hand if only they had one."

The man glanced up at me. He fixed his eyes on mine, then he let go of his breath slowly, like a rope uncoiling. The line of his mouth softened. He went back to looking at the nails.

"The boy's new," Bean said, "and from out of town." He waved his hand in my direction, both indicating, and dismissing, me. "Just what *do* you need them for, mister?"

"Kitchen door. Pine. One-inch thick."

Bean took a moment to think. He rubbed his chin. "In that case, mister, if it was me," he said, "I'd go for the two cents. Of course, that's just my advice." He gave me another wink.

The man laid one half cent nail alongside one two cent nail, and studied them carefully. He unhooked one thumb to roll the cheap one around a few minutes, and hooked his thumb back. Then he unhooked the other thumb to get a gander at the two cent, and finally hooked himself back to where he'd been to begin with. He stood there like a chicken with its drumsticks battened, all set to go in the oven.

"Of course, this is a big decision," Bean said. "Maybe you'd like a chair? Or one of those jewelers lamps from down the street? Take your time. While you're at it, take mine too. I got plenty of it." He finished with a lopsided grin so we'd know he was kidding around.

The man turned to him, his face flat as a custard. Then he went back to the nails. After a time, he looked up, slow and heavy, like somebody emerging from underwater. He unhooked both his thumbs. It didn't look natural on him, somehow. He fished out a coin from his pocket. "I'll have a dime's worth," he said to me. "The half cents."

"Okay, mister," Bean said, "it's like they say, you pays your money, and you takes your choice." He crossed his arms, square and tight, and took a step back.

I wrapped up the order, and handed it over. "Here you go."

"Much obliged," the man said.

" 'Night," Bean called out.

The man grunted. The bells on the door rattled after him. We listened to his clodhoppers go clumping down the stairs and onto the dirt road.

"Hicks," Bean said. Then we stood there a moment, not saying a thing. Bean laid his hands flat on the counter. He breathed, and regarded his fingernails. They were as pink and clean and neatly clipped as a young girl's. I seen a grown man with nails like that just once, a keeper of unclean animals in the wilderness of Shur. He'd completed the task at hand, he'd taken his gloves off, and was flexing his fingers in the sun, examining the tips for faults. Just moments before, his eyes'd been steady, and almost kind, as the squawking and the struggling rose, and then ceased (for one of his hares was diseased and had to be put down, and the keeper snapped its neck with a quick twist): the rest of his face forever escaped my gaze, as he was masked against such shame. Now, Bean's overall person, I could see, matched his hands, and the rest of his whole self: kind of spare, and tended to, and afflicted with one-note, meager vanities. There was times that just looking at Bean exhausted me, disheartened me, and make me sad, and want to sigh, and go listen to some music to assure myself that the world still contained such things as surely as it contained old Bean.

"Some folks don't know they're born," Bean said - then, soon as the words came out, he remembered what he'd been fixing to say before. He stabbed the air with his forefinger once more. "But they all know they're fixing to die." He chuckled. "I'm telling you, boy, enjoy this here quiet while you can, it won't last. Took out an ad in the *Crier*." He reached inside his pocket, and pushed a folded-up newspaper across the counter at me. One notice, near the bottom, was circled, and it read:

Closest at hand, for your nearest to heart.
Bean Caskets Inc.

"Came up with that myself," Bean said. "Pretty good, ain't it."

I said that it was.

"Only a matter of time before everybody in town'll be calling on my services."

"Death is what they call a growth industry, sir," I said. I was wiping the counter.

Bean's was smiling, but his eyes went a shade colder, like a shadow passing over water. It didn't do to show him too much wit. "Glad to see you've got a sense of humor about it, boy. Lots of folks hereabouts, they turn purple at the mention of this kind of work. Think it's unclean or something."

"Then they ought to read the Good Book," I said. "A man who touches a dead body, or a bone of a man, or a grave, ain't unclean for but seven days."

Bean weren't but catching his breath as I spoke. He picked up from right where he'd left off. "And they got a barbed wire animus against doing anything that ain't been done before. Now just the other day, driving around, I got to thinking, what law is there that the Compson fella a few towns over should get all the burying business in this neck of the woods? Nobody's got a monopoly on dying that I know of." He was reinvigorated and near jovial. The sound of his voice most always had that effect on him.

"How you finding this town anyhow, boy," he said, and I knew he weren't looking for my answer. He stood back and surveyed my face with critical intent. "A man can't wander the earth his whole life long, Jud. It ain't natural."

You don't know the half of it, I wanted to say but didn't. I just hoped he wasn't going to mention some unmarried cousin or another to me. Or maybe some gal with hair streaked the color of tinned butter who'd do almost anything for a new dress or a satchelful of groceries.

"Thank you, sir. I find just leading a clean and righteous life keeps me pretty well occupied."

"You are a godly young man," Bean said. "Like you dropped out of the sky or something."

"Thank you, sir." I glanced up at the clock. Just three minutes past six o'clock.

"Weren't a compliment, son." Bean looked at the clock too. He straightened up, slow and deliberate as if he were counting back a refund. "The only thing of the Lord's I got time for is His judgment."

The bells rattled again, and the door swung open. A woman walked in, and she looked pretty certain that anywhere'd be glad to have her, brightening the place up like a Christmas tree for any season of the year. She was pleasant-faced and broad-boned. Her hair was bright red, and looked like if you touched it the color would rub off in your hands.

"Sorry, Orville, I didn't think you'd still be having business," she said. She had a voice that was rough and smooth both, like a bolt of velvet somebody'd brushed the wrong way.

Bean looked at the clock and then at her. "Six oh-five ain't six-fifteen, is it, gal?"

"I could come back later," she said. She smooched goodbye to the air just above her collar, and smiled stiffly. "Or not come back at all."

"No. Now that you're already here," Orville said. He cocked his head in my direction. "You go on home, son. I'll lock up." He grinned with one side of his mouth, and venial sin congealed on his features like fat gone cold on a leftover lamb chop.

I said goodnight, and headed across the field. The ground was black and rigid with frost. It was a good mile and a half to the rented shack.

Now, that night began like most of the previous ones. I helped myself to a potful of greens, and a wedge of cornbread, and a glass of warm buttermilk. As was my custom in those days, I ate standing up, my coat still on. I expect it gave me the illusion I had an enemy I could flee, and a fate I could cheat. Then, my belly satiated, I installed myself in the broken-down rocker chair, and listened to the trains pass through, the Mobile and Ohio 10:03, and the St. Louis and San Francisco 11:47. You cited their comings and goings like scripture, only the timetables were a heap more reliable. Then I listened to the silence, and looked out at the dark.

An owl hooted in the blue-green distance, and that sound made me feel so doggone lonely that I got up and fiddled with the radio. It kicked in with a high-pitched whine, the sound of something stretched, and tangled up tight, and about to snap, and then I finally snagged WBIB. It was a station devoted to reading aloud from what it called the Word of God. It broadcast from a room above a furniture shop two counties over, and its voice was heard in the land only between the hours from dusk till dawn.

Now, the first time ever I actually turned on that radio what was left behind on the porch, and the sound of a broadcast reached my ears, I stopped, and heeded, and was astonished. A chill of joy and trepidation stole into my heart, as though I had ventured unawares into waters of unexpected depth; or wandered beneath the shadow of a high and holy thing. For with this instrument called radio, the voice of a man unseen spoke to the unseen multitudes, and was heard. The contingencies of flesh and circumstance seemed to melt away in its wake, and upon its descent, and what you were left with was a gift of pure spirit, borne upon the air, and made up of it. The announcer on WBIB, especially, had a voice intimate as only a voice broadcast over nighttime radio can be, dark and resonant as though fed deep on the knowledge of your secrets. It went slow, getting caught just now and again on its own twangs, and poured into the night like a pot of coffee into a bottomless cup.

And that night, as I had on so many nights before, I gave him a go, settled back, and amused myself with the misquotes. I was fairly gasping when he swung into the John 12:06, and my ear snagged on his words:

... because Judas was a thief, and had the bag...

Well, John and me was never what you'd call A-number one fans of each other. Of course, John never did give a thought to the families, aging parents and such, that got left behind from the road show. Being so transfixed with the love of the multitudes that his own gray-haired momma didn't even rate the glint of a cold nickel - one day we was passing through Galilee, she called me over, looked at the ground and chewed her gums to herself a few rounds, then finally asked me if I might spare a bit of something to tide her over. John was too busy just then chasing up the crowd to talk to her himself. The man couldn't even stand up but with a basketful of bread and a pailful of fish in his belly to balance himself out - good thing JC had those powers, I guess - but nobody bothers relating that side of things: Johnny out of breath, breasts wobbling like a woman's as he chased after JC and Peter going up the mountain to pray.

Well, I listened a bit longer, chuckling at a few old favorites that lay in wait like a stretch of barbed wire, only less beguiling, and finally I changed the dial. Then I lay in bed, radio WMEM, The Music Jamboree Station, playing by my side, and, hovering on the edge of sleep, I half-imagined a dream-missive was cutting across the corner of my sleep again, like a diamond scratched across a mirror.

I closed my eyes. The next thing I remember, I heard the rain fall. The rain was pouring down so deep and dark, the back of your mind got busy trying to conjure up what kind of inferno that kind of rain was worthy of dampening down - it was the rain that falls in a dream, or in ancient history, or in a prophecy; in the past, or in the future, or outside of time altogether, but never now. It was raining so hard that the sky and the earth looked to be becoming as one with the water, and since there has yet to dawn the day that fish can fly and birds can swim, the world looked to be going down in the flood for a second time.

And it was not just the water and the sky that looked to be combining. I stood and went out the back door, sleeping or waking I could not say, for the two had moved in on each other, in stalemate in a space behind my eyes. And outside, now, all the things of the earth were breaking loose and claiming their opposite state, converging on each other at speed. The clouds fell to the ground, and the dead leaves rose up in the sky. The weathervane spun off the barn next door and smashed to the earth, and the bulkhead door swung off its hinges to chase after the stars.

The radio inside was playing some song. The notes jangled into the wind-rough night as silver and jolly as charms spilt from a broken bracelet. Down below me I could hear a truck barreling down the highway, and I watched its headlights moving steady and fast. The brakes screamed, like they always did when a vehicle was going around that curve by the gas station. Only this time the racket did not pick up, move off, and fade away. The noise fixed itself into the night as stable and unyielding as a brick wall. The headlights beamed unmoving into the dark. The radio snagged on a single high note. Lightening split the sky asunder, and the sky stayed split, and glowed white. Black rain hung in the air and did not fall.

And all at once it stopped as quickly as it started - or started again as quickly as it stopped, depending like so much in this world on which end of things you choose to take up and call "it," the storm or its respite. The rain fell from the sky again, and pitched itself against the earth. The brakes quit squealing, and the truck moved on off down the highway. The tune on the radio played itself out, and the announcer's voice came on, unctuous as filched cream on a tomcat's whiskers: " 'Blue Moon of Kentucky', just gone half-past four here at WMEM." And the lightening cracked, and the sky went dark again.

Around me, bare cotton fields stretched off in every direction, flat as the back of a hand, and as like one to reach up every now and then, and slap you down. I guess I'd just been slapped but good. My shirt was drenched through with sweat that had gone cold, and rain my flesh was starting to warm up. The cloth stuck to my benumbed flesh. My time was at hand: I'd been through enough with the Almighty to know that much. I went back to bed, and awaited my destiny.

CHAPTER SEVEN

My mind was still muffled in sleep, when I heard the rattle and hum of an automobile. The clatter came closer, and stopped. A door slammed shut. There was a rasp and thud of heavy footsteps up to my door, and a knock. I rolled out of bed, made the two mother-may-I-sized steps it took to get to the front door, and opened it. Orville Bean was standing there, square in the middle of the porch, taking up as much space as possible, like he owned it, which he did. He was still in his tie, bright and tiresome as the punchline to a joke I already heard too many times, and his right hand was clutching a length of red string that further down was wound about a white shoebox. He looked like he'd come a-courting.

"Jud, I got a task for you. Thissy-here thing." He waved the box, and it dangled emptily in the air.

"Simple hole in the ground'll do. A still-born over on Old Saltillo Road. Number 306."

"It surely pays to advertise," I said.

He hunched out his shoulders and rubbed his forehead. The box bounced against his chin. Then he grasped either side of the doorframe and everything was steady.

"This one was luck, son. I just happened to be passing

by there - got business today in Memphis," Bean said. "I saw folks bustling in and out one of my properties, and at first I thought it was a fire. I pulled over and a gal on her way out told me what was going on. Good thing I carry those sample caskets in the trunk. I gave them one outright. And then sold them a burial plot on credit. Death's no reason a man can't go on paying me rent, now is it?"

He hung his head to one side and dashed the laughter out of his eyes onto the murky light. The eye I could see was watery and gray like a clam on the open shell. Then his head jerked up and both eyes were looking at me square. "You bury him in this here box, boy. A fancy casket don't do nobody any good in the ground - you fetch that one back to the shop." He released the door frame and took a step back. The box twirled on the half foot of twine hanging off his wrist. He frowned, and jabbed the box at my chest.

"Ye are like unto whited sepulchres, which appear beautiful outward, but are within full of dead men's bones and of all uncleanness," I said.

Bean looked at me, took a breath, and blinked. "That a fact?"

I took the box.

"Now this one's got a twin I expect you'll be getting to soon enough," Bean went on, "but so far it's hanging on. Good luck to him, is all I can say, he'll need it. His daddy's out keeping company with moonshine, and his mama can't hardly lift her head from the pillow, and even when the two of them are operating at peak capacity, what I mean is up to the task of standing upright, they still can't barely scrape together their rent."

I rubbed the side of my neck, and looked at Bean.

"Go by the house," Bean said, "and bury him before daybreak - if the niggers ever get wind of somebody left unburied so as to see another sunrise, they'll be sighting his ghost wandering through the fields in no time. And next season flatly decline to go out there and pick a single boll of cotton. It *is* a fact: niggers get an itch against doing a bit of work, which happens on the frequent side of always, and right away, it's a matter of the vagabond dead roaming the earth. Now, a white man, if he wakes up and don't feel like much work, he figures it's something wrong with his teeth, and gets himself to a dentist."

"I guess then they come to same thing," I said.

"How's that?"

"Some folks get hung up on a hole not getting dug, and others fixate on getting one drilled." I couldn't help it, living up to my other nomiker, "the Obscure," now and again.

Bean pressed his lips together. "That is one way to look at it, boy." He peered around me, into the shack. "You taking good care of this place?"

"Every square inch. Of course, it takes a lot of time keeping a place this big tidy, as you can imagine. As soon as I sweep my way over to one wall, it's already behindhand to start all over. Sometimes I commence cleaning in one direction, and I bump into myself cleaning from the other. In which case we switch pails and keep on going."

He frowned. "Glad to hear it, son. Only not so much of it. You just get over to the county graveyard. Priceville. Where there's plenty of other Presleys to keep him company."

"He got a Christian name?"

"If he's going to Priceville, son, it don't matter about his name. Unmarked and blank and kind of void is the way these folks go through life, and how they are most comfortable in death."

I could practically hear God's left eyelid closing in a broad wink, and His chin aquivering with what was His idea of a subtle joke: I was assigned once more to the paupers field, where strangers are buried and the dead go to rest unnamed. I guess I must have snickered out loud, despite myself.

"Didn't think I was funny, son," Bean said.

"You got a natural wit, Mr. Bean," I said. "It's a gift and I can't help myself laughing. But I'll see it all gets done, just like you say."

"Well," he said. "See you, son." I watched him head off slowly across the road. He stopped, looked back at the house, and scratched his head. I shut the door, got dressed, and made my way over to Saltillo Road.

The sky was a cold, still navy, and my breath rose in a misty coil in front of my face. I was passing through a cotton field that was tangled over with blackened stumps, like ghosts or spirits that got caught by the cold and frozen into solid. Far in the distance, a loose shutter was banging. I shuddered, and drew my thoughts closer around me. At the edge of the field, some jokester had thought to deck a cotton plant with Christmas tinsel and a few fake icicles. The tinsel was frozen stiff, and the icicles tinkled in the wind. Cold had found itself a sound, and I'd heard it once before, the only other time I had been as positively refrigerated as this; and that had been the first time I ever saw snow.

I was in a town to the north that faced out onto a dark unchanging sea. I'd been working all through the cold and starry night, fixing up some old wreck of a ship. Soon as I turned up in there, the town'd been hit with a plague. There were so many folks keeling over into banks of snow and such, that the living had no recourse but to load up old ships with the dead, and tow them out on the cold dark sea, and set the whole kitankaboodle alight. The pounding of the hammers echoed all over the yard, and it was as if our nailing was the only thing keeping the sky from tumbling down around our necks. I'd been crouched down all day. My knees were cramped, my fingers too, and clenched with cold. A horn blew loud and slow from the hill, and I knew my work day was done. Then the sound was gone, and the wind rattled through the frozen trees. I stood up, and found my body had turned into one solid stretch of ache. I rolled my neck backwards, and looked straight up to the sky - it felt like the first time that entire lifetime I'd looked up - and I saw the stars falling right out of it: stars we had yet to see, they were so new, and stars that nobody could see anymore, they were so old, and stars we saw every night, were falling loose all at once.

It was snow, which, wandering the more southerly latitudes, I had never seen before. The sky opened, and the snow was falling from it, shedding over the land a dispensation, like sleep, or grace, or an easeful death. I watched the snow fall, and fall quicker, and it was a cause for wonderment, and the wonderment eased my aching joints. They'll tell you that the rainbow is God's covenant with His people. But a rainbow's kind of watery and insipid. It's just an afterthought, evaporating. You give me my choice of covenant, and I'd take snow any day.

As I went walking through that Mississippi field, faintly petrified with cold, I looked into the sky, and wondered if it would snow that night. Then I saw the street sign for Saltillo Road. Setting my eyes back level on the horizon, I turned left. It was a pressed dirt road lined with a row of Bean's shacks just like the one I rented. In the front window of 306, an oil lamp glowed with a cold blue flame. I went up to the door and knocked.

A woman answered. She was so thin, the sins of the flesh could have searched a solid lifetime and never found a place of purchase on her. Hair was dry and limp as the silk on an old ear of corn, and nearly the same washed out color as her skin. Her eyes were pale too. She might've been in her fifties, and then again, she might've been twenty-nine, and led a pretty hard life.

"Mr. Orville Bean sent me, ma'am," I said. "It's about that baby -"

"You come right in," she said. "Mr. Bean's been mighty generous." She pulled the blanket about her shoulders an inch closer, and opened the door. "And didn't have us strain our eyes none by hiding his charity under a basket either," her voice snaked on behind me, kind of frayed and flattened both.

I passed by her into the front room. It was dark but for the one lamp in the window, and square, with an iron bed wedged in on the diagonal. A woman was lying under the covers, asleep, like the baby crooked under her arm. There was a rocking chair to one side, and the woman who opened the door perched herself on the edge of it, scarcely moving but that was enough to send a shadow slipping on and off the ceiling. Then I saw a white casket set on the floor by the window. The baby in it looked to be sleeping, too, and his breath if he had it, would be as sweet as flowers.

"I reckon I'll fetch him over to Priceville," I said softly. I scooped up the coffin.

The woman in bed opened her eyes. "We'll be keeping the casket," she said.

"What say, ma'am?"

"Not like it'll do my Jesse any good in the ground," she said. "And it's all we got to remember him by."

"Okay," I said. "Have it your way." I sure weren't going to ask her about any money. But if Bean didn't get the box back, he'd have his hand out for the cash, and I knew I'd have to take care of it. Well, I always do, I thought: one day my cash will run out (thirty pieces of silver ain't that much in the scope of eternity), and maybe then the good Lord'll see fit to retire me from this life. Because I could already picture myself taking the money out of my own reserves, and telling Bean, "Yessir, they paid me for it, counted out ten dollars one by one in front of me." Anyways, I stowed the casket back on the floor, brought forth the shoebox from under my coat, and transferred the body from one to the other. I was about to put the box top over him right then and there, but I caught myself in time, for surely that was too final and heartless a gesture to perform in front of the boy's own momma.

"Jesse, " the woman crooned, "my little boy Jesse." She reached her arms out toward him.

I tucked the fellow under my coat, so she wouldn't have to keep looking at him.

"I am sorry for your trouble," I said. And I was. I was sorry for everybody's trouble. Including my own, I am the first to admit.

The skinny woman got up from the chair. It swung back and the shadow on the ceiling snapped away shut. " 'Thy will be done,' " she said. The crooning kind of petered out. Then she shot me a look, and stole over to the door. Her hand rested on the latch. "It's a funny thing," she said.

"What's that?" I said.

"How they got a name for what somebody is when their mama and daddy passes on. Or their husband or their wife - like me, I'm a widow - but they ain't got a name for what somebody is when their little baby passes on, now do they?"

"No ma'am," I said, "They do not." And not for when their brother expires in plain sight of them, spatchcocked on a cross of wood, either. She was right: you get a name for this business of not having something, and it draws a circle around the nothing, and makes it into something. But like I said, I wouldn't know. I got the nothing, that don't have a name. It sits there, so useless as to be positively majestic, like a grand piano sunk to the bottom of the sea.

She pushed up the latch-bar, and nodded goodnight. If I had a hat on, I would have tipped it, and in any case, I slipped out the door, onto the porch, and into the night.

The walk to Priceville weren't so very long, but it made up for distance in lonely. The air was cold and emptied out, like somebody had been singing, and suddenly stopped. And my heart felt emptied out, too, for by then I had reconciled myself to the import of the storm, that I be called to the potter's field once more, and attend the dead amidst unmarked graves. Above me, the sky was black, and below me, so was the ground; and it was as if blackness was the substance surrounding me, and sky and earth were just the accidental forms it took. The entire way was as bereft of markers as the middle of an ocean, till, by the by, a signpost emerged, and through the murky light, I made out the words Priceville Cemetery.

An iron fence surrounded the lot. The only entrance was a ramshackle gate on the west-facing side. I entered, and headed over a small rise that was stubbled over with stiff grass. Through the dark, I made out the just-darker shape of a shovel. It had a busted-off handle, and was leaned against the trunk of a weeping willow; and, there upon its knobbled roots, I lay my burden down. The body was cold and little, and the whole boxful of it didn't rest more heavy than a whitecap upon the sea. I picked up the shovel, and set about digging a hole. It didn't take long to scrabble out one big enough. Then I bent over the box.

I was setting the cover on, the shadow of the lid had just swallowed the face up entire - when at that moment, the body seemed to stir, and gurgle.

Uncertain, I drew the creature square up to my face, and breathed at it, and I expect if anybody'd happened by, we'd have looked like two fellows commencing a heated argument. A shudder ran through his face like he was about to sneeze, only then he reached out with both tiny fists, gave me an appraising stare, and went quiet. I looked back at him through the murk, and a cold wind swept down on me out of nowhere. My neck muscles prickled, and I neglected to breathe. My heart felt like it had drawn to a stop between two beats. I wished he'd kept on gurgling, because I knew that when it stopped, the next move had to be mine, and I didn't have a clue as to what it was going to be.

Well, the first thing I done was panic. I ain't never before found myself out in the middle of nowhere with a chunnering new-born in my arms. And this one was so tiny, and near blue; and coming to life made him seem all the sicklier. I took my coat off, and bundled it tight around him. Then I feared he had not space to breathe, so I pulled the coat loose; then, afraid he would catch the perishing cold, tucked it in around him again. I held him close, but scared of crushing the life from him again, willed myself to relax my grip; then, terrified he would slip from my arms, redoubled my grasp once more.

My mind was all a-blubber with where I ought to take haste and deliver him. In vain, I tried to pluck from memory the nearest house I'd passed along my way, or surmise where a doctor might be found at this late hour. And all the while, I pictured his momma's face. I saw the shadows within it driven out by the descent of joy, like light, and her arms reaching out from her bed of sorrow to receive her new-born back alive, her heart so choked with rapture it'd near forget to beat.

When the babe first gurgled, my legs had gone all numb, but as I stood there, and thought on his distressed momma, they became warm again, as with an influx of blood. I stepped forward, gingerly, barely seeming to touch the ground at first. My mind weren't hardly connected with my feet just then, and bare two steps into my journey back to Old Saltillo Road, I'd near walked into that fresh-dug grave. I teetered an instant on its edge, a breath away from tumbling shin-deep into its small void. Then, just in time, something caught me. Like an unseen hand, it steadied my shoulder, and drew me to a stop; and I did not fall, but regained myself, and him.

I clutched the baby tighter, and stood looking into the empty grave. It did gape; and so too did my heart, yawning but in perfect marvelment. Hollowed-out, and hallowed, be that ground: a recognition came upon me like a benediction, and I kept myself unmoving the better to receive it. My heart went from soft to keen, from panicked doubt to elevated fervor; and, with a sense of profound duty bearing down upon me, it beat louder but more steady deep inside my chest. Had not this boy just risen from the dead? Did not an empty grave lay there before my eyes? In all my years, I had come across such a prospect but once.

I set the baby down upon the ground, and, overcome, I had to set myself down beside him. Though that night was dark, my heart was pierced with light; and not even a mountain of diamonds glittering in some winter sun could exert such near unbearable brilliance. So overpowering was the revelation that my soul was like to swooning, and a twinge of dizziness swept over my entire being. Providence had bestowed the gift of this boy's life for a second time; and Providence had taken care to deliver him from his momma unto me. It had summoned him outside the circle of ordinary life, and insisted he join, in that place, with me. And Providence had presented me with the last vista of my first lifetime all over again, the empty grave; made me totter on its brink, and drew me back from it at last. The Lord was sending me a sign, and with the prospect of a second coming, came the prospect of my second chance. The chill wind descended yet upon me, elating, and chastising, and holy. I dared not look upwards, to its source, but my shoulders squared to meet it, and my soul did gather, like a muscle wanting to flex.

There weren't nothing else to do. I buried the box in quick time, for I was bound to bring the boy home, and raise him as my own. It was the Lord's will, vouchsafed as clear to me as if my own brother had been standing there before me, in the shadows of the garden gate, waiting to receive my kiss.

CHAPTER EIGHT

I suppose I should have been grateful, the way he came to. There was no hunting around the marshweeds, a kiddy floating among the rushes, the sodden feet and obligatory exclaim of surprise and, of course, some queen who was able to catch herself a ritzy husband but couldn't have a child. Or another of his favorites, sticking a star up in the east and seeing how long it takes everybody to follow it. God spared me a measure of oldies this time, I'll grant you that much. Give or take the odd bluegrass tune.

I expect I hardly knew what I was in for just then, charged with the raising of a miracle infant. I set him down upon my bed. Then I warmed the critter up some milk and let him guzzle, greedy and fumble-lipped; and providing for his needs that night did seem so simple. Nowadays, of course, a man without a woman but with a baby sounds like one of those fool movie plots the big E got himself into and couldn't get out of till he opened his yap and hollered some songs. You'd be an idiot to try to get away with the set-up these days - soon as you knew what was happening, you'd get a knock on the door from a social worker with a degree from Mississippi State, and an opinion, and that's all you'd need. As it was, I shortly concluded that I must spirit Jesse out of town for a bit, so as to obscure the origins of his birth, and fulfill our linked and manifest destiny.

This last was foretold to me by a vision that played out before my half-wakeful eyes. After I watched him guzzle some more, look me in the eye, and fall asleep, I lit the oil lamp, and set myself down in the chair beside it. I took a swig from a brown bottle of my own. The lamplight wavered as if a wind from some unseen horizon was bearing down upon it, and it flickered, like the light behind your eyes when you totter on the edge of sleep.

The light made shadows, and the shadows trembled. I sat, my head bowed, as one stupefied by some knowledge about to be imparted. I turned my head, and in the shadows I seemed to see myself. I had a baby bundled up in my arms, and we were boarding a train in Tupelo station. The train went rolling down the tracks, a line of dark trees to either side, and a pyramid rose briefly on the horizon, and faded. Then the train came rolling back the other way, and it drew to a stop at the door of our little shack. The trees were stirring in the breeze, and just breaking into bud. The blossoms opened before me all at once, until I was faced with a field of brightness, and I saw a man before a crowd. He wore a robe of white so radiant it was like a length of snowfall stitched up with starlight, and he came into their presence singing. I saw the faces in the crowd, and the man inspired love, and something a shade beyond. And at that, I was jolted back into wakefulness, to a room full of dark. The lamp had just blown out. Thus it was ordained: a flight and a return for me and Jesse; and later, the boy to lead a movement of faith and love the likes of which the world had seen but once.

And the hope of the millennium quickened inside of me, and could not be stilled despite my best efforts. For it hit me like a hailstone to the heart: the second thousand years was drawing close, and would fall within the threescore years and ten of one just born – or one just born and died and come back to life. I could barely articulate in my own mind, the hope that if I were to deliver him to exultant manhood, and set him on the path of making known the way of the Lord, my ceaseless wanderings would be at an end. It was the sensation of busting out of a present that had already had its consequence, and felt like I was taking an exit out of time, and into eternity; like a dream, I'd say, but in a dream, you don't generally feel your feet slapping the cold hard ground in thin-soled shoes, or the rain fall smack in your eye, unless it turns out to be a piece of a star, that's the way dreams are. And mindful of how the knowledge of his marking out had near crushed JC even as boy, burdening him worse than any cross of wood, I vowed young Jesse would be raised innocent of his past, and fate to come: and neither by look nor word nor deed would I divulge this knowledge to him, or to any other.

I made to collect myself, and watched Jesse nestled up on the quilt. He was breathing regular and easy, and it was hard to picture him being marked out for anything more special than an everyday kind of life. His hands were raised up aside his head, and they stiffened into fists a moment, then went soft. The moon was a sliver of light wedged in one corner of the window, and the stars were scattered across the cold black sky as if somebody'd been playing with them and forgot to put them away. I could have used a nap myself. But I had to hitch my overalls back up, and head over to Bean's. Seeing to the practicalities that would allow the foretold to come to pass was still my lookout, as it had been from the first, and if I was to come back to Tupelo, I'd have to set my affairs in order. I kept my eyes on Jesse all the while I was getting ready. His skin was thin, and bluish white, like skimmed milk. He waved his arms about, as if fighting off sleep and wakefulness both, and by the time I'd fastened the hooks of my overalls proper, I'd swear that he was chuckling.

Bean was standing out by his porch, poking at the frozen ground. The sky was just beginning to drain itself of dark. He was holding a rotting onion up to his eye and giving it a dirty look. He lowered it when he saw me coming. I told him I had some trouble that needed tending to straightaway.

"What kind of trouble?" he said, a hard glint of interest in his eye. He had a toothpick sticking out of his mouth, and he jimmied it to one side. "You get some poor girl in the family way, boy?" His mouth jerked up at both ends in a semblance of a smile but his eyes just kept watching me.

"No sir," I said. "Nothing like that. It's my momma, down by Cairo way. She ain't doing too good, sir. I been meaning to tell you before, and now I ain't got no choice."

"That a fact?" Bean said.

"And my daddy's not been heard from for months. Lit out one night, said he was looking for work. Maybe he's found it - nobody knows but the good Lord, and he sure ain't saying."

"So what is it you want from me, boy?"

"I'll be needing to leave town tonight, sir."

Bean's lips made a line of gray. I pressed on. "I sure would appreciate it if I knew I was coming back to work for you."

Bean flashed his teeth, obliged by social convention to smile. "You been here less than four weeks, son. You tell me you're leaving, and I bet you can't even tell me for how long."

"I know it's a lot to ask. But I wanted to tell you what I had to do. And anyhow, couldn't just steal away, without coming by. I owe you that much."

"You owe me a heck of a lot more, boy," Bean said. "But I'll tell you what I'm going to do. You want my goodwill, you got to show me some yourself. You go on paying me that rent on the house, and if the job's still open when you decide to trundle back this way, you can have it back. That's the dead-level best I can do." He cocked up his eyebrows and levered the toothpick at an angle to match. "There sure are a lot of hungry men hereabouts who'd love to snatch up the job you're throwing over."

"And I expect most of them know just what kind of boss you are, sir." I kept my eyes round and my tone without mirth.

Bean raised his chin, as if his Adam's apple was equipped for sniffing out disrespect. "We'll just have to see, Jud," he said finally. "Most boys making your proposition, I'd just say, been nice knowing you, son, you're on your own. But there's something I like about you."

"Thank you, sir."

"As well as something I don't."

"They may turn out to be one in the same thing," I said, and before he could say anything, went on. "This here's the cash for that burial box. Those folks liked it so much they forked right over for it."

Bean's hand snapped up the roll of ones, and slipped it into his pocket. His throat appraised me once more. "You're a good fetch-it boy, I'll say that much. So maybe I'll see you and maybe I won't. February rent's due on the twenty-fifth." Bean turned back to his onion patch. "Good luck with your momma," he said. He pitched the rotten onion across the yard. "A boy's only got one of them."

Jesse and I stole away on the 6:38 AM heading south. Jesse slept the whole way through. When we pulled up aside a sign that read "Cairo," the train chugged to a complete stop, and we slipped out. I stood there in a yellowed field turned brown in the cold. I drifted amidst the coxtails and the timothy grass, and wondered which way to go.

CHAPTER NINE

Six and a half weeks later, when I returned to Tupelo with Jesse in my arms, I knew I might have some explaining to do and I was pretty well prepared. A stint doing odd jobs in Cairo - the oddest was when there was one *heh-heh*; I saw humor had never gone out of style in Egypt land - left me time to ruminate. I had fled into Egypt with my father, mother and brother a long time ago, and I was something of an old hand at the business.

I knew it was time to return when the light lingered longer at dusk, and mustard greens showed up as the side dish in the Pharaoh Diner luncheon specials. As the man tells it, "Out of Egypt have I called my son" - say what you like about the Almighty, He certainly is a card.

As I had noted upon my first glimpse of the M&O timetable, the names of the towns and the hamlets echoed the landscape of my first ramble on this earth. I could travel from Nazareth to Memphis all in a single day, and this whole state was like a jumbled up atlas of time, as much as of place, and mostly it felt each one was in suspension, and abeyance. Just browsing over the schedule as we rolled back towards Tupelo, into the deep blue south, the south as deep as your dreams, my first sojourn in a Cairo-land flickered into vision, in the dark in back of my eyes.

That time, we were coming into town by donkey. We'd been in the country more than three years solid by then, roaming around and having many adventures with leprosy and drought and famine and such. JC's bathwater had cured a girl a town back, and when the news hit and the local idols fell to the ground, and smashed into a million pieces, Joseph somehow got the notion it was time we pack on up and move on. The road was dusty, and the trees hung listlessly to either side of us, like the heads of thirsty beasts languishing by a fence. JC and I were sitting on the second donkey, atop a bag of clothes, and we were jabbering away.

"Next time you take a soak," I said, "you ought to bottle the water up and give to the sickhouse."

JC grinned. His front tooth had gotten yanked out the day before, when he held the goat's rope in his mouth, and the goat spied an ox up ahead, and gave off with a start. "I poured it into the ground this morning, and up sprung a fountain," he said. He had a lisp. "Tall as you or me."

"That big?" I said.

"Uh-huh."

"Mama ought to have washed our own clothes in it," I said. "Leastways a handkerchief."

Mother turned her head around to us. She was lurching with the gait of the donkey, but her mouth stayed flat and level, like an unforgiving horizon. Her face shone with sweat so fine it looked like a kind of light. "Jud?" she said.

"Yes, mama?"

"You hush up."

"Yes, mama."

Mother turned around again. I pulled my hat down lower and hushed up.

JC said, "See, you better do what I say." Then he started humming, a kind of thin, piping babble that always hinted it would run out of breath but never got around to it, and that would have driven near anybody crazy. I kept still. When he was rounding the end of the second chorus, he stopped in mid-bleat. "This'll be some fun," he said. He propped himself up on the donkey, his feet restationed under his butt, and reached his arms out. "Lookyhere, we'll get us a lick of that honey you're so crazy about. I saw her put it in the bottom of that bundle." JC fooled with the backstraps on the donkey in front. A bag of provisions started coming loose.

"You keep still," I said. "I am tired of getting an earful on account of you."

JC ignored me and kept right at it. His mouth was scrunched to one side, so intent was he on his labor of foolishness, and he kept at it until the bundle hung by one twist of the strap. We looked at each other and held our breath, like that would help. We watched the strap go slack. The bundle spilled to the ground. A flask of wine rolled out, dashed against a stone, and cracked open. JC jumped back and sat himself down again. The donkey ahead stopped short. Mother cried out. She slid to the road like a parcel of laundry spilling into the river, put her head against the donkey's neck, and burst into tears.

"Traveling's hard on a woman," Joseph said afterwards, when he'd come around the back to us. He tried to smile, but his face wasn't buying, so he settled on a wink. "Us men, we got to understand. Your mama ain't used to this kind of life."

"I know that, daddy," I said. I called him that on purpose, because it seemed to make him feel good, and besides so far as I was concerned, he deserved the title more than most other daddies I heard tell about.

"He ain't my daddy," JC said sullenly, and he stared into the falling dark.

"If he was, we'd all have ourselves an easier life," I said.

"An easy life don't mean a darned thing, son," my daddy said. He was fixing the halter. He paused a moment. "But come to think of it, neither does a hard one." His mouth folded into a small grin, and he went ahead to lead the front donkey.

A little while later, an old man came towards us on the road. He said as we approached, he could hear a great noise, like the sound of a king with a great army and the trumpets sounding. He looked all around him and saw nothing but night. JC and I stayed in back. The old man took a step closer to my momma and daddy. His eyes was blue, and one had a milky patch of white slipping all over it. He was looking up at some particular patch of sky high over my left shoulder. His mouth was loose and wobbly.

"Now where is that king?" he demanded. His voice was as cracked and worn-out as a tract of parched earth. I looked into his eyes more close, and I reckon he was near blind.

Joseph put his hand on my mother's arm. "Well, sir," he said, "I reckon he'll be coming along after us." And the four of us, we stayed on the road, and went on into the city of Memphis.

And there was a Memphis on this very train line, if you stayed with it the whole way, and Canaan and Bethany and Shiloh to boot. I read those names as I hurtled through the darkened land, Jesse in the crook of my arm, as heavy as a piece of ripening fruit, and again I felt a stab of recognition and hope through my stomach, my heart, and any other internal organ you could name, and the thought was taking form and knitting itself up, like a wound you been carrying around for some time - that for better or worse, the first was nearing the last, and my time had come.

The train pulled into Tupelo on a March morning washed soft and gray with rain. I gathered up Jes, and dropped by Bean's Hardware. Bean was in the yard inspecting some lengths of timber. A woman was with him, taking her leave but lingering on. Her voice was high and light, and it tingled in the air like a wind chime. That jar of pickles'll be a right treat, she was saying, and her voice went up as though she was asking a question. Bean was finishing the last of a candy bar. He gave a mighty last chew, and a big swallow, and he licked the ends of his fingers, indicating, I knew, and I wonder if she knew, that he didn't consider himself to be in proper company no more. The woman was spindly, and yellow-haired, and dressed all in brown. When she turned, I saw her face was sweet and desperate, fragile as a half-crushed flower, and it was full of bright-ish things that swept upwards then down - lips and brows and lashes. Bean did not give her a glance as she picked her way among the lumber. I nodded as she passed, and she looked right quick at the ground like nobody was supposed to see her, so they couldn't, and hadn't, and she hurried on.

Bean seemed a mite surprised to see me. He didn't bother looking at Jesse none.

"You sure are lucky, boy," Bean said. "Another fella done taken your job - and for a dollar less a week." Bean paused and grinned like grinning was a poison spreading through his system and he had to sweat it out. "But wouldn't you know it - his daddy got sick and right off he went, just like that. Ain't that something?" He swallowed his grin, and it went down his throat where I had no doubt he could burp it back at will in some poor working man's face. His eyes finally fell on Jesse, then he frowned, and looked back at me. "Job's yours if you want it, son. Start next week," he said. "At the new wages."

I said okay, and went on home.

The trees were just into bud, weak, waxy and yellow-green, and when I turned the key in the door of my shack, it was just as my vision foretold. Jesse gurgled and laughed. I chucked him under the chin and he chunnered. I would have to remember henceforth to address him not as Jesse but as James, after "Jesse James," a name I chose on account of that man was yet another betrayed by a confederate, only I had nothing to do with it, so it made me feel absolved and kind of pure just to look at him. I wrote out his name and looked at it: Jesse James Iscariot, to use the scribblers's form of my surname: a handy-dandy formulation of betrayal spelled forwards and backwards, done and undone.

CHAPTER TEN

I told the folks who would listen, Mr. Greenfield, who ran the grocery shop a few streets over, and his wife, to name two, how it turned out my mother had been in a family way when my daddy left her, and how, advanced in years for such an event, she had passed away giving birth. And how my daddy was to never know about his second son, having himself passed away the month previous, and how, of course, I now had to take over. And how my daddy had gone north looking for work but the weather just carried him away, it was so perishing cold, and the people's manners up there even colder. I told them how terse the landlady's note had been, as if every word took a year off her life, and a dollar out of her bank account. Her one concern was seeing that the room's rent was paid up in full. The day I let loose with that one, I came home and found a fresh rhubarb pie slipped in with my purchases.

As far as everyone else was concerned, I had myself a little brother. But so implicated was I in his life, I felt more like I had a son. I allowed, late that first night back as I fell asleep, as to how I might do better than God Himself managed on that score, not meaning any disrespect - because when in my entire dark pilgrimage on this earth did I ever have time to be disrespectful? In the beginning, I was too busy listening to my parents, or my teachers, people who knew better, and later on, I had to build cribs, and shutters, and tables with my father. Some of those pieces came out better than others, I admit, especially when in the middle of piecing the thing together, I had to run out to look for my brother and see what trouble he was getting himself into, bobbing along in the desert and upsetting the locals. Of course, I didn't have time to cook up my own doctrines, and parables involving mustard seeds and yeast and whatnot. Maybe that's why I was in such disfavor. Nobody ever stubbed their toe on a slipshod parable, or caught their sleeve on a slapdash figure of speech - I should've gone into the parable business myself. That's where I really went wrong. Nobody's ever hung helpless from the arms of a metaphor.

Anyhow, one day soon after my return, Mrs. Greenfield came by the house, concerned, she said, on account of my being in possession of a young one. She looked like she'd been leading a good life on this earth, and she had a solid accumulation of flesh to prove it. Her full name was Mrs. Lucy Oleta Greenfield. She laid down every syllable precisely and proudly, like a formal place setting of silverware, and I could tell she didn't get much occasion to say the entire thing out loud since everybody hereabouts had already known each other since before they was born.

"Over the years, I have minded a number of little children in town, Mr. Harricut," she said. "And I love doing it - it don't even seem like work." She paused. "I charge seventy cents a week."

"That sounds fine, Mrs. Greenfield," I said. I was holding him in the crook of my arm. "I expect Jimmy'll think so too."

She leaned over, chucked him under the chin, and said, "Ain't you cute!"

He gurgled, rolled his head back, and looked at me.

"Well, little Jimmy," Mrs. Greenfield said, "I best be on my way." She stood and straightened her skirt. It was made of some stiff, shiny plum-colored material. "It *is* a Sunday." The "is" came out a little scented, like she'd rubbed it with lemon polish. Then she added, real casual, "I belong to the Assembly of God Church. Maybe I'll see you there."

I nodded but said nothing. I looked down at my feet and set them to work nudging each other like a pair of high-spirited pups at play.

She headed down the porch steps, turned, and squinted up at me in the winter sunlight. "There are plenty of other churches in town. I'm sure some nice people go to them too."

So early each weekday morning, she fetched Jesse, and gathered him into her little brood. I wondered if anybody in town would catch on, and notice anything amiss or familiar about the infant in my care. But no one ever did. When I was on my dinner break, I'd walk in town to get a newspaper, and by the end of second week, one or the other of the men sitting by the courthouse was saying howdy to me, and asking about my boy.

And whatever she was telling folks about me, Mrs. Greenfield also took to telling me about Bean: a story here, with her head cocked to one side as she buttoned her coat; a detail there, as she accepted the money I owed her, folded her hand over it, and deflected attention from its existence and recent transfer. One time, she began asking me about my folks, but sensing it was a topic too painful to bear, as I looked first at the floor, then out the window, and sighed, she made up for it by spilling more of her Bean treasury, to which I came to add my own information, and judicious insights and surmises. She rented from Bean too, she told me, like we was fellow sufferers of some bodily affliction; and we took to fashioning a chronicle of Orville Bean the way the

69

preachers gave their sermons, call and response. She'd say a thing, and I'd repeat it, and she'd say what she'd said in the first place only adding to it, and in my mind I'd add my own bit in, too.

By the time Bean was born, Mrs. Greenfield began, his daddy was already in his sixties. Old man Bean had made some money long back buying up a few shotgun shacks, and thereby more or less owning the folks who rented them as well. He had a single broad black brow like a handlebar mustache that had risen over the years, and it seemed to get blacker as his hair went white. Whenever Bean and his son ventured out of town, folks mistook young Bean for his grandson. Bean took on the term "Grandfather" as if it had been a military title, and allowed it to be affixed to him like a sash across his shirt, and a row of beribboned medals.

Old Bean's greatest satisfaction in this life had long come from keeping accounts, tracing the fate of the last penny, and marking its whereabouts definitively, in India ink on a ruled ledger. But that weren't but the shorthand form of what put his world in order, which was the very notion of accountability. Folks in town believed in God Almighty, and read the Bible. Old man Bean believed in criminals, and read the Police Gazette.

Early one fifth of July morning, when young Bean was about twelve, a workman found the father sitting by himself on a bench facing the courthouse. He was at a right angle to the statue of the Confederate soldier boy. Old Bean's head was bowed, and his feet were splayed, and he had a crime gazette spread put aside him. It weren't till the workman nudged him, to say, Mr. Bean, those fireworks last night sure were something, couldn't get enough of them, huh, that his corpse slide a few inches down the bench, and then, having made its point, stopped. Bean's momma, when she got the news, was tending an apricot-colored azalea in the front yard.

She was frail and delicate; you felt she was something

not meant to be used every day, like a set of bone china with irreplaceable parts. She was the only child of a lawyer down in LaFayette, a widower, who'd lost all his savings buying up the chance of a lifetime: a goldmine in Alaska. Even years later, the very name of the state was said to make her shiver as though she'd been chewing ice and loosened a filling: she felt cold, and terror, and a delight she could not explain. ("Ecstasy?" I suggested, but Mrs. Greenfield looked at me willfully blank like I'd said something dirty, so I said "Delight," and nodded, and on she went.) Just then, among the azaleas, hearing of her widowhood for the first time, with her sun hat still atop her head, casting a halo of shadow over her face, Mrs. Bean went upstairs, not to weep, not to moan, but to tidy the closet.

She took out the mister's suits, gathered her sewing basket, and sat on the edge of the bed, threading the needle, and stitching hems long into the night. She was heedless of her son's weeping in the next room for the first few hours, and of his silence thereafter. The next Monday, she put a for-sale ad in the paper, Fine Men's Suits, alterations extra. (Mrs. Greenfield's mother had seen the notice herself, and how the ladies of the town did talk, outrage mingling with curiosity but not outdone by it.) There were no takers, and the fine suits hung in the closet, mended, refreshed, and untenanted.

And from that day, she was different; relaxed and released, as if a corset round her very self had been taken off, and she could breathe, if she had the discipline, and the taste for it, and could only get the rhythm right. She began to dote on young Bean, or would have, if her heart could have mustered the energy, and his heart suppressed its contempt. As a widow, her first move, and near her last, was to take to her bed.

She'd send her son off to the shop with a detailed list in hand, that left nothing to chance: violet water in a little bottle with a stopper shaped like a dancing angel; a heart-shaped mirror no wider than the palm of her hand, and backed with lavender satin, to keep under her pillow; a box of licorice torpedoes in yellow and white, that rattled like candy at the picture-house. Anybody walking by the house, if he looked up at the window of her bedroom, would have expected her to expire there years later, and gently, amidst the white curtains that fluttered like the wings of a moth by the flame, and the dead scent of cologne.

Nobody was home that day, the day of the fire, as it was also the day of the county fair; nobody except Mrs. Bean herself. Some folks say she lit the stove to make coffee and forgot about it; others say she set it deliberate-like, to get rid of those suits any way she could; or for the excitement, as the thrill of violet water was only fleeting and intermittent. The old men who sat in front of the courtyard chewing tobacco and remembered, said it was to banish forever the chill Alaska had cast over her entire life.

Whatever, Bean, by then in his late teens, came over the crest of the hill around five in the afternoon. He was carrying a stuffed pink rabbit he'd won at the duck-shooting booth, and no girl to give it to. He saw the smoke, and knew it was his daddy's house, and his momma inside it, and the concerns came to him in that order. ("That's what his barber swears Mr. Bean said," Mrs. Greenfield related. "Menthol pomade all over his face and him lying back in the chair, and out the words came like he'd breathed them in a long while ago and was only just then getting around to breathing them out.") In the end, they had to identify her by the shape of the mirror she was crouched over.

Bean knew his momma had been weak, indulgent, and by the end, almost childlike. And so, as far as Bean was concerned, no woman could ever hope to live up to her. He proved it, with a string of girls for whom shameless would be an improvement, implying at least that they were acquainted with the concept of shame in the first place. No woman could die up to Mrs. Bean's standards either.

While he bought the occasional gift for his gals, and indulged them with a pair of silk stockings or a half-dozen cans of stoned peaches, Bean pitied them in his good moods, and despised them in his bad. He had conjured them up into his life in his mother's image and likeness, only these ones with their trinkets and mirrors and scents never seemed to do the decent thing, and incinerate.

The Beans weren't the only folks Mrs. Greenfield had to tell about. It turned out that she knew that Mrs. Presley, on account of they went to the same church - she worked at the steam presser in the downtown laundry, maybe I'd met her sister, she was minding the house the night that I'd had to go by? Mrs. Greenfield told me that the Presleys was good country folks but nothing seemed able to help them out of the hole of poverty and misfortune life had dug for them. Mr. Bean himself sure weren't likely to help - for one thing, a cousin of Vern's had bested Mr. Bean in some local election a while back, and Mr. Bean, well, he just weren't the type that could forgive that. He took someone else's success as a personal slight, and it weighed his heart down ten times more than any success of his own could ever hope to lift it up.

She was fixing to tell me more, but I happened to glance at the clock, and she took that to mean something, and stood up and said, goodness, where does the time go? In my case, of course, it don't go anywhere, it just keeps coming around.

When I come home nights, Jesse cried some but not a lot. I supposed he liked me. Well, why shouldn't he, I thought, I'm only the emissary by which he was brought back to this life. Not to mention the one who cleans out his pants and sees that he's fed and has a place to sleep. Of course, that's no guarantee of anything. Joseph my daddy did that and more for JC, but JC never did bother too much about him.

In these, the baby years, Bean took a shine to me. I had a craft, and it weren't solely with the wood. When I reminded him how oh yes the Presleys had paid right up for that fancy casket, wouldn't have it any other way by the time I'd finished - how many times in your loved one's life, I told him I'd said, are you called upon to buy them a casket, it's not a burden, it's a singular privilege, Bean shook his head and smiled.

"Wondered myself how you wrangled that one. Inveigling no-accounts what can't even spare a sheet big enough to shroud a cat, to hand over cash - you got a flair for this business that can't be taught," he said. He took a step back to look at me better, and appraise. "Yessir, that is a fact."

It was a business I had plenty of experience with, but I didn't tell him that.

Bean set me to work building a whole series of caskets. Bare southern pine, unsanded, felt lining; pine sanded, and varnished teak, or painted white (your choice), with pink satin lining; caskets shaped straight as a ruler, and fancier ones that widened near the halfway mark, "so the beloved's arms may lie comfortable in eternal rest," Bean said. Bronze fixtures and engraving were optional. Bean's favorite was a luxury model, mahogany lined in lavender brocade. He'd gotten a sharp deal on the fabric when a factory over in Jefferson went bankrupt. He stepped into the backroom where I worked, and fingered the fabric, and just stood there and took in a deep breath, of sawdust, paint, and furniture polish.

"This place has the smell of profit," he said. "Sweetest perfume there is." And then, with a wink and a nod, he'd dubbed me, "The Casket King." He loaded the coffins into his truck, the lids flapping open, and carried them far and wide across the state. He became the supplier to a string of funeral homes across the county. He scanned the papers, and kept informed. When an epidemic of influenza hit, he took the opportunity to unload advance orders. Then the next year, he tried to interest the county jail in a government contract.

"I used your line, Jud," he told me. " 'Remember, sir,' I said, 'Christ himself died a condemned criminal.' And the jailer chuckled, put his feet up on the desk, and said, 'But that one didn't tarry in the grave but three days. What we got here, Orv, is more the Barrabas type, you understand me. They're thieves and cheats, and serve a few years. Nobody dies in my care, if I can help it.'"

But towards the end of the second year, Bean had got himself a construction contract to build a new prison wing the next county over, at Parchman.

"Crime is a growth industry," Bean said.

"And punishment," I said. "That's where the big money is."

CHAPTER ELEVEN

By the time that prison deal rolled around, I had already made my acquaintance of the Church of God and Mrs. Greenfield and the Presleys; caught myself a glimpse of Jesse's own brother; and faced up to a few of the natural elements the state of Mississippi could throw at a man.

It was around nine o'clock one night in April. A Sunday. Jesse was just a year old. I was sitting out on the porch, and he was nestled in my lap, lolling his head around, half-sleeping, then, getting bored with that, trying out his voice. He made cawing sounds into the failing light. They sounded lost and searching, like an echo of something that itself had skipped town a fair while ago. Jesse called once, then listened a moment, and tried again. The sky was lavender, and the smell of honeysuckle was thick in the air. The wind blew, hot and dry. The Baptists had gathered on some unseen corner. They were still singing, and the notes wafted by on the wind.

Didn't it rain, children,
God's gonna send the water from Zion
He's gonna raise heaven up higher
It's gonna rain

The singing rose into the falling dark. The sky was as gray, translucent and tender as a soap bubble. The wind picked up. I was looking down at Jesse, when somebody called out, "Why howdy, there, Mr. Jud. And little Jim!"

It was Mrs. Greenfield. She was walking along with Mrs. Presley, who had E in her arms, and a kind of worn-out, pleasant-faced man. The wind went still. The stillness was more ominous.

Mrs. Greenfield introduced everyone - she appeared to take great joy in following the finer points of etiquette, and added a syllable or two to my name. I stood up. A pinched nerve pulled me back down. "Got a stitch in my side," I said.

"Oh you know what that means," Mr. Presley said. "The devil's playing the fiddle, and broke a string so he's plucking one out of you." He chuckled companionably, but no companion took up his offer, so he shut up.

Just as his mouth was settling down straight, an angry twist of red and black flashed through the sky like a heated wire.

Mr. Presley stood there with his hands in his pockets and looked worried. His shirt collar flapped in the wind. The women kind of huddled together, with little E sheltered between their Sunday hats. He was hollering. Jesse perked up his head and looked at him, then lost interest, and chewed my shoulder.

"I would hasten my escape from the windy storm and tempest," I said, availing myself of Psalm 55.

"You got yourself an idea there, son," Mr. Presley said, looking up at the sky which was, obligingly, lowering to meet him more than halfway.

The wind blew harder, and hot. A school bus came steamrollering up the street. It rumbled noisily and swayed from side to side. A few yards ahead of us, it pulled over and stopped.

"Uncle Noah," Mr. Presley said. He ran toward the bus.

The door folded open. The sky darkened. Noah stood on the steps of his vehicle. His brow was black and straight.

"Get in," he ordered. "All of you." And we piled aboard.

The whole time we were rattling through the streets of Tupelo, I was studying E, nestled up against his momma. He didn't look any brother to the prince of peace that I could see. Of course, folks had said near the same about me and JC. This E boy was flush-cheeked and almost podgy, and he didn't look, even then, much like Jesse, who was pale as moonlight, and kind of fine-featured by comparison.

I looked down at Jesse, and touched his brow lightly. I was beginning to fathom how infinite pity could be. It's hard to forget what anointment means, when you've already seen it close-up, and shared a room with the one chosen, when you've watched him wake up flushed, and terrified from a bout of sleepwalking. Or after he's struck a boy dead just by wishing it so. I guess I'll have to tell you about that sometime, because the four official scribblers in the retinue weren't up to it.

Noah pulled up by the Assembly of God Church. It was flat and low and woebegone, like an ice cream stand in the off-season, pining for a lick of paint. We rushed inside and us menfolk braced ourselves up against the south wall. Mrs. Presley sat in a corner holding E. Mrs. Greenfield had hold of Jesse. She was in the center of the room praying. Jesse stared over her shoulder at E, and E stared back. Jesse took a soft-fisted swing. The shadow of it fell over E and he cried. Mrs. Greenfield went on praying, *Oh Lord have mercy*. I heard the sound of a thousand freight trains crashing into each other. The collision was bearing down on us. A chicken was running around just outside, I watched it from the window facing. The chicken ran, squawking, in circles, like something possessed. Look upon us, oh Lord, Mrs. Greenfield shrieked. Jesse's head snapped up like somebody'd slapped him, but he chortled. I looked at her, the wall behind me was groaning, and I looked back out the window. The chicken was still running in circles, screeching, only now it was entirely shorn of its feathers.

Then the wind went still. The tornado had come upon us, a beast breathing down our necks, and now the beast was moving on. The sky lightened. The wall stood fast. From the window we could see fires blazing down along the main road, and folks rushing out with blankets to beat them down.

"The Lord has spared us," Mrs. Greenfield said. "Praise the Lord!" I took Jesse from her, so her arms were free to rise in rejoicing.

We all stepped outside, cautiously, looking upwards as if the sky might be fixing to tumble down on us. We made our way down the road a few hundred yards, stumbling and uncertain, like we was tied to an invisible string and getting jerked along. Then we were all standing in the patch of dirt that was somebody's front yard. It was Mrs. Greenfield's. Her house was still standing, and untouched by fire.

"The Lord's sending us a sign," Mrs. Greenfield said. Her eyes were intent but glassy and strangely focused in the murky light. She moved her head the way blind folks do, listing first to one side, then another, then suddenly rigid and upright.

Of course the Lord has sent us a sign, I thought: be a skinflint and a slumlord, and the Almighty'll make sure them rickety houses you rent out to poor folks go unscathed through the mortal storm.

"Oh yes he is," Noah intoned.

"God took my firstborn son from me," Mrs. Presley said.

Jesse raised his head from my shoulder and wailed.

" 'I will smite the firstborn in the Land of Egypt,' said the Lord," Mrs. Greenfield crooned. She turned her face in my direction but didn't seem to see me.

Well, Jesse had been first smote down, and then resurrected straight away on top. Pride and pity are a potent cocktail, and I expect I was intoxicated on a long cool one of those as I looked down at Jesse and rocked him back and forth.

" 'The firstborn of both man and beast - I am the Lord' he said," Noah thundered.

"But He saved my Elvis," Mrs. Presley said. "And to him was given the strength of both their spirits."

Jesse stiffened up like he was set to bawl something fierce. I hugged him and he simmered down.

"The Lord's just saved your son a second time," Mrs. Greensfield said. "Carried him through the howling storm."

"The Lord's a-talking to us now," Noah said.

"And we better heed," Mrs. Presley said.

"He's sending us a message," Mrs. Greenfield said.

"To embrace the church whose very walls kept us in the embrace of life," Noah said. "The embrace of God's eternal love."

"To hold true to that church in thanksgiving," Mrs. Greenfield said.

"And everlasting devotion," Mrs. Presley said.

"I called out, save me Lord! And he did," Mrs. Greenfield said. "He shined that light down from heaven right onto my soul."

"We were lost and we were found," Noah said. "Let us pray." Noah bowed his head, and raised his arms out like the glowering wings of an archangel who's had it with singing and the harps, and simply means to get down to business.

I shrugged, and said to myself, "Here goes." One church that claims it follows my brother is pretty much the same as the next, so far as I'm concerned. I don't mean no disrespect, but if you grew up with JC as your brother, and had Jesse in the house waiting in the wings, I expect you would feel pretty much the same.

Mr. Presley winked at me. "The Assembly's church suppers are the best in town," he whispered. "Coconut cake, jellied salad, and chicken with all the trimmings." Which you can bet were real treats, since around Tupelo, folks filled their bellies with a mess of greens, or a bowlful of grits and cheese, maybe fried squirrel if they was lucky with the shotgun that day. I hadn't had victuals so noteworthy since my sojourn in Darktown a thousand years before.

And like they say, out of the mouths of idiots. Because it was at those church suppers that Jesse and E would soon commence revealing themselves to an unsuspecting world, in unsuspected ways. Just babbling on that day about the angel cakes and lemonade and so on, Vernon got me to thinking: this food thing was like JC himself, telling us that time at dinner to break bread in memory of him, and, sap that I was, I asked him who was going to do him in.

But bread doesn't do justice to my memory of JC, not even when it's sopped in gravy. In my mind, he was mixed up with a taste of something else entirely.

CHAPTER TWELVE

The taste of licorice, that's what I remember. Sweet and bitter, it lingered on your tongue like the promise of revenge, tickled it like a secret yearning to be told, and blackened it like the vestiges of sin. When we went running through the fields, JC and I used to carry a handful of anise seeds in our pockets. The licorice taste filled my mouth, I swallowed, and it became part of me forever, like guilt. They say guilt consumes you, but that ain't the whole story: you got to consume *it* first, to get things moving. JC had a pocketful of anise seeds on him, the day he struck his first boy dead. The anise spilt out all around him like the stuffing from a sawdust doll, and he wept.

We'd been playing down by the river, me, JC, and John, and James. Well, JC was playing, I was watching, and the other two were impersonating happy buddies as best they could. They were already wise to what JC could do when riled, ever since they'd heard about the time he was playing hide-and-seek, and he'd gotten irked at a fellow for peeking. Straight away, that fellow hobbled away limp-footed. So they'd taken to doing what they were told: laughing at his jokes; saying oh what a good idea to his suggestions, and trying not to sound too sing-song when they said it.

It pretty much always got to that when we played with JC: we were halfway in a daze, like the way you feel when you've been spinning around in a circle, and need to keep going, because you know if you don't, you'll fall to the ground, and your stomach'll fall a few feet further.

It was the first day of spring. Warmed by the sun, and buffeted by the winds, the afternoon lay before us like cloth of linen washed, beaten clean, and left out to dry by the riverside.

"I got an idea," JC was saying. John and James looked at each other. A thin white line of tension, from smiling just so, had formed around James's upper lip. John was out of breath. We'd just finished playing tag, as per JC's friendly directive.

"What idea is that?" James said.

"Let's make us some fish pools," JC said. He popped an anise seed into his mouth.

"I want my dinner," John said.

"Fish pools would be fun," James said. His eyes were almost amber, like blond raisins. They were hard to read.

"A snack would be good though," John said. He poked his nose in JC's direction.

"You just had breakfast an hour ago," James said.

"I'm still hungry," John said.

"You're always hungry," I said.

"What's wrong with that?" John said.

"You hunger after foolish things," JC said. "Someday you will know delights more honeyed than any childish treat." As he spoke, he got that whitish look in his eye, kind of glazed, like a day-old fish, the way he always did when he was saying something we could tell was supposed to be of great import.

"That so?" John said. "In the meantime, it looks like some folks hold on to their own treats pretty tight. As if sharing was never invented. I don't see how anybody - hey,

I can hear my belly rumble. Listen." He planted his paws on either side of his stomach, and looked up at us.

But JC had already picked up a forked stick. He was making a furrow in the ground. He dug a hole at the end of it, and channeled water from the river. John looked at James and shrugged. They each scrounged around for their own sticks, and did the same. Then JC stuck his hands in the clay of the riverside, and formed twelve sparrows. He always was a dab hand at the graven image. Didn't matter the flicker of an eyelash to him it was the Sabbath, either. He set them around the edge of his pool. I plunged my hands into the wet gray clay. John and James set to work on either side of me.

"I think I'll make myself a clay chicken," John said. "And roast it and eat it right in front of you."

"I'd like a turtle dove," James said, "so I can listen to it sing. And I'd make sure it was pretty one so I could give it to momma."

"Ain't you sweet," John said, and reached over to slug him. His elbow swung out, and knocked over my clay bird.

I was ready to swing back, when we heard a rustle in the willow tree behind us. It was Jonas, the schoolmaster's son, standing beneath the whispering branches. Jonas was a little older than us, about thirteen, but his voice was already as deep as a grown man's and his body was almost caught up to his voice. He pored over books all day long, wrinkling his heavy black brow, and if he had been shorter, or less broad-shouldered, he would have been beaten up on a regular basis. But as it was, as both a physical specimen and a figure of faith, he was muscle-bound and invincible.

Jonas stood there a moment and took us all in. He didn't want to miss a single point of outrage. "Was not the Lord's Sabbath made to be kept pure?" he boomed. Righteous wrath was one of his specialties. He tore a switch from the tree, and rushed towards us. He smashed John's clay work, then fell upon James's, and took a swipe at mine, half-hearted once he saw it was already wrecked. He scattered the pools we had built, and the water shimmered in the grass like a satchelful of spilt coins. Then Jonas let out a cry, and headed toward JC.

JC turned. He moved slowly, and deliberately, like you might see yourself moving in a dream. He seemed to take no notice of Jonas, but stood up, and clapped his hands, and a flock of sparrows seemed to fly out of nowhere. They twittered in the sky above us, and wove their song amongst themselves like a net high above. Jonas was advancing on the pool of water, his shadow fell tall, and his switch was raised high. JC held his palms out flat and the water vanished.

JC turned to face Jonas. Up to then, he hadn't bothered looking in that direction.

"As the water disappeared, so shall your life," JC said, and Jonas fell down like one dead.

"Hey, Jonas, you better stand up," John said. "It is the Sabbath like you say, heh-heh. You -"

"Shut up," James said. His face was white, and his eyes were wandering over JC as though he had never seen him before, and would have foregone the privilege indefinitely. JC took no notice of anyone. He just stood there, breathing regular, but a flush was spreading across his face.

"You shut up yourself," John said. "You're not the boss of me. Jonas'll smite you down if you're not careful."

"His smiting days are over," I said.

JC turned and looked at me. His eyes were bleached out and dazed, like he'd been looking straight into the sun.

"We better get on home now," James said. "See you." He grabbed John's hand.

"Hey, watch out," John said. James pulled him along, and they skeedaddled across the field like a ripple of wind.

JC fell down beside dead Jonas. The satchel of anise fell out and burst open, and he wept.

I myself have been deemed an associate Christ-killer. But knowing what I do, that term has a different

resonance and carries a different value. Christ isn't the
direct object, as the schoolmaster would say. He's the
subject. It took JC himself to lend a new meaning to that
phrase, as with so many others, and I guess that's why they
call him the Lord.

He was on the ground sobbing a few minutes. I dried
his tears and dusted him off. I wanted to say it wasn't his
fault, but "fault," and the kind of talk that goes with it,
didn't seem much to the point. So I just held him tight, till
he lay quiet. Then he got up, and we walked home.

Of course, after that little episode, no one in the
neighborhood wanted much to do with him. Jonas's
parents got wind of where Jonas had been, and went to
our dad and complained. My mother stayed out in the
yard, where she was boiling a chicken for supper, and tried
to listen, the steam from the pot rising all around her.
Joseph told them he would talk to JC. I guess he did,
because a week later, Jonas's parents were struck blind. It
really was the case that everything JC says presently comes
to pass. So folks were a little spooked being around him.
Our mother defended him to the hilt, and said the power
of the Almighty was with him - who were we to judge?
Joseph at table, took another sip of wine, and said nothing.
He was getting good at that.

James and John tried hard to act friendly, like he was
still a buddy, but their hearts weren't in it. They were
mostly afraid. It was like that even when he was older, the
eleven surrounded him, but not like friends. They were
more like a cast around a broken leg. I was his only friend,
his beloved disciple, his twin. And after he chose me to
betray him, he decreed that I will tarry till the second
coming. Most else of my story, they x-ed it right out of the
scriptures. But I knew it then and I know it now. Of
course, we're talking eternity, where what you know, or
think you know, don't matter a lick of spit. That morning I
was first at Parchman State Prison, working on top of the
roof, a licorice-flavored cough lozenge dissolving slow and

bitter on my tongue, and the story that I've just been telling you, along with a few other ones, all came back to me.

CHAPTER THIRTEEN

I was standing up the roof of the penitentiary, swinging a hammer into a row of nails. The lozenge was melting and making a store of black-tasting liquor in my mouth. I'd been saving it up. Then I swallowed. I looked out over the plantation beneath me. The overseers raised the crop, and beat it down, and raised it up all over again the next morning - only the crop was convicts.

It was October, a year after I had encountered E and family in the eye of the storm. A Saturday, just around noon. The men from the old wing were still working in the field. They were each swinging a hoe, in unison. When I stopped hammering, I could hear the chink of the metal and the *huh* of their breath, and they were singing soft and low, the sound of gray mist rising from the earth, groaning with no beginning and no end. The prison overseer rode about the grounds on horseback. His hat sat wide and low so his face was hidden in its shade, and he cast his very self about that field, roaming and hovering like a shadow of the Lord over the misbegotten.

Jesse was playing inside the red house they kept for the visitors. A lady in a faded dress had took charge of him. She had on a pair of men's loafers held together in back with carpenter's tape.

"You're a lucky boy, Jimmy. Your daddy ain't no common criminal doing time," she said, fake sugary, and accusation sunk deep in her eyes like dregs at the bottom of a cup of coffee gone cold. "He's an employee of Mr. Bean." She let the screen door slam behind her and Jesse. I went around the side of the building, and climbed the ladder to my post.

Yellow Hicks was already there. He was at the far end, sitting astride the central beam. He had his chin tipped up to face the sky, like it was talking to him. Yellow was what you'd call a simple fellow, and folks said he had been so ever since he came back from a prayer meeting by the riverside when he was five years old, and caught a case of brain fever.

When I mentioned once to Mrs. Greenfield, pretty early on, I think, that this fella Yellow was doing a few odd jobs alongside me, she sucked in her bottom lip and rolled her eyes up at me, and said it was a such shame. But for Mrs. Greenfield, shame was like joy, or a deep inhale of breath, or a helium-filled balloon on parade day: you was meant to let it go into the world.

Yellow lived with an old aunt who seldom ventured further than her own front room. She and Yellow were the last known members a line that was not so much in decline as completely through the process, and beyond it. So bereft of income or estate had been the family that Yellow's mother had had to sell the family silver while she was expecting him, and, according to Mrs. Greenfield, some said that disgrace so weighed on the mother that it was the cause of his affliction. And some said that's why his birth-hair was silvery-white before it went yellow, because she longed so much after the silver she'd had to pawn, and that longing colored and etched itself onto the very child in her belly. She took her wares to the next county, where she hoped the engraved initials would not be recognized. When she came back that afternoon, she found the house was dark and still. Her husband had packed and gone. And one day, before Yellow was yet six, she done the same herself. Yellow was handed over, not squalling a bit, nor even mouthing a single word, to her older sister, and he was living with her still.

Over the years, I'd known a number of fellows afflicted same as Yellow; especially I remember one, who was called Ben. I most always liked them, on account of they reminded me that folks in general ain't as smart as they might think, and that 'smart' in any case ain't so very much to shoot for. And I expect they reminded me of my brother; because while he weren't a dimwit, he was different, and marked out, and fixated on other things from most folks. I'd look at him and know that no matter how much I loved him, the world was going to throw things at him I couldn't never protect him from; and the knowledge made my insides shrink, and go hollow. A fellow like Yellow never made me nervous, or go gushy, or bullying, the way he seemed to with other folks.

"Hi there, Yellow," I said.

"Hi yourself," Yellow said, not moving a muscle. His voice was flat and toneless, like it had fallen into disuse.

I settled in on the beam. "Looks like you and me, we'll be nailing this roof up."

"Sky won't hold," Yellow said.

"You worried the sky's going to fall down on you," I said, "you set it an example nailing in this roof." I was used to dealing with crazies.

"Rain's coming," Yellow said. Which is why I guess folks insisted he was nutty: it wasn't so much on account of he talked crazy, it was on account of he talked sense when you least expected it. Yellow dropped his chin down, picked up his hammer, and took aim.

I could hear Bean on the ground, below my swinging right foot. He was yakking away with one of his buddies, I could tell by the tone of his voice, kind of boastful without even trying.

"- gal done okay by me."

"Oh I seen her looking at that automobile of yours," the other man said. "Hankering like. She be waiting for the day she can lay her little hand on all your belongings."

"She can go on waiting," Bean said. "Best thing she knows how to do."

"Ain't you taught her nothing else?" the man said.

Bean snorted. "Nothing her momma ain't done before her. Matter of fact -"

And his voice went on and on, like it was a separate animal from him, sprung loose, and would-be wily. It got caught up in the whine of the saw-wheel, snagged on the belt, chewed up and spit out. Then it continued just as sure of itself as ever.

"- man what can't even read his alphabet," Bean was saying. "Makes you stop and think, now don't it."

"It surely do," the other man said. He spit a fair distance into the yard.

"Where's your boy at, Jud?" Yellow said.

"He's with that lady in the red house," I said.

"He is a good boy," Yellow said.

The sawmill started up again, in low gear.

"Hog wild - he ain't nothing but an old pig at the trough," Bean was saying. "Just last week."

The saw-wheel ripped into higher gear. It was chewing his words up, tearing the limbs off them, and I couldn't hear what they were saying anymore.

I went on, my neck pressed up close to the sky, and pounded the next few nails in. The pounding was echoed all around, from other crews pounding on roofs going up around me, way up high. I watched the prisoners swinging their shovels down below, and I got caught up in their motion as if it was a game of skip rope, and I was calculating when to jump into it myself. I felt a rush of vertigo, so I lay down my hammer, and rested. The pounding echoed, blotted out the sound of anything else the way looking into the sun blots out all other light and fills your eyes with dazzle. The pounding wasn't coming from the work around me.

It was the hammer of ages, and I knew because I'd heard it that first time, when I thought I'd be free of him, when they nailed him up. I watched it from a distant field, where I'd climbed to the top of a whispering tree. That day, there was a hammer that kept pounding and pounding, as if some god were walking on the top of the sky, except he didn't ever go further away, or come closer to, or really sound like he was moving anywhere at all. It seemed like everything, the sun, the wind, the tides, just stopped while he was up there on the cross, and from the pounding, the sky would crack in two. You've heard what I've heard about that day, but you ain't heard the all of it, cause I ain't told it yet, and weren't telling it even to myself just then, when I was hanging off Bean's convict roof. By the time they came and found me that day, I hear tell I was hanging from the highest branch. Only with me on it, it was bent low, groaning, and swept clear to the ground. But part of what they ain't told you is, how when they came back with a knife to cut me down, I had already stolen away. A family trait you might say. And the pounding went on the whole day long, till the night sky went as dark as the sea and looked fair to tumble into it.

I must have nodded off or something, because the next thing I knew, Bean's voice was calling, "You fall asleep up there, Jud?" I was near to slipping off one side of that roof, when I felt somebody pulling at my shoulder. I straightened up right quick. Yellow was beside me, his blond eyelashes like a cat's whiskers doused in milk, unnatural white, and a-twitching.

"You okay, Jud?" he said.

That's all I needed, to be rescued by an imbecile. But I suppose I should have been grateful. The way time worked around here, the past crashed right into the present, hurtled into it, like a bully going down a slide, colliding mightily into anything in its path, such as myself. Time was as like to take me to the top of a steeple, where I could see all things in a single moment, and then push me off it, and the only thing between myself and unordained annihilation was something like a nail catching on the seat of my pants to stop me, to keep me suspended, as I was meant to be - in time, not on a cross. I guess Bean's voice and Yellow's tugging was that rusty nail scratching my butt, and keeping me dangling on this earth so as I could go about my business, which was also the Lord's.

"No, sir," I called down. "I'm just checking my work. Making sure everything's securely in place."

"You want to make sure your own place around here is secure, you better check a little less and get done a little more," Bean said.

The other man down beside him laughed.

"I ain't joking," Bean said.

The man shut up.

"And while you're at it, send that addle-pated halfwit straight down," Bean said. "We got a whole yard here needs sweeping."

"Hey, Yellow," I said softly. I didn't know if he'd heard Bean. He was staring up the sky again. "Mr. Bean needs your help. Says you're the only one can do what he wants."

Yellow looked at me sideways. Silent and right-angled and stiff-jointed as if he was made of wood, he clambered off the roof.

I hammered in a few more nails, and wiped the sweat off my brow. A Greyhound bus was pulling into the prison yard. It glittered like cold fire in the October sun, and lumbered towards us. It slowed down and finally chugged to a halt a few hundred yards from Bean and the makeshift sawmill. The doors folded open, and a four-foot dingy-sheeted ghost, with a couple of lop-sided eyeholes, stepped off. All you could see of him were his shoes; mini-version of the clodhoppers folks hereabouts favored, and striped socks. His momma tumbled out after him. She was clutching him by the hand. She smoothed down her dress, dashed the hair out of her eyes, and tried to smile. Then a pint-sized witch, and a paper-faced phantom lurched out into view. They seemed to share a momma in tow, only this one didn't try smiling. The kids were in dress-up, and the earth was playing at rendering up its dead. I attempted a grin myself, but my lips got caught on my teeth halfway, my mouth was so dry. Yellow was swinging his broom a few inches above the ground, and the witch girl pointed, and ran towards him, and made like to take the broom from him. Yellow backed off like a scared dog to the other corner of the lot. He raised his head every so often to keep an eye on her, and I watched his lips jabbering away.

The sawmill went silent.

"Have to be visiting day," Bean was saying. He snorted.

"Those kids'd be better off working in the fields alongside their daddies," the other man said. "Teach them not to wind up the same way."

"Uh-huh," Bean said, without enthusiasm.

"Do them better than a whole year's worth of schooling," the man went on. "Do them better than a weeping and a wailing with their mommas. Do 'em a heap -"

"Hey, Jud," Bean shouted out, "Seeing as it's Halloween this month, what you going as? How 'bout as a worker because I am sure no-one would ever recognize you."

"Just catching my breath, sir," I said.

"Catch it right quick. I surely do miss the sound of that pounding. I expect to set back this next half-hour with its sweet sound echoing in my ears."

Bean chuckled and the other man joined right in, a mite too loudly and a little too long.

I hammered the last of the nails in short order. Then I packed up my kit, and went down the ladder. Bean was standing there by himself.

"Got a big order this week, Jud," Bean said. "Luxury lined coffins fit for the men of God. So rest up that sawing arm. I've said before -" A child wailed from the direction of the red house.

Jimmy, what you got yourself into now? a woman's voice was saying.

Jesse let loose with another wail. I dropped my kit in the dust and tore over to the red house.

"Man's turning into an old mother hen who ain't got herself but a single chick," Bean said. He chuckled. "Saddest sight I ever did see."

I pushed the screen door open. Jesse was standing up in the arms of the woman with the heavy brown eyes. She was cradling his feet. Jesse's face was red and he was squalling something awful. I took him from her. He looked at me and rolled his head in anger and hurt.

"Jimmy decided to go for a little crawl," she said. "Out in the yard. Seems to me like somebody left loose nails around, cause Jimmy got himself scratched up."

I was bouncing Jimmy against my shoulder. I pushed down his sleeves, he cried out in fresh outrage, and his hands were grazed. I run my finger across a reddish mark over his wrist. It was still sore, raw as a rope burn.

"His paws got scraped something fierce," she went on. "Must have rolled around, 'cause he's even got a scratch across his neck. I am sorry for the little fellow but if you men can't show more care than to give it to a simpleton to sweep up after yourselves, it can't be up to me to do it for you. I only got two hands, not to mention that there's an entire busload of children running riot."

Jesse was reworking himself into that stiff-fingered fury he'd been perfecting since his soft pated days. "Hurt," he said.

Son, I thought, it'll all get worse before it gets better, and to tell you the truth, even better don't seem like such a hot deal, all told.

"You don't stop that racket now, you won't be able to stop when you're of a mind to," I said. "It's like what the fella says about religion."

The woman snorted.

"You got to get it when you don't want it," I said, "so you'll be sure to have it when you need it."

Jesse thought it over, sniffled once or twice, and hushed up.

"Now you ain't going to make a complaint about me, are you, mister?" the woman was saying. "I do my best, Lord knows, and like I say, that simpleton fella, it's really -"

"No, ma'am," I said, gathering Jesse up. "Complaining ain't my style. I am too busy fulfilling destiny to have much time left over for the business of bewailing it." I turned to go out the door.

She looked at me. "Hey, mister, it's only a scratch," she said, as the screen door swung shut behind me.

It was always disquieting to find myself called back to the day I stood watching my brother from the top of a tree. I hunkered down the whole bus ride home from Parchman, ignored my workmates, and contemplated just how disobliging this business of revelation is.

You take the case of JC himself. I didn't take it too hard the day Jonas fell down dead, nor the nights thereafter, when JC stood at the foot of the bed with a single piece of bread, or with a stick in his hand, writing things on the floor: practicing, I guess. After I saw that, and had some idea of what was going on, I brought JC a sick dog to heal. Of course, I had fixed it to find a dog whose sickness would wear off its own accord anyway, just in case. Now when JC found that out, he laughed. He threw one of his shoes at me and chased me clear around the yard. I don't recollect him laughing too often. Once, late at night after one of his marathon question and answer sessions in the temple, I woke and saw him sitting on the floor looking out at the sky. He was crying. His forehead was flushed, and the heat was creeping across his face like shame. But the trouble was something he couldn't even say, and I held him till he fell asleep. I prayed to God that he would let me take JC's place, a mouse-sized portion of duplicity gnawing away in the back of my mind because I knew just how often the Almighty had ever seen fit to change His course on account of a plea from one of the image-and-likeness set, but I felt the need to say the words all the same.

Such were the thoughts that occupied my mind as we rattled home along the highway. We entered the town of Tupelo, and passed the town dump, then the colored section, and a section where some poor whites lived. Until finally we entered the hour of the day, and the sector of city, where the power and the light were manifest.

The lights along this stretch of road glowed white and radiant. The bus jolted sharply as it went past Ed's Gas Station near the center of town. The E on the sign was smashed out and the lit-up G listed to one side like a boat with a bad leak. Jesse woke up and took a swing at the air. He looked like he was fixing to wage some kind of revolt against heaven, hell, the weather, and the Republican Party, and I can't say that I blamed him. In fact, I'd say in that particular regard, he was pretty darn precocious, though of course, folks always think that of their own. And besides which, you have to know your God before you can transgress Him. I have personal knowledge of that fact, and I was willing to bet it was only a matter of time before Jesse would, too.

CHAPTER FOURTEEN

Folks like to tell each other how time passes, or flies, or slips away, or some such, but that don't strike me as doing entire justice to the matter. These early years with Jesse, they more collected, like, outside my doorstep. They took their time - they *was* time, years accumulating themselves slowly, silently, without notice, on my threshold, like snow falling in the night. You look out your bedroom window in some dark hour and it's still building up; and you fall asleep secure. And then you look out a while later, it's melted, and you wonder where it's gone to.

The years of Jesse, and my remembering them, were different from my years with JC. Those years with JC, from the first I ever recalled them, was more like something stored, like rainwater in a deep barrel. When you stirred it, the water swirled dizzily, heavily; you might glimpse a particular incident, swirling in a spiral like a colored leaf, lost in its own languor, and slowly drawing to a stop.

I looked at Jesse in those years, and I wondered if I was a changing man. I ain't never been what I'd have called cold-stone bitter - more like, I'd say, my soul got its nose out of joint some time ago and ain't never been set straight since. A long time before my coming into the state of Mississippi, my heart had been but barely ticking, like a clock gone rusty by the sea, that sounds the hours thickly and tardily upon the salt-scented air. Lots of times, folks'll try to tell you how they came to get their heart into things again. They'll be holding their child for the first time, or their mother for the last; and their heart, they tell you, "just melted." Well, first off, I am not the melting type. Because, second, and on top of which, it don't do for a man in my position to melt. Melting leaves a mess behind, most generally for someone else to clean up. I am, and most generally have been, that somebody else. It ain't much, I will grant you. Maybe it ain't what I would have signed up for if I had had a choice, but all the same, I am it.

So what happened weren't a matter of melting. It was pretty near the opposite: a case of something consolidating, coalescing, and taking shape over and around the boy, and in time, my shadow embraced him near as closely as it did me. I cradled Jesse in my thoughts. At night, I looked in at him, and silently I drew the shadow-tips of my fingers towards the shadow-tips of his. I listened to him breathe, his chest as frail as a sparrow's, and the sound calmed me, and made me whole. I've heard folks tell how they felt when they seen the ocean for the first time, how they was astonished and silenced, maybe, before that discovered stretch of blue: well, watching Jesse asleep in his bed was like a sighting of that ocean to me.

Some nights, I stood in the doorway, my shadow swallowed up in the surrounding dark, and rendered as secret and unfathomable as Jesse's dreams, and I made witness to his sleep. Once or twice, I stayed there till the sky turned pink, and the sparrows rose, small black shapes atwittering, and the shadow I cast emerged bit by bit against the light. I always knew folks loved their children. What I didn't know, and weren't prepared for, was how they fell for them. In regard to Jesse, I was near as intense and skittish as an unripe suitor. My feelings for him hamstrung my heart. In that dark bed, his face lay there, as luminous and fragile as a candled egg. I thought of one of them races you run holding an egg in a spoon, and it did occur to me: no matter how much you may want to, you can't hug an egg close, without that you destroy it. And so, in his presence, I drew back from him; and in his absence, I drew near. And, there, he was most often giggling, or trying to stand and toppling over, or dangling off the rooftops of my mind, while I sanded a coffin or stacked a shelf or ran some such errand for Bean.

I tended to young Jesse carefully and well. I washed his scalp, and scrubbed his ears. I listened to his infant chatter, and answered him in good plain English. I took heed of Mrs. Greenfield, my head listing to one side, as she told of his doings, his attempts to stand up unaided, and take a step, or say a word, or swipe a dishcloth out of her hand, and toss it across the porch. I saw he had clean clothes, and was fed proper. I let him cry when he needed, and his rage spent, I set the shimmer of a silver coin to catch the interest in his eyes, and lead him to a place of sleep. I dandled him on my knee, the radio playing softly into the early night. We sat there as the trains passed through, and I wondered if they rolled on into his dreams.

And all the while, I guarded him carefully, like a mistake.

I was bound, I guess, to misread him and the signs attending him; and maybe the miracle I should have faced was that after a certain point there weren't none. Because whatever you might expect, or I might wish or pray, I cannot say I am a man saved by love nor loving. I reckon maybe I could have been, this time, and that is the greatest shame of all. But mine ain't the story of faith but of faith's shadow; of a man who learned to cast a shadow, and that you can't cast much else but.

*   *   *

So time mounts up, and Jesse was coming up to five years. I figured it was time he met his Maker, in the place and manner folks hereabouts most generally did. He'd taken to pointing out letters in the newspapers, and asking what word they were spelling, Mrs. Greenfield said he was a quick study, and she'd not seen many children take to letters so fast, and so tenacious-like. Once, when we was out walking, me and Jesse, he pointed to the Church of God, and asked what that building was. And he went up to the sign, and felt the letters on it like a blind man; and so it just felt like it was time.

I weren't full of reverence so much as curiosity, on two counts: I wondered how they worshipped their Lord, what notes they struck, and words they invoked, and I wondered what young Jesse would make of it all. I admit a third consideration percolated in my heart: I would look upon the congregation and know what they did not, that one day my boy Jesse would lead them.

At dinner one Saturday night, I told Jesse where we were going. The next morning, he was up a few hours earlier than was my custom, poking at me and asking when we were getting a move on. He'd slipped on his overalls, and put his shirt on over that, and matched the top two buttons with the bottom two holes and it hung so off-balance it was as if he'd been born on the side of a hill and had never shook off its malingering influence.

I turned over and drew the bedcovers up tighter. "You're in such a hurry, Jes, I reckon you ought to have got a move on yesterday."

Jesse yanked back the sheet and bopped me on the elbow. "Com'on," he said. "Right now." He hopped on his right foot, then his left.

"You think that church'll just melt away if you don't get there, don't you, boy?" I said, and soon as I was saying it, I was thinking that, in the long run, it doubtless would.

"Hurry up," Jesse said.

"Okay," I said. "I'm hurrying. Fetch your shoes and

we'll get going."

Jesse went out to the porch. I clambered out of bed, hitched on some trousers, and stumbled into my boots. I went out the door and found Jesse on the stoop struggling with his shoes.

"Like this, Jes," I said. "You scrunch up and aim your toes like a rabbit going down a hole." I pulled the shoe up, snug and neat around his left foot. I yanked on either end of the shoelace. "Then you wiggle your ears like this, and you tie them up trim and tidy like the top of an Easter bonnet."

Jesse giggled. I put the other shoe on him, buttoned his shirt up right, re-fastened his overalls, and then we were ready. "Okay, boy," I said, "Let's meet our Lord."

Jesse walked ahead of me. I followed, and scanned the sky for signs. It was bright and hollow, and revealed nothing. Jesse turned the corner to the church. I watched his shadow edging around the grounds, then I looked up and watched him. His left shoelace trailed behind him, and I trailed behind it. When he saw the church grounds, he broke into a run. I looked up at the sky, and turned my eyes on the church but the sun was in them and I could see nothing else. When I turned and saw Jesse again, he was standing still, waiting for me to catch up. I stopped and blinked. Then I saw the church more clearly: flat and square and squat. The yard in front was brown, and yellowish October sunshine dappled over it, kind of weak and hopeful, like an invalid's smile. In back of the church, among the overgrown reeds, languished a shallow pond, still and black and ungleaming. Folks were milling around outside the little church, smiling and nodding to each other, like they had found themselves one happy day.

Jesse clasped my knee with both arms as I headed into the church. We were passing through the shadow of an elm tree, when Mrs. Greenfield spied us.

"Howdy!" she called out, shading her eyes with one hand and waving with the other.

I nodded at her without looking, and kept walking. Jesse kept pace, and we clambered stiffly, man-and-child creature joined at my calf and his chest, into the church. It was empty. I aimed my knee towards the first two seats on the left, Jesse followed, disembarked, and then we sat down.

Jesse squirmed and looked around. "What is this place?"

"You know what it is," I said. "It's a church. It's where God lives." There goes the neighborhood, I thought, and chuckled, remembered myself and shut up. Let's just say that in the course of my long and lonely sojourn on this earth, I had not been what you'd call a devout attender of church or temple. I'd seen cathedrals built and I'd seen heretics burned, all in the name of that fish-eyed brother of mine. He mostly hated having a fuss made over him - used to run out the backdoor when our birthday came around to avoid the commotion wrought by his own family, so it was a safe bet what he'd have made of all the to-do carried on in his name. Even the four scribblers can't escape that truth. Like after he fed the multitude that time with a five loaves of bread and a few fish, he didn't stick around for the prayer meet they were all clamoring for. In preference, he went up a mountainside just to avoid a crowd scene.

And of course, I myself had had enough of prayer services from the day JC confounded the elders. I was remembering that day, and a little bit how I felt watching in the shadows as JC disputed on all subjects. When I looked up, all the chairs in the little Tupelo church had filled up. Vern and his wife and boy were on the other side of the room, and there were folks swaying in all the aisles. Noah was up at the front, taking up a lot of space, and his voice was booming, taking up a lot of air.

"Brothers and sisters," Noah thundered, "The Holy Spirit is among us. Every minute of every day he works in us and through us."

A crooning rose through the middle of the church. The faithful stood, raised their hands and beat the air.

Every minute of every day! they shouted.

"And Satan too! The Devil, he works the same field and in the same hour as the Holy Spirit! He tills the same earth and trawls the same waters! Oh brothers and sisters, tell us of your struggles against Satan! And your encounters with the Spirit!"

Let us bear witness, Lord!

And then they were all clapping. Jesse joined in, till I fixed him with a glance and he went still. They were swaying a bit too, like there was some music in the air they could hear but we could not, speeding up with their clapping, slowing down, then back up again. Just listening to that clapping, and thinking of trying to join into it, irritated me. It reminded me of trying to follow JC's line of reasoning, because right when you thought you had it down, it switched on you entirely. Like first you were supposed to go easy on adulterers, and then you're practically bullwhipping the market folks out of the temple. When I used to try to follow JC's train of thought, I felt like I was trying to hum along with a tune that kept changing and slipping into another key and turning a corner into the wind, and finally got lost altogether. I gave up round about the time that woman bathed JC's feet in perfumed oil. Why not sell the oil and give the money to the poor, I asked. And why not? I never could get it right with him. Neither could you, I bet.

I was still stewing on that one, as the clapping built up and dissolved around me. Noah's voice crashed like a felled tree across my thoughts.

"Come on up, people of the Lord! Let us proclaim our joys and sorrows, and the struggles of the Spirit against Satan!"

Folks were lurching and Jesse stood up on his chair to see, and a few swung their way out of the main mass of swaying faithful and rolled on up to the front.

The first one was a woman, thin and white-faced and looking like life had scuffed her up second or third time around the block. Mary Magedelene, and I know this personally, was never in fact so hangdog in all her days.

"Tell us, sister Claretta!" Noah said.

She took a gulp of air, and kind of jumped into her voice like it was a deep cold tank of water, so treacherous and thrilling was the act, that her face bobbed up with amazement. "Last Wednesday, I was sitting on my porch and I felt like I was a-coming down with something. My head was hotted up, and my hands broke into a cold sweat. Like the Devil and the Holy Spirit were in battle in my very body!"

Cast that demon out!

"And I thought of Christ our Lord, and the eternal torments he bore! I tell you brothers and sisters, that Devil just flew right out of me! He couldn't take the goodness of our Lord, and knew when he was outdone, and flew, into the evening sky and out. And I raised my arms and beat the air to scare off Satan, and he did skedaddle."

Hallelujah!

"As he passed out of me, a glass that was sitting on the porch step, there was nobody by it neither, well, it tumbled to the ground and broke."

"Satan has a thirst, we all know that," Noah said. "Couldn't touch the glass except that he destroyed it - but he couldn't get at your soul. No, ma'am, that vessel is in the hands of the Lord, never to be snatched or dashed; nor emptied nor broken! Praise the Holy Spirit, brothers and sisters!"

The singing began, like an entity not so much emanating from them as conjured up by them; and the clapping on the off-beat, a rhythm distinct from the top-level one of the singing, as thunder is from lightening, but connected. It was music that had crashed through the floor of heaven.

Gonna lay down my cross, pick up my crown

One of these mornings

A man took his turn to testify. He was robust, and sure, like he had been up there before and by now the power of the Lord had entered his very bones. "You say Satan has a thirst. Well, I'm here to tell you he tempts us to share in that sinful thirst. And sometimes we are led astray. I found myself last Saturday night with a little flask of hootch in my pocket. I was walking down South Chickasaw Street, feeling no pain, not in body, no, paying no mind to my soul. It was dark, darker than the deepest pitch that lays on any road. Don't ask, my brothers and sisters, how I came to be out in the night so late with a bottleful of demon water half of it stowed in my coat pocket and the other half within my belly! Whoever led me on that path, it was the Lord who brought me back."

Tell it, brother!

"I was passing through the darkness, and I felt afraid. Cold, like a mighty shadow was passing over. Above me was the sign for the old StepRight shoe factory. The windows were dark. But as I was walking past, a lamp lit up in the window! The light shone down on me. I was pinned in its beam like it was judgment from heaven, and it cleansed me. I took that flask of mine, and emptied it on the ground, and I tell you, that lamp burned brighter and brighter. It glowed down the whole length of the road, and it picked up that stream of evil liquor and burned it all to a path of light. That is the work of the Spirit, to turn the machinations of Satan into the instruments of godliness! And that path of light led me straight home, and I was still seeing it when I opened my door and took myself to bed."

"To slumber in the Lord," Noah boomed. "No sweeter dream than that."

"I am the light of the world, sayth the Lord," the man proclaimed.

The lord is my light and my salvation!

"He shall bring forth thy righteousness as the light," the man rejoined. "And thy judgment as noonday."

Noah put one hand on the man's shoulder and pushed himself in front. "Truly the light is sweet," Noah thundered.

"Hey, I like them sweet things," Jesse said.

A woman standing right ahead of us turned to look at Jesse, and smiled. Her eyes were shaded by the brim of her big straw hat. They looked kind, and sad. "It's like the Lord tells us, walk as children of light."

Jesse smiled as though somebody had just handed him a silver dollar and a chocolate bar. "I walk alright."

" 'Of light,' " I said. I tousled his hair. "The trouble is, Jes, a light just burns until there's nothing left of it."

"And sweet too are the fruits of the earth," Noah was saying. "Let us share together the foods provided by the ladies of the church. In the words of that beautiful hymn, let us break bread together." He was singing from the word "break" on down, and folks joined in with him.

Then I noticed that Jesse had somehow got his laces undone just sitting there. I sat down to set things straight when Jesse laughed and pointed up front. E had broken away from his mama and daddy, and was up at the front. He was singing at the top of his lungs which would have been about knee-high on a grown man but were still pretty powerful. He didn't know the words as such, but crooned along.

"A child shall lead them," Noah said. He laughed. The sweat gleamed on his face. "Serve the Lord with gladness. Come into His presence singing."

He has come into Jesse's presence singing, I thought. I watched as Jesse picked at his shoelaces, gave up undoing the left one and started in on the right.

The church folks were all smiling at E. They were beguiled by appearance, and blinded. They were ignorant of Jesse's identity, and my own. I looked at those folks grinning and hollering around me. I wondered what they would have made of it if they'd have known that Judas Iscariot was in their midst. Then I smiled, too, but my smile was knowing without any effort on my own part. It is a fact that when you been roaming the earth like I have life is pretty much one forlorn process of having your suspicions confirmed. But in that moment, I was proud, for our time would come, mine and Jesse's, and of that I had no doubt. I imagined the knowledge fairly glistened upon my whitened brow, and amid the noisy cavortings of the devout, I discreetly bowed my head as though in worship.

They were into another song already, arms raised high, hips shaking, shoulders twitching. This moving around business JC never could have kept up with. He couldn't dance, and he couldn't carry a tune. But hereabouts, as in my hometown, folks was watching for signs, even if they got it wrong and they were always fixating on a light blazing up or glassware breaking or some such: JC himself could find several dozen clues to life just staring at a mustard seed.

Still in song, folks rolled their way out of the church, into the yard laid down with a tablecloth and the cloth laden with food. Jesse ran ahead of me and stuck his finger into a half inch of yellow frosting on an angel food cake. I stood by the pond and watched. With his mama beside him, E ran right by Jesse, but neither took much notice of the other. E stood a half-head taller, I saw, and his brow was taking shape dark and sturdy like it was printing up in boldface. Whereas Jesse's frame was slight, and his small face shone pale and fragile (for rising from the dead must surely take it out of a body), and as transparent as truth; and I was content no one would guess they was even related. Jesse moved on to a peach pie, and E reached up his hand to grasp his mama's. I looked into the black unmoving water, but found no reflection.

When the afternoon had grown heavy with shadows, and darkness ready to fall, Jesse and I moved to go on home. Jesse had been hanging out by the cake table, gobbling up as many slices as he could, and saying a polite thank you after each one. I tried to arrange it so as we slipped out quiet-like, attracting no notice to ourselves, but Mrs. Greenfield spied us. She had a plate of lemon meringue pie in her hands, and it kept her from waving.

"Brother, we surely hope to see you here again," she called out.

They all looked to see us, a dozen hat brims turning in our direction, and they pitched a variety of goodbyes our way. Jesse and I kept walking, though I turned a small and perfect circle to face them once more, my hand raised in farewell. I saw my shadow circle around and meet itself. We were facing home, and we walked off in that direction.

We were crossing through an overgrown lot just beyond the church, not saying much, when I heard a couple of giggles rise up and then stifle.

"You hear that?" I said. We both stopped walking.

"Yep," Jesse said.

We were by a tumbledown picket fence that slumped and stretched in the middle of the nowhere we was passing through. The fence was overgrown with timothy grass that poked out all over it. I stood there looking, and my eyes picked out the motion of something, which then went still.

"Hey," I said. "What's that?"

There weren't no response but a quiver quick as a jack rabbit, only not quite as fugitive, as whatever was moving did not venture out into the field, but hunkered in deeper, and stopped. I reached down, and pushed aside a couple of pickets. They was half-rotted with termites and rain, and almost crumbled at my touch. In the bluish hollow below, the boy on top was the one I saw first.

"Howdy," he said. He clambered up, wiping his hands on the knees of his overalls and manfully making the best of a bad job. Then another boy emerged from the hollow, this one a little smaller, and finally a third, who was the smallest one of all.

"Howdy yourself," I said.

"Folks call me Reck," the first boy said, "and this here

is Mirth -" at this Mirth gave a quick nod of his chin, "and the puny one is Luck." Luck looked at us, scratched his knee, and yawned.

"I'm Jimmy," Jesse said, "and this here is Jud." He went up eye to nose to Luck. "We was both just at the prayer meet."

"We heard it ourselves," Reck said.

"Smelled awful good," Luck said.

"Course, if'n we got too close, Mrs. Greenfield, she'd see us, and start blubbering, and drag us on in -" Mirth began.

Reck swatted him. Mirth shut up, and Reck went on. "And pray all over us, and make such an all-around fuss, I reckon we'd rather get ourselves a slice of cake someplace else."

"We got plenty at home," Mirth said. He stuck his chin out.

"Plenty," Reck said. He looked me in the eye, steadily, man to man in charge of the young'uns. He shrugged with one shoulder, casual-like. "But sometimes a fella, he just likes to eat out."

"Save on the clean-up," I said.

Reck nodded. "It sure do."

"But don't it give you boys the whim-whams hanging out here in the dark?" I said.

"Heck, no," Reck said. "I ain't scared of no dark. Matter of fact, there ain't much that does scare me. I was just telling these here youngsters about a fella called Dr. Stingaree. Some folks call him Zogg, or Alzedi, he goes by a bunch of names, but he's the same fella, used to run a carnival show, where he made folks do what he wanted just by looking into their eyes. And now he's branched out, visitating a terrible but merciful death upon the condemned throughout the land. Now these two here," - he gestured with his thumb in the direction of Mirth and Luck - "it gives them the shakes to hear about it, but -"

"How'd you find out so much about that fella?" I said.

"I got a cousin," Reck said. "Lives in a lighthouse down by Biloxi, and someday, I'm gonna live down there too, right by the ocean, and the salt breeze cool my brow. Anyhow, he wrote me a letter all about it. Threw in some clippings too."

"He sounds like a real pal," I said.

"He's a heap more than that," Reck said. "He is my very own personal correspondent."

Then Luck started bleating, and he ran and burrowed his head into Reck's knee, and Reck looked at me with a well-what-can-you-do kind of look, and Jesse said, it *is* getting dark, Jud, maybe we better get on home. And so we all said, goodbye, goodbye, and the farewells ricocheted off the evening sky like stray shot, and echoed all around us.

·

CHAPTER FIFTEEN

That was the first time we met those three boys, but it sure weren't the last. I told Mrs. Greenfield the next day about how Jesse and I met up with them, and when she started up her talking, her chin was quivering at the mere thought of them boys, but she got so into telling their plight, and her chin steadied up right quick to keep pace with her mouth. And what she told me got mixed up into what I got to know about them myself, as they soon took to Jesse as their special pal. Before they'd even get to the door so as you could see them, you'd hear them laughing and calling and whispering, and they announced themselves in that way like ghost children out on the road, looking for their supper at the hour of dusk.

They was called the Lesses, two of them brothers, and one of them a cousin, but nobody remembered which was which, and they was bunched up in age like cars in a train wreck. They lived together in a tumbledown shack on the edge of Shakerag, where all the colored folks were. The Lesses were a regular disgrace, everybody said, and got by on their own ill-advised devices. They had no momma, and no regular daddy. Time to time, a man did turn up. You knew he was in town because the Lesses quit going to school altogether. You might run into one of them boys on the back roads. He'd say hello quick, and hang his head to one side, and there was either a shadow, or a purplish mark starting to steal across his jaw. Near as soon, you'd spy the man, rubbing his filthy beard, drinking moonshine, sleeping all day by the river, and becoming a topic of conversation at dinner tables and porches across town. And just as quick, he moved on.

Whatever their original names were, they had long been forgotten. They were called 'Less' on account of their habits of shopping. They'd go into a grocery store, and collect a basketful of goods: licorice whips, bulls-eyes, canned cream corn, hot dogs, vanilla wafers and such. When they brought their basket up to the counter and the amount was totaled, they were always short of the cash to pay for it. Big pout, chins trembling, they'd put aside the bag of crystal mints, then the can of tomato soup, each time calling out, "less the mints," and "less the soup." They'd been seen out in the hard frost with no shoes on; and whatever the season, snot dangled from their noses. Their hair met up with a razor but infrequently, and the razor in question looked to be as rough-edged and wayward a proposition as they were themselves. They would've been outcasts, if only they'd been taken seriously enough. As it was, they became Jesse's best friends: Reckless, Luckless, and Mirthless.

Reckless was the biggest, tall and stretched-out-looking for his age. His arms and shoulders was like a good length of leftover drain piping: expansive beyond any possible use, and hollow. He had freckles that spread out like a dash of nutmeg on eggnog, and a raspy edge to his voice. He was pugnacious if crossed, and he was most of the time ready to be crossed, walking around with his chin stuck out and his hands at his sides knotted up in fists. Alongside warding off potential aggressors, Reck pursued what he called his "investigations," or "researches," and he kept a record of happenings both in town and far away. It was his book of wonders, especially those involving mayhem, destruction, and death - how you got there and what happened to the body afterwards. "I endeavor to get the story right," he said, "and complete, and set down in my own handwriting."

Mirth was a year or two younger. He was moon-faced and fat-wristed, with skin as light and translucent as watered-down milk, and a lank mouse-brown shank of hair that lay limply on his brow. He took things serious, and he read the labels on their cans of corn and boxes of vanilla wafers, his mouth half-hanging open, and his lips moving; and in the same way, following the preacher's directive to heed the signs the Lord puts in our path, he pondered the meaning of traffic signals.

Mrs. Greenfield said she found him one summer night on his own, lingering by a walkway at the intersection of Lee and Elm Streets in the center of town. It must have been around nine at night, she'd guess; in any case, it was dark enough for cars to have switched on their headlamps. You can cross now, she told him, the road is clear. Mirth had one arm slung around the pole of a streetlamp, like it was his new-found best buddy. Around the high, white light, almost harsh in the soft summer night, flitted a cloud of moths. There was a sign affixed near the top of the pole. Mirth pointed at it.

" 'Yield to Light,' " he said, almost in a whisper. "Ain't that beautiful? And that's just what I'm doing. I been yielding here for a good long stint."

Mrs. Greenfield didn't have the heart to tell him the sign referred to a set of traffic signals not yet installed, and was, in any case, directed at drivers, not folks on foot. She took him firmly by the hand, looked both ways to set a good example, and marched him across the road. She was at the point of walking him the whole way home, Mirth twisting around to keep his eyes on the sign the whole time, when Reck and Luck turned the corner. It was lined with a boxwood hedge, and that's why she hadn't spotted them straight off. Reck took the matter in hand. "He did remember to call out thank you, that Mirth," she said. She reached down absently to smooth the hem of her dress. "And so did the little one. The lanky one just nodded though." She sighed. "I reckon that's his idea of being a man."

Luckless was the smallest, the youngest, and the quietest of the three. His eyebrows were the biggest thing about him: half-circles, like an owl's, and dark, as if they was penciled-in. He looked tired and surprised, as though the effort of showing such perpetual astonishment had tuckered him out early in life; and a little undone, too, by the world popping out around him with such bewildering variety, and wearing his eyes out with so much seeing to do all at once.

They was what Jesse carried away from his encounter with the worshipful. Oh, he liked the music, he told me when I pressed him, and the ladies were nice, and the pies were fine, and the preacher fellow was okay he guessed, but from that first encounter, it was them boys Jesse had on the bean. I could not help but consider them a something of a distraction and a nuisance, especially given what Jesse was, and eventually had to do. But, I told myself, Jesse ain't but a boy yet; and besides which, compassion is an admirable trait, particularly in a chosen one, and so I indulged him.

I had to indulge him on a darn near regular basis. If Jesse made noises about going to the movie house, he'd throw the Lesses into the pot at the last minute. If ever I brought up how it was a nice afternoon and the lizards might be hopping, let's go by the river and watch them; or how clear the night was and let's go look at the stars, Jesse would say why don't he ask the Lesses to come along too. We don't always got to bring them boys with us, I told him once, one arm halfway into my coat sleeve. Jesse looked me in the eye. No momma, no daddy, he said, his arms stretched out to either side of him for emphasis, and then united, like a boat jib suddenly pointed my way, they ain't even got a you, Jud.

Well, I said, scooping him up and dangling him down and tickling his ribs, that ain't just a crying shame, it's a laughing one on top.

And Jesse agreed that it certainly was.

CHAPTER SIXTEEN

There was a matter of crying shame that was soon to befall us, and it was delivered from the hand of Orville Bean. Maybe I should have known when I'd seen him come into work that day. His nose was positively aquiver with the prospect of a particular bargain.

Bargains in general weren't to Bean what they was to most folks, a means to an end. With Bean, they was the end, and an end without end, if you get my meaning: driving a bargain was like driving a car that perpetually manufactured its own gas. A look came into his eye when he spoke about a successful deal: it was as if the deal were animate, a creature like a race horse whose beauty and speed and profit-making ability were all of a thing and could hardly be conceived of separately. And added to which, he had conceived a resentment of E's family, which had long been at a simmer.

He finally told me about it himself, one steamy Indian summer day that a water valve burst in the town square and we sold the city a fair stretch of new piping: some cousin or other of Vern's had the sheriff's office in East Tupelo locked up since forever, and no matter what he owned, or who he bought, Bean never could seem to make a dent. As "a young buck, younger than you now, Jud," Bean had tried for the office himself - once, and failed. After that, he'd taken to "sponsoring" a fella to run. Over the past few years, Bean reckoned he had sold that town more coffins than he or his boy had ever got ballots, and he figured the only chance he'd have is if the dead got up and shuffled on off to the ballot box. The most recent go around, Bean's stooge had got bare four per cent of the vote. And the sheriff was quoted in the paper, saying why don't Mr. Bean avail himself of one of his very own coffins, and give his political career a decent and overdue burial.

"I ain't fit to be made a fool of," Bean said. His face was grim, like a leftover that was a-going to stay that way. "What you reckon I should do, son?"

"Well, sir," I said, "I reckon it's time you fired the pollsters, and hired yourself an historian."

Bean gave a slow, malignant grin that was all teeth and no heart, and I figured that's why it could last so long. He hung his head low. He had one of his crime gazettes rolled up in his hand, and he swatted the air with it. "Shucks," he said. Then he turned his face to me, and asked if I knew about how the authorities apprehended the Red Handed Bandito, and why he was so called. When I said I did not, he brightened up considerable. He opened up the gazette, and read me aloud the last couple of paragraphs of the case history, where sentence was passed (twenty years for the housebreaks, plus an extra three for shoplifting the trademark bottle of nail polish beforehand), and the aftermaths put forth. The policeman who had traced the tell-tale "Bossa Nova" shade of nail varnish to three possible cosmetics counters had since been elected sheriff of Calhoun County, Arkansas. The chief arresting officer had retired from the force, and now ran his own hardware shop - try as he might, Bean could not keep from giving each word of that sentence a hard, equal emphasis. Bean read the story slowly, with a delivery dramatic but measured, and paused a moment, like a preacher at the end of a scripture, before he folded the magazine shut. Then he closed his eyes, and directed me to restock the nut-and-bolt canisters.

What Bean went on to do weren't simply, I am convinced, the joy of skinning somebody's else wallet. So far he was concerned, it weren't revenge, nor jealousy, nor even city politics, nor yet the will to bully – at least at the outset. It was a matter of justice. Bean leafed through the crime gazettes, and how those stories stirred his blood from cool to lukewarm. It weren't so much he felt a cleansing revulsion at the doings of criminals; it was more that he felt an aspirational reverence towards the correctional authorities. I know a thing or two myself about the matters of misdoings and the sentence they carry, and the stories folks can make up about it, and I am satisfied of this one thing: what Bean came to see when he saw Vern was his chance to dispense the justice he'd only read about, and his daddy slipped out of this world browsing over. If it took making Vern a criminal to make Bean a deputy of social order, well, that was okay by Bean.

And with my unwitting, and witless, connivance, they both became just that.

It came to pass a week or two after our encounter with the Lesses. The morning dawned gray and close. The sky was the color of a dead fish belly, and the sun was diffuse, like it had been left inside the pocket of a shirt sent through the hot water wash. I was hard at work in Bean's backroom, sanding down the wood for a big order of caskets. Bean was leaning against his desk, facing me as he went through the paperwork and bragging about his big order and how he secured it.

"Yessir," he was saying, "A houseful of Jesuits down by Natchez, dropping like flies. What you make of that, boy?"

I stopped sanding, and looked at him. "From all you have been saying, sir, I expect the language itself will fit itself to this development like the shoreline to the sea."

Bean stuck a toothpick in his mouth and kept looking at me as if I hadn't said anything.

I went on, "And in a hot summer season, we'll be getting out the swatters, and saying to each other, why, these here flies are dropping like Jesuits."

Bean lip-wrangled the toothpick to the other side of his mouth, and looked up over his accounting sheets. "I'll tell you what I make of it, son." He rustled his fistful of number-scratchings at me. "Profit. It's all in here." He tossed the stack of papers behind him on his desk, gave them a hearty whack with the flat of his hand. He was watching me all the while. "I guess that influenza just seeped into their bones and if it didn't get 'em quick, it'll get 'em slow. Of course, I don't hold myself with men wearing skirts, but they are willing to pay hand over fist for their coffins. Eyes lit up when I told them there was a bulk offer. Goes to show you to one thing, boy - all the Jews aren't in Jerusalem. A boatload of them headed for Rome."

Bean commenced to hee-haw. I went on sanding, so that it rasped over and against his chortle, and then we both heard the bell on the front door rattle and the door push open, and swing shut. Bean, still chuckling, looked at the clock, and then turned and winked at me. "Coffins ain't the only thing I got on the burner today. You fetch that hick back here, and maybe you'll learn something."

Vernon was standing by the paint cans, hanging his head, hands in pockets, shifting on his feet, and looking feckless, as embarrassed as my own dad had been when JC commenced alarming the neighborhood. Maybe that's why I had always taken a shine to Vern.

"Howdy," I said.

He smiled. "It sure is nice to see you, Jud. I mostly forget you work for Mr. Bean, somehow, you're, uh I don't know, such a different sort of fella."

"Come on in the back room, Vern," I said, "Mr. Bean is waiting for you."

I held the half-door open. Vernon took a single step, then a fraction of another one, over the threshold.

"Good morning," Vernon said, like he was trying to talk himself into it.

Bean looked at the clock. "Afternoon," he said. "Ten minutes late, Vern. Now I like a man what keeps his word."

"Then we think alike." Vernon gave the idea of a smile a go, forcibly hearty, but it rolled off his mouth and shriveled up somewhere in the vicinity of his boot heels. "What I mean is, Mr. Bean, sir, that hog I sold you, well, we agreed ourselves a price for it."

"Yes ourselves we surely did."

"Fourteen dollar. Not four."

"That ain't my recollection," Bean said. "Jud, you ever hear me say anything about a fourteen-dollar pig?"

"No," I said. "Not a four dollar one either." I was sanding real slow. "Four dollar is one heck of a bargain, and the only thing you love better than getting a bargain is talking about getting one."

"This here's a copy of that receipt I wrote out," Bean said. He waved it at Vernon, who stepped up and took it. "Read it yourself." Bean chuckled.

Vern took the receipt and looked at it.

"It's upside down," Bean said.

Vernon's mouth twitched. He handed the slip back. "All I know is, Mr. Bean, we said fourteen for the hog."

"You said, son. I didn't. And you signed on four."

"It don't seem fair," Vernon said.

Bean gave a brief, mean smile, like the fugitive flash of pocket knife in the hot sun. "There's a couple of things I can't stand for in my underlings. One of them's greed. The other one's giving me sass. You keep on like this and I'll give you the heave-ho. I'll hire Yellow to clear out the warehouse. That what you want?"

"All I want's what coming to me."

"You'll get that alright," Bean said. "Don't doubt that

for a minute, boy."

Vernon just stood there, lumpy and inert, like a sackful of potatoes getting depleted one by one.

"I got work to do," Bean said. He shoved himself off from the desk. "Jud, see this scrap paper here, stack of old estimates, checkbooks and such? Take 'em on up to the trash heap." He looked at the clock. "I better get going. Those priests can't wait forever for eternal rest ha-ha." Then he said he'd be back by five, and left, the half-door swinging a few times behind him. Vern and I watched it till it went still, and the fan-shaped bit of shadow and light snapped shut entirely.

"Saw your little boy the other day," Vernon said. "Running like the wind. Got himself a nice appetite there, too."

"Oh Jimmy's a handful," I said. "He sure loved that church meet. I couldn't get him to stop talking about it. The cakes and the pies part anyhow."

"You never know what'll led them to the Lord," Vernon said. "Now, my boy, he can't wait to get to church meets and commence his singing. And folks all seem to like it, too. Gets them all joining in till he gets so good, they stop to listen to him all on his own."

"That a fact?" I said, a few degrees cooler than I meant to. I could not help thinking, of course, of how Jesse had it all over E, but that nobody but me knew it yet. Then I was immediately ashamed of my own small-mindedness, for how could I begrudge the man taking whatever pride in his life he could.

"Like last night my boy drew us a picture," Vernon said. "Looked like one man making a barbecue with another man beside him getting ornery, and a big man up in the sky smiling down. He said it was Cain and Abel and God, and the sacrifice part was like the church supper." He chuckled ruefully. "Only then Elvis started crying and said he missed his own brother that his mama's always talking about."

"You don't say," I said. I picked up my sandpaper, casual-like, and recommenced my labors.

"Better get to work myself," Vernon said. He shifted onto his left foot, and stopped moving. "I could take care of them papers for you."

"That's okay," I said.

"Heap's on the way to the warehouse."

"You got enough to do," I said.

"No sense in you wasting your time, Jud."

I put down the sandpaper. "There's no sense in wasting anything," I said. "You know what Vern? Why don't you take that paper home yourself? Looks like you sure have a use for it."

Vernon looked like I'd caught him at something, he was standing so still and silent, caught in mid-inhale.

"Give your little boy something to draw on," I went on. "Do sums. Or maybe draw some more pictures of our Lord. Or that hog you got squizzled on." I figured it was the least I could do after Bean had showed himself so scurvy.

He was suddenly up to the task of exhaling. "That's a real nice idea," he said. "Thank you kindly."

"No need to mention this to Mr. Bean," I said.

"Of course not," he said. I thought I saw him wink but maybe it was just a splinter of sunlight in his eye, or mine.

CHAPTER SEVENTEEN

That night fell deep and starless, and my sleep was troubled and full of dreams. I saw a ladder, reaching up aside a building that had no roof, and I heard the pounding of a thousand hammers. The blazing sun caught on their edges, and the earth looked scorched. I heard the singing of men at work, and the singing became a wailing over the land.

When I awoke, I was standing out in the road. The moon was bright and my shirt was wet. I was caught in a terror as fearsome as if I was lost on an uncharted sea. I didn't know where I was, nor how I got there. I was one heap of nullifications, shivering and perspiring under the soft black sky.

My brow was glistening with sweat that started out warm but was going cold fast, and in that same sensation, I felt a wave of shame and dread creeping over me. When JC and I were little, sometimes one or the other of us wet the bed, and knowing we was to get yelled at when the sun rose, we lay there, feeling kind of lost, the wet warmth beneath us staying wet but going cold in the flat light of five in the morning. The Almighty had His ways of calling me back. Just foisting a passel of dreams on me wasn't good enough - I had to tread the earth through a fair number of mine as well.

I turned and saw I was a few good ells distance from my house. The front door wavered. There was something like a low-flying spirit hanging around behind the hinge. It gleamed milky white in the night, The door swung open, revealing Jesse, who cried out, and trundled towards me.

"What you doing?" Jesse said. He tugged at my shirttails.

"Just taking a walk same time as I was getting some shuteye and searching for the stars," I said. "It's a genuine time saver. You ought to try it."

"I was watching you and talking to you but you kept on like I thought you was dead." Jesse stuck both his arms up at me. I scooped him up. He tousled my hair.

"I guess you talked me back awake," I said. "You could hire yourself out as a human alarm clock. Just need to wind you up every now and again." I grabbed the top of his head like the fern end of a carrot, and give it a little twist.

Jesse laughed and brought his nose up next to mine. "Let's go get us some root beer."

"Sure," I said. "We'll do that in a little while." I spun him around like an aircraft over my shoulders, and carried him in circles back towards the house.

"This here is what you call a flight," I said. "When you were little, we fled Cairo-way, just like I done myself when I was little. You remember that?"

"Nope," he said.

"Well, we did. We went down by Cairo, and lived to tell the tale. Let's wing by Mrs. Hadley's clothesline." I spun him up in that direction. "And by her rickety old fence, and into her flower border she's always hollering about." I dipped him face downwards into an azalea and plucked him back up. "Or how 'bout going face to face with that twinkle-toed pig she got?" Mrs. Hadley kept a hog that high-stepped around the swept yard like a lady in new pair of pumps.

Jesse was giggling. For someone marked out, he had a real nice temperament.

"More," Jesse said.

We spun around, from a hacked-out tree trunk on one side of the clearing to Mrs. Hadley's azalea on the other; the first one was Jericho and then it became Bethlehem; the second was Memphis, until it became Jerusalem. We were spinning around like that, the sky getting lighter and lighter, Jesse calling out the destination, till we were buzzing around the broken-down pump out back of our shack, and Jesse yawned.

"Is it a little while yet?" he said.

"Nope. It won't be until next week, or maybe the one after that. I say we both get some sleep that don't involve wearing out our feet."

It wasn't until I'd put Jesse under a quilt and laid back down in bed that I remembered the dreams that had so disturbed me that night, and I felt uneasy and displaced, like I'd been walking on spilt sugar, or followed by somebody else's shadow.

The next afternoon, I was in the back room waxing a deluxe casket. I sat back on my heels, and regarded my progress. Mahogany ain't never been my favorite wood to work with, to tell you truth. It's damn near self-important with its own opacity. If I had my choice, I'd have worked more with maple. It's got shadow and sun swirled right into it, and works up supple as a yard of silk. I'd just rocked my weight back to the front of my feet, when Bean came in. He struck the countertop with the palms of his hands, and grinned.

"I knew that addlepated hick would fall for it," he said.

I went on waxing. "What's Yellow got himself into this time?"

"I ain't talking about Yellow," Bean said. "I'm talking about that no-account rube, Vernon Presley."

I slowed down my rubbing. "You rent him one of

those false bottomed-casket numbers for when the time comes?"

Bean grinned again. "Fool pinched one of those old checkbooks of mine. He wrote himself a check, like I reckoned he'd do. He just cashed it down the Savings and Loan."

I put down the cloth and sat up now, a little straighter, and worried.

Bean went on. "I knew once I mentioned them checkbooks, he'd be nosing around, waiting for his chance to swipe one of them. And he sure did."

"That must be a great satisfaction to a man such as yourself," I said.

"Jud, I expect we're both of us students of the human condition." Bean fixed me with those eyes of his, the color of a shucked oyster, and leaned back on the counter. "You can learn a lesson here, boy. This here is what having power is." He waited.

"What's that?" Playing straight man to the spiritual big cheeses was my main and most practiced skill.

"It ain't making people do what you want." Bean paused and savored his words. "It's getting them to do what you want theirselves. Like it's what they were wanting to do too. And that fool sure did."

"What did you tell him?" I said. "Four dollars for the hog, or fourteen?" I was feeling pretty sick but was ready to grin companionably as required.

"I never said fourteen myself. Not a once. And that ain't the point, now is it," Bean said. "On account of a man what can't read got no business signing his name, do he? And what he's gone and done now is a clear matter for the law. Probably hung out by the heap waiting for you to dump them bank books." He heehawed. "I bet he was feeling like he could make himself at home round you."

"Maybe he did." I swallowed hard on nothing.

"Prison's the only place for him," Bean said. "I was trying to do him a favor, buying that hog. And this is how he repays me. For plenty of folks hereabouts, four dollars is a solid week's wage." He'd be telling this story in court, and he was practicing it, to get it in good shape. I bet he was imagining himself quoted in police notes somewheres, and in a witness box taking the oath. The whole internal spectacle no doubt made his insides shiver with impacted delight, and I was reminded of his momma and her tooth at the mention of the word "Alaska."

I could taste the wood wax on my tongue, bitter as a taunt. A hog had laid old Vernon low. I had attended upon his downfall, and delivered, unbidden, the instruments of deception into his hands.

At dinnertime, I headed out into the street, dragging my faint shadow after me. My heart was heavy and my senses dazed. A fellow said howdy, I think his name was Charlie, and I think I said howdy back. Leastways I nodded because I saw the shadow of my chin dip down and up. The sunlight drifted down weakly, at a slant, and my heart sloped down with it.

CHAPTER EIGHTEEN

I saw the story in the paper a few days later: how Mr. Vernon Presley was found guilty, and sentenced to the county jail. Bean got to testify in court, and he was quoted in the newspaper. A few of his buddies in the key of sycophant had come into the shop when the paper came out, and Bean read his testimony out loud for them. His right forefinger perforated the dead air: " 'Now, where I come from,' I says, 'a deal's a deal, a man's word is his word, and four ain't fourteen any more than a firefly is fire -' I could tell they liked that line, so I gave it time to sink in - 'all I am asking for of this court is simple justice.' "

Two of the buddies gathered around was brothers. One of them managed a cotton mill, and the other one wrote for the *Crier*. They were stocky, broad-shouldered, and low-lying; and each of them was wearing a whitish suit, with a tan-colored shirt underneath. They stuck to each other side by side, and from the corner of my eye, they looked like a pair of saddle shoes, or basset hounds. The mill manager spit a little when he talked, and the other one sweated no matter what he was doing.

Just watching Bean in front of them that day, I felt I

was watching a man who was losing some less obvious sense, not sight or hearing, but touch maybe: or inside of him was diminishing some organ or gland that we don't know what it does or even have a name for it until we come across somebody where it's totally withered away. He was a man ascending to the podium of his own conceit, and from its heights, he looked down upon his fellows, and judge them. And he did.

"Simple justice," Bean repeated. He looked the two brothers each in the eye. "I looked at them just like what I'm doing now. Then I said, 'For judgment I am come into this world, sayth the Lord. And for judgment are we gathered here today.'"

"That's telling them," the spitter said. Bean frowned, mindful of the trajectory, and stepped back.

"You said it," the sweater echoed. He had a handkerchief pressed to his right temple. "And I done told about it." His mouth cracked into a grin, revealing a row of childish square white teeth. His wide fair forehead gleamed.

"Man such as yourself can tell them what's what, and they'll listen," the old man said. He was skinny and pink-faced, and all the fat he had on him looked to be collected in a turkey wattle round his neck. It was wobbling with emphasis, and his voice wobbled too. "I know how to *keep* accounts, alrighty, but Mr. Bean here knows how to make them stick."

"This town sure don't need a fella what's hog wild on the loose," the spitter said.

They hucked it up, eyes on Bean the whole time. Bean permitted himself a smile, then his mouth went straight. The chortling subsided.

"Justice ain't a pleasure, fellas," Bean said. They stood up an inch taller, as if pulled upwards by the same string, and waited. "It's a singular duty," he concluded.

Their shoulders relaxed, and they agreed that it surely was, and thanked him again, and told him he'd stood up for his rights so fine they were thankful he weren't their adversary. Bean stood there accepting their praise without comment, like it weren't no more remarkable than sunlight, or air. Then they looked at the clock, remarked on the time, and nodded goodbye. Bean watched them leave, and breathed deep. I wondered where he'd stashed his next candy bar, but his mind looked to be still on higher things.

The bells jingled, and a man came in. He said his hound been sprayed by a skunk and he needed a can of kerosene. Bean had to move out of the way so I could reach the can. And I was glad because I felt that by displacing him I'd made some of that praise fall off of him, on to the floor, where I swept it up later and threw it on the trash heap, where the checkbooks should have been.

On my way home that night, I took a detour through Cornwillow Street. Across the road, I saw E on his momma's porch. He was bawling his eyes out and taking in all the air he could and flushing it out of his lungs, and starting all over again.

I kept walking on the shady side of the street so no one would see me. I passed by a candy stand on Chicksaw, and bought a nickel moonpie for Jesse. I got home, said hello to Mrs. Greenfield, then in short order goodbye, and set out supper for me and Jesse.

Jesse was eating his greens. "Tell me a story," he said.

Okay, I said, I will. I got down my Bible, and flipped through it. "There's lots of good ones in here. How about this one? Cain and Abel." Preoccupied, I fell back on the doings between brothers.

I told him the story. Cain was a farmer and Abel was a shepherd. "Cain knew his folks were pretty hard up, the crop hadn't been great that year, so for an offering to God, he scrounged around and came up with some moldy carrots. Abel turned up with the whitest, fleeciest sheep of his flock, and offered them to God, then Cain had the temerity to get jealous of his brother. His brow went black and he got mad."

"What's temerity?" Jesse picked up a collard leaf and popped it in his mouth.

"It's insolence," I said. "Like when I tell you to use your spoon for your food and you go ahead and use your paws instead. Anyway, one day Cain and Abel were out walking and Cain turned on Abel, and killed him."

Jesse swallowed one big collard green lump. His jaw dropped open. "Why would he do that for? They're in the same family."

"I reckon he was so jealous he couldn't think straight. He knew Abel was God's favorite."

"But they were brothers."

"So what?" I said.

"They could take turns being God's favorite," Jesse said.

"It don't work like that." I knew that for a fact. "So God sent Cain from his homeland, to wander the earth like a lost dog."

"Is that what he's doing now?" Jesse said.

"Him or else somebody pretty much like him," I said. Of course, the funny thing was, some us get to be a vagrant on account of *doing* the Lord's bidding. "And this one may come up to you on a lonely road, but don't be afraid. He's okay. He don't wish you no harm, or anybody else either."

"I don't like this story," Jesse said.

"Well, then I'll you another one. It's about brotherly love, too."

I told him about Jacob and Esau, adding as was my custom details not in the Bible because it needed doing. I was skating pretty close with this one, Esau and Jacob being actual twins, too, but the telling bug was upon me, had bit pretty bad, and I couldn't help myself. It was all I could do to keep from grinning.

"Well, Jesse, this man Isaac was married to a lady named Rebecca, and one time she found out she was going to have a child, and more than that, two of them. She could feel them squabbling away in her stomach before they were born." I kept talking fast so Jesse didn't chime in with questions of a type I was not in mind to answer. "So Rebecca asked God what was happening and he told her, 'Two nations are within you waiting to be born, two rival peoples, and the older shall serve the younger.' Esau was born first, a right hairy little mite he was, then Jacob, who was clinging to the first one's heel."

"I wish I had me a brother," Jesse said.

"You keep listening, and you'll know better what to wish for. Esau was a hunter. He liked to roam the fields with a shotgun and bring back all kinds of meat for roasting, which his daddy Isaac sure enjoyed. Jacob, now, he was a quieter fella. I expect he might wear glasses and read a lot of books. Kind of stoop-shouldered from carrying them home. His momma favored him."

"Wish I had me a momma," Jesse said.

"I know you do, boy. So one time Esau came back from hunting. He was famishing hungry, ready to drop from it, and Jacob was cooking up some red meat stew. You could smell it cooking from a mile way and the closer Esau got, the wider his belly gaped. So he asked his brother for a bowl of that stew, and Jacob said, well, Es, you want a bowlful, you'll have to give me something."

Jesse pondered. "Esau have a bicycle?"

"No. Nor a catcher's mitt, or a train set or anything of the kind. But what Esau did have was his birthright. On account of being the oldest."

"And what's Jacob got?" Jesse said. "A birthwrong?"

"You catch on mighty quick," I said. "What Jacob had was a hankering to take over from his daddy when the time came. So he said to Esau, I'll gave you a bowlful of this stew if you give me your birthright. Esau was close to fainting, he was perishing of hunger, and he said, okay then, that birthright won't do me no good if I die here and now of starvation, so he swore an oath, and chowed down.

Jacob sauntered off, knowing he got a good deal, and later on, he was the granddaddy of all twelve tribes of Israel."

"What kind of stew was it?" Jesse said.

"Chicken meat, I expect. Or goat. But that ain't the point of the story. And I know something else that's good. It's got chocolate all over it."

Jesse hopped down from his chair. "Where is it?" He headed over to my coat, reached up and turned the pockets inside out. He scampered to the chest of two drawers, and pulled out the bottom one.

"Before you pull this house apart, I guess I better tell you. On the window sill, looking out like it wants to be put back in the sky."

Jesse went up to the sill, snatched the moonpie, and rolled it along the ledge. "We're going out to play," Jesse said. "Take a ride on that gate."

"You slip on that jacket before you go anywhere," I said. "And take care you don't fall off. I ain't fixing to tend to some little fool's broken neck."

Jesse went out the door. I sat at my table with the Bible. In a moment, I heard the broken gate swinging back and forth, and it sounded kind of mournful, like a low-flying gull who'd lost sight of the sea. I heard Jesse talking to the moonpie and asking it about which of the stars it liked best. That's all we need, I thought, an instrument of God who talks to a marshmallow moon like it was a playmate.

But soon I was mostly thinking about the stories I just told Jesse, scanning them closely as the night sky, and musing over the deceptions of brotherly love, and fatherly love, and other kinds as well.

I know how we're supposed to conclude Esau deserved what he got, or didn't get. But the man was hungry, and I always thought Jacob pulled a dirty trick. He knew how to drive a bargain, but so does Orville Bean. Hoodwinking his daddy as the daddy lay dying about which son he was, I guess Jacob went Bean a few steps better. But that's who the Almighty saw fit to heap with honor. That story haunted my boyhood. Sometimes when JC and I were both still living at home, I'd daydream about sitting by the side of the house in the gathering dark and the bluish cold, warming a pot of stew. JC'd be hungry, and I could get him to sell me his birthright as first-born. Our shadows would fall black and stark, and JC's arm would reach for the pot. I would watch not him but the wall behind him, his shadow-sleeve outstretched, and that gesture would silently and indelibly seal our fate. Or I'd daydream about my momma taking my part the way Rebecca took Jacob's, and scheming to have me win favor with my father. She would wear a blue sash at dinner that night as a signal to me that all had gone as planned, and JC wouldn't know a thing about it as he reached for another piece of bread.

JC never took too well to the story about Esau. I expect he didn't want to hear about a younger twin in the ascendancy. In preference, JC made one up about a prodigal son, and a more side-swiping, brother-bashing anecdote is hard to imagine. Because I was the one who stayed with Joseph and worked, and didn't get no fatted calf roasted on the spit for my troubles either. That stupid story almost put me in a mind to go out whoring just so I could be found, and they could throw a big party for me. But I was too busy earning our living, and honoring my father on this earth. You don't hear too much about me in connection with honor, I'm willing to bet, but then I ain't never told my side of the story.

JC did wear me down, with his remarks about going about his father's business and you can bet he didn't mean making anything useful with a hammer and a nail. Joseph got pushed aside. JC's handlers sure don't bother telling you too much about him. It was as if this man, who raised us as his own, somehow didn't rate much more than a mention. When JC took to street preaching, it close to finished my father. He lay sick for several weeks. For a long time before that even, no one had wanted his business: strangers might begin talking to him about making a table or a set of chairs, then realize who he was, and say, a grin splitting across their face like a rip in a burlap sack that couldn't help but widen, so you're the one whose son's causing all this fuss, and Joseph hung his head in shame. His face went gray and his breathing became forever heavy and slow.

As it happened, Joseph's own time came right around JC's. I know for a fact JC could have raised him up, like he did with Lazarus. But he didn't. He was busy with other things, loving the world more than he did his own folks. That was one time my heart scowled black against him. JC was too busy performing tricks to convince the multitudes: walking on water, multiplying bread - a regular road show that would have disgusted him before.

JC and me and our mother and the merry band had been preaching in Shiloh that day Joseph died. I remember JC was mouthing on about the family of all mankind, and the spreading shelter of the yew tree and some such. I was standing up against the sun beating down on me, withstanding it more like. It was oppressive, like a great weight, as if some abstract force like authority or responsibility that had been bedeviling your mind was being made concrete and physically intractable. The sun was so relentless, it was like to incinerate the things of substance forever and make of their shadows black and immutable shapes. I stood with my arms crossed, watching a one-legged chicken hobble through a broken gate. A pack of stray dogs were rounding after it, loose-limbed, affable, and murderous, yipping high-pitched and clamorous into the noonday heat. I reached down and chucked a pebble at them to scatter. It hit one mutt on the left flank, and ricocheted off the gate. Big John rolled his eyes at me to keep still. I was about to remonstrate in the way I knew he hated but couldn't answer, "Is not this chick a member of the family of life?", when the chicken stumbled and fell right over. It scratched at the air with its one scabby foot. Just then, a messenger appeared, raising the dust to our ankles, and announcing that he sought the sons of Joseph.

It's not as if the news bothered JC much. Or our mother, for that matter, because for a long time, the four handlers had encouraged her in their new way of thinking: Mankind! Eternal Life!, and they became her sons too. When they sprang that one on me, as I was sweeping up after dinner, I thought, well, that's great, eleven more just like him, stumbling along the desert and giving the locals scandal, and leaving me to smooth things over as best I could.

"JC's got such an insight into God's will," I said. My mother was still sitting at the table, looking at a spot of nothing somewhere to the right of her water glass. "He reminds me of that fella Jonas," I went on. "Maybe you ought to get together with Jonas's mother. Compare notes. How my boy tripped up the Almighty on a technicality, and some such. But oh wait, I forgot - Jonas isn't with us no more. Wonder how his momma's doing these days. I bet she remembers JC. Your boy's got more good works than you can shake a stick at, don't he."

"There's no need to be cruel," my mother said.

"There's no need to be nothing, when you come right down to it," I said.

"You know he isn't like other people," she said. "Why do you bear him such bitterness?"

"You got a point there, mother. Not being like other people ought to make him the most likable creature on this earth. But I guess I just got a bias against a fella who's so warm to make the world his brother. Especially as I am the brother who sees he eats now and again, and takes a bath and remembers to change his clothes more than twice a year. Of course, that just means I ain't got time to tend to important things like gawking all day at a field full of half-putrefied lilies and conjuring up some lesson it's supposed to be showing us all."

"You never used to be so mean-spirited," my mother said. She raised her head, and the whole of her face was cast in shadow. "It makes me so sad, Judas, to see one of my boys bear such ill-will against the other. You don't know the pain a mother's heart can hold."

"You better watch out," I said. "The next thing you know, the whole world won't just be his brother, they'll be his momma, too. I'd hold on to that title if I were you, with both hands, like your best wrap in a high wind. You'll excuse me now, I got our accounts to tend to. That's what I call love, mother: when somebody pays the bills now and then."

It was a fact: to satisfy those eleven, JC had to divest himself of every human contact but them - and I do dearly believe that's what killed my father Joseph, made his heart go sick and gray inside of him. That other day, when the hammer was pounding and pounding into the sky, and I stood at the top of a tree, I couldn't help but note they'd had to fetch a hammer and nail to build that cross, and set it up, and in a way my father's business was being done too. I remember hearing the wood creak a little, even from that distance, whining a bit with the strain, like a woebegone wind from a faraway place was caught within it.

I was hearing the same creaking all around me. I put my head up, and looked through the window in the failing twilight. Jesse was standing on the gate. The three Lesses was grouped around him. Their faces glowed. The sky was low, and the light, near yellow, and tremulous. Reck was in back of Jesse, so as to swing him on the gate, and Mirth was in front, so as to keep the gate from swinging out too far. Luck was hunkered down to one side, poking at the dirt with a stick, and by turns, looking up at them.

Reck was telling them about some man, face gleaming blue-black in the moonlight, who roamed the back streets of town at night, and he was called 'the Conductor.' Why they call him that? Mirth said. And Reck said, well, to listen to the Conductor himself, it's because he plays women like a violin section with a double bass thrown in, but you're too young to know what that means; and anyhow, my own reckoning is it's on simple account of his wearing a trainsman's hat somebody threw from the window of the M&O one Christmas Eve as it hurtled through on its way to someplace else.

"Why don't he go out in the day like most folks?" Jesse asked. He'd been fixing to propel himself forward but now he stopped, the top half of his body still bent forward.

"Is he a doer of evil?" Luck said.

"Fellas that seek the cover of night, Dr. Cobra, the Octopus and them," Mirth said, "most generally are."

"No," Reck said, "I expect he's a doer of nothing. Now, when folks see him, every now and again they catch sight of a little nigger gal up ahead of him. She got a yellow dress on, bright as a candle on a birthday cake, and she's rolling a barrel hoop aside her. She's called Mary May. She's out a lot these nights."

Jesse straightened up and sighed. "Quit yakking and push," he commanded. Reck ignored him.

"Don't her folks wonder where she's at?" Luck said.

"They think she's resting," Reck said, "moldering away in the ground, but I reckon she's had enough of that. She don't mean no harm though. Of course, she ain't so much the point herself, you understand; it's what kind of folks is able to see her that's the important thing."

"What kind are they?" Mirth said,

"Folks who've known some trouble," Reck said. "Or is going to soon. Folks who is touched by the hand of God."

"He travels the countryside, that conductor," Mirth said, "and he visits death on the condemned. He can make a man go mute just by looking him in the eye. And he got writing and pictures inked so deep into his very flesh that he can't never wash it off. Ain't that so, Reck?"

Jesse turned to face Reck. He was tired of waiting for the push that still hadn't come. "Push," he said. He stabbed Reck's shoulder blade with a finger.

"You seen the gal yourself, Reck?" Luck asked. He was hoping, voice listing to one side like the sail on a ship in trouble, but you couldn't tell if he was hoping for, or hoping not.

"No," Reck said, "I have not. At present, I am still gathering the facts." He gave the gate a small push, and Jesse swung out on the wind in front of them. Their faces were growing murkier, as if some light from within them was diminishing under the lowering, yellowing dark of the sky.

"You be putting them in the box with that mess of clippings you got?" Luck said.

Reck reached out and brought Jesse and the gate to a standstill.

"Ain't that man called by a bunch of other names besides?" Mirth said, "Zigg and Trog and some such."

"Sounds like a Saturday night picture show at the Lyric," Luck said. He sniggered.

Reck breathed deep, and tried to be patient. "First off," he said, "the Conductor and Zogg, that's the name, are different fellas entirely from each other. The Conductor ain't nothing but an old man traipsing around town with a ghost girl playing in his shadow, 'cause he got nothing better to do. But Zogg, well, he's a man with a mission, what takes him across the entire state." And to show that he himself had a mission too, he finally gave Jesse a mighty push, and Mirth stepped clean out of the way.

Jesse swung back close to the fence post, like to crash into it, and at that moment, instead of crashing, he stuck out his foot and gave the post another mighty kick and so kept himself and the gate in motion. The gate whined and creaked as it swung back a full arc a second time. I wondered if it would give way altogether. I went to the door. My shadow spilled out the doorway into the yard and lay there, a shade darker than the lowering sky. The Lesses were looking at each other, faces bobbing in the light like a trio of candles sputtering in the wind, and they called out, goodbye, Jesse, so long. The first raindrops fell, heavy and purposeful, and warm as metal when it's beaten. They scattered on the ground like a fistful of nails flung from a high rooftop. Jesse's feet hit the ground, and he was running towards me, for shelter. I pushed the door open. Giving him shelter till his hour drew near was the least I could do.

And up till then, I guess I'd figured that the least I could do was all I could do.

CHAPTER NINETEEN

You may ask yourself, how can you tell the difference between the twisted peculiarities that make up fate, and your misguided attempts to intervene and influence that fate? And the answer is, you can't, until it's too late. The interventions don't get anywhere, just sink to the bottom of time as if they never happened. That's most of human endeavor right there. Drain the river of time and that's what you'd pretty much come up with, a net fair to bursting with beat-up shoes and empty tuna fish cans and efforts to change the course of history. I've spent most of my time just trying to figure out where it's going, and to swim along with it.

So I did take upon myself the task of securing for E and his mother alms and comfort. I figured I could at least prevent Vernon and his family from upping stakes and heading out of this here promised land. There's a funny thing about "prevent"; it means like you get there first and keep something from happening. I wasn't so hot at getting there first. I mean, I was born second, and my whole career had been trailing the earth in the aftermath of a deed I was ordained to do. So just going around preventing a thing, like E and company skipping town was a new one for me. And the thought dawned on me, slowly developing like a day taking shape, that this time there was something I *was* coming before, and not after, and I thought I knew what that something was.

That Saturday, I bundled up Jesse, fished out one of them two silver coins I still had squirreled away, and headed off for a junk shop over in Bethel.

"Where we going?" he said.

"It's a surprise," I replied.

The air was soft, the sky was gray and the day had an edge of joy and recklessness beneath its dullness, like we were approaching the end of something, which, since it was the fall of the year, we were. I had my sights set on a fair sum, while Jesse walked along beside me, hands in his pockets, chunnering away to himself.

"The Lesses been telling you about some conductor fella," I said.

"Yep," he said, interrupting his tune, "Just some old man roaming around at night, with his little girl by the hand." He stuck out his lower lip, and gave a resentful look. "I wonder why *she* gets to be out all hours." Before I had time for an answer, he picked up humming right where he'd left off.

As we came in sight of the shop, Jesse was finishing up his song. He piped a final few pure notes onto the still, chilled air, deliberately and carefully, like he was setting toy boats upon a quiet lake. He stopped a moment and watched them float off, then he held out his hand for mine, and we set off up the stairs. The shop had scrolled shingles all cracked around the edges, and a sign with faded, cursive lettering. The bells jingled as I opened the door. I slipped out the coin and got straight to the business of securing providence.

"Haven't seen one like this in all my years," the junk shop owner said. He was squinting through his eye piece and holding the coin up to the light. "Where you'd say you picked it up?"

"I didn't," I said.

"Been in your family for years, I expect." He was a stiff, spare fellow. He held his limbs so close I expected them to click when he moved, like he'd contracted a case of lockjaw that extended all the way down.

"Yes," I said. "I've had it a long time."

He took off his eye-piece, snapped off the light, and looked at me. "I never seen a coin like this - I collect them myself and this one has me flat-out stumped. It don't look like real coin to me somehow. So old the markings just rubbed right off."

"What can you give me for it?" I said.

"Looky here," Jesse said. A shaft of light like a yellow pencil at a slant marked him out. He was standing by a table crowded with junk and pointing upwards. On top of a pine dresser, there was a toy trumpet propped up next to a guitar and some odd pieces of china. I read the scene clear as any handwriting on any wall, and vividly it flashed into my mind an image from my revelation, of a young man amazing the crowd with songs of joy and wonder. And in that moment I knew that if Jesse be willing, I would forfeit the plan I had gone forth with, and instead my coin would purchase for him the instrument raised up before us.

"All it's got going for it is the value of the metal," the shopkeeper said. "And the curiosity."

"You got a figure in mind, mister?"

"One dollars and a half," he said.

"You know it's silver," I said.

"If you say so."

"It's got a real interesting history, that piece," I said. "I doubt you'd believe me if I told you."

"I can't put a story in the bank, son," he said.

I already knew all about that, up close and personal, and how a pocketful of parables won't do much to keep your body and soul together - in fact, it does pretty good at driving the two irrevocably apart.

"Look it," Jesse said. He had scrambled halfway onto the table, and was jimmying an evil-looking wheel and whisk number towards himself.

"What in tarnation is that?" I said.

"A rotatory hand mixer," the man said. "Popular with the ladies."

"You see any lady here?" I said.

He smiled briefly. "Your wife would truly find it a help."

"He ain't got no wife," Jesse said. He aimed the thing at my shin and made it whirr.

"Oh. I am sorry," the shopkeeper said. He started fiddling with some tablecloth lace on the counter that didn't look to need no fiddling with.

"Is that gadget what you've been bleating about there, boy?" I said. "I thought for sure you conceived a hankering for that trumpet up there."

"Nope," Jesse said.

"Make a joyful noise unto the Lord, with that one," I said.

"I'd rather make us a cobbler with this," Jesse said. "Cook some victuals good as Jacob in that story."

"So you're going into the birthright business," I said. "Wish I'd run into you a long time ago."

The man looked up right quick, and if he'd had a second more, he'd have concluded he was hearing a crazy man babble.

"But, boy," I went on fast, "you think we got the money for a little doodad like that?"

"I'll tell you what," the shopkeeper said. He straightened himself up. "Seeing as how the little fella's taken to it, I'll throw in that mixer for a quarter. Worth three times that."

"Okay," Jesse said. "Let's take it on home."

"Won't see another one like it," the shopkeeper said. "Not at that price."

"This something you got a positive need for?" I said.

"Yeah," Jesse said.

" 'Yes, sir,' " I said.

"Okay," the shopkeeper said. "I'll wrap it up for you."

I gave the trumpet one last look. It's time had not yet arrived, for truly a man can fulfill but one errand of the Lord at a time. "Don't trouble yourself," I said. "He'll carry it as is, won't you, boy?"

Jesse brandished the mixer and beat up the air within a twelve inch vicinity of his face pretty good. He hooted, and ran to the door. The man counted out the money, and handed it to me, one dollar and twenty five cents. He dropped the last nickel into my palm.

"Thank you," I said. I turned to go, then looked back at him.

"You take care of that coin, mister," I said. "You'd be amazed at what it's bought and sold over the years."

He nodded without smiling. The glass door swung through the cold air and shut, like a thin screen of ice congealing in front of him, and it glittered in the failing light.

We set off home, under a sky of shifting rose and amethyst. We could hear the shouts of some young'uns playing a few fields over. Their cries criss-crossed the air, and echoed, till they fairly surrounded us from all sides. I took a short cut through an alfalfa field, without thinking precisely where it would lead us, and Jesse and I wound up along the east wall of the Priceville graveyard. The sky had deepened to navy by then, and the shadows were falling thick as autumn leaves, and dark as moleskin. I looked close at Jes, and just then a flock of magpies burst into flutter, and took wing, squawking as they rose, and reeling as they squawked. Jesse aimed the rotary beater at the sky. The wheel was whirring like it was from the innards of a runaway clock gone nutsy and mean and set on shooting to ribbons the stuff of time it was meant to measure.

CHAPTER TWENTY

I dropped the cash I had secured on Vernon's front porch early the next morning, the pale dawn glowing coldly. E and his momma stayed on living in town, I saw, and I heard tell the momma got herself a job in the Loverton cotton mill over on the east side of town that had had its ups and downs but was presently operating dead-level flat, which by contrast to its overall average, was looking like an up. They looked to be eating enough to keep body and soul in one piece, and still they abided within the promise of the power and light in the valley and its environs; and in this respect I was well pleased.

As I tended to Jesse that year, I knew that one time soon, fate would be coming for him, for in him the promise of power and light was redeemed. I could feel it in my bones as the days grew shorter, and the trees outside his window began to rustle through the purple night; and I felt it just as strong when the days lengthened again and the sparrows gathered twittering on trees so young and tender a yellow green it made my heart ache. And through that year, Jesse and I made our way to the church neither so regular as to make it expected, nor so infrequent as to make it strange. Most times I said we was going, Jesse made me promise to let the Lesses come over afterwards, or leastways not turn them away from our door should they appear. It was not my place to discourage his compassion, especially in the direction of the least of all brothers; and it was one price to pay, but then I'd seen worse.

In the shadows of the Church of God, I stood, and watched, and waited for some sign to flicker across Jesse's face, or else the complexion of the skies. I heard the singing building up and falling down all around me, and I watched folks gyrate and their shadows play on the wall like waves of water splashing; and though I watched the shadows fall upon Jesse's face, I never yet saw one take hold there and transform him.

But then, this one day came, and I thought I saw a transforming shadow pass over him; though maybe it weren't but a shadow that fell loose from the folds of my own memory, ineluctable, and indelible.

That morning, it was a Sunday, I woke with an ache in my heart, like something was weighing on it and needing lifting. The sky was gray, and the air was steamy and still. I rose and dressed Jesse for church, and we walked slow, and in silence. The birds on the trees clung there by their claws, almost wilting, and declined to twitter. The rain, when it came, would be a blessed relief from the weight of the air. It was the first close day of summer, and the ladies held fans that were magnified in silhouette upon the walls, and beat like the wings of hovering angels. In the gathering heat, a soapy, sweaty smell rose from the flesh of the faithful, and lingered. Outside, the sky was clamped down heavy as a lid on an unwatched pot.

Already as we arrived, the whole church was singing, and emoting to it like as to expire. Preacher Noah was standing at the front, and he'd made his hand into a fist, and beat time in the air. And then E was standing there beside him, and then E's voice struck out on its own. His voice cleared a path through the air upon which other voices gathered and proceeded and ascended towards the ceiling. I looked at Jesse, who was sitting beside me open-mouthed, as if he could hear and see better that way and take more of everything in. The song had a kind of *plunk-plunk-plunk* rhythm like you was riding on a donkey on a road that rose steadily up a steep mountain, and Jesse nodded his head in time, and raised his face up like he was following the ascent.

And I stood there, that ache in my heart still waiting to lift, and feeling the weight upon my chest of being who I was and nobody knowing; and of seeing Jesse's brother not Jesse exalted by the congregation; and of remembering my brother soaking up all the glory due him, then as now. Noah beat the pulpit in time to the music, plunk plunk plunk, and it sounded like a bowl of water filling drop by drop.

And that sound did echo in my memory, for JC's teacher had a leaky roof, and he kept a banged-up pot onto the back corner of the temple. It was set into a steep and craggy valley, that temple, and it always felt like it existed in the shadow that lingers before a rainstorm, and the pot was just sitting there, waiting to be filled drop by drop.

Over the Tupelo Church of God, the sky broke, and the rain came spattering down the windows, and it sounded on the roof. Folks raised their hands high, as if in greeting and supplication, and they trembled amidst its descent.

That other day, the rain had come spattering down upon me. I was stood in the doorway, and waiting under the darkness cast by the thick door beam. No one saw me. JC was standing in the middle of the temple, the teacher was sitting, nodding his head like he was conducting music that only he could hear. JC was holding forth, and the water dripped in, slowly, to a filling pot. He was answering at some length, and the folks in temple, even kids who hated him, and made his life in the schoolyard a torment, they was all listening to him, their mouths emptied of their own words, and their ears filling up on his.

Watching from the doorway, I felt a twinge at my belly, thinking to myself how I could have told them that, knowing I would have been walloped if I did, but also knowing, at someplace darker inside myself, that I never could have come up with what he was saying. The crowd was all looking at him. I stood there in the dark, my heart filling like the beat-up pot bit by bit with jealousy, only of course jealousy don't really fill your heart, it's more like an acid that eats it alive till it ain't but a hole barely beating. JC was giving better and better answers. I stopped hearing the separate words after a while because the whole thing got to be like when a singer slips so completely into a song, goes through the high notes like a swimmer moving through treacherous waters unscathed. It's a positive joy to behold, if you can just forget about yourself, and quit plucking at your own sleeve with notions about how maybe you could do it yourself, too, if you hadn't been kept so busy all your life feeding the chickens and washing down the yard and nailing together most of the workable joinery your daddy's shop ever saw fit to turn out.

Hearing my brother speak just then was like hearing a singer clear a high note, and I was feeling the same kind of split run right through me: like somebody's singing, so fearlessly that I can't help but drop what I'm doing, and the singing's outside of me altogether and I'm jealous of it - and then that the singing has everything to do with me, and I'm joyful, both at once, and the song just seems to hang there a minute in the air.

And then in the little Tupelo church, E was singing:

And the sun refused to shine
And the blood ran down
And the dead got up, child, from the grave

I looked at Jesse, and I swear it was as if those last words had unlocked some door deep inside him. His eyes turned a lighter blue, and he was breathing out the words of the refrain, tipping them out on the air, before the rest was even singing them, *I'm glad salvation is free.* Not for me or my brother it weren't, I couldn't help demurring; but then I was drawn down the shadowy slope, back into the waters of my own reflection.

When JC was done holding forth, the schoolteacher had quit nodding his head. I expect he was hearing things he didn't know himself. The crowd was beginning to murmur amongst themselves. (And in the Church of God, folks was on their feet now, all aquiver with their singing and their worship.) JC's teacher rustled around, and took hold of the cane he kept aside his desk. The water kept dripping in, and the pot was getting full. (And up in front of me, Noah raised his fist high above the podium, beating time). The teacher raised the cane high. I saw the shadow of it fall first (And Noah was now crashing his fist down upon the wood), and then the teacher was striking the cane across the desk with a single almighty thrash. In my heart, I was gleeful, with a gift-wrap made of penitent, because I thought JC was about to get his comeuppance.

Soon as that cane been lifted across the desk, I stepped forth out of the shadows. I was all fired up to tell JC in front of everybody that his momma wanted him to head on home, and I imagined how they would all laugh. But just then, the teacher turned his face, round and faintly glistening, to the crowd. He said JC's learning was excellent and marvelous, and everyone had better fall silent in its presence, or else have the weight of his cane fall upon them. JC raised his throat up. It was lily-colored and quavering, but his jaw was steadfast, enough to cast a shadow in the yellow light. I slipped back onto the threshold. The rain was still falling. Then I turned, and went on home alone. Nobody ever knew I was there, and just hearing my mother brag about JC even weeks afterwards made my insides twist up, like they was all full up of an emptiness that was heavy as water.

But the moment Noah smashed his fist upon the wood that Sunday in the Church of God, and the folks near applauded young E, who was quavering out the final notes, the weight upon my chest did lighten. For I realized it was less an ache than a hunger; and with a rapacious sort of pride I fixed my sights on the day to come. And then I done something I ain't ever done before: I pushed Jesse, by which I mean to say, I encouraged him, to go to the front and give witness with the others swaying their way up there.

"Jesse," I whispered into his ear, "why don't you step forward and lead us in the worship of the Lord."

Jesse looked at me. He snapped his head down, grabbed hold of my knee, and buried his face against it. "I ain't doing it," he said. He kept on saying it, too, in case it hadn't sunk in yet. His voice was muffled, but the folks right in front of us turned and smiled down at him.

I divested my limb of him, and said nothing. The boy ain't even started school yet, I thought to myself, and maybe I'll have to wait. But my will was resolute now. Meanwhile, in front of us all, Noah had raised E up onto his shoulder. They was crooning a new one now:

Were you there when God raised him from the tomb?
Sometimes it causes me to tremble, tremble, tremble.

And their two faces glowed white, like a flower and its offshoot trembling in the light of dawn, and they glistened; and the boy was exalted by the crowd, for they knew not who was in their midst.

*   *   *

That night at home, Jesse told me flat out he didn't never want to step forward in that church. He was in the other room, and I was at the sink, wiping a cloth over a couple of dinner plates. Why not, I asked him. I hate talking to a bunch of folks I don't even know, he said, them all looking at me. His voice was stifled as if he had swaddled himself in bedclothes from head to toe, on the steamiest night of the year. I turned my head to look in, and that's exactly what he had done. He was lying there like Lazarus waiting for the command. And I just don't want to, he said, through the muslin. Well, boy, a time comes when we all got to do things we don't like to, I said. Then I went back to the dishes.

And from that day, I scanned heaven and earth, and kept solitary watch for a sign to mark the advent of Jesse's mission. I thought it might come in the form of a tornado, blackening the landscape for miles, ripping off the roof of the house, lifting up a thousand windows and letting them fall with a single mighty crash. Or fate would come in the form of a flock of blackbirds, swooping down from a winter's sky and mysteriously settling around Jesse, like a constellation slipped to earth, and from its configuration, he would divine its import, and out of their twitterings, fashion a tune. Or fate might come in the form of a tall dark stranger, a preacher with a wide-brimmed hat who whistled a hymn as he made his way up a shadowy street that rustled with stately elms.

Fate came alright, but it was in none of these forms. Fate, such as it arrived at all in those years, came in the form of that unwieldy rotary whisk Jesse had scavenged from the junk shop. Jesse palled around with it all week, beating imaginary cake batters and such, then one day I came home and found his nose buried in a grease-spotted, spiral-bound book, *The Red Rock Cookery*. It had a crowing chanticleer embossed on the cover, and was peppered with black and white illustrations of coal-burning stoves, diagrams for carving a turkey, and step by step instructions for separating an egg. Mrs. Greenfield told me she'd run across it when she'd been sorting out a cousin's attic, and she thought Jesse might like it, because she'd never seen a boy take so to learning letters like him. And I thought to myself, well that's because he's a child of the Word; but I smiled, thanked her, and kept still.

Jesse said he wished somebody would read books like that *Red Rock* out on the radio. He took to asking me to read from it, in preference to the usual story books, even the Bible. I guess that made a roundabout kind of sense, as the recipes in it for roast goose and lemon chiffon pie were every bit as fanciful to us as a slipper made of glass, or gold spun out of straw. On the never side of seldom would we have the money to spare for a roasting chicken, or the coconut for a three-layer Lady Baltimore cake. But I read aloud to Jesse, and he'd lie on his belly full of greens and corn pone soaked in buttermilk, and dream about delta shrimp sputtering in a skillet.

"What's shrimps?" Jesse asked. He rolled over on his back and stretched his arms above his head.

"They're creepy crawlys, like bugs, only they traverse the bottom of the ocean."

He rolled on his back and looked me dead in the eye. "That don't sound so good."

"It ain't," I said. The boy was a constant wonderment to me. I reached over for my own book, and cross-referenced it for him. "Scales and fins, see Jesse, that's what you want in your fish food." Long ago, I'd learned to stomach pork, as I had near had to, to survive in most parts, but I had my limits.

It crossed my mind that not having a momma was maybe beginning to take its toll on the boy, that he was turning out a mite too sissified, whether for his good or my liking I never did quite weigh that one out, reckoning them to be about the same in any account. Maybe I had coddled him too much, fearing for his mission and the weak heart inside him. But I asked myself, what's wrong with a boy liking his food, or liking to make it even more than eat it?

And it looked like the Lesses had asked themselves the same thing, and come to the same conclusion, several nights a month. They took to appearing around our doorway, as if they could somehow smell the food cooking that we was only reading about. They mostly favored the moment betwixt and between, neither day nor night, the sky a still and darkening blue.

Sometimes they gathered round under the window, when it was open of an evening and our radio was on and the sound of it wafted outdoors. Somebody on the air would tell a joke, and Reck would laugh loud and hearty, and Mirth would bark out one laugh, drop it right quick, like it was a mouthful of something too hot, and say, uh, what's that one mean, anyway, Reck? Reck would tell him to hush up, and Luck would say, hush up the both of you, I'm trying to listen. And Reck said, you hush up so loud next time, Luck, that somebody's bound to come out and chase us off.

Anyhow, sometimes Jesse went out to the porch and asked them inside, or went out there himself; other times, I told Jesse to respect their privacy to the extent of letting them make of our patch of dirt their own home parlor, and work to maintain the illusion by pretending as if we didn't know they was there. The time would come, I knew, when Jesse would outgrow the Lesses as all other childish things, and go forth in fulfillment of the vision, and I would welcome it; but until such time, I saw fit to indulge the boy in his strange whims and unlikely affections.

CHAPTER TWENTY-ONE

One night, after we'd just had our supper, the Lesses came by. It was the clove of seasons, late summer disappearing into early fall; and of hours, afternoon slipping into evening. Jesse was sitting on the bottom step, whirring away with his rotary beater at some imaginary batter or other. The last light of day shone over him. Reck emerged from the dark line of trees, then Mirth and Luck appeared in turn, and they all called out 'howdy'. I expect I may have sighed, but I imagine it got chopped up by the whirring of the beaters and Jesse didn't hear. Reck asked Jesse what that contraption was, and Jesse told him, and Reck said, okay if I have a go with it, and Jesse said sure. So Reck took the beater and stirred up some air with it, then he pointed it at the ground and used it to mow down a little patch of buffalo grass. Hey, Mirth said, standing up, his shadow raising like umbrage to an affront, but Reck laughed and went on mowing. Jesse sat there and calmly watched, not even moving, and Reck handed him back the beater.

"That thing got teeth in it like a monster," Mirth said.

"Like that Trogg creature," Reck said. He added, real casual-like, "You see that poster at the Lyric, Jesse? *Revenge of the Trogg-a-Beast?*"

"Yeah," Jesse said.

"Tonight's the last night they showing it," Reck said. "You fixing to go?"

"I don't know," Jesse said. He turned his head, and called into the house, where I was sitting in front of radio as if its voices were a breeze that might refresh me. "Am I fixing to go, Jud?" And I heard Reck add that once it starts getting cold nights, the Conductor took up a kind of residence at the Lyric, keeping himself warm and rested before commencing his nighttime wanderings. Mirth said, oh yeah, you got him under observation, and you said how no picture-house in town would ever let us in on our own; and Reck told him to hush up; he'd heard it was a good picture was all, don't you think so too, Jesse?

Well, the upshot was, I got finagled into shepherding the whole bunch over to the Lyric, for the 7:05 showing - Reck happened to have the times handy, since he'd noted them down in his little notebook of investigations into the events of the neighborhood and beyond. He took care to get the details right, a sight more than many scribes I could mention.

Well, I said, putting on my jacket, I can tell you what kind of seats we're getting, boys. What's that, Jes said. And I said, the cheapest ones they got, pressed up to the ceiling, and the folks who sit in them are closest to God, and that's why they're the children of paradise.

Soon as we reached the box office, the Lesses and Jesse hung back on the sidewalk, and when I turned around, my eyes fell upon a shadow, so unwavering as to belong to an object immovable and inanimate. My eyes followed it, and in the end, met up with the pale, unblinking gaze of Yellow Whitehead.

"Jud," Reck said, "this here is -"

"I know who he is," I said. "Yellow's one of Bean's regular handyman. Howdy there."

Yellow looked at me, steady and blank, and barely

nodded.

"Yellow lives a few houses down from us," Reck went on, "and he's being saying for some time that this is a picture he'd sorely love to see. Only he ain't as blessed as us Lesses, with each other to pal around with anytime we like. Ain't that right?"

Yellow nodded more deeply this time, and slower.

"I imagine your boy here may feel the same way himself from time to time," Reck went on, looking right at me. "With Yellow, though, it's worse. Kids are scared of him. Run when they see him coming, and yell mean things at him. It don't bear thinking about."

Jesse turned and looked up at me, his chin kind of wobbling. So I sighed, and said, okay, so long as you don't expect me to spring for popcorn too. And I bought another ticket. The lady in the box office took one look at Yellow, and charged the child rate.

I headed into the theater proper, where it was dark, and the door was so narrow, they had to fall into single file behind me. I went past five or six of rows of seats, was about to turn left and settle us all down, when Reck said, "Jimmy, now, weren't you saying about where you wanted to sit?" and Jesse said, loud as he would at home, "I want to be a child of paradise, Jud, and set up on high." We was shushed from either side of the aisle. There were more folks setting there than I had thought possible, and I told him to keep quiet. Then I lead us out towards the front again. I blinked in the electric light a second.

"Yonders the door to the crow's nest," Reck said. He was pointing down a dark hall. "Puts you as high up as you can get in this theater."

Okay, I said, and I led us down it. Jesse was at my side and the rest of them bobbed along behind me, Luck the last in line and keeping Yellow quiet, and holding his hand now and again. We went up a short flight of stairs, and I opened the door. The space beyond was completely dark. I heard a critter scurrying along the floor. A rough and skinny and longish tail brushed by my ankles, and just as fleeting, it was gone. Right then the projector up back started rattling. A ray of light was sent forth. The cartoon went up, and I could see better. The seats were straight-backed and unforgiving, bare slats of wood like they was made up of rulers chopped up and hastily nailed together. And the faces, when they turned our way, reflected the light from the screen off them, and did not just drink it in, milk in water, the way the faces of white folks do: they were all colored folks up here. One man turned. He was wearing a conductor's cap, and Reck led us his way, and ducked down one seat back. We all filed into the row, Yellow was last, face set like it was carved of wood, shoulders the same, only his eyes flitting inside his head a bit.

We'd just settled down when a little boy aside Reck turned to look at him. His mouth dropped open, and his eyes blinked then grew wide, a few times over, like they was drowning in dark and incredulity, and gasping for light like it was air.

"What you looking at?" Reck hissed.

The boy looked at him another moment. "You all don't sit up here," he said.

"That's exactly what we is doing," Reck said. He got out his notebook and pencil.

The Conductor turned our way. "You folks, you most generally sit down there."

Reck leaned forward into the light. "Where's Mary May?" he said, cutting in quick, a knife-blade of a question.

The man looked at him a second. He lowered his head, and touched his fingers to his cap.

"Why's he so sad?" Luck said.

Mirth punched him on the shoulder.

The Conductor raised his head. "Down there's got the view," he said.

Jesse looked at me. "Ain't up here what you said was closer to God?"

"I did," I said.

"And up here is the children of paradise, what are dear to his heart?"

"Yep," I said.

"Ain't us folks dear to him too?"

The Conductor snorted, and the door opened. At first I thought it was some picture-house man sent to straighten the ruckus out, but it was a young negro gal. She wore a pink dress and her hair was in tight plaits that stuck out all over her scalp. She was hurrying down the side aisle. Her head cast a shadow on the screen and it grew as she approached. It all but blotted out the canary bird in tap shoes, who was telling about his plan he was hatching after the cat that been chasing him, and then the shadow-head slid down and off and was gone.

"Mary May?" Reck said.

"Her dress ain't yellow," Mirth whispered.

"I ain't telling nobody my name," the girl said. Her voice slapped the air like a challenge.

Reck scribbled in his pocket-sized notebook, his nose close up in it. "Well, if it had a-been yellow, and we could have seen her," Reck whispered, "I reckon we'd all be in trouble."

The cartoon was ending, and the place went dark, and the girl must have mis-stepped herself in the aisle, because when the picture flickered into light, and she looked up, it was straight into the face of Yellow, his gaze unblinking, steady as a block of wood and barely more animate. She screamed. Yellow's neck roiled around, he was like to bellow, when Mirth put his hand on his shoulder and said real soft, hey, Yellow, weren't that cartoon really something? You ever wonder if birds and cats and such can talk, only we just can't hear it, I wonder if they understand us any, and Yellow looked at him, and went calm. His lips blubbered silently like a drowning man going down for the third time.

"Boys," I said, "we better move on down a little lower.

Folks want to watch the picture in peace." I stood up.

"Then we ain't the children of paradise no more," Jesse wailed. It was like somebody'd handed him a gift, and yanked it away.

"Don't worry son," the Conductor said, "They ain't only in the picture-house." He watched us go out the door. We went downstairs and I made them set down quick in the first seats we found, and they kept quiet.

Outside on the sidewalk, Reck made us all pause under a working streetlight. The other Lesses bobbed around him at the light's edge. Reck noted carefully in his book what had happened. He ignored Mirth's instructions to put down the plot of the cartoon, and he wrote in conclusion that the rest of the evening passed "without incident."

CHAPTER TWENTY-TWO

Sometime before, I had concluded it was my duty to point Jesse towards his own destiny, and lead him unto the right path. In the shadowy portions of a house of worship, where once again one brother was raised up and another was ignored, my ambition for Jesse took root. It grew like some strange flower that blossomed in the dark; and it matured, bit by bit, into stranger, more marvelous fruit.

And so, with the faithful of Tupelo, I abided; and I stood up through their misreckoning. Amidst their swaying I was steadfast; and against their blindness, my eyes was lit with certainty. And, truly, I knew I was a prophet in my own country, for I was without honor.

As it turns out, I was pretty much without it in my own house as well. I received such indications, and the most telling arrived in the form of a silvery little five and dime birthday geegaw. Jesse was approaching his sixth year; the September to follow, he was enrolling in institutions public; for in the ninth year of the rule of Franklin Roosevelt, Ross Lawhon being superintendent, Jesse was to enter school; and it was funded by the taxing, every one unto his own city. It would be as it was with JC in the temple, who amazed all that heard him: in school as in church, all would be soon astonished at Jesse's understanding and his answers. So, for Jesse's sixth birthday, I made more of a fuss than previous. For us that year, it eclipsed Christmas, which I had long been in the habit of letting pass with a minimum of commotion; though in time, I could see a day the two events would be celebrated as one.

In the weeks preceding his birthday, I took to wondering out loud about what gift I ought to get him. Let's see, I'd say, I bet Jesse wants a basin and a sponge for his birthday, to help out with the clean up, I know he's got that on his mind. Or I got it, a dustpan and mop. And Jesse would laugh ha ha ha, like the swift short sweeps of a broom, as if my joke was a little pile of trash that his cackling whisked out of the way straight up. Then he'd chime in, eyes round and very helpful, about some spatula or vegetable peeler or whatnot, and where he'd seen it, and how it didn't cost hardly nothing at all.

I smiled; and that week I went out to the five and dime, and bought him a harmonica. I hadn't set out with a mind to purchase it, but I liked it as soon as I saw it, for surely that harmonica would inspire Jesse to songs of praise. And further, the instrument came alive not with the strumming of a finger or the scraping of a bow, but with the influx of human breath; and truly it gave forth songs of pure spirit.

When I gave Jesse his gift, that night after dinner, he pulled away the old newspaper I had wrapped it in like he couldn't wait to get at it. When he saw what it was, though, he said, real faint-like, oh thank you. His mouth made a small flat line, and he put the harmonica right down. It lay there on the table, gleaming in the watery winter light, like a thing always already in its own silver coffin. You don't like it, I said. It's okay, Jesse said. By then, he already found his rotary beater, and had it in hand. What were you hoping I'd get you? I said. I been telling you about all kinds of things, he said over the small metal whirr. His eyes were almost pugnacious with accusation. Ain't you heard a word I been saying for the past week, he went on. And I had, but I hadn't listened, because he weren't yet speaking the kind of words he was cut out for. I picked up the harmonica, and began blowing a little riff for his and my amusement both, but secured only my own, and the riff rode, airily and jaunty, above Jesse's beater that he kept on whirring.

That Sunday, I headed us over to church. The dead grass crunched under our feet, and the harmonica was stowed away in my shirt pocket, almost hidden, like one of Bean's candy bars. Its weight was a comfort to me, as was its position, square over my heart; and I half-hid to myself the intention for which I bore the instrument.

Low was the light that day, and low the ceilings of the Church of God upon us. We watched as E burst into song the way he near always did, and I stood trying not to glower. The folks all loved him, of course; they were clapping in time to him as his voice ascended the notes with scarcely a falter. He was about to launch into yet another lyric of faith and inspiration, but he had to stop and catch his breath, and that's when I made my move. I took out the harmonica, and blew a short sharp riff.

Then Noah stopped clapping. He looked out among us, and held out his arms like to part the Red Sea. He called out, "Who makes such a sound unto the Lord?" Folks murmured, glanced at each other and shrugged. At the interruption, E looked around him like the sun had all of a sudden gone behind a cloud. I watched him trundle back to his appointed place, and he sat back down. His momma dandled his chin a moment, and her eyes were shining like gray water in the half-light.

I held Jesse's hand up for him, and I said, this boy here, he did. Jesse snapped his head around. He looked at me like I'd delivered him into captivity. I ignored the look, and propelled him towards the front of the church. Then I slipped back to my place in the shadows. My face was glowing, I could feel, but only faintly.

"Now, brothers and sisters," Noah was saying, "I'd been telling you a while back about how I outdid temptation. Outjumped and outsmarted him." In case we missed the point, he jumped side to side in front of us, as if he was fording a stream by leaping from one trickily gained stone to the next. "I just got outta his way. You know how to outsmart temptation, too, don't you boy?" He thumped Jesse on the shoulder. "By making a noise unto the Lord so joyful and so mighty it knocks the Devil out of his boots! What else you do to outwit temptation, son?"

Jesse looked so small and white up there. It was though I was watching him from a great distance, and he was drowning, gasping for whatever breath he could, and all the air he could find was heavy with prayers and singing and supplications.

"I like to cook," he said finally. His voice was tiny, pinched, and piping. I felt like I had two hearts beating inside of me. One of them was fit to bust with pride and the anticipation of glory. The other near broke to see him like that.

"Cook?" Noah boomed. "But boy, a pie or a cake can't ward off the devil, not even if you bowled it straight at him." He made an exaggerated motion of pitching a ball along the ground. Then he straightened up, dusted off his palms, and laughed. His face crinkled up like an old apple. Jesse's face shrunk a little more, and his head drooped low. Everyone else was laughing by then too, the laughter going through the church like a sprinkling of rain, so Noah made like a thundercloud before the burst, and redoubled his seriousness quick before his strength was spent and dissipated. "The lust of the eye and of the flesh is how the Devil gets in! He seizes upon our lust like an intruder upon a weak door, and he breaks right into our soul! Brothers and sisters, keep your house in order! And fill its chambers with light so the devil flees before such brightness!"

By the time Noah got to the part about the intruder,

Jesse had already bolted from the church front. The faithful were enraptured. Every eye was focused mid-distance, on some certain thing not visible to any other, and all hands were raised up, trembling, placating, and rejoicing all at once. I thought Jesse would hunker down beside me in his seat, but he rushed right by me, giving me a dirty look as he passed. He ran out of the church altogether. The door slammed on its rusted hinge, but I wager no one but me noticed.

Well, it was a start alright, and whether he liked it or not, Jesse had spoke to the people. It came with a price, for Jesse refused to talk to me again until I agreed to do a few things. We had to make a red velvet cake from the book (like I ought to have done in the first place, he said, seeing as to how it was his birthday) and invite the Lesses over to eat it. And then I had to swear never to pull that going forward stunt on him again. "I ain't fooling," he said.

I was putting him to bed, He was lying there with his chin sticking up at me in the dark. A chink of moonlight edged in, and found out the whites of his eyes.

"Jesse," I told him, "you have my word." And my lips found his own, and I kissed him

CHAPTER TWENTY-THREE

So I held off from presenting Jesse to the world just then. In the Church of God, I stood in the shade, and to one side, and kept myself in check. But whenever we was heading over there in those months, and the sweet smell of honeysuckle drifted our way, or the call of an owl echoed through the gathering dusk, I knew we was headed in the right direction.

A direction, of course, ain't the same as a route or a destination, and I figured that one out soon enough. We was downtown, Jesse and me, one Saturday, the April after he turned six. The sun was shining and the warmth weren't that of a winter's day anymore, but of the next season entirely. A mockingbird called, and another one joined in, and their cries unraveled in the air like thread off a spool, getting picked up and woven into the just-green branches of the trees. The air smelled of moist black earth, and that earth itself seemed almost buoyant, and it gave every step you took a spring to it.

Jesse had wanted the Lesses to tag along that morning, but I told him we weren't always to wait on them. And he hung his head, but then he pulled on a pair of red socks, the last of the bunch on account of I didn't get a wash done, and finally his shoes. We walked downtown, and Jesse tried to whistle in time with the birds, and couldn't, and so tried laughing in time to them instead. At the five and dime, I picked up a few household supplies. I was up at the cash register in no time. Jesse was haunting the kitchen goods aisle, and every so often he'd stand at the end, and hold up a colander or a grater or somesuch for me to see, and say how this one sure looked like a real bargain, now don't it. Finally, when the cashier lady was nearly done adding up my bill, I told him to hold on to those measuring spoons he had in his paws and bring them on up to the counter.

The spoons was small and cheap but they rattled importantly, like a set of keys joined on a ring, and they seemed to make him happy. We set off down the street. He was looking at the markings on the spoons, and talking on about some stew or another he thought we ought to try, the Lesses would like it too, and it did yield a right lot of servings.

Uh-huh, I said. That's a nice thought. Of course, there's always a church supper coming up, and if it makes so much as to feed the multitudes, don't you reckon that's the place to take it?

No, I don't, Jesse said. He had the smallest spoon held up to his right eye, and he went on: I ain't fixing on feeding any but my friends.

You can make a lot more friends, I said, if you were willing to feed them. Lady like Mrs. Greenfield would surely like it. Make something from that book she was nice enough to give you.

I see enough of her as it is, and I ain't looking for more friends, Jesse said. I've got enough to do with the ones I got already.

We were going on like that when all of a sudden, from on high, noise broke right through our words. It was loud and squawky and sounded as if God was dragging His fingernails across the blackboard of the world.

That's when we saw the sign:

WELO
WORLD FIRST EVER BROADCAST
TODAY

The sign was propped up on the sidewalk, against the front window of Buford's Dry Goods Shop. A man was leaning out of the second story window, with an elastic, lopsided grin that looked like it'd been stretched out of shape from overuse. "Folks, that weren't nothing but a fuse blowing," he said. "Won't take a minute to fix."

I looked around me, wanting to fix the moment in my mind, for I knew I was about to witness a manifestation of the Power and Light in the Valley and its Environs. A gentle breeze reached down and refreshed my brow. Jesse had stopped dead, for there were a dozen or so folks in our path, standing around, waiting for something to happen, I guess. A clown was among them holding a bunch of balloons.

When he saw Jesse, he padded over to him. His oversized shoes flopped to either side. "You're the fella I been waiting for!" he said. He made his voice high-pitched, and it kind of balanced in the air like a ball atop a seal's nose. You wondered how long it would stay put.

Jesse reached up for my hand, and held it. "How's that?" Jesse said.

"You got them red socks and they match my nose, and that's why I'm picking you out of this here whole crowd to speak on the radio, to folks all over town. Ain't that something!"

Jesse looked scared. I squeezed his hand tight.

A bug-eyed little man who'd been standing in the crowd, his hands in his pockets, piped in. "Shoot, Jeff, I got a little boy at home myself who'd have been tickled to talk on radio. You ought to have told folks something."

The clown wiped his forehead with his hand, and some

white stuff came off. He looked at it on his hand and frowned. "We ain't been set up but three days, Hal," the clown said, "and we ain't had this a-here idea for more than one. And the boss sends me out just now and tells me, find a young'un for a minute's chatter, folks always think a young'un's cute." He had slipped back into his regular voice, and right then he realized it, so he had to say something quick in his clown voice to re-establish himself. "Don't that sound like a tonic, boy?"

"I don't know," Jesse said.

"Well I sure do," the clown said. He winked at me, and I nodded. He gave Jesse a great pantomime wave of farewell, which Jesse ignored by setting his neck straight and looking straight ahead at nothing. The man I'd seen in the window was down in the doorway by then. He gave his stretched-out smile, and his face was sweaty and pale white like a glass of warm milk on the turn. He put his hand on Jesse's shoulder and led him inside. I followed them, and watched as the door closed behind me and snapped my shadow in two.

They had the radio set-up on the second floor. You had to make your way up a narrow dark staircase, and through a storage room that was lined with bolts of unbleached muslin. The air was warm, and full of motes that spiraled in the slanting light. Jesse was sat down at a chair by a desk, and they pulled out another one for me. A man was already sitting there. His blondish hair was slicked back the color and sheen of a pine varnish; and his tie was bright green, and I expect he was announcing to the world thereby that he was some kind of character. He asked Jesse his name and age, and Jesse answered proper. Jesse sat facing me, even though he was talking to the man in the tie. It made it easier for Jesse, and the man in the tie didn't take no notice. Then the man said, "My name's Charlie Rowen. Pleased to meet you, partner."

Rowen fiddled with the dials, then he pointed at Jesse with both index fingers, and said, "From downtown

Tupelo, live, it's WELO's first ever broadcast! And I got here somebody who's been dying to speak to you all! What's your name, son?"

"Jimmy Harricut," Jesse said. He was a mite prim, and his voice was wavery but I was proud of him. He was trying not to sweat, and he sat up straight.

"You how old, son?"

"Six," he said. "Same as a minute ago." He was getting irked, just enough that it was overcoming his nervousness.

"Lawd have mercy! Folks, I swear I would have put Jim-Jim here closer to 39 years of age or so, a midget who's been leading a real clean life ha-ha! Now what brings a fella like you to town?"

"Me and Jud, over there, we came in to do some errands, and then he got me this set of measuring spoons."

"I am looking at them right now, and folks, let me tell you, they are a fine example of the item. What use you got for them, Jim?"

"For making cakes and stews and such. Got my eye on pineapple upside down cake if somebody'd bring home the right things to make it with."

Rowen chuckled, and his face doubled up and collapsed on itself. The rest of the world was no doubt about to join him in some ecstatic conspiracy. "Most boys I know ain't into that kind of thing at all. Leave it to their mommas."

"I ain't like most boys," Jesse said, and I smiled. "And I ain't got no momma." I sat back in my chair, and one of the legs scrapped sharp against the floor.

That last comment of Jesse's weren't what Rowen was expecting and it threatened the fun, and so Rowen punted it out of the conversation quick, and it seemed like he was looking for a way out of the fix himself. "That is a sorrowful shame, son. Now I can think of something else these spoons are good for. Hand them here, and I'll give it whirl."

Jesse handed them over, and Rowen tapped out a little

tune on a patch of desktop, just knocked it out like a bit of nailing done in time and with spirit.

Jesse cocked his head to one side, and at first I thought it was the spoon playing itself that had got to him. And then his mouth opened as if some brand new thought had occurred to him, and astonished him, as if it had just glided down from the heavens, and hopped onto his shoulder to sing.

Jesse looked at me, and he said, "You know what Jud?" His sound was still on. I could hear how he was talking too close to his microphone at first, and the sound of his lips was amplified an instant out of recognition, then went quiet. "I wish I was far away from here, because then if I listened to Charlie Rowen chattering on and playing the spoons, why, just being able to hear it would really be something."

We all laughed, and with a half tablespoon and a quarter teaspoon, Rowen nailed the final three beats home.

"I'll tell you, son, lots of folks have remarked as to how they like keeping a distance from me," Charlie said. He heaped a big laugh into his voice, and chuckled a few times so as to dissolve it. His voice, still jovial, went a few notes deeper, like he was confiding a secret, between just you and him. "Now, WELO got hopes of putting on a regular Saturday jamboree someday, where any of you out there can come on down here, and play and sing and be heard all over this county. But right now we got a word from our kind sponsors. Next time you're doing the dishes, why not try -" He went on chattering like that, and mid-way, he looked up and pointed at Jesse with both forefingers and drew one of them across his throat. The man with the worn-out grin stepped out of the shadows, and divested Jesse of his radio apparatus.

That was how radio got hold of Jesse, and set my soul afire. All the way home, my heart was joyous, and so light it near to capsized in my chest. Jesse was tapping the spoons around like a set of castanets, and jabbering about his plans to go down there one Saturday and read them a recipe like they never heard before. Usually that is the kind of thing that frays my nerves so long I could trip over them, but this time I barely heard it. My thoughts were drawn to the higher places, whence the voice of God is sent. For as it says in Romans 10:17, "faith cometh by hearing, and hearing the word of God . . . and their sound went unto all the earth, and their words unto the ends of the world."

I had just witnessed the means by which Jesse could speak, and, unseen, be heard. His voice would level the crest of the highest hill, and fill the depths of the steepest valley. In the light of day, and the shadow of night, the word would be sent, and the word would find its people. And the word was borne upon the air, and was made up of it. The word weren't flesh, as fat John insisted, and well he might; it was voice and breath, rendered over to the world. The power and light in the valley delivered not just a wall of radiance by night, but a covenant of sound, and it spanned from earth to heaven and back again. Its passage was cast in imitation of the first covenant, a rainbow; and more than that, it was in imitation of Christ. And the power and light made such glory possible, and what men called radio weren't a diversion but an observance, and a manifestation; and I knew Jesse had found his own church at last.

It came upon me too why Jesse got so tangled up about talking in that old style church, and what he said seemed so garbled and paltry. It weren't just that the folks at church was the kind of catch you get from a too narrow casting of nets, though that was true enough. And it weren't just that Jesse was scared of talking to a crowd of folks in front of him, though that was part of it too. The real point was what Jesse'd been saying up there with the radio fella, about listeners and talkers needing some distance from each other for the glory of the medium to be revealed.

It echoed the words I'd said to myself in those very

first years, and my feelings for him had near hobbled my heart: absent, I found him; present, I drew myself away. For so too, in his presence, the faithful would not recognize him, and would keep their distance, and he keep his own; but in his absence, when his voice did carry from a place they could not see, they would at last embrace him. It would be as it had been with JC, who, seeing the multitude, went up a mountain to open his mouth and speak and teach.

Jesse would vanquish the limitations of all flesh; not with the flexing of muscle nor the shedding of blood, but with his voice, and the expiration of his breath. Through the power and light in the valley and its environs, he would make the people of the world his witnesses.

CHAPTER TWENTY-FOUR

And so, of a Saturday, Jesse would lead me by Buford's Dry Goods shop.

"Maybe you're fixing on sewing now, too?" I said once, early on, but he didn't bother to answer.

He pulled me along by the hand. Charlie Rowen was letting folks stand in a roped-off half of the room and watch him broadcast. By noon, the place was always crowded with folks anxious to wait there, half-hushed, until they was called up by Charlie Rowen to applaud or laugh or hoot. Most every Saturday, Jesse so wanted to get a move-on down to WELO, he mostly didn't even tell me we had to wait for Lesses to hook up with us. And more than once, we saw E there, by himself, and intent. There was a hillbilly singer who showed up at WELO pretty regular in those days, a long thin blue-denimed streak of a fella, with a kind of whiney reedy voice, sounded like it been pieced together with a rusty needle; and always sounded far away, even if he was standing right in front of you. His singing, even the first you heard it, come to you like something you weren't so much hearing, as half-remembering. And whenever he stepped up to the mike and commenced to warble, E raised himself up on tip-toe, and stood so still it was like he'd stopped breathing altogether. Jesse took no particular notice of the acts as such; he preferred to hum along to the sponsor's jingles. I felt the humming rumble low and inside of him, as I stood beside him, my hand on his shoulder; and already I could feel his presence taking shape.

Like: one time Charlie Rowen was at the mike and said, soon as he signed off that afternoon, he was going to pass around some Wright-Rue chewing gum for all the kiddies gathered around in front of him:

Wright-Rue, Wright-Rue,
It triples in bulk, it surely do.
Break a piece off for a friend,
To Wright-Rue there is no end.

"We gonna do a pass-around, though, folks, we need a tagline for it," Charlie Rowen said. "Now if'n it was you" - his hand went swooping through the air for he was not yet sure who it would wind up at - "what slogan would you give it there, little fella?" He was pointing at Jesse. Jesse was too startled to answer.

"Give ye them to eat," I called out. Folks around me kind of stirred, and gave space. I saw my shadow spill out, uncrumpled now, and freed-up, upon the floor. Jesse looked up at me. He nodded, sagaciously, as though I had proved myself. And Charlie Rowen wiped the sweat off his brow, and said that sure was a slogan and half. He was so flustered for a moment that he clean forgot what was to going to be on the next week's show. And Jesse stood and looked on, straight and true, amid the murmurings of the crowd that settled down only bit by bit, like water growing still.

CHAPTER TWENTY-FIVE

Soon enough, the summer arrived, with a flat blue-green haze of trees, and a warm sky, that came together like they were of a piece, and set a-humming. Evenings I sat out on the porch, it felt like time had stopped, and the only thing passing through weren't seconds and hours, but the night train into Mobile.

That summer had a kind of theme tune that ran right through it, too, like a snagged-up thread, the static from the radio when Jesse tried to tune into WELO. Besides the show on Saturdays, it mostly broadcast only twilight to dawn, and a lot of times his search was fruitless. But it was clear he had found his way to saying the Word, and I was well pleased.

Still he hankered after the Lesses; and more than once, when I saw them three trooping towards us in the distance, emerging, scattered and rag-tag, against the dark line of tees, I wished they'd pass on by. They had a way of stalking towards the house, and pausing a moment in the clearing. They'd dart another stretch, then go still again, waiting, full of breathing and quiet resolve, like catfish at the bottom of a tank; and finally they'd flit ahead all over again, right to our doorstep, as I stood and watched, and sometimes sighed. But I had not the heart to prevent Jesse from performing a kindness to the least of all brothers; and it pained my heart to see Jesse disappointed.

Reck'd been busy following his own path, occult and misbegotten as it was; and I found that out one summer's night they came trooping over. The air was heavy with the scent of lilac and honeysuckle, and so sweet as to hover on the edge of rotten. The blackberries by the river had ripened in the sun close to dropping off when your shadow so much as passed over them. Reck's notebook of researches had fattened up considerable, too. Before that night was through, we was all brought within the ken of an ambassador of death, for his voice did reach our ears.

The smell of honeysuckle was thick. The air had gone still, and felt embalmed. I'd been struggling to snag a station on the radio, any one at all, on account of Jesse asked me, but what I got was a tangle of high-pitched whines. I gave up when I heard Jesse call out howdy, and I went out to the porch. Mirth emerged first. He was clutching a lard can that brimmed over with huckleberries. Luck scurried alongside him, trying to help by reaching up to clutch one side of the can, but only succeeding in dragging it downwards and scattering a few berries to the ground. Reck came last, his eyes on the horizon. He had hold of his notebook.

The book was so thick now, it gaped open, and as he dropped it down onto the porch, a scrap of newspaper fluttered out. Jesse picked it up, and had me read it as far as it went - it was two-thirds of a recipe for gem cakes - and then he took the scrap from me, put his nose up to it, and said, well, what happens after you fold in the flour? Reck snatched it away from him in a hurry. What kind of goober do you think I am? he shrieked, and he turned the piece over to show what the scrap was really about: a postage stamp-sized picture of a verified mummy that was making the rounds of the county fairs in Alabama.

"I got it all in here," Reck said. He tapped his book.

"Mummies, the Conductor, the putrefaction of bodies, and so on."

"That cousin still writing you?" I said. Mirth shoved the bucket of berries my way. It rasped along the flooring. I reached over, flinched a handful, and popped them in my mouth.

"He sure does," Reck said. "Matter of fact, he is as much interested in my findings as I am in his."

"Hey," Mirth said, "I just thought of something funny." He saw how we was looking at him and waiting, so he reached forward and nabbed a few berries. He propped his chin back, held them up a few inches from his open mouth and dropped them in, one by one. Then he put his chin to horizontal, and looked at us. He was ready. "Cousin Paul, he writes with a pen, now don't he?"

"Yeah," Reck said. He grabbed hold of the side of the lard can and dragged it his way. "So what?"

"Well, he lives in one them, too."

"You hush up," Reck said.

"I thought only hogs and pigs and such lived in pens," Luck said. He reached out for the bucket but his arm was too short so he gave up.

"This ain't that kind of pen. It's a bigger word too," Mirth said. He screwed up his face, and tried to remember. "Pena - penta -"

"Oh," I said. "A Pentecostal camp."

"Yeah, that's right," Reck said, looking up quick, then looking down to fiddle with the binding of his notebook.

"What's that?" Mirth said. He had smears of purple by the corners of his mouth.

"They got a few of them by the coast," I went on. "Where folks settle together, and do their work, and look out over the ocean and feel the night sky lowering over them like it was God's own bed-comforter."

"They the children of paradise?" Jesse said. He sat up straighter.

"Yep," I said. "They sure are. Nobody but God would

179

have 'em. That's true of plenty of other folks too though."

Luck reached his arm out again towards the berry can, but it still weren't any closer. He sighed. "Huckleberries ain't my favorite anyhow," he said. "Mostly, I favor the raspberries." He looked off into a distant and raspberry-filled horizon.

"I like strawberries myself," Jesse said. "They're good in a cobbler."

"Blackberries is best," Mirth said, "so long as you keep them bitty things out of between your teeth." He bared his fangs a moment to demonstrate, and turned in the direction of Reck, who sat there still fiddling with the fastenings of his notebook. "Hey, Reck, what berry's your favorite?"

"I can guess that one," I said. "It's a chokeberry, on account of the deadly associations of the name itself. I bet there's a chokeberry somewhere that done an awful deed, and is just waiting to have itself written up and exhibited at county fairs. 'Nature's Sweetest Instrument of Death.' "

Reck looked up and frowned. "You ain't so smart after all, Jud," he said. "On account of the berry I got most time for is the li-berry ha-ha-ha." He grabbed a handful of berries and popped them in his mouth all at once.

"You got me alright," I said. I sat back, and pictured Reck slipping into the town library some afternoon, when he'd cut out early from school. The tall greenish windows would halt the sunlight, and make it dim and muted. Reck sat at a back table somewhere, poring over newspapers and almanacs, pursuing his research, and snipping out bits when the librarian was busy shelving books at the other end of the room, say, in the social studies and handicrafts section. I bet he knew to sniffle loudly to cover the sound of newspaper tearing, or wait for a truck to lumber by.

We went on eating the huckleberries. They were sweet and tart both, and their juice burst forth easily and dark, and stained our lips as deep as words of deceit, or desire.

"You know, WEMS's got the mystery theater on

tonight," Reck said, after a bit, kind of casual-like and turning to me. "It's about ready to start right about now."

"Hey, you listen to radio too," Jesse said. He turned his head and looked up at Reck. Jesse's forehead was luminous in the pearly light. "We got a pretty good one. Few nights back, it caught a station all the way from Jackson."

"Son, you have spoken on the radio," I said. "And you're down there near every week, and someday soon I reckon you'll be the star attraction on that jamboree show."

Jesse looked at me, kind of pole-axed and happy at the same time, like I'd said something he dreamed of but had never dared put into words. He sucked in his lower lip and I watched his little chest raise and fall with his breathing. "Yeah," he said, and I watched him kind of put the thought, so precious and perishable, back on some high shelf in his mind for safe-keeping. Then, all business and everyday interest, he turned to Reck. "What kind of set you fellas got?"

"We ain't," Luck said, and Reck cut right in.

"Radio's okay," Reck said, and he gave a small shrug like he could take it or leave it. "It's what a fellow in my line of work calls a research tool, and I won't deny it's got its uses, but only a goober would be hellfire for a jamboree. Now, me and my brothers here, we don't got call for it the way you do; I mean, a fella without a single soul but old man Jud here to keep him company."

Jesse took the thought in, and I watched it hit him in his eyes and settle there and magnify like a pebble thrown into a pond.

I raised myself up. "WMEM's all the way from Memphis, Reck," I said. "It won't be easy." I slipped inside, and commenced fiddling with the dials. The signal that came weren't from Memphis, but considerably further. It fluttered into recognizable words but fitfully, and them words soon splintered into smithereens, as if the signal had got snagged on a high and spiky treetop on the way over and could not break free except in stray bits and shreds. .

. . . anybody touched by the hand of God gets cut down by the hand of man . . . being that I am one hand . . .

"What was that other word I was thinking of?" Mirth said. "Penat- ?"

"Hush up," Reck said. "I'm trying to listen."

. . . condemned man just gets that scent on himself. . can't help smelling it, and nobody can scrub it off for them. Not with carbolic, or boiling water, or a tears of a momma's love. . . I smelled it down in Lucedale, and over in D'Lo . . .

"Why, that there is Dr. Zogg talking," Reck said. His eyes opened wide, and his neck muscles went on alert, but he was steady and maintained his purpose. He reached for his notebook, got out his pencil, asked me to estimate the time of day, and took some hurried notes.

. . . like they just ain't meant for this world. Down in Simpson County, we got an expression, a man . . .

I kept fiddling with the dials, to get the signal in better, but it weren't no use. Finally, I called Reck in to take over. Then I went back out. I sat on the porch, filling my belly with berries, and letting the whine of the radio stir the still summer night and catch itself up, choking, on the dark line of trees.

"That man is the future of criminal execution," Reck said from the shadows inside.

The signal never came in proper. It went from whining high to whining low, and back again, but Reck kept at it, in the bluish murk, like a solitary captain at the wheel of a stalled ship.

Jesse and Mirth and Luck and I said nothing, and scarcely moved in the gathering heat. The heat was so heavy and dense, it took on a color, yellow-gray, and collected around us like a tub of lukewarm water filling drop by drop as to overflow if we stirred a muscle. We went on eating berries from the same pot, tasting them on our own. The fruit lay in my belly, and I could almost picture it there, gurgling and dark, and amid that sweetness, and the pale yellow sunlight, I closed my eyes. The aftertaste of the berries rose up the back of my throat, and the memory of another sunlight swam behind my closed eyes.

That other day was purple, too, on account of the pie, and yellow on account of the sun; and it had the smell of salt and rosemary, which to me is forever the smell of desire, and of remorse. I was on a bank high above the water, and a stray wind ran through the reach of sea grass like a shiver on an arm, and lost itself in shadows. I was sat down, leaned up against the wall of a shed. I breathed in the smell of cut grass and salt water, and my fingers were stained purple with the blackberry pie I'd polished off for lunch. Them berries was sweet and tart and dark, like a secret being told. They made my mouth pucker, and before one spoonful was gone, long for another, just to keep my mouth from having to change its shape and lose the taste that went along with it.

My girl was sitting there beside me. Her dress was the color of hyacinth. I remember how the breeze stirred its folds, and when they was touched deep enough inside, they rendered up the smell of crushed rosemary. She wore two slender silver bracelets on a single wrist, and when she moved, they jingled like a chime so soft it seemed from far away. I fancied I was in love with her; and in such moments, in those years, I could fairly picture my heart opening up, like a door in a walled-up garden, within all flowers and springtime. But over time, I've seen that such love fades like it was written in water. In my mind now, this girl's name is an empty space, as luminous as a splash of moonlight, and as undefined, same as her face. I can't recall either one of them. It ain't her I remember so much as her brother Ben, and the pain I took up on his account. Ben got into my heart the way a creak gets in a door, and resides there still, like a break waiting to sever the thing in two.

So we was sitting there together, her and me, high on a slope above the water. The dark grass swayed and let the breeze run through it in little paths that arose out of nothing and merged and vanished. She was telling me about how she'd gone and let Ben have that ribbon I'd got her, on account of he liked it so much; and how I done a nice thing myself, setting aside that afternoon to spend with him. I nodded, and my insides gurgled with satisfaction. The sun beat down upon us, and its heat was like a mantle. She reached for the pie plate. Her bracelets jangled, and caught the light. *A real sweet thing*, she said, *it gives a good feeling, how much we do for him*, and her eyes was cast down, and their color was hid from me. And there stirred within me desire, and I thought abstractedly of the good we done, and both feelings mingled into one; and carried aloft as by a swell, generous and fine, I took her in my embrace, and she yielded, warm and breathing, and I lay her down upon the grass, and the shadow of my face was lowered over her eyes.

When I next looked up, I heard the water lapping against the bank. A passel of boys was going by. They had fishing poles slung across their shoulders, and their shouts echoed across the cooling sky. On a far levee, somebody cast a last line into the water. It made a silver glint in the air, as if a tossed coin had etched its path upon the wind. I stood up. A cloud passed over my heart. My insides went dark and cold; for I knew I had broken the promise I had given in the heat of the morning.

I'd been out mending a length of fence on the edge of the watchmaker's property at the time. A flock of gulls wheeled overhead, and their cries fell from their beaks, and was lost to the hollow sky. Two hours before noon, and the sky had already scorched to white. Ben was lurking up-fence from me. He was bulky, and looked to be as immovable from the inside as the out. He had a woman's hair ribbon wound around his hand, hyacinth blue, and pretty as a bit of tune; the week before, I'd picked it out and given it to his sister. It shimmered like the wind, and dangled down to his boot-top.

Ben's back was broad and his neck was thick, but his eyes were as mild as watered-down milk. He'd been waiting by that fence awhile, I guessed. There was a group of boys on the other side. I could see their motion between the slats, cut up, like the sideways view of a deck of cards. Every now and again, they called out Ben's name, loud, like it was a ball they was taking turns batting out of a park; and each time he heard them call his name, his neck gave a short sharp jerk. e moved one slats-width down the fence, and stopped. He waited, bulky and silent.

Then the gate swung open, and the boys emerged. I was facing the sun, and in my eyes, they were in silhouette. They looked like a brace of black stick figures twisted out of iron, each with a much smaller stick figure thrown over a shoulder, and that skinniest bit was a fishing rod. The tallest of the boys called out, "Hey Benny Ben Ben."

Ben turned, slow and deliberate. His hands made fists which he raised in front of his chest, and his eyes opened so wide they looked a shade lighter.

"Want to go fishing with us, Ben?" the tall boy called out.

Ben gave a smile. It was so homely and so unguarded it near broke your heart. His eyes closed, and he nodded, yes, yes, though he could not get the words out.

"We're going to have the best time," another boy said.

"Go fishing all the live-long day and have a fry up," the tall boy continued. "It sounds just like heaven, now, don't it? I bet you'd like to come along, Ben, wouldn't you?"

Ben near stamped his feet, he was so happy with the prospect. Joy had him in its grip.

"I knew you'd want to come," the tall boy said. He paused. "Well, you can't." He swung the gate wide and let it slam shut. He walked past Ben without even looking at him.

"We ain't taking no idiots."

"Yeah," one of them said.

"And how," another called out.

"Like an old dancing bear, ain't he?" That was from the youngest-looking one of the gang. His eyes went round as he peeked up at his buddies for any takers.

"Idiots is bad luck," the tall boy said. He was a little ways ahead by then. "Besides which they are idiots."

Ben watched them go by. His head was set there facing them like an empty cannon, and it did not move. Then his shoulders hunched up. He was crying.

I went on mending the fence so as to give him some time. Then I looked up and said, "Hey, Ben. I got an idea last night. How about you and me go fishing sometime?"

He sniffled.

"Seems like a waste of a summer day to do anything else," I went on.

He looked at me. His eyes were the color of cornflowers. He rubbed his nose with the flat of his hand, and the ribbon drew up and danced in front of his belly. His gaze was as flat as paint drying. "When?" he said.

I laughed. "You don't waste a minute, Ben, or a word neither. Let's say after lunch. Meet you right there." I pointed down the slope. "That big flat rock shaped like a diamond."

Ben looked at me, then down the length of my pointing arm. His eyes followed its direction across the grass and down the sandy ridge, and then they went back the same way, all the way to my eyes again. He nodded.

"Okay then," I said. I turned back to my fence-mending. Ben lumbered off into the blue-green fringe of woods. I watched him, getting swallowed up, noiselessly, into its depths, and then he disappeared. Overhead, the shadows of the gulls swooped and fled, and their cries rebounded emptily against the hard high sky.

The next time I saw Ben, he was in the shallows of the creek, just where the water turns brackish and reedy. It weren't but a few hundred yards from the diamond-shaped rock, where he must have waited, while his sister and I slept our guilty sleep through that white-skied afternoon. My eye caught sight of a narrower stream running within the water, like a current with a different color, and degree of warmth. We got closer, and I saw that narrow current was his sister's hair ribbon. By then, she'd already spotted Ben. He was lying face down in the water. The ribbon was still wound around his hand. It had come loose, and floated out into the tide, where it drifted with the ebb and flow, like the murmur of a living heart. Then somewhere up high a seagull cawed, and its cry got tangled up with Ben's sister's, and both cries flew up higher, to the treetops on the bluffs, and got caught worse the more they kept trying to break free, like a trapped and snarled-up thing.

Then something slammed shut. I opened my eyes. The radio was still whining.

"That Dr. Zogg really is something," Reck said. He came back on to the porch. He was shaking his head and rubbing the back of his neck like a growed man. "I got to write a whole new entry."

CHAPTER TWENTY-SIX

So that summertime passes, and by its end, we'd had enough of them in all that Jesse had reached the juncture where his path crossed that of public life, and he was registered and enrolled and his named inscribed upon the ledger; and he had now to put on his overalls and go to school.

It weren't an easy passage. I suppose some of the questions he got hit with I should have thought about beforehand and prepared him for, but I was a novice in the business of bringing up a boy raised from the dead, and keeping him in the dark about it to boot. When I came back from work that first day of school, Jesse's head was still hanging low, like a disheartened dandelion, and his bottom lip stuck out fat as a pouter fish's. He was hunkered down on the front step, and refused to say goodnight to Mrs. Greenfield. She was shaking her head at me, and said she'd done everything a human being could think for the boy, including trying to tune that fool radio but she couldn't get nothing to come in. She buttoned up her coat, and snapped her pocketbook shut. The clasp glittered in the thinning light. I ducked my chin at her once on Jesse's behalf, then once on my own.

"Howdy, Jes," I said.

He kept his head down, and put his hands over his face. "I ain't going back," he announced.

"Back where?" I said. "Cairo-town? You get tired of building them pyramids in the sand?"

"That school place."

"You got thrown out already." I loitered beside the step, and plucked out a blade of timothy grass. "How 'bout that. Most fellas, it takes them a week or two at least. Took me ten days but I had some help."

"They laughed at me," he said. His voice came from deep within his fingers. "All of them was laughing."

"You are a funny guy, Jesse," I said. "You can't blame them for seeing that. I expect it means they like you, the same way you laugh with the fella on the radio." I hoped to God he hadn't told about his hankering to bake.

He whipped his hands out of the way, and turned his face up at me. It was angry and red and stuck out of his neck like accusation made flesh, a semi-tamed animal clenched up in front of my doorway. "Soon as I told them, my name is Jimmy but my daddy calls me something else, they all laughed. And one of them said first off, he ain't your daddy, your daddy run off up north. Then they was all saying it at me, and what kind of goober gets called one thing by his daddy who isn't, and another thing by everybody else."

I perched down beside him. "I bet they said it in kind of a nay-nay sing-song kind of way," I said. I jostled the grass in the air like I was conducting an orchestra of bullies. "One of them picks up the cry and trying to stop it's like trying to catch the call of the whippoorwill in your cupped hands. Voices and whispers and such, well, they are born fugitives. Slippier than a shadow. You ever try to catch one?"

Jesse burrowed his head back in his fists. I waited for a sob and that hiccupy gather of the shoulders kids give off when they start crying, but none came.

"Jesse," I said softly, "I am not your daddy." I drew the blade of grass just above his ears, a caress so light he did not feel it, like I have read the breath on angels attends upon the blessed unawares. "But that don't mean I don't love you like one, Jes. Maybe even better."

"Where's my daddy gone to?" He put his hands on his knees and looked at me dead-level. He had eyes steady and unblinking like my semi-natural born brother had, only Jesse's were a warmer shade of blue, and they made you feel exhilarated and gratified both, like when you wade in the ocean and stumble into a sunned up strand of water. Jesse's eyes didn't seem made for hiding anything, not from them, and not within them neither.

"Your daddy couldn't face being on this earth," I said.

"Is he with my momma?"

"I imagine he is. He asked me to help him out and look after you for him. And I am gladder than I ever knew I would be that I said, yes, surely I will."

"What kind of kin was he to you, my daddy?"

"He kind of adopted me, Jes. A long time ago. Out of the goodness of his heart."

"That makes us brothers."

"I reckon it does, in a roundabout kind of way."

"But you're so old you're like a daddy anyhow. Nobody else I know got a brother old as you."

"I reckon they do not." I made to knock off his hat even though he wasn't wearing one, then I settled with roughing up his hair. "I call you Jesse because it's what your daddy wanted you called."

Jesse rolled his head around to accommodate my scalp rumpling. "Why don't everybody call me that?"

"The Jesse name's kind of a secret you share with your kin, but nobody else. Same as you share your blood."

Jesse turned his wrist over and planted his right ear over his left pulse.

"See," I said. "Your blood ain't saying nothing. And it ain't going nowhere but around inside you."

I planted his thumb on the pulse spot. "You feel that?"

Jesse sat there like somebody with a conch to his ear listening to the sea for the first time. He cut down on his breathing, and his eyes were wide and calm. We sat there on the front stoop. The sun had gone down. A truck rumbled by on the highway below.

"I'm going to make you a deal," I said. "It's so fine, that Mr. Bean himself his eyes would glint up and he'd snap it right out of my hands like a crocodile with an empty belly."

"What's that?"

"Jimmy's got to go back to school, but Jesse, now, he don't have to go back there ever."

"I ain't stupid," he said.

"You ain't stupid," I said. "You're my brother."

Jesse smiled as if he had caught the joke.

"Only sometimes you are my son. I get mixed up."

Jesse whooped and raised his arms over his head, shaking them like they was a treetop caught in a high wind, and then he ran down the steps.

I chased after him. He ducked by the fencepost. I made like I couldn't see hide nor hair of him, but when he went to sneak out, I grabbed him by the back of his overalls and it made a handy-dandy holding fixture. He tried to run, his shadow feet hitting the ground but his real ones not.

"Now about Mrs. Greenfield setting off tonight," I said. "What do you reckon you ought to have done?"

Jesse stopped churning, and looked like he knew what was coming but stood his ground as best he could, considering he was three inches above it.

"When a lady makes to leave, you get up yourself," I said. I hoisted him up another inch.

"Okay," he said. "But I ain't fixing to be no sissy boy."

"And say goodbye loud enough so she can hear it. I ain't talking about being a sissy boy."

"Yessir."

"You wash up and in a little while, we'll have ourselves

dinner," I said. "And then maybe I'll see about tuning that radio to WELO." I set him loose and he hit the ground running.

"Remember," I called out after him, "there's a 'man' in 'manners.' "

A sheet was flapping on Mrs. Hadley's clothesline. The air was bluish, and streaked with chill, like a remnant of smoke gone cold. Jesse was running through it towards the house, and his shirt rippled on the wind. I sat out on the step myself. The Baptists were having a dunking down by the river, it sounded like. The light turned deeper blue, and fell on the trees, which were glowing white, and the washing on the clothesline, the roads and houses, and the stars. The whole world was getting baptized in blue by night. Blue and white were bleeding into each other, like the sky and the river and the air were getting mixed up. The washing glowed bluish-white on the line, and flapped like a wing without a bird.

I'd known the sky itself to open once with a flutter of wings. We were gathered by the water. JC and I, grown men by then. We'd gone to find our mother by the river, as Joseph had asked us to, and wait for him there, so we could all walk home together. Every so often, he got the idea we should try to live like the other families in town. When he let that one loose on me, I said, of course, not every family can a boast a son who could make a boy fall dead just by wishing it so, that's a dinnertime topic and a half right there; but Joseph went on smoothing the wood like he hadn't heard me. Our mother was taking out the washing, and when she saw us on the riverbank, she pointed to a ledge, like we was still kids, and told us to sit there and not get into trouble. It was a little late for that.

I was skipping stones across the water and thinking about JC and me when we were little, how I taught him to swim and he weren't no good at it, mouth blubbering up in the water like it was a separate creature, drowning, but I kept trying with him, diving in after him, and showing him how to get through the water. JC was standing there looking into the river, and it's funny: eyes that in a child are wide and round, ready to take in the world, in an adult just look kind of untenanted, like a vacant lot scattered with broken glass.

I watched him staring out over the water, and I fell to remembering all kinds of things I had lost over the years, all jumbled up, that dog JC and I took in one winter, a yellow jug shaped like a circle on its sides that mother kept in a front window in some house or another, things I could scarcely recall and them becoming ever more precious and more numerous the further they receded from my recollection. You reach a point in your life, sometimes it's the end of childhood, sometimes it's the onset of middle age, and you find your past has grown into a kind of hinterland inside of you, from which you are forever exiled. All the things that made it up, the bits of bric-a-brac, the blanket your mother laid out special when you were sick, the wobbly-jawed hound who used to greet you of a night, have disappeared, and so has the you which was you when you lived in it. The only things that recur are certain slants of light, and that's why they haunt you as surely as a ghost.

So JC and I were standing under a cedar, its shadows wavering like a passel of snakes in the water. Mother tumbled the washing into the river. JC had burnt a hole in his shirtsleeve the night before, and, his mind fixated on matters of the spirit, had barely noticed what he'd done. But I knew how such waste would dishearten momma, so I'd pulled the burned sleeve inside out, and twisted the whole thing in a knot. I was watching her, wondering if she would find out.

"Look at that," JC said.

A few hundred yards down the bank, there was a weird looking number in clothes that hadn't been washed in some time, dunking folks' heads in the water. His hair had been uncombed for so long that it looked to be growing in circles around his scalp. I was always worried if he weren't careful that JC himself might wind up in such a state, unkempt and disreputable. Folks were standing in line for the waterworks, some of them humming and others throwing in a holler every so often, as if it was called for, like punctuation in a run-on sentence. On my stretch of the bank, mother was opening up the stripy shirt, and starting to draw in her breath, when JC headed off towards the weirdo. That's all I need, I thought: a professional in the line of peculiar for my brother to tag after, dragging me in tow with him.

JC got himself a place in line, it looked like, and when I turned around, Joseph was standing there next to me. His lips fluttered, and he was a little out of breath. "I got the job," he said. "Making them chairs and tables. Means work for you and your brother too."

"That's good, daddy," I said. "I'm real glad to hear it."

Mother was holding the shirt up to the light and sighing fit to bust. Over by JC, a pigeon was flying straight down at him, and even from that distance I could hear it was flapping something fierce.

"It was my fault, ma," I said. "Leant too low over the candle and up it went."

Then I heard someone say, you are my own dear son, and I am well pleased. I thought it meant me. Sometimes I still do. I turned around. Joseph was patting me on the shoulder, and when he saw me, he pulled his face into a smile, only his smile seemed shadowed with regret. There were deep creases around his mouth, and his shoulders were stooped. For the first time, I saw he was an old man. There were streaks of gray running through his hair, like smoke from a fire that was running low. Above JC, the pigeon kept on flapping, and right by where I was, my mother was back pounding the bluish cloth with a rock, the water rushing around her, and the washing hung over the branches flapping wetly in the wind.

CHAPTER TWENTY-SEVEN

All this while, that Jesse was starting school and discovering the radio, Bean and his business empire had been flourishing over the land. I was assistant and witness both to its ascendancy. It ain't easy being first deputy to a fellow who styles himself a visionary. I'd done it first to that one hung up on matters of eternal life, and now to this one stuck on the business of death. Bean's prison-building and his casket-making went clear across the state, all the way up into Memphis. He had the convicts felling the timber, and the timber lining up to make coffins, and new prison camps. For life and death sentences both, he had the market cornered. I told him that one day.

"Huh. I always knew there was something I liked about you, Jud," Bean said. He was pocketing the remark like spare change. We were out by the workhouse at Parchman on this Saturday, Bean and Yellow and me, and one of Bean's men, and the spring rain was falling heavy and relentless, dampening down the smell of lilac that lingered in the air with the smell of the sawdust rising off the floor. The gate was hanging loose from one hinge and it scraped against the ground. I was batching up the planks in lots, and tying them with twine. "But then again," Bean was saying, "there are a few things I never could figure. Like how come you ain't got no woman?"

Bean's man laughed so hard, his shoulders hunched up around his neck. His head was shaped like a pumpkin with a long jagged gash, like a knife been dragged through a custard pie, along his left cheek. "Wouldn't mind a tumble with that blondie waitress I seen you with," he said.

"You can have her," Bean said. "I been served."

The man's shoulders hunched up again. I weren't laughing and Bean looked at me, and went on. "But you ain't, now have you, Jud?"

I was snapping the twine off across my fingers and it cut into them. I tied the length off and knotted it around the wood. "It don't do, not with a child to look after."

"How's that boy going to know about life if he never overhears any of its goings on," Bean said. "You can have my cast-offs, if you got a mind."

Yellow joined in the heh-hehs the way he always did, a mite tardy and a little scared that something was happening without him.

"Looks like Yellow knows all about what I'm saying," the man said.

"Why don't you explain it to us, boy?" Bean said.

Yellow stopped giggling.

"I know something even more peculiar than a man without no woman," I said.

"What's that?" Bean said.

"A man who's got plenty of women but ain't never had a child."

Bean's eyes turned a shade colder, like a razor turning in the light as it's sharpened on a stone.

"Of course, I've only read about such carryings-on in the good book," I went on. "Some folks'll try and tell you, barrenness is a curse meted out by an angry Lord. But I don't imagine the Lord is like that." He ain't, for the sole simple reason He ain't interested in the things that folks are.

"That Bible'll sure keeps you safe, Jud," Bean said. "Especially if you take care and carry it below the belt at all times. And keep it shut. The book I mean. Plenty of carryings on inside of it, I am still referring here to the book not your pants."

"Plenty of begats in it, too," I said.

"Jimmy, you leave that pot of soup alone," a woman's voice was saying. Jesse was in the children's keeping house.

Bean looked at me and grinned. "It's an established fact, a woman gets her belly puffed up but once, and forever after, her voice is raises a few keys just so she's fit to go screeching after the young'un. That true of men, too, Jud?"

The man laughed. Yellow opened his mouth and cockadoodledoo-ed into the air. The sound ricocheted off the roof.

"I was talking about men," Bean said. "Not an imbeciled idiot. Now when you're done batching them planks, Jud, load them on to the truck. Have to get them across the state by Monday." He checked his watch and looked at the rain fall like he was calculating its speed and what it would fetch at an open market. "I'll get you one of the paying guests. They're always happy to help. If they ain't, I help them wish they was."

"Okay, sir," I said. "I sure could use a hand."

Bean and his man and Yellow headed out of the yard. I was flexing my rawed-up fingertips when the broken gate swung as open as it could and scraped into the ground and got stuck. When I looked up, Vernon was standing in front of me. He couldn't seem to find a spot comfortable enough to rest his eyes on, though he was searching all over for one, and I thought for a minute he wasn't going to say howdy, but instead make like he didn't know me. He weren't ashamed so much as embarrassed, and not for himself, but for me having to see him like this.

"Hi, Vern," I said.

"Jud," he said finally. I guess he'd decided my left shoe

was the least rocky eye-rest in the vicinity.

"I hope you're doing alright," I said. "It can't be easy for a fella."

Vern stood there, his face white and round and bland like a bowlful of cream of wheat going cold.

"We better get a move on with this wood," I said. I hoisted one end of the plank over my shoulder. "My boy's here today, and he's been making a regular ruckus."

Vern shouldered the other end of plank. "My boy's coming visiting today too, and his momma."

I was set to push off towards the truck, but Vern lagged behind so I stopped. The gate scraped against the ground again and Bean sauntered in taking the wrapping off a stick of gum. He'd put on his city coat. The buttons glittered in the grayish light. He'd changed his shoes, too, and they squeaked a bit as he walked. He was going to some Chamber of Commerce meeting or another. The rain was pouring off the roof ledge. Vern's shoulder must have slumped because the plank was pulling down on mine.

"What's that squeaking?" I said. I thought I'd try and make Bean with his new shoes feel conspicuous.

Bean grinned. "Sound like a pig, don't it?" he said. He popped the gum in his mouth, and gave a big chew to break it in. I could smell the peppermint. "Now you and pigs go back quite a ways, don't you, Vern?" Bean chewed and worked himself a mouthful of peppermint liquor. Then he swallowed and I watched it go down his gullet.

Vern's end of plank tugged upwards a moment, and went still.

"You know what, Vern?" Bean said. "You ought to gather together all the pigs you ever deserved to be busted for, and get them all to squall, and start yourself an all-hog symphony orchestra. Music to gobble prison grub by."

I hoisted up the timber and made a move. This time Vern followed. He weren't steady and the timber was bobbing around.

"Oh, there's nothing like the squeak of a new pair of

shoes," I said. "You remind me of Jim there, Mr. Bean. I was looking at some footgear for him, soles as thick as a gum eraser. I reckon your boy has near the same kind, right, Vern?"

"I don't rightly know," Vern said behind me.

"Jim screamed when I showed him a pair in the paper. Right good buy, but he said he wouldn't be seen in shoes with tassels and dots punched out in a pattern like the swirl in a cinnamon bread. Like he was some kind of girly doll."

The plank bobbed up. "Now my boy, he don't mind fancy things a bit," Vern said. "Looking at them anyways."

"Why not just steal them, he's his daddy's boy, ain't he?" Bean said. He took a step towards us, away from the sound of the falling rain. He put his hands on his hips and shook his head, like we were the sorriest sight he ever did see in a lifetime spent appraising the manifold varieties of human folly. "Just cackling away together, like a hen and a gelding in the same pen." Bean took a deliberate chew and pulled back his lips to grin but the crinkle did not reach up to his eyes. They were a flat grayish-blue. Then he crumpled up the gum papers and dropped them on the floor. "Sweep up in here after you've loaded the truck," he said. "And mind your gabbing don't slow you down none." He walked out the gate and it swung halfway behind him, stiff and purposeless, like a wing severed off an archangel and fell to earth.

We shouldered up the planks and brought them to the truck. The rain was falling steady and swift.

"And they say the Lord is a stern taskmaster," Vernon said.

"But His undertakings ain't so extensive," I said. "And His concerns nowhere near so personal."

CHAPTER TWENTY-EIGHT

That weren't the only encounter of the day either. When I went to fetch Jesse that afternoon out of the kiddie coop, I nodded to the caretaker, and was like to walk past E who was playing out in the center of the floor, trying to make a top spin and failing. I set it going right. "Thank you, sir," he said. The air was heavy and soft, the light was dreary, and the floor was full of greenish shadows. I dragged my own one, like a coat out of season, across to Jesse.

He was in the corner, stacking up blocks and knocking them down. The top clattered to the ground, and he turned and looked at E, irate and round-eyed. That boy's noise was spoiling his own.

"What you been up to?" I said.

"Nothing." Jesse burrowed his chin into his collar.

"That boy troubling you any?"

"No," he said.

"He been laughing at you at school?" I said.

"Nooo," Jesse said. There's nothing like irritating a six-year old with the full force of your own stupidity, because it comes right back like a boomerang and hits you in the forehead and marks you for life. "Soon as they see him coming," Jesse said, "they laugh at him instead."

"Then he's the shoofly boy, like that pie in that cookery book of yours. Set it out on the picnic table and the creepycrawlies all head towards it instead of the lemon meringue. You ought to like him on account of that alone."

The care lady brushed the hair out of her eyes. She was stood at the sink and she was shuffling some dishes onto a drying rack. "Mister, those boys can't seem to get out of each other's way," she said. "One turns to run and the other is standing in his way, and not like he was fixing to either but somehow he just is."

Jesse pointed at E. "His daddy is a thief," Jesse announced.

E went on fiddling with the top like he hadn't heard, only a little too much like he hadn't heard.

"Now Jesse," I said, "I know his daddy and I have never met a kindlier fellow. You got to learn folks have feelings same as you. Let's go over to him and you'll see what I mean." Jesse stuck his lower lip out, but I hauled him up on my shoulder and brought him over to E.

"I ain't getting down," Jesse said. "Not till you take me home." He clung to my shoulder like a monkey on a tree.

"That ain't no way to talk, boy," I said. "I ain't budging till you learn how to behave proper."

We stood there, overlooking E, casting our shadows on him lightly but as present as breath, and E glanced up at us, then went back to his labors of play.

Jesse was pummeling my chest with his fists when the door swung open, and E's mother stepped over the threshold as careful and cautious if it might jump up and hit her. She straightened the skirt of her dress, and smiled nervously as she looked around. I seen my own momma do the same, days she fetched us from the schoolroom and weren't sure what mischief her sons got themselves, and her, into that day.

Soon as he saw her, E jumped up. The top fell out of

his hand and crashed to the floor, he was in such a hurry. He rushed up to her and she dandled his head a minute like a baby lamb's. Then he looked up and took her hand and swung it slowly like one end of a jump rope. "Momma, can I get you something?" he said, softly. "You want a glass of water?"

"This boy sure is special," I said.

Jesse's head popped up out his collar. "What's so special about him?"

"You will notice he looks after folks," I said. "Don't go around putting them down."

"All God's children is special," his mother said, polite and evenhanded, like she was handing out mints from her pocketbook, and able to be generous because she knew in her heart that hers was the most special.

I leant down, Jesse still tight around my neck, casting his shade beneath me; and I whispered to E, "Son, you are touched by the shadow of the Lord." He looked into my eyes. He had heard me, and he nodded.

Jesse could tell I'd been saying something to E, and he took a swipe at him. "That boy's got his own daddy," he said, turning his nose square face to face with mine. "And a momma too. He's got enough of his own people right there."

"You know what?" I said. "You sound like Mr. Bean, adding up who's got what, and how much, and how it compares to your own little pile of peas. I'm going to take you home right now so you can get to counting." I nodded goodbye to E's mother and the care lady, and headed out.

Jesse started clambering down my sides.

"Knock it off," I said.

"Ain't I supposed to stand up to say goodbye?" Jesse said. "That's what you said. You said -"

"Just hush up, after you say goodbye," I said.

"Goodbye," Jesse said, into my neck.

"Mind you don't bash your head," I said. Jesse craned his neck out to look out for a low beam and almost got whacked by the doorframe. We both were out the door, straight into a spray of steam rising out of the laundry shack.

CHAPTER TWENTY-NINE

Jesse and I weren't exactly a bookish pair, but it was a fact that in that year, the printed word increased and multiplied in our house. I had a Bible, which I hardly needed to read no more, imprinted as it was in my mind, and then Jesse got hold of a handful of old cookbooks. He'd scoured some from beside a trash can on the way from school one day. The pages was speckled with mold and curling up. Reck took one look at them and said they were a waste of time, and mighty girly besides, but if that's what Jes wanted, he knew a place he could get them not only for free, but in a heap better shape. Where's that, I asked him; oh, just a place where I do some background research, he said, you have to be a member there. I told him no thanks; the last thing I wanted was us to get busted on account of Reck clipping the *Grill and Gruel Cookbook* or some such off the shelves of the public library.

But there was another kind of book Jesse took a liking to that year. And he read them the way a fat man eats: when he was with people, when he was on his own, when he was walking to school, when he was out fishing. He squirreled bits away in his coat for later, and traded for new ones with Mirth. Mrs. Greenfield told me she'd seen him almost walk into a fence, because he had an open book in front of his face, and paid no mind to where his feet were headed. They weren't the cooking kind of book with measurements for cups of flour and teaspoons of nutmeg, either. Jesse was a reader of comic books. Or one comic book in particular: *The Spirit*, that came as a supplement with Mrs. Greenfield's Sunday newspaper.

The ink stained his fingers. At first I thought it was some marking of the divine, and looked heavenwards and began to pray in my heart. Then I saw how easy it washed off. That's how I first got wind of what he was up to. I caught him a few times, when he was supposed to be asleep, crouched up by the blackened window and slanting a comic book against it, his eyes as wide as he could make them to take in all the light that they could. Well, he was a person of the book alright, and someday he would be spelling the words that belonged to him alone.

One night, it was a Friday, about an hour after I put him to bed. It was the time of year the sky got dark by six, and the train sounded more forlorn than ever. *Are you cut short by the ways of men? Are you seeking but have not yet found –* the man on the radio was saying, till I switched him off, and the sound snapped shut. The place felt kind of empty, the light outside was growing watery and dark, and I could hear a whippoorwill calling far away. Forlorn ain't just a state of mind, it's a sound, and a color of the sky, too. I was surely glad to have a bundle of warm and breathing flesh in the other room.

"You asleep, Jes?" I called out.

There was a pause. "Yes," he said.

"Oh. That's too bad. 'Cause if you was awake, I was going to read you one of those comic books you are always carting around. Mrs. Greenfield found another one for you. But since you've -"

Jesse appeared in the doorway. His hair was tousled and a patchful of it stood up in back. He was the greater-crested Jesse.

"I ain't sleeping now."

"Okay then." I got the comic book out from my coat, and sat back down. Jesse climbed into my lap, and I looked at the title. *Denny Colt and The Secret of Wildwood Christmas.* The cover showed a darkened field under a purple sky, with a sliver of moonlight stuck up in the corner like a shaved-off nickel. There were a bunch of lumps standing up in the field, like bales of hay. "What's this Wildwood place, anyway, Jesse?"

Jesse popped his thumb out of his mouth. "That's where Denny Colt lives."

"In the middle of a cow field?" I said.

"It's Wildwood Cemetery."

I felt the skin on the back of my neck get ready to take a walk at that one. "Quit sucking that thumb, boy. You keep it up and one day you're going to swallow your hand whole. What kind of goober lives in a cemetery, Jesse?"

"Everybody thinks Denny's dead. Only he ain't. And at night, he ain't Denny no more anyhow."

"What is he then?"

"He's the Spirit."

"What kind of spirit are we talking here, Jes?" I said. I was waiting for him to popfly the word Holy at me.

"You get to reading like you said you would, mister, and you might find something out."

"I guess you got a point. And looky-there, a nose too," I said, giving it a little twist. I hunkered down an inch or so in the chair and started reading.

What Leniford Ruthless, leader of the town gang of smalltime riff-raff, doesn't know is that the graveyard he's been using to store his stolen goods, isn't deserted. It's the home of Denny Colt!

Winter moonlight streams down over Wildwood Cemetery. Hidden in the shadow of a gravestone engraved with his own name, Denny Colt keeps warm - and keeps watch on the city he has made his own. By the abandoned shed where he has stashed his ill-gotten booty, Leniford lurks. He has not caught the holiday spirit - but maybe soon the Spirit will catch him!

That copper's had it in for me for a while, but I'll nab him good this time. I pointed. "That's Leniford Ruthiless, with the Central City Gazette in his mitts. See, Jess, the headline: Commissioner Dolan to Open Fair." I went on reading aloud:

The whole family of Dolans'll be at the Christmas fair, and I'll move in and clear the place out in no time. Deck the halls alright heh-heh."

"Nuts," Denny thinks to himself. "I'll make this town safe for Christmas if it's the last thing I do!"

Having awoken from his state of suspended animation at the evil-doing hands of Dr. Cobra a year ago, Denny has found that the shadow of supposed death provides the perfect cover to don the mantle of crime-fighter. Even if it means leaving behind the one girl he'd ever loved.

And so, on Christmas Eve -

The Dolan family is busy with its holiday preparations. Daughter Ellen is putting the last touches on the Christmas cake, while Mrs. Dolan gathers up the gifts for the local orphanage.

"Faith and begorrah!" the commissioner says. "We'd best be getting a move-on to the fair. I'd like to be there before the Easter lilies are in bloom, girls!"

As the Dolans make their way out the door, little do they realize that hidden in one corner of their shadowy yard is Leniford Ruthiless - and in the other, ready to play the ghost of Christmas Present, is Denny Colt!!"

"He the ghost of a Christmas present?" Jesse asked. His mouth dropped open and he thought about it a minute. "Like the ghost of a top or a sled or some such that got left behind somewhere. And starts spinning and going down hilltops all on its own." He started whirling his hands around, and I could tell he was picturing specter toys picking themselves up in corners of empty rooms, and sleds pitching themselves down snowy fields with blue shadows playing over them.

"No," I said. "It means it's as if Christmas for that year was made into Denny, into a person. Made flesh." After I came out with that one, I made sure my eyes hotfooted down the page but quick with my tongue moving along in close pursuit.

A brief tap at the window - and Leniford alights into the Dolan's home. In the darkness, he brushes against something as prickly as wolf's tail and cowers - until he realizes it's the branch of the Dolan's Christmas tree.

Meanwhile, Denny - now in the guise of the Spirit - has gained entry through the bulkhead door. Down in the basement he begins to have fun at Leniford's expense. As a general rule, Denny has learned that those who seek the cover of darkness are either on the side of good as himself - or rank and utter cowards.

I grinned. "I'm not sure about that one, Jes."

"What's happens next?"

These chains will make a nice clanking sound - if a little unsettling,' says Denny.

Upstairs, Leniford pauses. "What is that?"

Down in the cellar, Denny begins to moan in an eerie fashion he has picked up as a graveyard regular. "Oh what evil do I see here! I must leave my grave to avenge, avenge -"

With a loud crash, Leniford drops his bag of booty to the floor. "Halloween's the time for ghosts - not Christmas!!"

Lightfooted as an Indian, Denny now bounds up the stairs and stations himself behind the Christmas tree. He begins to shake its branches, which move as though alive. In a quavering voice Denny says: "I have come for you this Christmas."

"For who??"

"Youuuu. . ."

"Must be an echo in here," Leniford says. "Gulp."

"I heard you plan your evil-doing under the moonlight, disturbing the peace of the dead. You - Leniford Ruthiless!!"

"What - how - whooo - ?"

Before Leniford can finish his sentence, The tree heaves forward with a mighty crash.

At this, Leniford falls in a dead faint.

"Lenny, you'll make the best Christmas present Cmmr. Dolan 's ever had!! I'm going to wrap this nasty number up in the most festive

ribbon I can find."

Leniford is soon decked out in a bright red bow.

Jesse let loose with a cackle. It burst on the air, and floated in smithereens a second, and then disappeared by the time I turned the page.

Back outside now, Denny waits again in the shadows that have for so long been his only home. He looks through the window of the warm and welcoming front hall, waiting for the Dolans to return. At last the front light goes on, and Denny hears their exclamations.

"Look what Santa left behind!" Cmmr. Dolan says. "Gift-wrapped too! I'll bring him downtown myself. Oh - but that means we won't be going caroling straight away like I promised you, Ellen."

"I can think of one stool pigeon that'll be singing pretty tonight," Denny thinks to himself.

"Oh, dad, don't bother yourself," Ellen says.

I was getting into the thing myself and tried to make my voice a bit higher, Ellen-style. *"This is the best present ever a girl could have - Central City made safe, and Christmas with my family, and that is fact!"*

Against the cold and darkened glass, Denny breathed quietly to himself. "And it is a fact, Ellen Dolan, that I will love you to the day I die!"

Jesse sat there in my lap, silent and not moving, and thinking the whole thing over. It rested in his mind like a Thanksgiving dinner in the belly of a tranquil man.

I allowed him a decent pause, and then I said, "So, boy, what did you think?"

"It was okay."

"Thanks, boy," I said.

"I liked number 56 better, *The Tale Of The Dictator's Reform.* But 52's good too, with Denny and the airplane that goes to Washington DC."

It was plain how Jesse liked his books larded with numbers: citation style, like the Bible or the serial comics, or measurements of teaspoons in his cookbooks. Jesse was sitting there citing these comic stories like JC in the temple citing scripture and law. Now that would be something, if trial lawyers and preachers referred to these books of Jesse's, numbered and versed as they were, in making their speechifying. I could already picture big John staying up all night with a sofa-sized snack of bread and cheese at his elbow, writing out the latest adventures of The Holy Spirit: "Judas has made potter's field his home – but what Judas doesn't realize is that the field has also been home to the Holy Spirit! And the Spirit is willing!!" Or some such. There would be a Christmas special, and an Easter annual. John would oversee the sales of them, and take detailed but inaccurate accounts. Sometimes a blob of butter from his fat fingers would obscure the total, and I'd catch the blame.

I was starting to chuckle and get irate all at the same time, one of my main proclivities in life, but caught myself. "The ghost and graveyard part didn't scare you none?"

"No," Jes said. He sat up a little straighter. "And I'll tell you what's more, they're talking in there about Halloween. Well, it's coming up and what I want to do is, I want to hang out at the graveyard and make like we're Denny Colt. That would be something, huh?"

"Something don't begin to tell the story," I said. "Don't it seem kind of a spooky thing to do? Goblins and ghosts and spirits roaming the earth, and us camped out in a field that don't yield no crop but moldering corpses on a regular basis?"

"Denny does it. So can we."

"I suppose 'we' means them Lesses too, don't it?"

"Nope. Denny don't bring a crowd. Only his single sidekick and loyal cohort."

"I guess that'd me," I said.

"Yep," Jesse said.

I made one last try. "Jesse, what about bobbing for apples?"

"I want to go to Priceville and make like Denny Colt." Jesse prepared to stick his thumb back in his mouth but paused. "A boy who's dead but ain't."

I had to wonder an instant just what this boy knew and what he didn't, but his eyes were clear and his brow untroubled, so I let the matter rest. I knew I'd wind up taking him, though. The boy wanted to go. Maybe it was some appointed hour they forgot to tell me about - I was always good at getting folks to those.

But before that Halloween wish could come true, and we both overheard something that was like to change ourselves forever, first a matter of Bean came due - and after that, a man whose living was death itself, in a way of which Bean could only dream, crisscrossed the land, and my life, like a tune in the wind.

CHAPTER THIRTY

For a while now, Bean had been coming down hard on his convicts. A few weeks back, a shop down by Natchez had returned two coffins, claiming they were below standard, and that their customers, if they was paying for luxury, demanded luxury. The lid joints squeaked, and the lining weren't glued in right, and the whole contraption looked like a giant jim-crackery jewel box you get at a carnival for hitting a target square in the middle with a weighted–down softball. Bean sniffed when he got the letter, said that whatever a yahoo knew about a luxury, a dead one knew even less. But all the same, after that Bean became so attached to notions of "luxury," "quality," and "craft" in relation to his coffins, and convinced that's where his fortune in this business lay, that he took to inspecting them for fine detail. He drew his hand along the length of each coffin, testing for splinters, like a white-gloved lady of the house checking the mantle for dust. He stood opening and closing the lid so many times, it was like watching him have an argument with the thing that he just couldn't seem to win. One time, after he'd found himself a particularly poor excuse for joinery, he lined the men up and demanded to know who was responsible.

Vernon's chin wobbled like a jelly salad that had just had a slice cut out of it. No one stepped forward, and just to show who was boss, and that men were held accountable for their deeds, Bean set them to work through the night, destroying that week's output piece by piece: plucking out each two-inch nail, keeping count to make sure all the nails had been pulled, rebatching the lumber, and resawing all the uneven cuts.

By this time, Bean had the north of the state cornered; that is, embalmed, en-coffined, and interred. His burial empire stretched from Tishomingo county to Lafayette. From Jefferson to Jackson, there was no one that keeled over but with Bean or an appointed representative thereof hovering nearby like an angel of God but with considerably more commercial intent. Far away, men were waging war, and it did prove a positive boon to Bean's enterprise. He got a government consignment to build a prisoner camp over the next county, and provide for any "death needs" on top. And all over Lee County itself, townships harboring a prison, a hospital, or an old folks home were deserving of a special hit, or "bite of the apple," as Bean put it, and were graced with a Bean funeral home showroom. Often it weren't but a coffin and a placard set up in the local carpenter's shop. Smaller towns made do with a broadsheet publicity number, which Bean directed me to draft.

"Mind you don't get too fancy on them," Bean told me.

We were in the backroom of the shop one day. The sky was still blue but low, like the brow of a man with something on his mind. Bean was trimming his fingernails with a penknife, and speculating.

"But mind you don't leave it too plain neither," he said. He raised one eyebrow and flicked a nail clipping into the sawdust. He gestured towards the coffin I was nailing together, a white pine 7-footer, and slapped it on its side like it was the rump of an amiable old girlfriend, and said, "Make this ahere coffin the final object of their aspirations.

Now what do you think is the way to do that, son?"

I put a nail in place, gave a good tap to hold it steady, and said, "Well sir, for starters, I wouldn't be forever hunting up yards of mauve silky stuff and off-cuts of pink sateen either. Begging your pardon, Mr. Bean, but not everybody wants to be launched into eternity decked out in the end-of-bolt remnants of some mother of the bride get-up."

Bean raised his chin so that his Adam's apple was aiming right for me. "Well then, boy, what would you do?"

"I'd make a fair portion of the coffins a whole lot cheaper."

Bean laughed and flung another clipping to the ground. He shook his head. "Jud, my boy, that is why you are the hired help."

"I didn't say I'd sell them cheaper, sir. I said I'd make them cheaper. Wouldn't get hung up about perfect joints and neat edges and so on. I'd make them simple and spare, the way they build their churches around here. I'd line 'em with plain fabrics, unbleached muslin and such, stuff you can get right in town, and costs a lot less." I pounded the nail in and looked up. "And I'd make that its positive selling point. Like Christ in all his glory."

Bean stuck his chin out another inch and started rubbing the sides of his neck. The thought of another sharp deal to pull had him all atingle and the sheer longing was like to cause a muscle cramp in his gizzard any second.

"What I'm saying is, Mr. Bean, use the words you describe 'em with to bump up the price. Not the fancy wood or the fine cloth or the painstaking craft, because each of them things cost you a fair penny."

Bean stood there, his hands clasping his neck. He was looking off into the distance and then he turned to me. "You find us a Bible quote to back that up for these hicks, and maybe then we're talking."

"They wrapped him in the simple cloth and laid him the sepulchre which was hewn out of a rock." Luke weren't never an actual scholar of the textile trade so I took my liberties here.

"I ain't got a quarry, so better soft-pedal that last bit," Bean said. He was back gazing off into the distance somewheres, to a land where burials were Baptist-style but Episcopal-priced, and coffins of cheap and simple make went lumbering into the grave as if on an assembly line, and by the same mechanism, money went pouring into his bank account. Then he looked me full in the face. "I like it. Of course, I already got a warehouse full of them velvet and silk lined numbers."

"That's why Lord sent us the Jesuits," I said.

"And kept 'em down in Natchez I hope to tell you, not a soul under the age of seventy-one, God bless them, or should I say His Holiness the Chief Papist." Bean flashed his teeth, then snapped them shut along with his penknife. "Never could understand the appeal of a man in a dress and a jew-looking beanie to top it all off. You do up a one-sheet on this, and I'll look it over." He noticed a bit of nail was hanging loose from one his thumbs, and he picked at it and flung it loose. He looked up. "On your own time, mind."

He was already reaching in his pocket for a candy bar. I heard the paper rattle telltale as an adder. He went out the door, and the bells on the door chimed after him. I waited until the sound had gone away and then went back to work.

That night I ransacked the Book for quotes that might get folks in a mind to hanker after the simple instead of the fancy in the matter of tombware. Jesse sat at the table beside me, drawing pictures of a house and a shoe and such, till I told him, Draw one of Denny, and he ducked his head down and notched his tongue over one corner of his lip, and set to work. The radio was on, and he sang along to it every so often like somebody walking along a shore ventures now and again into the water. And I was glad I had bided my time, but, surely, with the waning of another year, his own time was drawing near.

At the end of the week, I put in an order for muslin, at the Loverton mill over in east Tupelo. The woman behind the counter shook her head, and said above the noise of the machinery something about how it's funny, the business of death making some folks a pretty fair living, and keeping many a body and soul together.

I stood there a moment amidst the whirring machines, clacking away like there was an end and a purpose to their doings, and I wondered what in my case it would take to have body and soul finally and forever set asunder, as is in the end the story with most everybody else.

As it turned out, Loverton weren't but small potatoes in the business of death making you a solid living. I refer here to another interest that came to overtake Mr. Bean in those years, the appearance of Jimmy Thompson, aka Dr. Zogg, carnival huckster, hypnotist, and executioner in a new-fangled way to the state of Mississippi, purveyor of its first electric chair, a conveniently portable model.

But that weren't awhile away, closer to Christmastime, when the sky is dark, and lights to look at, whatever their source and implication, are ever so beguiling.

CHAPTER THIRTY-ONE

Though the sky was still blue and it weren't but late afternoon, the moon was stuck up in the sky just like the cover of Denny Colt had showed, and the air touched our faces heavy and soft like it was made of velvet. The trees were already pretty bare, and when a wind came up, the branches rattled like bones. I pulled my coat closer around me, and held Jesse's hand, and we entered the gates of Priceville Cemetery on Halloween night, just like Jesse wanted.

Jack, jack o'lantern your face is all aglow, Jesse was singing. *When you are lighted, your crooked teeth all show.* "Too bad we didn't get ourselves a pumpkin. What did you used to do on Halloween anyhow?"

"Pretty much what I do everyday, Jes," I said. "Wandering the earth, and haunting folks, mostly myself. Bobbing for apples is optional."

I set up what I elected to call "camp" in order to get into a Jesse-style mood over the event, but camp weren't more than a couple of blankets and a bag of sandwiches. We were pitched up by a gravestone that was cracked in two, and it read:

Joseph Wilki

1850 - 1
A man who
And was love

"It's a waste of time bobbing for apples," Jesse said. "A chocolate bar, or a moonpie, would be different."

"Jes, you look here. Where do you think that other half of the stone has gone? Don't it seem like a broken heart and this poor Joseph fellow won't be able to rest until he finds its missing part?"

"No, it don't," Jesse said. "It looks like a cracked-up gravestone, and I would like a sandwich now please."

I rustled one out for him, and parked down beside him. There were luminous clouds drifting over the face of the moon like the inside out of a shadow. The ground was curdled with cold, and musty-smelling with moldering leaves, and the air felt chilly and expectant.

"Listen," Jesse said.

There was an owl hooting in the dark, and it sounded far away, like it weren't sounding from a remote place, but a remote year. I pulled my coat closer around me.

"Denny Colt must have fun living like this," Jesse said. "Every night of his life."

"I would expect a fellow gets lonely," I said. "Living a deep dark secret like he does, he must want to go to Main Street on Saturday high noon and scream out who he is to all the assembled shoppers of Central City, and they'd spill their oranges and soap powders and such on the sidewalk in the confusion."

"Then he wouldn't be the Spirit no more." Jesse said. "There's worse things than being lonely."

"Like what, Jes?" I said.

"Being a bully. Or a goober." Jesse turned and faced me straight on. "Or a convict."

"Jes, a convict ain't but a fellow who's had a conviction sometime or another. And a conviction ain't just proof that somebody is guilty of something, it's also means somebody believes in something - and a lot of times, though folks don't much think about it, the two come down to the same thing. It's like -"

"Shh," Jesse said. "I hear somebody."

I hushed up and listened. A truck was whining its way above us on the piece of highway we couldn't see. A gust of wind took up with a flock of dead leaves on the ground and swung them around before it got bored and ditched them and moved off someplace else. A hound dog was yapping in the distance. You could practically see its yaps filling up the air around it like a forest of sound springing up out of nothing. Then the hound was silent and the yaps was felled and the air went empty. The light was getting murky, and the woods beyond looked mournful.

"I hear something," Jesse said.

"Maybe it's a ghost, Jes." Leaves were rustling like they was being walked on. "But ghosts is lighter on their feet, if they was to have them, which I wager they do not. I expect it's a fox, or a squirrel."

The rustling got closer and stopped, and Jesse stopped breathing, maybe to make whatever it was feel more at home, and I have no doubt would have given his heart a rest from beating, too, for added hospitality. Then we heard something else, and we didn't think it was a fox or a squirrel no more.

"I had a bad time in school today," a voice was saying. It was from the rise above us, it sounded like, and we couldn't see anything, but the voice went on, a boy's voice, I would have guessed, maybe about Jesse's age. I surmised he was a Halloweener with some of his pals in tow, though there hadn't been but one set of feet rustling.

"I was wishing you was here with me and we would be helping each other out," the same voice went on, "and we would be helping our momma, too. Today when I went out into the schoolyard and saw them boys, the mean ones, circling round me and no one was there to help me, I was thinking of you, and how if someone was to treat you like that ever and I could see it, I would change into

Captain Marvel in a flash and deliver you from their evil clutches."

Jesse's eyes went round and his mouth hung open. "It's that funny boy Elvis," he whispered.

"Why don't them boys like me anyhow?" E was saying. "Can't they see I'm just like them?"

"Who's he talking to?" Jesse asked.

"Himself," I said. "It makes him feel better."

"It don't make me feel better," Jesse said.

"I wonder what it's like to be buried here," E went on, "in a place that don't even bear your name." From the sound of his voice, I'd guess E was heading past us to the east side of the field. "I wonder if you feel the way I do, like you lost something somewheres, you can't rightly say what or where. Sometimes when I am listening to the radio and a song I like comes on, I get to wishing that you was there with me to hear it. Like when we have peach cobbler, or go fishing for lizards and such, and I think to myself, now weren't that something, Jesse?"

"He ain't talking to himself," Jesse said.

"You think he's talking to you?" I said. My heart was floating into the vicinity of my throat, and like to choke it up entire. I weren't too keen on having my boy find out he was supposed to be dead, Denny Colt or no. And I doubted it was the Lord's plan either, seeing as to how He had gone to such lengths including myself to have them brought up apart in the first place. Of course, the big divide ain't between the living and the dead. There's a bigger one between the haunting and the haunted, which is to say there ain't no divide at all. You may as well try to wrestle the wind out of the air, or the whitecaps out of the ocean. There ain't no way.

"I ain't his brother," Jesse said. "I ain't nobody's brother 'cepting maybe you, and that's a funny enough business right there."

E's voice was trailing off. He had been walking straight above us and by now sounded like he was almost past us.

"I got to go home now, Jesse," he was saying, "but I will come back for you forever."

"That boy is crazy," Jesse said. "Wait till I tell the whole school about this."

I asked him why he would want to do a fool thing like telling everybody and Jesse said it would make sure the boys at school had somebody to laugh that wasn't him. I told him there was worse things than being laughed at, and he said, like what. Like being a bully, I said, it's a heap worse than that convict business you got on the bean. And Jesse said, yeah, that's another reason why I don't like him, his daddy is no good. And what do you suppose they say about your daddy, I said. He shut up.

"What he was doing, Jesse, weren't far off from somebody on the radio. Just talking into the dark and making as if he is certain there is somebody listening."

Jesse pointed out that fellows on the radio do not make out like they are talking to one particular person who ain't there, and they are not wandering around a cemetery when they do their shows either.

"Yeah," I said, "What kind of a dope would spend his time in a graveyard?"

Jesse snickered and said yeah, what kind of a - and then stopped and frowned.

"Maybe that funny boy is just like you," I said. "There ain't nothing wrong with that."

Jes said there was plenty wrong with that, besides which it just weren't so. Then he snagged himself another sandwich and bit into like he was closing the conversation right then and there.

I sat beside him looking off into the sky, which was getting cold and purple and brooding. My chin sunk towards my chest and bobbed up again soon as it touched down. The faraway lights flickered in the dark, ahead of my eyes or behind them I could not say. My mind drifted free of this earth, and I was gazing on the world years ago, a-teeter on the brink of the past millenium. Rumpus was nosing the curdled ground, and running in circles, excited and gangly, like he'd done when he was a pup on the scent of a rabbit. Ambrose the clockmaster was there, come down from the mountaintop: he'd pronounced that night the night of the second coming, when the workings of time would cease. He stood apart from all of us, in a clearing at the edge of the burial ground. He wore layer upon layer of rough dark clothes; and above the ragged drapery, his head looked white and shrunken. Though he'd kept at it over ten year or so, his beard was just a shadow that crept across his pointed chin.

Ambrose weren't the most exacting timekeeper I'd ever run across either. One Sunday morning, the first of summer, and the heat rising in a mist, he'd rung the morning bells an hour long of its mark - anybody who bothered to look close could see that by the slant of the sun. Another time, a glowering Friday with the hint of snow in the sky, he brought the end of day forward by about the same margin. When I'd pointed it out, he shrugged, said, "Time is but an indirect measure," and poured himself another shot of whiskey. He added that at least he'd always got the day of the week right, so far.

The night mist was swirling around us as if the clouds had fallen to earth and were wandering across its face. All the folks in town had gathered, and we were waiting in the shadow of tall pine tree. Some kids had contrapted a swing in it the summer before, and it rattled, empty and useless, like a skeleton, caught by the wind for an instant then just as quickly cast down. The wind was up, and looked to blow that tree aside like the mast of a ship in a stormy sea. The leaves were brown and mulched down underfoot, the branches were bare, and you could feel rust peeling off the world.

All along the hilltops, there were bonfires burning. The smoke was rising, and with it, the singing of the assembled crowd, a sound like something issuing not from the throats of men but out of the dark and broken earth. Ambrose stood watching, and I was watching him. The fire picked out his deep-set eyes, and they were dark and aching-looking, as if something had just been extracted from them. He drew a jug out of his coat, and took a quick swig. Then the jug went back into hiding. I could already picture JC tottering among the living and the risen dead, pressed into being the life of the party, and determined to outdo himself in joy.

The crowd was chanting one chant as though from a single creature, so big that you could only see its breath; and they were saying, over and over: "Time has ended, the Lord has come." The chant was rising like billows of smoke into the sky, getting mixed up in it, until there weren't no more sky unless you were also meaning smoke, and no smoke but that you were also saying sky. Then I looked, and saw.

The sun had already begun to rise. It was like a wagon wheel set over us, and its next turning looked like to crush us underneath it; and if I could have reached on up, and held it back with my own hands, I surely would have.

But day broke, same as it always had. When I saw the sunlight sifting down, I knew how brightness falls as sinister as a shadow, and warmth takes hold as numbing as a chill. Rumpus was barking. It was the first time I'd noticed the gray on his muzzle. It glinted in the slanting light. Time was going on, and a dread came over me. Rumpus was running at the fire, taking in big mouthfuls of air and not giving a single one of them back. He barked, again and again, like nothing could stop him. But I felt I had to stop *something*. I rushed towards him, I was beside him, his neck was in my hands, and I -

"Hey, what're you doing?" Jesse cried out. "You fixing to kill me?" He wrenched himself away from me and stood up. His face was white and round.

"Jesse, Jesse," I said. I moved to clasp him to myself, and he flinched. I was all fixing to wail over the things I've been known to do in my time.

"You okay now, Jud?" Jesse said. His voice was softer. "You've been having one of those night terrors, ain't you."

Yes, I said, I surely have. I put my arm over his shoulder, and said, aren't we lucky, Jes, the night is nearly over.

That night with Ambrose weren't ended for me entire yet, because another thousand years is always set to come around: but in certain particulars it ended a lot of things. Like with Rumpus, after that night, the years seemed to collect in him quicker, like they was offcuts of heavy stone, and his body weren't but a broken basket. It was like the chill of that night had entered his bones and made them stiff. He couldn't hardly keep pace with me when we went out roaming the hills. He sought the shade, and fell down to sleep within it, and he woke up grumpily, in slow and lumbering stages. Blueflies grew lazy in his presence, he stirred so slowly. They droned heavily around his head, until I moved to bat them away as much for his dignity as his comfort. And, finally, one morning, he did not stagger to his feet at all. When I stooped down to him, his tail beat the floor a couple of times, like he was saying he was sorry, and it weren't my fault. I buried him in the forest he loved so much, out in the glade where the clover bloomed; and the next year, I done the same for Ambrose, downed by a fever.

That go-around, I didn't bother even trying to hang myself. A man can make only so many futile gestures, and I'd already made my share.

Or that's what I used to think, before I landed in an alfalfa field somewhere in Lee County. If ever I thought the state of grace was a tough proposition, I guess I just hadn't tried the state of Mississippi.

CHAPTER THIRTY-TWO

What Jesse carried away from that night in Priceville Cemetery where he was supposed to be buried weren't nothing about E, or himself, or my own little set-to, but the bit about the radio. He said he was fixing to tune in a lot more because that way he knew for certain that the man doing the show had somebody listening. I said that was right nice of him. But of course I knew it meant more. For the power and light had opened as a road before him, and he was already proceeding down it; and through it, he would soon proclaim the word of God.

Jesse was still a little fella though, and while I did not let on, I knew he got a mite lonely and scared, especially at night, and it was a comfort to him to have somebody to hear at night - somebody what made sense, too. It weren't the music shows Jesse favored, like I would have expected, so much as the talk. He liked news, dramas, and story-hours; weather, crop reports, and ads for food products like Sunblest cake flour and Bourbon vanilla flavoring. Song shows like the Bluegrass Hoe-Down and the Tan Town Club was okay: he sang out loud with them, then outpaced them, or fell behind them, and seldom ended up actually alongside them, like a terrier trying to keep step with a team of Tennessee walking horses. But what he really seemed to warm to were the lead-ins and the lead-outs. He hushed up when they came on, and, intent, breathed with quiet resolve.

Jesse got the idea that when he grew up, he would get himself a job reading Denny Colt comics on the air. I asked how would he get around the lack of pictures, and he said if you read with the right expression, that would tell everybody everything. He could add in some stuff about how the door was opening, or it was raining, or the fish bowl had just smashed in two.

Then you ain't reading, I said, you're writing. And he said, now I ain't listening, I'm talking. I guess you have a point there, I said. What's that? he said. That it ain't no good to be doing just one side of thing, I said, it's like breathing in all the time and never out. Jesse tried that one for a few seconds, then gave up.

Jesse also said he would bring cookbooks to the air, and I said I could just hear it, Jesse leading them through the Lady Baltimore Cake like it was a longish short story with a beginning, a middle, and an end, precise and to the point, and marked out nicely with numbers and specified quantities. And Jesse said, for a follow-up, or a lead-in, he could read a math book. Right, I said, just call it the Book of Numbers and around here you're guaranteed some kind of audience.

I was joking, but I had to admit that when Jesse did his arithmetic homework, I sat up and took an interest, partly because he was fulfilling my theory about him and books with numbers salt-and-peppered through them. But I expect it was more than that, because I myself favored some of the deeds and procedures therein more than others. Addition and subtraction, for example, weren't but small and simple potatoes, putting things in a basket and taking them out. Division and multiplication, on the other hand, was more linked somehow, pieced together like a good piece of joinery, or notes in a song. I even took to division's neat notation, the way it looked on a page, and so did Jesse. When he was just starting up with this business at school, he thought the symbol ÷ was a picture of a see-saw at rest, and thereafter he was convinced it told a story. $^{42}/_7$ meant 42 had something on 7, or was mad at it over something, or maybe cared about in some special way: he couldn't tell, but the numbers for him were like characters from books, or people he knew, with a past, and a future, that were forever in peril of having their fate rewritten.

Jesse took less to the second symbol they had in there for division: he looked at the 4 divided into 12 and he said it looked like the 12 was a fellow buried down in the cellar and he was looking out at you from a window in the earth, and the 4 stood there not knowing, or else not caring, hands in its pockets, outside, whistling. I tried to say, well Jesse, to me it's like the 4 has come calling at the 12's house, and is standing at the door asking to go out and play somewheres. That seemed to go over pretty well until a few pages later, when Jesse was told in big black letters, like the warning on the bottle of morphine:

DIVISION BY ZERO IS UNDEFINED.

I was surprised they didn't hoist a skull and crossbones over the page. What's they mean by undefined, Jesse said, and I said, they mean it's something so God-awful you can't even begin to try to name it. In case we weren't sure exactly what was being forbidden, they showed a zero where the 4 had been, and drew a big slash across the whole affair. That was when I saw what Jesse was saying, only it was the zero on the outside that struck me like the look in JC's eye, when he'd hang his head and half-turn away, and the eye that I could still make out got round and full of something nobody else could see, or else maybe just emptied of what everybody else could get a gander of. It was like that divinity of his worked like a zero when a zero is where it shouldn't be, dividing up where it can't, and unsettling the whole equation.

The words of the warning struck me as neat and powerful as an amulet. I wish I'd had it handy when JC was growing up and even later, and people hooted at him for his all-around weirdness. I could have pulled it out at any moment like a pocketknife of truth, let it glint a moment in the light, and cited it like a point of law that carried its own enforcement: division by zero is undefined. That would have shut them up. I'd sure rather have been making statements of that sort, with a law and a logic and a point, than the ones big John thought were so deep, mostly on account of he had thought them up hisself. It ain't enough to exclaim, it's a mystery! and start equating things like 'word' and 'flesh' that ain't the same, as soon as you find you're in a tight spot. You got to do something with that tight spot, make a story of it if you can't explain it outright. Denny Colt knew that much.

And them numbers and notations, along with his fixation with cooking, brought Jesse nearer to the word he would soon be proclaiming, for one misty morning that fall, he located a curious fragment that yoked them both to the plowshare of the Lord. I was standing on the porch, my shirt half-buttoned, waiting for the sun to make itself felt; and Jesse came out, and slammed the door behind him, and before I could say anything, he'd shoved a page of newspaper up at me.

"What's that saying?" he asked.

I looked at the page. There was a story on growing snap beans, and one on a cotton mill in Oliveta that'd caught fire, and at first I weren't sure what had got him going. Then lower down and in tiny print, I saw; and I smiled to myself, as I began to read it out to him:

Alabama Scripture Cake

Judges 5:25	1 cup butter
Jeremiah 6:20	2 cups sugar
1 Kings 4:22	3 cups flour
1 Samuel 30:12	4 cups raisins and figs
Genesis 43:11	1 cup almonds

Genesis 24:20	1 cup water
Isaiah 10:14	6 eggs
Leviticus 2:13	pinch of salt
Exodus 16:31	1 glug of honey
1 Kings 10:2	good pinch of spice

Follow Solomon's advice for raising a child: Proverbs 23:14.

"Ain't that something?" I said. And it was as if my heart had within it a quantity of yeast, for it did rise and lighten: Jesse had revealed unto him a pieced patch of citation that translated his dubious interest into the language of the Lord (and not a crumb of it come from them self-appointed scribblers who clutched to my brother, neither). And Jesse agreed that this recipe really was something, said it was like a code a spy would use, and his secrets never be found out despite they would throw him a darkest dungeon and threaten to slit his gizzard.

We went inside, so I could get down the Bible and parse some of them references out for him right then and there. I wanted Jesse to see the words printed out upon the page in front of us.

"See, Jesse," I said, "Judges 5: 25: 'she brought forth butter in a lordly dish.' Right there." Jesse looked at the page, and told me to move my finger so he could see. I sounded out the words with him. "Jeremiah 6:20. Let's see." I flipped ahead: " 'the sweet cane from a far country.' "

And Jesse made me go down the whole list entire. He was entranced. When I was finished, he sighed, and looked defeated, until he thought of something. Nothing would do but that Jesse fetched the scissors straightaway and had me cut the recipe out for him. He folded it and put it in his shirt pocket, just over his heart, and kept it there all week.

That Saturday, we went to watch the WELO broadcast, and we stood shoulder to rib cage in the front row, folks packed in close behind us, penned up in one-half of Buford's second-story warehouse like livestock, only less meaty and more mute. Charlie Rowen was on air yakking away about some spaniel that could bark in time to a record of grand Italian opera, and had anybody ever heard of a thing on this earth that was smarter, Jesse tipped his chin up, and said to me, "Well, I got here a cake recipe that speaks the Word of God." Folks next to me heard him and grinned, and looked at me understanding-like, and I whispered in his ear to hush up just for now, Charlie Rowen was doing his broadcast.

But Jesse's words evidently carried, for the Lesses, who'd been hanging out in town by some shop door or another, heard the radio playing; and Mirth told them he bet it was Jesse he'd just caught a small earful of. They headed over that evening, and instead of saying howdy, Mirth asked Jesse what in tarnation he'd been talking about. Jesse's mouth made a soft round "o," and his glance fell down to the floor an instant before he looked back at Mirth. I expect he was wondering whether to tell his secret, it was so grand. But he reached into his shirt pocket, took out the clipping, and flattened it on the table with his hand.

Luck drew near, and Jesse started explaining the cake to them. He asked me to fetch down the Bible so they could see some of the verses cited for themselves. I did as he bid; and I looked on, well pleased. Reck stood grumpily behind us. His shadow fell over the opened page of the Bible. He crossed his arms, uncrossed them, stretched, yawned and found no position that was satisfactory. He sighed loudly once or twice; and he barely waited for a pause in Jesse's talking, while they searched out a second citation and couldn't find it, before he cut right in and loudly started telling us all about some swamp that swallowed folks up whole and made their remains glow green as old cheese.

I stood back and indulged the interruption, for I knew that nothing could deter Jesse from his path of power and light, so firmly was he set upon it. I thought even the Lesses basked in the glow of such power and light, and, that season, they were drawn towards our house and the sound of our radio like small animals towards a fire on a winter's night. I was not set to thwart the little creatures of the shadows, for their presence was yet first testimony to Jesse's glory. Most nights they come, all four of them boys hushed up to listen to Lexo's Mystery Theater and the TimTam Club.

And then, sometimes, Reck would read to us from his book. It was a source of error and amusement, instructive by way of contrast with Jesse's endeavor, and I took to thinking of Reck's efforts as a treatise on how a fella might get the details accurate enough, but be chasing down the wrong story altogether; exacting, but at the same time, harebrained. Of course, in the matter of accuracy, he was way ahead of the four scribblers my brother got stuck with, leastways in effort and resolve. Reck labored to substantiate his findings. He had found out, for instance, there was such a thing as life after decapitation, and he read us out an example. There weren't much to say to it, though, and after a pause, I asked him what was happening with the Conductor. Reck said that investigation was still ongoing, but wasn't it something about that dead man's eye still winking a half hour after the head had been cut off. As we sat there in the failing light, and Jesse passed around a bag of gumdrops, we all agreed that it was.

In that stretch of months, I pretty much forgot to scan the sky as I walked to work, and look for signs. Mostly, I no longer remembered what I had been dreaming the night before, and I quit wandering in my sleep altogether. Imminence seemed mostly to have sunk back into my eyes, or faded into the light of ordinary day; and I'd say now, it was near the best time of all.

But of course, imminence, as I have learned to my sorrow, is pretty much always just around the corner.

CHAPTER THIRTY-THREE

Around the time Jesse was radio-fying, Bean was taking a sniff in the same direction. It weren't for amusement, nor redemption, but in pursuit of the only version of those things that he understood: lucre.

"You were right, Jud," Bean said, "about something a while back." He was leaning against the counter watching me stack some new cans of paint. It was in a mid-morning in November and the sunlight through the window lazed over him like a pat of butter on a flapjack. Bean had a toothpick in his mouth - I reckoned there was a nick of caramel on a back tooth still plaguing him - and he jimmied it as far left as it could go, and indicated. "Stow them big cans up yonder."

"What would that be?" I said.

"About words bumping up the cost of a good."

"Thank you, sir."

"But you were wrong about the way to do it." We both waited for the space of time it would have taken me to say, "How's that, Mr. Bean?", and he continued. "Take your average hick, Jud. It's stretching things for him to read more than a half a page of a funny paper. Brain-strain. Writing it out for them is no good." He took the toothpick out of his mouth, and stabbed a tidbit of air with it for effect. "Talking to them, telling them like children - that's more their speed."

Bean said he'd had something in the works for a while. He'd been angling to have the state's first Christmas lighting done in this town, and his the hand to switch the lights on; and he'd further found out that the jamboree radio show WELO kept gabbing about was going to have its first broadcast the Saturday before Christmas, in the courthouse three doors down. Bean knew because Charlie Rowen rented from Bean, and he had fallen two months behind in his house payments - a fact of which Bean appraised him last Thursday. Rowen had sat facing him in the back office, Bean reported, and related on top how the man's godawful patter-patter at last ran out of steam, and his feet churned slowly under the desk, mashing the air sideways instead of making tracks on solid ground. Bean also swore Rowen's fancy hair oil went from slick to dry in the course of the conversation. I am a hard man, Bean told him, but not an unreasonable one. It turns out the only thing Rowen could stump up on demand was a fifteen-minute slot on WELO, the all-day special the Saturday before Christmas. And Bean swiftly pocketed it, as part payment, mind.

" 'The Bean Burial Spot', " Bean went on. He paused to let it sink in. "That won't be what's the show's about, Jud. Just its name, and we'll have an insert here and there to remind folks who I am, that sort kind of thing. Rowen says everybody's doing music, and I reckon my slot ought to be some different kind of thing. Ticky-talky if you follow. You'll have fun figuring it out. But it don't matter if you don't."

"You'll be doing the talking yourself?" I was willing to bet the thought of talking on air to all those folks made Bean the slightest bit jittery, because it did me anyway.

Bean gave a smile, quick and involuntary, as if my dullness never did cease to amuse him. "Jud, that's what I call a hired man's chore," he said. "It's like minding the counter, only one that sits out there on the airwaves." The figure of speech raised his spirits, and with them he hoisted up his nostrils a notch, and decided to tell me about life. "See, if I was to get up myself in front of a bunch of hicks, it'd look like I had to. I'd be no bettr'n a -"

"- politician," I cut in.

"Yeah," Bean said. I doubt that was what he was going to say, and he drew himself back, and looked at me. His face went stiff.

"One what was in danger of getting somewheres with the electorate," I added.

He kept his eyes on me, and considered. "Them cans you been stacking up?"

"Yes, sir."

"Take them all down." He fiddled something out of his shirt pocket. "I want them over in that-there corner." He pointed with the butt-end of what he'd fiddled out, a chewed-down lollipop stick. Then he went out the door, and the bells rattled.

And so the power and light descended that much closer to me, and glee did fill my heart. As I shifted the cans of enamel, I could practically feel the glory and the promise in my fingertips, though as yet I was to be but a hired man proclaiming the grave-making of a stony-eyed chiseler. And my tongue was still, but it itched all the while to speak, and tell young Jesse of the news.

I was putting Jesse to bed when I did. Jesse was near stupefied. He got that day-old fish look in his eye same as JC used to when some idea or another struck him, and I bet he feel asleep a few hours later with that look still in them. And when I got up the next day, I found him sitting at the table with his chin resting in his paws, looking out the window at nothing, his mouth hanging open so as to create room for more all-around nothingness.

"What you thinking about, Jesse?" I said.

"Our radio show." Before I could remind it him it

weren't ours, or even mine, but Mr. Bean's, he went on. "I'll read some Denny Colt and tell folks about Wildwood. Then I'll put in a recipe for a lemon daffodil cake. Or else the Scripture one. Folks'll like that." He hushed up, but his shoulders was shaking, like a dog's, when it comes up from a dip in the river.

"A fella can tell all kinds of stories," I said. By then, I was by the stove, fixing myself a cup of coffee.

"Oh can I, Jud?" The words floated out of him, light but intense. I turned around. He had got himself perched up on the chair to face me, and he was positioned there like a body praying. "Can I go on the radio and tell everybody all them things?"

Of course, he was so dead set on what he wanted that he'd fastened on what I'd said as some kind of promise. Well, why not let him think so, my first thought was, if it makes him happy; then chewing on its heels: why not let his mistake here lead him to proclaim himself. And then it was clear why the Lord had thrown Bean a show, and seen I was given charge of it. Elation is a delicate thing, and though visited to many, endures only in the house of the circumspect. So I weighed my words as careful as Bean would, if they cost him something. "All kinds of things get told on the radio, and I reckon us two got to give them a chance to get heard," I said. "Just don't go telling folks what we got in mind."

Jesse's shoulders gave another shudder, and he didn't even seem to mind when I told him it was time to get dressed for school.

You can bet I weren't fixing to have Jesse take to the power and the light, only to prattle on about whisking egg yolks and the doings in Wildwood and how to make a cake even it was drawn from scripture. I had my own ideas for him: he would fulfill the words of God, and proclaim them. I even suggested to Bean later that same morning that his show be Bible-based. I pointed out it followed on from his other ad piece that put his product in proximity to Scripture; it was popular, and it weren't too taxing.

Bean said, well, maybe for a short lead-in; but he was waving his hand around the whole time like that stuff didn't matter to him one way or another. He said he knew now what he wanted on his show: Dr. Zogg was to be in town the day the show aired.

"Dr. Zogg?" I said.

Bean dropped the local paper on the counter and pushed it in front of me.

STATE DEATH DOC TO VISIT COUNTY

"Says here he loves doing radio," Bean said. "I am just thankful that I got a show of my own for him to do it on."

"But so far, you been associating your products with the Bible," I said.

"God's mercy is nothing without His justice." Bean jabbed at the upside-down headline with his index finger. "And this-here chair of his combines justice with mercy. Plus, folks'll tune in to hear him, Jud." He paused. "I myself have always had a nose for criminal justice." He raised his nostrils as if to demonstrate their abilities.

I watched them quiver, and paused as though I too heard the baying of the bloodhounds in the distance, and the firing of shotguns, and the cries of "Halt!"

"You may recall, for instance, that I all but enacted a citizen's arrest in the matter of our friend Vernon Presley. Now, a different man might have looked the other way, made a deal, but so far as I am concerned -"

"Business is business," I said.

"I was going to say, boy, that justice is justice," Bean went on. "Of course, justice usually turns up a pretty penny. That has been my experience."

Mine too, I thought, 30 solid pieces of coinage at least.

*   *   *

That night after dinner, Jesse sat himself at the table with some pencils and a book of foolscap. He said he wanted to get started on his radio piece straight away. We kept the radio playing alongside us, for inspiration.

From time to time, I glanced down at his paperwork, though he told me I weren't supposed to, and his handwriting jittered unevenly across the page. It struck me as pitiful as a cripple attempting a jig, and you'd smile to keep from hurting his feelings. Jesse said again how he liked to listen to radio so that the fella talking on it wasn't there alone. He made me think of JC, and how that one used to talk into the darkness sometimes at night when he couldn't get to sleep, and how lonely a fellow like him can get to be. So far, Jesse seemed less of an out and out oddster, but he was still marked out, and it near broke my heart to look at him and know it, and him not know it.

I remember one time I went out in a hurry to fetch some wine for dinner, because JC had forgotten it, and I couldn't face seeing my mother bite her lip in consternation at his forgetfulness. The day was just failing. My shadow was dark, but not as dark as the night thickening around it, and it soon melted into the road like something dropped into a vast and reflectionless sea. The street echoed with the sounds of crates being packed away, and I hurried around the corner, to the market place. There weren't but one shop still open, and I bought up the last bottle he had. As I made to hurry home, I heard some voices across the square. A woman was standing in front of one of the stalls, one arm around her son and the other raised against the men gathered in front of him, as if she could ward off their voices with the palm of her hand. A gaggle of shopkeepers was yelling at the boy, and he was shifting his feet on top of a litter of shards - it looked like he'd had a run-in with some pottery - and lolling his head around, and looking off into the distance like he didn't know what was going on. The mother was telling folks not to mind, he'd been touched by the hand of God - of course, by that she meant he was flat-out wrong in the head, like Yellow Whitehead or some such. That ain't an excuse, one man said. And I thought, well, if that ain't an excuse, what is?

All these years later, I reckon I was still scouting around for one. As I watched Jesse that night, scratching away in his book of foolscap with words I knew he would never be speaking, I was by turns exalted and uneasy, for I'd hatched the scheme to inveigle the boy upon the air, and join as one with the power and the light. I knew that was where he belonged, but I had delivered a brother before, to where he was wanted, and the whole thing still sat ill upon me. Whether my scheme with Jesse was borne of desperation, or duty, or pride, I can't rightly say; and flatly deny the need to choose amongst. But I can say this, as I watched Jesse scribbling and concentrating alongside me, I resolved that he would not know his hour had arrived, so sudden and glorious would it come upon him.

CHAPTER THIRTY-FOUR

The day the man first came into town, a Friday noon, there was a commotion in the streets. I was inside minding the counter. The window shade was at half-mast, and outside, I could see as high off the ground as Bean's red bow tie. It was bobbing around, scrabbling here in front of a lemonade wagon, and heading off there to have a look-see about the cotton candy. I imagined the bow-tie was yakking of its own accord, buzzing around like a bumblebee, herding folks this way and that, and telling them what to do. I went out onto the front steps. The bells chimed after me.

"Yes, sir," Bean was saying, "Santa Claus is coming to town early." He had pushed his hat far back to the top of his head, and it sat there as if dropped on him from the sky. "No, sir," he went on, "don't mean maybe." I had never seen him so jovial-like, and it was as if the scent of legitimized death had perked up his nostrils, and intoxicated him like a long lazy swig of moonshine on a summer night. There was folks lining up on the road to either side of him, noses all pointing down the street as if a giant hand had brushed them that way. Bean stepped out in front of everybody. Then he spread his arms out as if he was sailing into a big, well-deserved yawn, only he didn't finish yawning and fold himself back up, he kept his shoulders there like permanent. His shadow fell on those behind him, and I am sure that just having a sector of humanity so marked out by his presence made him feel more in control of the situation, and all-around companionable. "How 'bout that," Bean said to his shadow-bearers in general. "Dr. Zogg in town. Can't wait to see his show myself." It weren't likely to be the kind of show Bean was hoping for: it was the off-season, Zogg told me later that day, his turban slipping off to one side. Like a fool, I believed Zogg, because I figured he was the professional in the matter.

Anyway, Bean crossed the street and pointed at me. "Jud, what you wasting my time for? You can stand there with your mouth full of nothing, but not on my nickel." A grin crossed his face like the grimace when you down a dose of cod liver oil. "Join the crowd. Fetch that boy of yours out of school ahead of time, why don't you. I don't expect we'll be selling much paint the rest of today." He slapped his knee and gestured down the street, flinging an arm-sized chunk of shade upon it and thereby claiming it for himself. He looked back at me. "Mind you minus them hours off your timesheet before you lock up."

I closed up right quick, and light-footed across town towards the schoolyard. The sunlight was piecing itself together on the ground like a jigsaw puzzle laid out by some mighty and indecisive hand. The air was sprightly, like the fizz from a fresh bottle of ale. I was making my way across the courthouse green, just beyond the statue of the Confederate soldier boy, when I was waylaid by a half-dozen prize sheep. They butted my side and bleated, and their driver, a fat and affable fellow, stopped, shoved his thumbs into his belt, presented his red flannel belly, and told me they was on their way to the livestock show and not to mind, they wouldn't hurt a lamb ha-ha. That's better than most shepherds manage, I said, and a smile crossed his face. He nodded, and waved me on. Then I was crossing the street to the school, and near got run down by a van hauling a giant plaster strawberry ice cream cone, and trailing bits of music behind it.

Soon as I'd reached the top of the school steps, I could hear Jes's voice. He was reading aloud, a story about the good Samaritan. I followed the sound. He was telling about the priest passing right by the man in trouble. Then I stopped outside his classroom door. I was standing in the hallway. The light was sad and yellow, the kind of light you find in engravings in old books, or on winter afternoons, where the sun ain't but a memory lost in a sky made of lead. I breathed in the smell of chalk and pulpy paper and wet paint. There was a singing lesson across the hall, and each time the pitch pipe sounded, it was a tone higher, like another flight in a staircase had suddenly appeared. The class clambered up and down it best they could. After they finished one scale, they were silent.

"Elvis, you will kindly stay within key," a teacher's voice said.

"Yes ma'am," the boy mumbled. Then the pitch pipe sounded a new note, and they was climbing upwards again.

Jesse was up to the part about the Samaritan giving the innkeeper two silver coins, to take care of the beat-up fellow brought in from the road.

"That was fine, James," the teacher said. "Just fine. Now who do you like best in the story?"

"The innkeeper," Jesse said.

"The innkeeper?" I could hear the raised eyebrows in her voice, mildly angled and insinuating, like a word in italics in a page of block type.

"Uh-huh."

" 'Yes, ma'am.' Why's that, James?"

"Yes, ma'am. I feel bad for him, 'cause he's the only one what didn't get a chance to prove how neighborly he could be. The Samaritan man just up and gave him money straight away, like the Samaritan thought he was the only one that could ever know about helping out folks in trouble. Maybe the innkeeper didn't take it though. It don't say."

"The story isn't about the innkeeper," the teacher said. "Don't you think the Samaritan's the good example here?"

"He's okay. But the innkeeper, he's more like Denny Colt. Mostly he don't get a second thought, either, and few folks know his name proper, but still he helps folks out, in ways nobody knows."

"I am not familiar with Denny Colt," the teacher said. I could hear whispers and giggles amongst the school kids, stirring about on tether, like goats with bells on them, and ready to break loose.

"Denny Colt lives in Wildwood Cemetery," Jesse said, "and he keeps the peace in Central City. He -"

"Miss, you'll excuse me," I said. I stepped in over the threshold. Everybody turned to look at me, and they shut up. "My boy Jim and I, we have important family business. Needs tending to right away. You understand."

"Better than James understands the story, Mr. Harricut," the teacher lady said.

"Maybe he's gonna see his daddy," a boy in the back row said, snickering. His yellow hair rose atop his long skinny face in a short mean quiff, and he had a nasty, self-assured air that most folks need a few more decades roaming this earth to attain. "It's about time, ain't it?"

Jesse made like he hadn't heard, and stuck his chin out a fraction.

"John, that'll do," the teacher said. She nodded at Jes. "You are excused, boy."

"There's no excuse for him," the boy said. He was doodling on the paper in front of him. The teacher made like she didn't hear, she was kept so busy locating one particular piece of chalk, and the half dozen ones by her fingertips just wouldn't do.

Well, I have to admit, I thought Jesse understood the story just fine, and it felt good to hear him take a different slant on things, and not be afraid to tell folks about it. I was a little disquieted on his account, too, of course, as folks don't like different rubbed in their faces, and most often take it as a personal insult. Once Jesse and I was out in the schoolyard, I gave his shoulder a little pinch like I was a clothespin, and it was a clothesline, and I said, "Jesse, you read so good. And held your ground too. I'm proud of you, boy." Added to which, I have never much held with stories about fellows getting silver coins, because the folks so depicted are given short shrift at best, if not outright maligned through eternity. "You ought to speak up to folks more often," I continued, lightly as I knew how.

"I just pretended I was talking on the radio like I'll be doing anytime now," Jesse said, "and it weren't so hard." Then he put in his hands in his pockets, and looked up at me and shrugged. That was his way of rounding off the compliment business. "What family stuff we got doing?"

"Having fun," I said. "It's about time, ain't it?"

Jes and I headed the short way back into fair day. Jesse pulled me along to cut corners whenever we came across one. We was cutting round the corner with the old lumberyard on it when I began hearing sounds as of a distant battle in the air above us, drawing closer. I heard a faint pounding every now and again, and the roar of a crowd rising and falling around it, and into it, fugitive as the play of shadows over water. I was looking up the sky above us, recalling battles and bands of angels and walls going tumbling down at the sound of a trumpet. A whistle blew. The roar of a crowd surged up like a mighty wave of the ocean, and subsided.

"The Angels've pulled out all the stops," someone ahead of and above us was saying. His voice was a hollow boom from on high, and fell upon us like crackly light from a distant heaven. "But then those Disciples are never far behind."

"Oh those boys pack some wallop, alright, Ike!" This

one had a hearty chuckle in his voice. It caught in his throat like a belt buckle across a fat man's belly.

Jesse stopped in mid-step. He held one foot above the ground and turned his head towards me slowly. "Who's that talking so loud?"

"Maybe it's God," I said. Jesse looked at me like that one was too dumb to even answer. I went on. "Who else has a voice that can fill the land like that, Jes? Who else takes such an interest in the doings of angels and disciples?"

Jesse lowered his foot and listened. He looked around him like somebody hunting, or being hunted.

"Dan, the folks at home ought to get a gander at some of goings-on at this fair!" the first voice was saying. "The ballgame's just the beginning, and many of our fine sponsors - "

"That there is a radio broadcast," Jesse said. "Live." He pointed to a pick-up truck a few hundred yards ahead. Two men was set up in back, each of them with a set of what looked like bee-stung baseball mitts slung over their ears. Jesse kept looking first into the ball field, and then at the radio men. I looked up into the pillars of light, dim this time of day, and saw some speaker-boxes been wired around them, so the whole ballpark would hear the broadcast of what they were seeing in front of them anyway.

"You know what, Jesse?" I said. "I don't know whether to watch the game, or listen to them fellas tell us about it instead."

"I reckon we can do both," Jesse said. I said okay, and we can buy ourselves a hamburger and a root beer, too. We stood in line at a snack booth, Jesse turning around the whole time to keep his eye on the radio folks, I had to ask him twice if he wanted ketchup. Then we set down on the edge of the field. Jesse went real quiet, and ate careful as if a misplaced munch would upset the game unfolding in the sound waves above him. I stretched out, the mid-

November light sifting down, warm but a mite steely.

They was going on hitting, and the hitting sent a sound through the air, a pop then a thud, like a turkey getting shot mid-flight. Foul, someone called out, and I laughed. The ball went through the air again, and someone called out, strike two. They that was watching commenced to roar, and Jesse and I joined into it ourselves. I jumped out while the roaring was still going strong, and like to shake myself off of the sound the way a dog shakes the water off from a dip in the river. The Angels had been up and the next thing was, someone called out, strike three, and they spilled off the field like nails out the bottom of a worn-out sack. The Disciples went up, and one of them was swinging the bat.

"You ought to get on the mound yourself, Jud." Bean was saying. I blinked and looked up. He was standing there beside me, a white potentate in the pale gold sun, his shadow falling over me near full. "You built up a real good swing on that saw."

"Oh no sir," I said, sitting up. "Sawing wood in two is one thing, and piecing it back together, but striking the air is useless."

"Getting a strike sure is useless." Bean walked away. The pale light fell back on me, warmish, but more like the remembrance of warmth than warmth itself. "That ain't what I'm asking you to do," Bean's voice went on. "You better learn yourself how to hit, boy."

I was sitting straight up by now and facing the field. Yellow Whitehead went up and they all laughed. He swung, swatted nothing but air, then he was running straight ahead of him, past the pitcher, into the outfield. On the field, they stopped a minute, then they were throwing down dark things, their hats and mitts and such. They were laughing. Their faces and throats were tipped back, and were pale and exposed-looking as a bunch of boiled eggs with the shells peeled off. Yellow was running around the field like a cartoon dog with his tail on fire. He ran off the side of the field, whooping the entire way.

The next man was up, and I heard the bat hitting the ball and "Foul!" It got hit again, and that one was good and the man ran. We cheered, and I was thinking about hearing Jes speaking out at school, and wondering what he would sound like on a radio, if I heard him in some faraway place. The ball got thrown and caught, and thrown and caught all around the field, regular and steady, like the sound of water collecting drip by drip.

Jesse was standing up, and a roar stirred around us like a newly conjured creature. Against the faint flat light of the sky, a metallic squawk blared. It sounded like somebody'd sounded a note, and run over it, and squashed it, and left it splat on the airwaves to die a slow and lingering death.

"It's a home run!" the loud voice said, "Ike, how 'bout that! The ball sailed up - right up to the sun!"

Now I could not help being jealous in a residual kind of way of somebody being able to hit like that, so effortless it seemed, because I knew I never could, but I could see how good the hit was, too. I was looking into the dullish sky, straight at the sun, and I guess my jealousy and my awe cancelled each other out because the ball just seemed to hang high in the air a moment. It like to crack the air in two, and I felt a spilt run right through me, between joy and jealousy, same as I did that time JC amazed them all in the temple. He stood before them, blooming like hothouse lily in the steady yellow light. And I stood on the threshold, in the shadows, unremarked. I headed home alone, my insides empty, and heavy as water.

But now, with Jes, and the future envisioned for him, I weren't a bit jealous. I had more an achy kind of pride, like I'd left my heart in the pocket of my shirt and sent it through the wash wringer, and my heart emerged battered but intact; faded, water-logged, but a heap less grimy. When I looked upon Jes in the church, or heard him in the schoolroom, I'd felt only pride, and love, and the will to share his message with the world. Didn't that mean my heart was cleansed, and my own redemption could not be far behind?

So just then, with Jesse beside me, watching the ball game, and each of us downing a root beer and taking turns cheering, and sometimes cheering together, the day made me feel glad and expectant, like somebody'd made me a promise. Only at that point, I could not know who would be fulfilling it.

CHAPTER THIRTY-FIVE

We watched the men spill off the field, the Angels had won, 4-3, and I said, well Jesse, what do you want to do? And Jesse, who'd been watching not the field but the radio men, and seen they'd pretty much packed up all their gear, shrugged like he was saying, it don't matter, there's nothing else going on now.

"Well, that is a fool answer," I said.

"I ain't said nothing," he said. He kicked at a clod of dirt.

"There's a ferris wheel, a dodgem, a sheep judging, a singing contest, a show with Doctor Zogg, a freak show -"

Jesse stopped kicking at the earth, and looked up. "What kind of freaks?"

"Lady with a beard, I guess. Real short folks, maybe a tall one. Siamese twins -"

"The ones that are joined forever?" Jesse said.

I said yes, and Jesse said that's what he wanted to see. And though I weren't pleased, I said, okay, but I want to get a gander at this fellow called Zogg, why don't we wander through the fair ground and stop at whichever one we come across first.

The crowd was thickening up, and we walked through,

taking in the smell of diesel, and cotton candy, and candy apples, and hot dogs frying in their own old grease. It was like all these victuals was being made not for folks to eat, but to inhale, take into their noses, and let linger in their hair, and folds of their clothing, for weeks to come.

I was looking up at the hill opposite the fairground. It must have been about three o'clock, and the sun was behind the hill, and in a flash, the hill was swarming, as if the ground that made it up was disrupting. First they rose up in black shapes against the afternoon sun. Then they tumbled down the hill, and streamed into the fairground. All the schoolchildren in town was released that hour.

"Hey, Jimmy Jim," a voice called down from the hill. I shaded my eyes, and saw it was that nasty yellow-quiffed character. The sun touched his hair; it already stood up like something afire, and now it had the color too. "Where's your daddy at, Jim?"

"Com'on," I said. I started walking. "We don't get there soon all them goobers'll be blocking the view." Jesse caught up with me, and we was walking, his shoulder at my elbow.

"Why's he so mean?" Jesse asked. "I ain't done nothing to him."

"Being mean don't got nothing to do with how a body treats you," I said. "It's something you just got, like blue eyes, or a rickety heart."

Jesse said he wished he'd got it, and I said, no you don't, because if you did you would turn into someone else entirely, and what good would that do you, you'd have trouble even deciding which one was you. Jesse kept his hands in his pockets but loosened his shoulders a bit and thought it over. They was pitching roasted peanuts aside of us. Just after we were finished crunching our way over the shells, we saw Zogg's booth.

It had a rough plank of wood with his name scrawled across it like he'd been running out of both time and paint. The booth weren't but a tent set on a little rise on clotted earth, and it had a ripped green curtain, the color of moss with mange, and I was willing to bet that if you grabbed hold of it too tight, it would stick to your fingers. Nobody was around outside. You can't hardly knock on a tent flap, though I tried. Then we just went on in.

"Dr. Zogg?" I said. It was quiet and dark, and greenish, like the underwater of a mountain lake.

Zogg looked at me, and nodded. He was sitting at a low, little card table set up at the far end of the tent. He had a long skinny nose, crooked so badly that if it had been his spine, he never could have walked, and as it was, made me wonder a second which way his face was looking. He was in his undershirt, and his long slack belly made an outline like a creeping foothill that'd gone out for a stretch, and weren't too sure about coming back. He had a turban on his head, listing to one side. It was of dirty pink silky stuff, and starting to unravel. And he had eyes black as a bird's, and tattoos up and down both arms. At first, I thought his arms was bruised or mangled, they was so thickly figured. They looked as if the workings of his insides, arteries and veins and such, was imprinting themselves on the out. I was working double-shift to keep my eyes set square on his face.

Jesse whispered, "He *wallpaper* himself?"

Zogg cracked a smile. It even reached his forehead. "Permanent-style, boy," he said. "Can't steam these here beauties offa me but by flaying me. Not that some folks don't relish the idea."

"Dr. Zogg -" I began.

"You can call me 'mister'." He waved his hand. At least the palm was still white. "Or plain Zogg. Sit down, I ain't busy. I can tell you your fortune, if you like, or pour you a drink." He pointed to a jug beside one of the table legs. "Have a seat. Got some orangeade somewheres for the boy." He got up, rustled up a few glasses, set them on the table, and poured us each a drink. Jesse's was bright and conspicuous, like a potion in a fairy tale. "Taste like sunshine, don't it, son?"

"Yes, sir, it does," Jesse said.

"Always did prefer the moonshine myself." Zogg winked at me.

"Thank you kindly, Zogg," I said. I took a swig. It was rough as wet sandpaper skimming over my gullet. "My name's Jud. This here's my boy, Je- Jim."

"Howdy."

"Local paper ran an awful big write-up of you, Zogg."

"Yeah."

"You read it?"

"Yeah, I read it. And I'd've polished my boots with it, if I were a boot-polishing type. Papers don't tell much. And what they do, most generally are not the parts worth minding."

I took a small nip of whiskey, to smooth over, and seem real casual-like. "What would those be?"

"How condemned men just seem to trust me," Zogg said. He was looking at me full in the face now. "They take one look in my eyes, and they know they have found a friend."

"We have a friend in Jesus," Jesse said. His glass was empty.

"I'm sure you do, boy," Zogg said. He was still looking at me, not blinking, and not smirking neither, just steady, like he was biding his time. "Only these folks I'm talking about, they need another kind of friend. Jesus is your friend for life. Well I reckon I am their friend for death, and I don't know another soul who can say that. You know what I mean, Jud?"

"Son," I said, "You do me favor. Here's a nickel. Go fetch me a bottle of Nehi. Chocolate or grape. Get yourself one too. I'll be here chatting to our new friend." Jesse took the coin and slipped it in his pocket. He looked at me like he was going to say something, but I kept looking at Zogg, who watched him go, and as soon as he had, started talking again.

251

"I gave my first fry-up oh about a year ago. Nigger down in Lucedale. First cold night of the year it was. Sky was purple, the crows that'd filled the trees all atwittering at three was gone entirely by five, and the air had a real snap to it. Come nightfall, the warden brought a bunch of niggers into the yard. They had to stand there and watch. The whole time, setting up and all on the raised platform that was waiting for me, I didn't once see the whites of their eyes. They had to be there, alright, but nobody could make them point their eyes at me.

"Now to my customer, I said, quiet-like - I was washing his right ankle, and the top of his shaved head, with salt-water. Same strength what you'd use to cure a ham hock, it gives the clamps a better grip - boy, I said, this'll be quick. You are in good hands. I will never leave a mark, and I sure appreciate your trade. And he looked at me, beyond scared, and his sweat had gone from warm to cold, and from wet to dry, and it mixed in with the salt from my dosing. The smell of death was on him. Yes, he said, I believe you do. He looked straight at me, and his was the only eyes that looked at me that whole night. Then I slipped a hood over him, and they was gone too.

"Now, it ain't hard to set a man up in that chair. Ten to one, he's that far gone, he's not a-going to fight you. The buckles on the straps was new and stiff, of course, and that was the fidgetiest part. But, you want to know, I've had worse trouble saddling up a swaybacked horse. When the time came, my hand was steady. His weren't. They kind of jerked around a few seconds, like a raw egg slid into a hot skillet. Then they stopped, and his head slumped as far down and forward as the strap across his forehead would let it. Niggers didn't make a sound. They didn't look at me, or at him. Which I guess made some kind of sense. But what got me is, they didn't look at each other none either. Their heads was up, but their eyes they kept to the right or the left, or down. I only caught a glint here and there of them eyes, like silver dollars scattered on a plowed-up field, and found out by moonlight. They was filed out same as they came in. And then all I saw of them was their breath, regular and warm, like the breath of beasts in a frozen pasture.

"The warden came up to me, he was wearing a new pair of shoes for the occasion, and they squeaked, and he said, you done fine. I said thank you sir, and made to shake his hand, but right then he noticed a spot somewhere on his right shoe, and made to rub it off, and he said, folding half his face into a smile with all the juice run out of it, 'Excuse me, Clara'll just kill me,' and he moved on off. 'Don't worry,' I called out after him, 'I sure as shit won't.' His shoes went squeaking down the hall, like he'd been soaking in a puddle, and I cracked up. 'Pilate washed his *hands* of the affair,' I called out after him, 'not his feet.' Heh-heh!" Zogg finished chuckled, and fixed me with his black and fathomless eyes. "So what you think of that, mister?"

"Well," I said, "it's a good thing you're so easy a talker, on account of I work for Mr. Orville Bean. I'm the one what's doing that radio show he asked you onto."

"I am right tickled to make your acquaintance," Zogg said, "and plumb relieved it's you I'll be chatting to. Between you and me, I can't stand a fella who waits on my every word, like to snap it out of the air soon as it's set there and swallow it whole. But you - well, you got the kind of ears a man just naturally spills the truth into." Zogg raised his empty shot glass, and briefly saluted me with it. "Course, I first met old Bean that night I been telling you about. He was down in Lucedale sniffing around the jailhouse, looking to unload pine boxes, I expect, at a volume discount. He came up from the yard, he'd been standing in the shadows, watching the whole thing. He shook my hand like I was visiting royalty, and looked like he was working overtime to keep them nostrils of his from quivering like a little baby rabbit's. I told him way I figured it, we was in a similar line of work, looking a make a honest nickel out of death; and he brightened up considerable. I reckon he'd pay a fortune for me to tell him the story I just told you. He'd been there all day, snorking around for a bit of money, and all night too, for a bit of blood, on account of the excitement. Cold blood is more his taste, is my guess. He figures it's cleaner. Folks ask me how my work's done changed me. Well, it ain't. But I can tell one thing I do different now, and it brings me back to you, Mr. Jud. No matter how cold or hot or steamy or raining like the time of Noah it may be, I am sure to open my windows before I lay myself down to sleep. I don't want no ghost of a fried man rattling round my room. I noticed something when you walked in here. Right now, it's the state's off-season. Won't have call for me till the new year. But when you showed up, the tent flapped up good. Like a storm was brewing inside its folds, if no place else. That's when I said: mister, I want to tell you. So I have."

"This part of your act?" I said.

"No. I'm a hypnotist by trade," he said. He took a final swig. His eyes were blacker than ever, near bouncing around my face like clef notes on a sheet of swing time, and almost as merry. "Sleep's for show, Jud. Death's for tell."

"And for keeps," I said.

"If you're lucky," Zogg said. "It may surprise you, Jud, but I preach the word."

"I seen a lot of preachers in my day," I said, "and I ain't surprised. What church?"

"They got plenty what preach the church of life everlasting. I preach the church of death expeditious."

"Christ died for your sins," I said automatically.

"He lived as a man, Jud, and the measure of a man's life ain't so much the number of his years as the accumulation of his sins, and so I ask you, who died for his sins? *He* did. In which case I am leading these fellas to follow their Lord's example. And I lead not by word but by deed." Without moving his head a fraction, Zogg's eyes shifted from my face to the flap of the tent. He blinked, and then Jesse was coming through the flap, with a bottle of soda in one hand, and a fistful of nothing in the other.

"You okay, boy?" I said.

"Saw a sign for that freak show," Jesse said. "We don't got more than a half-hour to get there before it closes."

"You better get a move-on," Zogg said. "I got some things to put together myself." He stood up and straightened his turban a few degrees. "Thank you kindly."

"Thank you, Mr. Zogg," I said. Jesse mumbled the same, and we slipped out of the tent.

"That's the fella Mr. Bean wants on his radio show too?" Jesse said.

"Yep," I said, and left it at that. We was walking towards the north side of the fairground. The sky was cold, and almost milky, and our shadows fell onto the stubbled ground. A man in back of a hamburger stand was pouring a panful of hot grease into the earth. The grease hissed, and disappeared into the hollow, with a small satisfied glug. Some folks was starting to pack up, and when they hailed each other across the grounds, the calls sounded lost and forlorn, like echoes that had meant to come right back to where they'd started, but got themselves trapped in a corner of a stall, or the crook of a tree. Stragglers was drifting around, and a couple of them jostled me as they hurried by.

I felt out of sorts, and unsettled, like I was walking on spilt sugar, or somebody'd shortchanged me at a till. I wished we were on our way home. I sure weren't sold on what we were set to do, gawking at a sideshow. For starters, there's lots of things stranger than pointy heads and living skeletons and such: because a freak ain't so much about how some folks look, it's about what other folks got a hankering to see. And for another, I didn't want Jesse to get a gander of some Siamese twins joined at the hip, and start bleating about how he wanted a brother, making me uncomfortable, and stirring up my recollections of always being on the lookout for JC so he wouldn't get roughed up too bad, which is funny in light of what I went on to do, I guess. And that got me thinking about Zogg some more. But Jes and I were already in spitting distance of the show. I could hear the barker, not his exact words, but the tired roll and sweep of his touting, and there weren't much help for it.

"This is it," Jesse said. We were in front of a big dark tent. A ticket man was slouching on a barstool outside the entrance. His arms reached near down to his heels, and his small feet swung clear off the ground. He had a face like a monkey, with worried brows, wrinkled up and almost bluish. I once knew a cardinal who looked like that, forehead puckered, sleeves spilling out over his arms: his mistress was over six foot tall, when she wore her best powdered wig; and in profile, their daughter was a right ringer for the dauphine - not that it did them a lick of good in the end. The ticket man did not move a muscle, and regarded us without interest.

"One adult, one child," I said.

He yawned, took the coins and dropped them into the box. He gave me the tickets. Then he said, looking far away, into the darkening fairground, "Ten minutes to closing, mister."

Inside the tent was dark, like being in the bottom of a canvas schoolbag. It smelled of stale cigars, and piss, and a peppermint stick that'd got stuck to the floor and melted away. There was some gawkers further on, and their hoots echoed back to us. Jesse was looking around like he didn't know where to go first. His eyes filled up on what light they could. "I want to see-" he said.

"I know what you want to see," I said. "Let's just walk around the place, and take in all we can." Which was bound to be a lot more than I wanted, and a lot less than Jesse craved.

The featured folks was set up on separate platforms

raised a few inches up from the sawdust floor. They mostly seemed to take no interest in what was going on around them. The first one we come across, the bearded lady, was half-snoozing. Her beard spilt over her chest, and nodded away like a tamed ferret.

"Yes, indeed-dy," a wandering dwarf cried out, "this little lady from Budapest got whiskers Uncle Sam would envy - and you can throw in Santa Claus too. She's sold her beard clippings to the world's finest wig makers, destined for the scalps of European royalty."

The dwarf wore a lemon-colored suit. He roamed the floor, every so often pulling a handstand or a cartwheel. Soon as we were aside of him, mid-handstand, he sprung right-side up, and followed behind Jesse. He imitated Jes like a mincing shadow a couple of steps. Then he pulled on the back of Jes's overalls and when Jesse turned, he said, "Hey, mister, what're you looking at - you never see yellow before?" He shrieked with laughter, and trundled off.

That was when the crew up ahead turned and looked at us. One of them was that mean number from school, John. His quiff looked whiter, and sharper-edged. He came a few steps toward Jesse.

"Hey," he said, "Jimmy *is* a freak, now ain't he?" His pals hung back, but snickered, and showed their teeth in the shadowy light. The boy, encouraged, went on.

"Jesse, they're called the ignorant 'cause you ignore them," I said. I'd been through this kind of scene with JC, where at first, I'd try to pretend I didn't much notice somebody was being mean to him, so as not to embarrass him. I took a step or two away, and watched the sword swallower. I made sure I was facing a different direction to Jesse, while still keeping him within my field of vision.

"I mean, you ain't got no momma and ain't got no daddy," the boy went on. "At least these a-here freaks are freaks on account of what they got. But you, you're a freak on account of what you ain't got, and that's the worstest kind." He'd been advancing the whole time, and by now his shadow fell over most of Jesse. "Hey, but don't look so sad, Jimmy-Jim," the boy said. "We better watch out for old Jimmy, fellas, come Judgment Day. Cause you know what they say: the freak shall inherit the earth, haw-haw!" He said the "freak" word real loud to emphasize it. It popped out like a cork in a shook bottle, and bounced all over the ceiling of the tent.

It woke the bearded lady. She opened one eye, then the other, and hopped down from her stage. The back hem of her black gown trailed behind her like the tail of a serpent. She stole across towards the other side of the tent, and was soon swallowed up in its darkness. The yellow-suited dwarf put his fingers to his mouth and gave a short low whistle. A dwarf, and then some other folks, emerged from the dark at the sides of the tent: a human skeleton in a red union suit, a pinhead in a smocked dress and a pink hair-bow even though she was near bald, and a trio of midgets dressed as colorful and cheap as notes from a toy xylophone. Soundless as the night falling, they closed in around John and Jesse. I was heading over that way myself, but they was quicker, and silent, like nuns. John's pals melted away, easy as shadows.

"The freak shall inherit," the dwarf was saying. His voice was nasal, and high-pitched. It wavered forth, handling the words as though it was juggling them, keeping them in the air with a measure of difficulty, and a flourish of bravado. "Both of you together."

Then they each picked up the last part, and said in turn, one with a low voice, one that was squeaky; one with a voice that was raspy and slow as a warped saw on hard wood; one that was fast and bubbly, like a brook running with soda water, and astonished at its own effervescence. All the while they were closing in tighter. They were pushing John against Jesse, and Jesse against John, like them boys were both slated as the cheese in a game of farmer in the dell gone haywire and nasty.

That's was when I'd had enough, and was set to enter in, when I spied a man advancing from the other end of the tent. He was already nearer to them than I was. I noticed he had bluish looking arms. As he got closer, I saw it was Zogg. He waded into the group. The folks on the outskirts parted to make way for him. The pinhead girl dropped a curtsey. She fiddled with her hair ribbon, and it came off in her hand. Soon the group weren't nothing but outskirts of its former self. Zogg looked steady at John, who wavered like somebody'd hit him with a four by four. He wandered away. I've heard of someone charming the birds off the trees and such, and I imagine the notion makes most folks think of springtime and gardens and sparrows tying blue bows in the sky with their beaks, and singing. But charm ain't to do with pretty; it's to do with power, that gets into you, and makes you itch from your insides out. That's what Zogg had. He fixed eyes with the freaks, one after another. They each nodded in turn at something he didn't seem to need to say, then they scattered like beads of water on a hot griddle. One of them was humming with a high-pitched kind of tonality, and it sped up to a frenzy by the time he'd spun completely out of sight. Only Jesse was left standing there, breathing patient and normal and making like nothing had happened.

This was my second meeting with Zogg. His eyes were darker and more merry than ever.

"Never did get to see them Siamese twins," Jesse said finally.

"I reckon we'll live," I said.

And that's when Zogg, friend of the condemned, giver of ablution in their last hour, saw fit to smile.

*   *   *

Soon as I was back at work, Bean asked straight off, did I see Dr. Zogg.

"Yes, sir, I did," I said. There was a load of varnish had

come in, and I was stocking the shelves. "Went by his tent, and we had ourselves a little chat."

"Of course, I have talked to the man myself," Bean said. "Extensive-like. On the night of his first fry-up, as he says. Oh he certainly is a card." Bean chuckled. You could tell Bean reckoned theirs had been a meeting between equals, citizens of the world who knew just how much death could profit a man. Bean was faintly basking in its memory. "When I told him about my line of work that night, he said - he was patting himself on the belly - when you think about it, Mr. Bean, our own bodies ain't but the coffin of all the chickens and pigs and rabbits and such we have in the course of our lives consumed, guts within guts, and all fit for interment. Wonder what you'd get for your own cadaver, Mr. Bean, he said, you'd have to polish it up and solder it down I expect. We both laughed. Quite the huntsman, Zogg is, in his off hours. Most of what he eats, he's bagged and skinned himself. Says he never leaves a mark on them critters either."

"Ain't that a kindness," I said, and went on stocking the shelves.

Bean went quiet a moment, and his voice came back, a shade or two colder. "Few days, and we're on air," he said. "Looking forward to it, ain't you?"

"Oh yes," I said, "and so is my boy."

"He's a bit delicate, ain't he?" Bean said, appraising his fingernails and frowning.

"No, he just takes things awful serious, but he's a handful of fun too."

"Never did put much stock in fun," Bean said. "It don't last, and long as it does, it distracts, unless it's serious fun, now that's more my type. That's what I like about that Zogg fella."

"Fun ain't the word for him," I said, but Bean was already headed out the door, and the bells chimed behind him.

CHAPTER THIRTY-SIX

Jesse and I woke up early that next Sunday, with a stitch of hunger in our sides. I got myself to the stove in short order, and set to boiling us up a pot of greens and fatback. "Careful," Jesse said, "don't want it to scorch none." He had his nose in the Red Rock cookery book. He put it down in a hurry, though, when a passel of whispering came to hatch right outside our door like a nest of new green snakes.

I gave Jesse the spoon, and went to the door. The Lesses were bunched up just beyond it. They were tumbling over each other like socks in the laundry wash, and jabbering softly the whole time. "If we make enough noise, Mirth, they'll have to -" "Knocking's the easiest -" "This is dumb. Folks don't mind none -" They stopped short soon as I came out.

"Just boiling up a pot of greens," I said. "You fellas eat yet?"

Luckless said yes, and Reckless said no, right at the same time. They looked at each other, and butted heads. Mirthless sat on the porch like a puddle of a person and giggled. A breeze came up, not yet cold, but carrying within it the intent of winter, like a knife inside the coat of a thief. The leaves on the oak across the road stirred, and the greenish shadows they cast on the porch shifted slowly till they was dizzy, and settled back down. Jesse poked his nose out the door. The rest of him followed. The smell of fatback on the boil tinged the air with oil and salt, and bore the smack of a small, sure something to look forward to. Jesse said howdy, ducked his head, and kicked at the floor with his feet. The Lesses said Howdy back, but forewent the kicking.

"Sure have got a mess of food on the go," I said. "I'd hate to see it go to waste."

"I guess we could help out, if you want," Luckless said.

"But if'n we do, we got to have some root beer on top," Reckless said.

"That's your carrying charge," I said.

"Yep," Reckless said.

"Well, okay. You boys just set out here, while I finish rattling them pots." I could hear them talking outside while I poked at the greens, and got out the plates and some forks. Luckless asked Jesse, "So you going to talk on the radio yourself?" I guess Jesse couldn't stop himself from telling them, but then I figured, those boys was so woebegone, they didn't have nobody to tell.

Jesse said he sure was, and had a lot of things to say about Denny Colt and an apple upside down cake, and it was going to be something. I bet it ain't, Reckless said, and Jesse said, well what do you know, you thought the capital of this here country was Jefferson. Maybe he thought they meant county, Mirthless said, and Jesse said, that don't matter either way, and Reckless was just out of joint because he wanted to be on the radio himself. I sure wouldn't want to have to talk to old man Bean, Luckless said, and Reckless said, he ain't so much, the only fella what comes close to give me the shivers is that Zogg character. I saw him at the fair putting folks to sleep. Oh he'll be talking on the show too and Jud knows him pretty good, Jesse said, and Reckless said, I bet Jud knows the president of the United States besides, and Jesse said, well, if he did, he sure wouldn't go looking for him in Jefferson. Then it sounded like they collided into each other.

When I came out, carrying a couple of plates of greens, they was still tangled in a heap, moving barely at all, like stew on a slow simmer.

"Jesse, you better tell your guests it's time to eat," I said.

Jesse's head was under Reckless's shoulder. "Let me go," he said, kind of muffled, and Reckless lifted himself off. Jesse stood up. "We're going to eat now," he said.

"Got them root beers ready?" Reckless said.

"They'll come later," I said.

We all set down on the steps to eat, and the sun was warmish but muted, and you had to sit still to let it get to you, and so we abided, and let it gather around us. Mirthless was beside Jesse and moved to steal a bit of fatback when Jesse weren't looking, but his balance was no good, and he fell off the step and landed on the one below. He held on steady to his plate the whole time.

"You okay?" Jesse said.

"He was aiming to pinch your dinner, you dope," Reckless said.

"I've been done worse by," Jesse said. He pushed a forkful of greens off his plate down onto Mirth's, who chowed without saying a word, or raising his head.

Luckless sighed. He picked up a twig full of pine needles, and commenced to sweep it over the floor beside him. He looked up. "Hey Jud, what's going to be on that radio show anyway?"

"I got some ideas." I didn't look at Jesse none.

"Who cares?" Reck said. "Local radio ain't fit but for snot-babes like Luck. Now, my book of researches got heaps and heaps more kick to it." He raised it aloft, for emphasis, but Mirth and Luck and Jesse weren't looking at him. Their brows was tense with thinking, and they looked off to a patch of blank mid-distance.

"I reckon I'll start first with a Denny Colt story," Jesse said finally. He put down his fork. "A Christmas one, and Denny can see a star stuck in the sky above Wildwood, guiding him through the falling snow."

"I read the latest Denny," Mirthless said. "It's about how it rains so bad, for one solid week, in Central City and some buried booty washes up in Wildwood, and nobody knows whose it is, until Denny Colt straightens the whole thing out."

"I bet it gets buried all over again," Jesse said. He was staring straight ahead at nothing, the plate balanced across his knees.

"Yeah," Luck said, "He lays it to rest to keep peace in the town. How'd you know?"

"Jesse has a real ear for Denny," I said.

"Like I lived it myself or something," Jesse said.

I was reaching for my fork and my hand only wavered a spilt second if that.

"I bet Mr. Bean'll be awful interested in Denny Colt," Jesse went on. "He catches evil-doers, who most generally go on to become convicts, and on top of which he lives in a graveyard, so there's coffins all over the place."

"Except nobody makes any money," I said. "Wouldn't make any sense to Bean. What's that fool move about putting treasure back into the earth?"

"Way Denny does it, I expect it's proper," Jesse said. "In a casket so nobody suspects anything. Maybe one for somebody they all think is dead but ain't, just like Denny himself."

"I'll tell you what," Mirthless said. He was holding his fork in the air between his mouth and his plate, and his brows were arching a tiny bit higher. "That's better than the way the book had it."

We went back to eating, slowly, like it was a task that took some thinking about. Reckless said he hoped we was done talking about the stupid radio show.

By the time we'd done with our platefuls, the day had

warmed up considerable. The sun was soft and gold, the color of half-beaten toffee pouring from the saucepan to the tin. Jesse and the younger Lesses was chattering about swapping some comic books. I sunk my chin upon my chest, and closed my eyes. I liked just sitting there with Sunday lunch tucked inside my belly, and Sunday light drifting down over me, and Sunday afternoon kind of talk buzzing around me. So that's what I did, for what seemed a good long while.

"This day's like a sparrow that was flying south, and got trapped by a mean wind." It was Mirthless talking. I opened my eyes, and he had his face tipped up towards the sky, scanning it. "And now it's fallen loose," he went on.

I straightened my back and raised my chin and said, "Mirth, it's the stealing of scraps that makes a poet. I knew a dog once, a water-retriever type that got lost in the city and scrounged out of slop buckets, and he couldn't bark but without he came out with a sonnet like you'd find in Shakespeare."

"Mirthless is a dog," Reckless said. "Ha-ha-ha."

"Leastways he ain't an itch," I said. "You ought to try it yourself sometime."

Jesse got up and slipped inside and fiddled with the dials. By the time he came back out again, the signal, wherever it was from, was coming in clear enough, but the fella on it was having a heck of a time thinking of what to say next.

I guess we uh got us a song coming up soon I hope heh-heh about uh well songs make the world go round they say huh? oh a commercial first? Okay folks -

"I hope to God Zogg and I can keep up a patter better than this fella," I said.

Jesse poked his head up, and looked around at his buddies, and announced to them all, "You know Dr. Zogg spent a whole afternoon talking to me and Judd once, and I bet he's looking forward to doing it all over again on our very own radio show."

Reck stuck his head up high. "Well, as it happens, I know a few things about Zogg myself." He crossed his arms and sat there looking at us; and he shut up, so somebody would have to favor him with a request to go on.

"Like what?" Jesse said.

"Like Luck and Mirth and me was going by the fairgrounds oh day before last maybe, and what did we see but Yellow standing out by the freak show tent. It was starting to get dark, folks was hurrying home, and Yellow was awful upset. Snorting breath like it was water in his nostrils, and panicked to get it out. And Dr. Zogg stepped out from beside the tent, and laid a hand on his shoulder, and steadied him like a runaway horse. One of them dwarves was outside, and he pranced right up to Yellow and held out a chocolate bar to him, and when Yellow made to take it, the dwarf snatched it away and laughed."

"Mean rattling kind of laugh, it was, too," Mirth said. "Sounded like a stick dragged along a stretch of fencing."

"It stopped short, though," Reckless went on, "when Zogg reached right over and took the chocolate away, and gave it to Yellow. The dwarf stuck his chin out, like as to kick somebody with it, he was so mad. And Zogg just looked down at him and said, 'Man ain't got many pleasures left in this world.' Then he told Yellow, don't fret none, Zogg himself was going to take him out shooting one day, like the big boy that he was. Of course, that morning, I run across Zogg myself. He was out in the woods with his shotgun. I saw a flash of white through the trees and I thought it was a running deer, but turned out to be the glint off his rifle. I was glad he didn't catch sight of me none, because I couldn't make out hardly a hint of actual meanness to him, and that near spooked me worse than an evil grimace. It was like he was out doing his job or something, and we know what that is."

"Yeah, we sure do," Jesse said. He set about unpicking a knot in shoe-lace, and doing it up proper. He frowned in concentration.

"Anyhow," Reck went on, "soon as Zogg promised Yellow an outing, Yellow calmed down some. He stood there practically inhaling that chocolate, and got it all over himself. 'Look like he's been touched by the hand of Hershey's,' Zogg said, and gave him a handkerchief. It was white and it kind of glowed in the dark. Yellow took hold of the hanky in one hand, like it was a treat he'd get to later, and went on guzzling the chocolate bar, which was in the other. And Zogg shook his head and laughed."

Jesse looked up. He'd got his shoelace tied up again, but one end dangled long and loose. "Of course, what's touched Yellow is the hand of God."

"I reckon Yellow's been slapped by that one," Reckless said. "Like this." He stood up and rushed over to Jesse to demonstrate. Jesse stayed sat down, but he swung his arm upwards at Reck. I got up and stepped in between them, as if I was wading into low but turbulent waters. I told them to settle down. And when they did, and there was relative quiet for once, we heard the radio again, though the signal was getting weaker; and the fella was saying:

. . . course, Christmas ain't just a season on the calendar, it's a season of the heart, and those boys down in Biloxi convicts though they . . . building a...

Luck started singing real softly to himself, something about the Erie Canal. Mirth joined in for a verse, while Reck hemmed, and hawed, and glowered at them. The veins was starting to stick out on his neck and hollered at them to keep still, he was trying to listen and take notes on a place of historic interest. But by then the signal was pretty well lost, and by time I brought out the bottles of root beer, it was gone altogether. We downed them root beers in silence, and I reckon we were all feeling the air was a mite colder than it had been.

CHAPTER THIRTY-SEVEN

In the weeks that followed, I could already glimpse what was coming up. I saw it in the pale color of the sky that went thinner and thinner through the day like silver stretching, and the hint of winter in the air that lingered, and hesitated. It was an advent sky, and I looked up into it, and realized Jesse would soon be casting the words of the Lord upon it. Already that year, the heavens had been filled with the broadcasting of Christmas songs; and their sound did reach my ears, which were as if on tip-toe. My heart filled with solemn expectation. Though in years previous I had passed the day with little fuss, this one approaching would mark the coming of the power and the light, and of Jesse being known unto the people. I believed Jesse himself was tinctured by such divine perception, though unawares.

Like: one day soon after our encounter with Zogg in the woods, Jesse came home from school with a picture he done. He showed it to me, a five-pointed yellow star atop a tree, and waves of light emanating from it, to guide the wise men on. It's real good, I told Jesse; and was glad I didn't say a thing more, because then he asked me which part I liked best, the radio tower, or the signal up top, what was sending out stories and jingles across the land. So he revealed without even meaning to, how the advent of radio was cast in the image of the birth of Christ, the way men here did celebrate it. I looked down at the picture, then across the table at him. I tried not to let it show too much in my eyes that his time was at hand.

"Oh and we had a Christmas gift draw," Jesse said, "and so we got to go and buy a something for that goober I got stuck with."

"Who'd you get?"

His face sunk in on itself. "That crazy boy Elvis." Jesse got out his book of foolscap, and sat down to work some more on his radio paper. Reck's research book was pretty good, he allowed, but his was going to be better because he was writing it all up himself, and not just copying stuff out. And plus, I pointed out to Jesse, he was going to talk to whole households full of people, whereas Reck couldn't corral but us and his brothers.

"He's been stinky about my radio show," Jesse said. "I ain't going to tell him about it no more."

"He's jealous," I said. "And once you know that, he can't hurt you none."

As if in agreement, Jesse picked up a crayon, and scrawled across the front of the tablet: *Mine - Do Not Read.*

It weren't but a charade on my part, for I already had in mind what his radio address was going to be. But when Jesse was finished writing for the night, he made me put his tablet away careful; and to keep things smooth, I did as he asked, and laid it out on the front windowsill, like a body in state. I weighed it down with the harmonica, but Jesse hated that thing, and insisted I take it off his work. So I took the harmonica and propped up against a corner of the floor. Jesse couldn't see it from his pillow, but I could.

It glinted in the moonlight, and in the dawn; and it became, in that season of Christmas, a talisman of Zogg, for the silvery glint of him was already part of my memory, and foreboding: for the day Jesse first spoke unto to the multitude was as well the day I had to speak on air to Zogg. I pictured him as Reck had done, the day he'd spied Zogg in the woods, disappearing through a grove of beech trees, a whistling going with him, and the metal on his hunting rifle glinting now and then through the branches, when the sun hit it right, until it was gone. He trailed through forests of my mind with that flicker of gun-metal to him, like tinsel on a tree; and in a semblance of a smile, showed his mismatched teeth. They was like a handful of torn-out nails being held out to you.

*　　*　　*

Straight the next day, I could not help but notice that the season had taken over the town. There was a rope of silver tinsel strung across the doorway of the Strand movie house. It dipped and rose in a line of defeated but persevering scallops, and caught the winter sunlight. On my lunch break, I saw a man from the city laying a string of bulbs along gabled roof of Koehner's, then on across the street, to the drainpipe of Tempner's Beauty Shop. Old Mrs. Tempner came out and watched him, and tugged her shawl closer. She called out to watch himself, that pipe was fresh-painted last month. The utility man nodded, and tipped his cap to her, and near lost his balance in the process. But still, the line of lights held steady. In the afternoon, when we weren't looking, somebody stuck a bunch of poinsettia and winter-wonderland type stencils on the front window of the shop. Just as I was ready to go home, Bean directed me to take a bucket of warm soapy water and scrap the things off.

"I got nothing against the season," Bean said. "But a man's window is his window."

There's no way to argue with that, and soon I was a-sloshing and a-peeling. I had particular trouble with the top hat of a snowman in the far left corner, and there it stayed, suspended on nothingness, at a jaunty angle. I tried pulling at it, and some came off but what remained hung there like a music note that had got separated from its tune, and just looking at it put me in a mind to do something fun, and of the season. I decided to fetch Jesse, and take him to what shops was open, so he could get his offering for the Christmas draw.

Mrs. Greenfield was already waiting on the porch when I came home. She said Jesse'd been a sweet little lamb all afternoon, quietly set down, flipping through one of her old cookbooks, and reading a section or two out real fine, and writing a few words down in his little book of foolscap. But when she'd picked that notebook up, she said, Jesse let loose with a squall.

"He's getting to be a regular little man," she said. She was already down the front steps by then and she ducked her head to one side as she buttoned the collar of her coat. It was made of lightish cloth that glowed blue in the fading light. "Wonder if he ain't missing the Church of God some."

I was stood on the front door threshold, and regarded my feet. "We all try to find our way to the Lord," I said, "and mostly we get there, sooner or later."

"Try sooner," she said. She jutted her head towards me and mock-whispered. "As a kindness to the babysitter." She raised her hand in farewell, and set off down the darkening road.

Jesse weren't expecting a shopping visit down Main Street, but by the time I'd told him and turned around, he'd already got his coat on. As we were walking downtown, we saw the peaked roof of Koehner's, rising up in the distance. Jesse pointed at it.

"The kids at school been saying there's going be a Santa outside Koehner's. Tree beside him and he'll be sitting in a chair on top of a sled, and I go up and tell him what toys I want. On the day we do our radio show."

"Well, you won't need to ask him for nothing," I said.

"Because you'll have had your Christmas by then, talking on the radio to the whole wide world."

Jesse tugged at my hand and kept up his chatter, that couldn't he at least ask for a bicycle too, and finally he wore me down and I promised. By then we were on North Main Street. The lights were coming on, and their luminance was hard and white and unflinching. I felt that we were entering a zone of truth. It was defined by the deep and purplish dark, like a wilderness, from which we had just emerged, and into which we would soon return. A few shop fronts was lit up.

"We'll try the five and dime," I said. Jesse took my hand and we crossed the street over to it. There was a rope of red and green tinsel hanging over the door way, and around the shop window. It looped over a toy rifle, a red wagon, and a baby doll with hair the color of butterscotch. We went in, and the bells on the door rattled. The aisles lay before us like miniature streets lined with shiny goods, that all glittered or talked or smelled like something it weren't. The floor was the color of an old rag, and sticky, and the place smelled of pine cleaner and old penny candy. The light was yellowish, and tremulous as a bowlful of water.

"What kind of toy you think your Christmas draw would like?" I asked Jesse.

"Who cares?" Jesse said. We were heading down the sewing notions aisle. At a display of gift-wrapped monogram handkerchiefs, we turned the corner; and there, we near collided, nose to nose, with E.

He looked at each of us in turn, and gave a sly smile. He had a toy rifle in his arms, and to mark our approach, he pointed it towards the sky like a sentry. The butt end hit the floor, and a pink bullet of some variety popped out its top. He giggled. Jesse rolled his eyes.

"Howdy," E said, so soft I wondered a moment if he'd said a thing.

Jesse looked at him.

"Howdy," I said. I kneed Jesse in the back. He mumbled something, and turned away to fuss over some toy trucks on a shelf.

E's momma was a few yards further down the aisle. She stood direct under a bare bulb, and the light cast sorrowful shadows under her eyes. Soon as she saw me, she bobbed her head and sent an embarrassed smile of greeting my way. Then she went on with what she'd been saying.

"And you're liable to kill all your little playmates with that thing," she said.

Jesse half-looked at me and snickered. "Like he got any," he said, real low. Then he scurried off into another aisle. I stayed put.

"Ain't there nothing else you like?" she went on.

E drew towards her. I made like I was looking over some rose-scented padded hangers laid out in a bin beside me; and I saw their two shadows converge. I looked up and E was pointing up at the end wall. It was decorated with little silver-foil stars, and above them all, a giant one, wide as a man-hole cover. Amongst them, was slung up a few other toy weaponries: an archery set, some pistols and a few other shotguns, and a boomerang; and then on its own, a guitar. It stuck out from a hook in the wall. It was suspended by its neck, and the neck had a red ribbon around it. The ribbon was the biggest thing about it. The body weren't much bigger than a fiddle's, and the shoulder strap was as skinny as a shoestring.

E's momma shook her head. I weren't looking at her, but I saw the shadow wobble from side to side. I took a step or two closer, and commenced fiddling with a rack of stuffed teddy bears that had santa hats glued onto their heads.

"Maybe like birthday and Christmas rolled into one," E was saying, quiet-like.

"But it's more'n two whole days's wages," she said. She stole a look around her, as though she might have embarrassed anybody what could have overheard. She put a hand on E's shoulder. E looked at the floor. Then he peered up into her face.

"You know what?" E said. "You look tired, momma. I'm going to take us on home." He took her hand, and led her around the corner. They were so different in height that her arm slanted sharply down. He led her forward. I watched them thread their way through the cleaning goods department, then the gardening aisle, and the candy section, then they were at the front of the shop. The door opened and the bells chimed as they went out.

Jesse was in the kitchenware aisle. He was stood before a wall full of gadgets. His mouth was hanging open.

"See anything, boy?" I said.

"I like this here pan, what the sides come off of when you want them too, and a thing that cuts a pear in eight. And the bicycles, they got them over there." He indicted with his head.

"Bicycle? It's mighty generous of you, wanting to get that for your Christmas draw."

"Nooo," he said, like I was stupid. "I meant for me."

"We ain't buying for you this time," I said. "Supposed to be about giving, Jesse."

"So why ain't you giving me something?"

I just took a breath and went on. "Now your Christmas pal -"

"He ain't my pal."

"- looks like he's got a hankering after this here thing." I pointed up at the guitar.

"That's too nice a gift for that boy," Jesse said. He poked his chin up at me.

"And his momma liked it too."

Jesse had a round tin in his hands. He held it out. "This here is the one I like."

"You can go on liking it," I said. I headed off.

"I hate that boy anyway," Jesse called out. There was a whine creeping into his voice.

"I don't want nothing to do with him," he called out. His voice was straining like it was about to break into a howl. "I only got stuck with him."

"That's too bad," I said, moving off. "I'll be down the back counter seeing you give him a nice gift." I was already in the thick of the seasonal goods item aisle.

Jesse ran out in front of me. He stopped at the first bin he came to. It was heaped with little net bags of chocolate coins wrapped up in gold foil. He reached in, and threw one to the floor. It landed with a soft crunch.

"Buy that for him!" he cried out. "It's good enough."

He turned and ran to the next bin. It was piled up with perfumy candles that was shaped like Christmas trees and holly and poinsettias and such, and gave off a riot of synthetic scent, pine-like and spicy. Jesse reached in with both hands, and flung two of them down in front of me. "And them things too!" His face was red; and his hair was so sweated up that it was sticking out. He was looking straight at me. I kept walking, and went right past him.

"He got his momma to take care of him," he hollered, "and his daddy to steal him something good."

I reached the back of the shop, and I went on ignoring him. Jesse was howling, all the while that the item was taken down from the wall, and was rung up; to when I made him pick up and put away what he'd thrown on the floor; and all the way home, down the streets that was lit, and the ones that weren't; and through most of our supper too.

But by the time I was wrapping the gift up in old newspaper, he quit sniffling. He came up behind me, and spoke into my elbow.

"I could draw a few things onto that paper," he said. "Make it look a lot better."

It was late, and he should've been in bed, but I unwrapped the gift, and pressed the newspaper flat. Jesse got out his crayons, and he drew some stars and a couple of trees, and some ribbon; or anyway that's what I thought they were. We set the gift on a shelf high up in the house; and before we went to bed, we both stood and looked upon it. And with Jesse I was well pleased; for he was learning to act as a savior ought.

Jesse got to thinking some more about Christmas, it looked like, because that next morning, he told me we was to do the holiday right this year, and on top of which, include the Lesses as much as we could, since they didn't have hardly nobody. I asked him what did he have in mind, and he looked me and it was as if he had so much to say he couldn't get one word out proper. Mrs. Greenfield left one of her housekeeping magazines behind, and Jesse had been studying it. He daydreamed over wreathes made out of shiny plaid ribbons, and Christmas trees constructed from pine cones and sprayed gold, and racks of cookies baked in the shape of stars and candy canes and snowflakes, and decorated each one specially. He said he'd got an idea from some story he heard on the radio: he and Lesses were to form a procession, and march from the edge of the woods into our house, singing carols all the while; and once inside, each of them was to step forward, hang a single ornament on the tree, while the others went on singing the refrain.

I could imagine what Reck would have said to that one, but I let it go. "What tree?"

"The one we're going to go out and get," Jesse said. "A full-size one that reaches to the ceiling."

So far with Jesse, I'd just lopped a branch off the bottom of a pine out in the woods over the highway, and set it on front porch, with a blanket to shore it upright. It reminded me of the way Jesse had come to me around that time of year, though he didn't know that. At the time, it used to satisfy him. But this year, nothing would do but a standing-up, tall tree. He stretched his left arm up to show me just what he meant.

"Jesse," I said, "there's no way we could fit one as big as that inside our house."

Jesse didn't say nothing. His arm was still straining upwards, indicating, but his brow came down low, and his lips pursed up in a tight tense line, and his cheeks puffed out like a blowfish.

Well, soon enough he'd be learning to put all childish things aside. So I said, "You know what, Jes? We'll get one that big out in the woods, and we'll leave it there, but we'll put a star on its tippy-top. And in years to come, folks'll wander by, out hunting or walking, and come across it, and wonder who put it there, and why. And it'll become a true mystery of Christmas."

Jesse's arm came down. His cheeks flattened out some. He was thinking about it.

"How about tomorrow night, and you can collar them Lesses into the deal if you feel like."

Jesse nodded slowly.

I spent my lunchtime piecing together a star shape out of a scrap of soft pine. I was thinking of flinching a tag-end can of gold enamel going dry, but decided against it, which was a good thing, as Bean came in and surprised me. He had a newspaper folded up in his hand and he swatted the doorframe with it in greeting. The shiny red foil of a half-eaten chocolate santa was poking a smidge out of his shirt pocket. I pushed the star to one side, and made like I'd been busy the whole time lining up the hinges on a soft pine model, extra-wide, that'd been hanging around in the back room.

"They say Christmas is a boon to the businessman," Bean said, "but can't prove it by me. Folks within a breath of keeling over get one glimpse of a dimestore santa, and it acts on them like a dose of tonic, or a reprieve from the governor. You know what, Jud? I like February. It's good for business."

Then Bean said he'd just been down to the courthouse, to nose around ahead of the broadcast and refresh himself as to what the place was like. He seemed exhilarated but contained; and I expect that breathing in the air of the very chamber where cases were heard and judgments rendered and sentences passed intoxicated him, not to joviality and high spirits, but to solemn rectitude, and a measured talkiness to go along with it: a philosopher who has at last breathed deep of the purest form of his lifework's particular theme.

"It will surely be something," Bean said. "Dr. Zogg himself, speaking in a court of justice." He looked out the window like he was picturing it. Then he turned to me, refreshed and refocused. "Town had trouble finding a lead long enough for my tree lighting. But Zogg has a generator he carts around with him, and he says he'd be tickled to provide the juice. That's what he calls it." Bean's face crumpled up with joy at the fraternity implied by Zogg's use of the term. "Matter of fact, I'll be running him over to Jefferson and back that day - he's got another speaking engagement lined up right after my show, and he thought at first he might not to be able to do WELO. So I said ferrying him over wouldn't be no trouble, it would be a pleasure, and he said funny how one man's trouble is so often another man's pleasure; and we both laughed." Bean laughed right then too, as if in reenactment. I kept working and declined to join in. Gradually, the rapture faded. His lips made a thin gray line. "So what you got ready for Dr. Zogg, boy?"

I'd been sorting out a drawer full of two-cent nails. I chucked the one I was holding back its proper bin, and then got the folded up sheet of foolscap out of my shirt pocket with a list of questions on it, all of them softball and most of them only lead ins for the kind of stories I knew for a fact the man kept on tap.

Bean scanned the page, but his mind weren't on it. "Of course," he said, kind of abstracted, "Dr. Zogg and I have a kind of understanding that comes of working in the world at large. Zogg, he ain't kept busy making a bunch of things out of wood. A lot of chairs and caskets and so. I ain't putting that down, mind you. But what Dr. Zogg does is more. He provides a service. And that service is justice."

"Oh," I said, "that's what he's getting at when he talks about his fry parties and so on."

"Don't let a man's levity blind you to his seriousness of purpose."

"I won't, sir."

"I'd hate to think you doubt my seriousness of purpose." His eyes went a degree colder and his nose headed a degree north.

"I never have, sir. I want you to know that."

Bean relaxed a bit. His eyes wandered over mine, like he was estimating their depth and tone and weight-bearing capacities, and finding them unremarkable, moved on. "His doings are so final," Bean said. He looked out the front window and straightened the foolscap out on the counter, his fingertips going in circles, while he talked. "That's another thing about him. None of this haggling I got to put up with. Done is done." Bean turned and looked at me. He made a gesture on the counter with his right forefinger as though he was dotting an "i" and crossing a "t". "I tell you, if I didn't respect him so much, I'd outright envy him." He pushed the foolscap my way.

I folded the paper back up, and put in my pocket. Of course, nobody has to keep to a script, even if he wrote it. Me and Jesse was proof of that.

CHAPTER THIRTY-EIGHT

The woods that night were blue and deep. The sun had gone down, and the sky was left there, gray and blank and faintly shimmering, like the windows of a deserted house. Somewhere far off, an owl hooted. I was trailing out in front, with Jesse by my side, and the Lesses fanning out. It was almost cold enough I could near catch sight of my breath, but as soon as I looked close, it was gone. Every so often, we heard the rumble of a passing truck on the highway down below. The light was so low, we had to work to make each other out, and the air was dry and cold. We called to each other but once or twice; and it was as if the sounds of our voices were at once disembodied from us, and made their own shape in the air; and so did our footsteps, as we traipsed over the hard black earth. The wind whooshed through the pines, high and low, and I wandered amongst them, from tree to tree. I done this once before, I half-remembered, when I -

"How about that one?" Jesse cut in. He was pointing to a sapling that weren't much taller than he was.

"That ain't a tree," Reck said. He hurried over and his shadow eclipsed them both. "I seen pencils with more wood on it."

"We ain't after the lumber, Reck," I said. "But the shape ain't much to brag about, and the branches are kind of threadbare and moth-eaten."

"That's the kind we always get," Jesse said.

"Well, this time we're after something else," I said, "like you said you wanted." We tramped on. Mirth ran ahead, then stood aside to let me pass.

"You got that puzzle ring on you?" Luck asked Jesse.

"Nope," Jesse said. "I was really hoping somebody'd got me that three-way peeler." He looked up at me. "We did our Christmas draw today."

Reck hollered up ahead, from somewhere we couldn't see him.

"How'd your gift go over?" I said.

"That funny boy said thank you and tried to talk to me, about where he'd seen it when he was mooning over the things on the wall, and was trying to get his momma to get him that boomerang if'n he couldn't have a rifle. Then some kids were laughing at him on account what he gave over. A little fire-truck that was dented in all over. You could tell it was one of his old ones."

"Then that's a true gift," I said. "Man ain't got many pleasures, and he gave up one of his."

But Jesse weren't listening. He was looking at Mirth, who was up ahead of us, standing like he'd been frozen, with his hands held to his mouth like somebody who'd just seen a fright.

"Caution," Mirth said. Then he stood up normal. "I read that on a sign today. New one they was putting up by the department shop."

The wind swept through the branches. In the distance, an owl hooted.

"I don't much like the woods at night," Luck said. He had his hands in his pockets and his shoulders were clenched. He was looking down at the ground as he walked. His face was pale and white in the bluish light. A shape was running back towards us, the color of a shadow, and near as soundless. It was Reck.

"Stop," Mirth said. He hopped onto a spot a half foot ahead, and stood still for a second.

"What are you scared of there, Luck?" Reck said. He was a little out of breath. "A ghost come out and screech at you?" He walked on a few steps, doubled around back, then pounced - "Like this - whooah-ooah!"

Luck stood still. His chin hit his chest, and his frown went down to his feet.

"Reck, you are one terrific big brother," I said. "If ever you get thrown out of school once and for all, you ought to start up your own. The Terrific Big Brother Institute. They'll come from all over the world to learn your trade secrets. How to be a bully in five seconds flat, without the use of gun or rope. How to make the youngest, who don't stand hardly taller than a ten pound sack of flour, cry - and laugh at him at the same time. Don't that sound like something to be proud of?"

Reck grinned like he didn't know what else to do, and stood there, his fist full of fingers and his mouth full of teeth. He was reduced to flexing his feet full of toes in protest. "I didn't mean nothing by it, Luck," he said finally.

Luck gave a single short nod.

"Apology accepted," I said. I looked around for Jesse. The light was dwindling, and like to soon run out.

"Where's that star?" I heard Jesse say. He was stopped in front of a good-sized pine, and looking up at it like a man seeing a big city skyscraper for the first time. Its branches swept upwards, prickly and full, bristling like a hundred wolf tails. Against the bright and hollow sky, it stood dark as a mystery, mighty as a river, and intractable as time itself.

"This a-here one, Jud," Jesse said.

Reck came up for a look, and the other Lesses followed. Mirth was walking backwards at the time, and he bumped into Reck, who reached out and punched him on his shoulder. Then Luck turned up and started sniffling, why can't he put the star up on the tree too? Mirth said, why don't Reck just hoist him up alongside Jesse, and Reck punched Mirth a second time, and then went ahead and did just that. Luck and Jesse was lifted up together, like a pair of little flames to light a candle, and each of them took hold one end of the star, Luck the bottom, and Jesse the top, and they moved it over the tree without being able to settle, like a magnet passing over a magnet.

"Hurry up," Reck said.

"Hurry yourself," Mirth said, jumping out of range.

Jesse and Luck's hands finally gravitated to the same spot, and they hung the star on the tree. They stayed hoisted up there a moment, till Reck said he couldn't take no more being a human crane, he'd rather be schooling bullies in their trade, and he lowered Luck down, who landed in a heap. I let Jesse stay up there a little longer. When I'd swung him back on the ground, Jesse looked up at the star.

"Pretty good, ain't it?" he said.

"Never known a wooden star stuck on a pine tree above the highway to look any better," Reck said. I play-made to swat him, and the shadow of my hand slugged the shadow of his head square-on, and he pulled away and laughed.

I was facing the spot where Reck had been, now, and there, through the branches, down by a ridge blanketed with needles, something was stirring. Maybe I'd seen a flash of color, or maybe I'd heard a sound. We all stood still a moment.

"That an owl?" Luck said.

"Maybe it's Yellow," Mirth said.

"Yellow's more scared of the dark even than Luck," Reck said.

First thing I thought, it was old Zogg, and the back of my neck prickled up, till the whole of my body weren't but prickled neck prowling out in all directions. I was on my guard, and near looking for a fight.

I watched and waited, then I saw: the Conductor was passing through. The brim of his cap glinted in the nightfall. He was humming a tune so garbled and scattered, it was like trying to read outloud a sentence that weren't but a string of punctuation marks.

"That crazy railway-hatter," Reck said. He ran on ahead, for a better vantage point, or to prove his research had since moved on to other subjects, I don't rightly know.

"Who's that gal with him?" Jesse asked.

Mirth peered back down the ridge. "Ain't nobody with him."

"A young gal," Jesse said, pointing. "See. She got a yellow dress on, and rolling a hoop alongside her."

"Nope," Mirth said.

Reck was running in circles up ahead. "We ought to trap us a bear," he hollered.

Jesse turned to me and Luck. "You see her, don't you?"

The thought of Zogg loose on that slope was still itching at me like a tickle I couldn't reach, and I didn't get around to answering. Luck, though, raised his eyebrows a smidgen. I think he was about to say something, when Jesse gave up pointing, and shrugged. "She's gone below the ridge now anyhow." He ran on ahead towards Reck, and, sliding the last few yards, collided smack into him.

Reck turned around, a rock in his hand, and said, "Why'd you go and do that for? I was making Mirth a sign right here on the ground."

Jesse's face wobbled like he was on the edge of contrite, but he didn't go that way in the end. "Not like you could read it in this light anyhow," Jesse said.

Reck threw the stone aside, and Mirth started blubbering, and saying just keep writing it Reck, it weren't Jesse's fault, he didn't mean no harm.

Then why don't he say he's sorry? Reck said. His chin jutted out of the dark at me.

Because I ain't messed up nothing worth doing, Jesse

said.

I was heading towards them, and soon as I reached them, I scooped up Jesse. He was still talking. He poked his head out from under my arm, and kept yakking. "I am sorry," he said, "that there ain't no way you can read a single word in this dark, and you ain't got the brains to admit it."

Reck ran up and took a swipe at Jesse's head that hit me on the elbow. "Sorry, Jud," Reck said.

Jesse stuck his neck out. "Apology accepted," he crowed. Then he ducked his head back against my chest, and there it stayed, all down the knobbly slope, the Lesses bobbing around us like they was tied to an invisible string that pulled them along.

CHAPTER THIRTY-NINE

That next day, the one before the broadcast, I had me a vision. I hardly sought it out, for my heart was already full of light, but still, it proved good. It happened upon me early in the morning, on my way to the hardware shop. The street was full of a wintry mist, soft and gray as if it just been laundered. I heard the sound of men at work, and the sound carried like sound over vast tracts of water, or time. I stopped, and squinted; and far down the road, I'd have sworn I saw Vernon. He was standing up in the back of a pick-up truck, and his face was mild and pleasant, like a sun that shines out of January skies. I was already like to be late, and I had to turn off that road straightaway to get to Bean's, but I gave one last look. By then, all I could make out was a lumber truck and a pile of wood stacked up high beside it, the mist swirling around it, and the echoes of wood getting moved and stacked and hit against each other like weapons in futile and ghostly battle. And I walked on, joy and trepidation both plucking on my nerves. Something there elated me, and the same thing then eluded me, for I was reminded dimly of some distant passage, the words of which I could not yet call forth.

Bean was already at the shop. By way of greeting, his

mouth twisted up like there was sour taste in it, and he started talking to me as though we was already in mid-conversation. "I've known more no-accounts and cheats than I can count," he said. "And now that Presley no-account's been sprung. 'Good behavior.' What you make of that, boy?" I knew I weren't required to answer.

"Hitching his pants up at home," Bean went on. "Well, won't get a chance to do much else, because there's not many willing to hire a convicted cheat such as himself. Leastways not for long."

"You'll see to that," I said. I set right to work on an unfinished piece.

"Won't hardly have to," he said.

"His boy -"

"That boy of his been a heap better off having his daddy out of the house. I done him a favor."

I settled down on my heels, and levered open the can of varnish. "You been giving that boy Christmas all his life, Mr. Bean, even if he don't rightly know it."

Bean said nothing. He unwrapped a stick of peppermint chewing gum and popped it in his mouth. He looked at me glumly a moment. "Mind you don't devote the entire day to fiddling with that thing. We ain't building a monument. We're burying a hick."

And as I set about my work, the fumes rose sharp from the varnish, and the words of the revelation I had perceived came forward in my mind, as if jogged free, and they were the words said of Barrabas: "At that feast was released unto them one prisoner, whomsoever they desired." Thus another sign was put forth to mark the holy day of Jesse's announcement. I thought of E and his momma, his father freed, and the joy in their own small house in this here little town. And heart was made steady in my chest, like a ship with ample ballast.

Bean's spirits rose too, as the day went on, for I completed the piece I been varnishing - the show model of his newest coffin. So now he had two coffins on display in the outer workshop: the mahogany number, grand as a concert piano and lined in maroon velvet that I'd just finished up ("the Presidential," Bean called it), and a small and whitewashed coffin, no longer than a tool box. He lay a sprig of holly atop each one. Then he had me hang a placard across them:

The Bean Burial Spot
Live on WELO

"Any way we can work these here models into the show?" Bean said.

"This ain't the right holiday," I said.

"What one you got in mind? Halloween? In case you missed it, boy, that one's gone and passed us by."

"I was meaning Easter, sir," I said. "Christ getting laid into the tomb and so on."

"Oh,. Bean leaned against a shelf stocked with wood varnish. "I get it."

"Right now, Mr. Bean, we are at the other end of the story, Christ getting himself born."

"Cradle to grave," Bean said. Then he raised his eyebrows, and repeated it, this time with emphasis and import and a suitably slowed pace. "Now there's our motto for you. Takes us from Christmas to Easter, with a clean sweep of my product line, and back again." Bean smiled and shook his head at the power of his own inventiveness. In the world of old man Bean, perspicuity belonged to those who profited by it. He commenced chewing the gum slow and easy, like he'd done a solid day's work in those five seconds.

And maybe he had, for in that season of my brother's nativity, I was brought back yet again, musing, to the season of his death and resurrection, and how it had outdone me; and though I did not know it then, how it would undo me all over again.

For plain as it was that this land did strike a resonance

with the one from which I first come, it was lately apparent that the seasons of Easter and of Christmas were merging as one, intruding on each other, mingling like chimes that sounded from alternate skies, and colliding like two planets; and with that, signaling the end of all time. I saw a tolling of a giant bell, suspended over all time and place, and the bell swung first into the season of resurrection, and then on immediate return, into the season of nativity; and so a note from one season was struck, and a note from the other responded. Perhaps it was always thus, but this time I had the ears attuned to hear. And as the bell tolled, and the focus of all holiness veered from a full-up crib to an empty tomb, so too lurched my fate, from omitted, to defamed - and as the seasons moved to merge as one, so too would my twin fates of ignominy converge, and the contradiction between them be undercut, and they both be cancelled out at last. Like unto a crucible, the holiness of all seasons was swept into this Christmas of Jesse: once again I was to betray the one who most loved me, but out of my love for him, and so that a greater promise be fulfilled. Let no man dare to call me proud, for I gained no glory from such service; and matter of fact, since ever I done it that first time, my name's been tantamount to traitor.

Traitor? The night I'd glimpsed that Vern was free, I lay abed for hours: sleep could find no purchase on me, but that word did pry into my weary brain. And when my heavy eyelids nearly dropped shut, I saw before me the way to Calvary, and the brook Kidron, shimmering dully, moving slow like a snake gone sluggish with its belly full; and I saw this as though from a high place, and through a veil of falling snow. I weren't no traitor, I avowed, for I loved JC.

And I did love him: he was dutiful and hapless, unassuming, vexatious, and obscure, imprisoned as much as empowered by his identity, such as the heroes depicted in those books Jesse loved; or as young Jesse himself. JC

289

had Jesse's eyes, his gait, his speech; the guilelessness of his heart did show upon his face as he lived, and died. When he rose, he fulfilled the scriptures, and redeemed the days, and his host of brothers, all except for me.

But this time, would not Jesse, still so young, yet already risen from the dead, deliver me from myself? Would not Jesse have pushed aside my sop of bread at that last supper; and at the last hour, by the garden gates, turned his face away and refused my kiss? That tree that provided our cradle wood, would not Jesse have cut it down before it grew, replenished, to furnish the cross they nailed him to; or else became the tree from which I hanged myself? Could not those three kings traverse the desert, and come upon not a manger, but a tomb, unused, the Lord not risen because never crucified? And the star they followed dissolve into the light of everyday, and then every night, as the promise of the power and light was fulfilled? Why could I not, with Jesse the author of my salvation, follow the trail of Calvary myself, and find at its end not a shattered body upon a cross, but my brother and me as babies once more, breathing sweet and easy under the tender gaze of our mother? And together Jesse and I would slip off the rope that bound our hands, and neck, and abscond from this world, and the account men have immured us in, and depart in secret, and in silence, to live as all men are bidden to, as brothers.

And then it was as if I was in some high place, where I could see all the kingdoms of the world and in a moment of time; and I was thrown forward, weightless for an instant, and free, before a dry thing snapped somewhere inside my head; and then I was sitting upright in my bed.

I weren't in a state to get much any sleep that night; and finally, in some white hour, I rose from the bed, slipped out to the porch, and put the radio on, real low. The voices were like scratchy waves in a darkened sea. I stood in the doorway and looked back at Jesse sleeping.

His face was a pool of soft light in the dark. I listened

to the intake of breath, and as I stood and watched, I knew it was his last night of such sleep, and such quiet breathing, for presently he was to be given over to the world. In my pocket, I had his words ready for him. I'd wrote them out on a sheet of tablet paper that rasped starchily, direct over my heart. It read:

There is nothing hid which shall not be shown; neither was any thing kept secret but that it should come abroad. If any man have ears to hear, let him hear.

The time is fulfilled and the kingdom of God is at hand.

It had come easy to me, and I liked it for a few reasons. It was short, and I figured it was about as much as he could handle on his first outing. It laid down who Jesse was, clear enough to those attuned. And it paid tribute to the power and the light, through which these tidings would be sent forth and reach the ears of men. I could already anticipate Jesse's voice, kind of thin and nasal, but gaining strength as he proceeded; and I would be there watching his progress through the words, like a swimmer's through high and treacherous waves. He would become a man before my ears, and my hope and pride would buoy him along. I had given thought to the practicality of timing as well: after Zogg was done talking, I was to read out a commercial message for Bean, then I was to give a short squib, tying together Bean Hardware and WELO, which I was supposed to prepare but didn't, because that's when I was going to turn the talking over to Jesse. After he read his statement, I'd ask Jesse questions about the Word that I was sure he knew, and he would amaze the listeners with his understanding.

Jesse stirred once in his sleep, and stopped breathing, and I wondered if I had woken him. He turned over, and gave a tiny snore. I saw his eyes were rolling under his lids, and I wondered what visions unfolded beneath them.

CHAPTER FORTY

From the beginning, that day passed like a cart in a bad road, with fits and starts and rumblings that in the end mostly went nowhere, but jerked at your nerves all the same. It was sound not light that brought me to wakefulness; and not a sound that emanated from the power and light, like at first I thought it was, a burst of tune from the radio that filled me with joy. My joy emptied as soon as I realized I'd heard a jay bird calling from a treetop. I opened my eyes then it shut up. A moment later started its racket up all over again.

I heard Jesse outside and the Lesses, whispering and jabbering and going silent, then talking all at once. I rolled over, and heard a car in the far distance. It stalled, and jerked back into sound and motion for a moment, then stalled again. I got up and stood at the window. The sun was a chilly gold-white, drifting behind a sky of thinned out lead.

But there was a happening, that marked the day out, from near its beginning:

Jesse was standing across the road, under a street light on the top of the rise, one of them lights that ain't never been put to use, not in the entire time we lived across from it. It was wired for the light but not hooked into it. Jesse was squatting down at the base of the pole, like he was pitching a game of marbles or some such, and the Lesses were arranged around him in a semi-circle. Luck sat on the ground, his feet straight ahead of him, twiddling his toes. Mirth was kneeling, his hands fluttering at shoulder-height from time to time. Reck was standing at the outermost point of the arc. His back was straight, and his arms dangled loosely, as he held forth on a side point to his research: if you had to be hit dead by a truck, which kind of truck would be the worst.

" - with it sprinkled all over you on the road like you was a fried chicken at a picnic," Mirth was saying.

"Or a potato chip," Jesse said.

"I am telling you, Mirth," Reck was saying, "it ain't that way at all. You take a man what's been dead for a less than an hour or so, and if'n you had him pickled in salt from the moment he fell dead, he wouldn't decompose hardly at all, so how could a salt truck be the worst kind of all? From my investigations, I would say -"

"A live chicken truck," Luck said, "'cause they'd peck all over you. Even your eyes." He had hold of a twig, and jabbed at Jesse to demonstrate.

"Cut it out," Jesse said.

"I'd say the worst kind of truck to be hit by," Reck continued, not condescending to notice the interruption, "is a gas truck. It smells, and that ain't dignified. And on top of which, it can catch fire."

As soon as Reck had finished saying the word "fire," a light descended from on high, in a small and perfect circle. It cast itself over Jesse. The streetlight, which had stood over us as dark as a spent match since the day it had been put in, was shining pure and radiant. Jesse alone was bathed in its glow, which poured down on him like white water. Mirth and Luck didn't notice a thing; one was busy scratching his elbow, and the other was trying to knock his heels together to some song I guess he had in his head.

But Reck, who was far enough from the spectacle to see it, took a footstep back. His mouth was dropping open, and he was half-turning his head as if to say something, but in that short meanwhile, the light had already dimmed, and went out. Reck rubbed his eyes, brought his lips back together, and said nothing.

Neither did I. But I had seen this thing when it happened the first time, and I could guess its import a second. All time was converging into one: Christmas, Christ is born; Easter, Christ is risen; and the next one: Christ will come again, and the power and the light would arrive to give such witness. Because I can tell you right now what's at the beginning of Easter, from the very first. It ain't the sun standing still on the first day, or the sun rising up on the third, or the angels waiting by the rocks. It's that light atop a hill a few days before, where even them eleven saw how white his robes became - but none of them had a clue as to how downright painful transfiguration can be.

JC told me afterwards it was like having your bones stretched and turned inside out and back again and the whole time you was hearing them wrenching from so deep inside you, it seemed like miles away. That day, he was trembling, though they didn't notice it. That day, too, I started to see in him how someone can be giving in and being wilful all at the same time. I saw how he wanted to fulfil the words he had been sent to, not so he could go on from there, not full of hope at all, but just wanting to end the thing. And in my own long course of years, there's been some days I felt the same way myself.

Well, it looked like Luck had poked at Jesse one time too many, because Jesse yelled at him to quit it for good this time. And he stood up and came towards the house.

Mirth stood up too. "Jud be cooking something?" he said. His nose was fairly atwitch.

"I reckon he may be," Jesse said without looking at him.

"I bet it'll be good," Mirth said.

"Mirth, you ought to learn yourself how to bark like a dog," Reck said, "on account of you already know how to beg like one."

"He ain't begging," Jesse said. "He's just stating a fact. You're pretty big on facts yourself, Reck."

Reck patted his notebook and said that matter of fact ha-ha he was.

"What you all waiting for?" Jesse said. He was heading across the way. "Jud'll be wondering why we all ain't clamoring at his table this minute."

"Wait for me-eee," Luck called out. He strung out the last word so long it got lost in the wind and blew away.

I guessed it was time for me to slip on my jeans and slap on my shoes, and get on out into the kitchen. By the time Jesse and them came through the door I had got out the skillet, and was fixing up some grits, with a side dish of greens. The Lesses settled themselves around the table, and Jesse slipped over and fiddled with the radio. They kept up their chatter. Reck was saying how he had got himself a new notebook for the occasion of hearing Zogg in the flesh.

"You finished up with the Conductor?" I asked.

"He's just an old man that goes roaming the streets," Reck said. "Now that Zogg, he's been somewhere, and done something."

"I expect he's planning getting a few things more done," I said.

"I saw the fella this very morning," Reck went on. "Stepping out of his van. It's got all silver sides, and his chair inside of it fit for display."

"That ain't the chair I am hankering to see," Jesse said.

"I want to see Santa," Luck said. "I got in mind a few things I need to tell him."

"You ain't been good enough to ask him for nothing," Mirth said.

Luck turned and stuck his jaw out like he was about to

talk back, but Reck went on like nobody'd said a thing. "Now, some paper down south's been calling Zogg the angel of death, on account of how speedy he goes about his business, and merciful. Then it goes on to squawk about how that angel done passed over their little town without making a single stop."

I busied myself stirring the pot. Jesse was twiddling the radio dials, and Luck slipped off his chair to join him.

"What you looking for?" Luck asked.

"Won't know till I find it," Jesse said.

He kept fiddling with the dials, with Luck by his elbow watching, and Reck went on about what he'd found out about reading papers from all over, as far away as Chicago city; hey, what state is that in, Reck? Jesse was asking, to be clever - when the radio gave a loud crackling sound, like it was struck by lightning from within,. Then it went *phht*. For a solid second, a flame rose from it into the still gray air.

"Watch out," Jesse cried. He stuck his arms out and pushed Luck to the floor. Luck sat there and looked around as if being dazed would require more focus than he could muster.

"That radio has sure talked back," Reck said. "Like that streetlight - it -" Then he shut up quick. Maybe he thought nobody would believe him, or it ran contrary to the thrust and inclination of his researches. He looked a little white around the mouth. "You okay, Luck?" he said finally.

Luck stood up and said he was.

Smoke hung lazily in the air above the radio set. We set down at the table, and the smoke drifted away.

"I'll get us another radio, boy," I said. "Don't you worry." Jesse nodded, solemn and white-faced. Over in the town square, I knew an angel of death was setting up shop. But I feared not, for sure as the dead would rise, the power and light would abide, and the voice of the righteous be heard at last. The Lesses and Jesse started to eat, and chattered amongst themselves.

In a space in back of my eyes, the streetlight Jesse had just stood under was still shining, and my mind was drawn back to the first occasion I saw such luminance. I reckon you have heard about me at the last supper, where my brother flat-out up and told us twelve that one of us would betray him. The eleven were chattering over their platefuls, looking around the table and wondering who it would be. I leaned upon his bosom, the disciple whom Jesus loved; and I rallied, took my turn, and asked him, is it me?

"And I expect a red bicycle goes faster than a blue one anyhow," Mirth said.

Reck snorted.

"You said it," Jesse said.

But I hadn't said it. I had asked it. Then he broke bread, and gave it to me first. That's how he marked me out.

Jesse asked for somebody to pass the plate of greens down our end of the table, but Reck was holding forth on the ways the Egyptians preserved their mummies, and took his time passing the plate along, and passed it in front of me first, and I didn't make a move, till Jesse said, Jud, hurry up.

Be quick about it, he told me. And that's when I knew I had been set up. Other folks had got a chance to go and sin no more; and Peter got three chances and more. But he had said what he had said. There was no way out, not just for him, which everybody knows about, but for me. He couldn't be resurrected until he was crucified, and couldn't be crucified until he was betrayed, and I was the only one he could trust to do the dirty work. No matter what I did from that moment at dinner, I betrayed him: by handing him over, or by not handing him over. That night, it weren't JC who took on himself the sins of the world. It was Judas.

"Jud, you hear a word I been saying?" Reck said.

"He's got things on his mind," Jesse said. "Practicing his lines."

"Yep," I said, "I been through them more times then I care to say, but I got to go through them again."

Reck started talking about some fellow who'd been buried alive for ten days up in Canada. That sure is a big city, huh? Jesse said, and Reck reached across the bowl of grits to swat him, and kept on talking the whole time.

Them eleven were all jabbering away when I went out. Darkness had fallen. I walked farther and farther down the narrow streets. The sky was black and the road was white. I heard singing from the distance, then all was silent. In windows on high, I saw people sitting together to eat. Far below, I walked alone. I was cold, but when I put my hands to my face I found it was bathed with sweat. I felt like every opposite in the world was out at play that night, and switching over, inside me and without, till the road went black and the sky turned white, and it was morning.

He was giving me my own transfiguration. The jealous was being pulled right out of me, wrenched from my bones and wrung out of my blood. It had been buried there so deep I had almost forgotten about it, but I guess JC hadn't. I could feel JC cleansing me even if he killed me doing it. By the end of the night, my face gleamed like the morning sky; weakly, like a convalescent recuperating. And then I was standing by the gates of the garden. I kissed him, but it weren't to betray him. It was to forgive him.

The sky went low and stayed dark straight through the middle of the day. When the sun should have been its highest and the shadows fallen their longest, there were no shadows. The light never changed through all those hours. The sky stretched out almost purple, and there was no horizon between it and the dark, still sea.

After a while, I climbed to the top of the tree. I felt like I could see the whole world from there. In the stillness, my brother cried out, and what he was saying felt like he ripped out of my own throat. He weren't just some god almighty type either. He was my brother, even if he tried to make the whole damn world his brother instead, and cast me out, alone, forever. When I heard his cry that day, I saw the words rise in black letters. They formed a string across the sky where the sun should have been blazing like the eye of God but wasn't. I had thought ahead, and brought along a good length of rope.

Jesse was shaking my elbow. "Jud? That string of lights you got for Bean's tree, where you been keeping it?"

"Stashed it behind the shop counter," I said.

It's a good long length, Jesse told the Lesses; and Jud got it shaped into a star for the tree's tip-top.

Jesse had out his file of foolscap. He carried it folded up in his hands so he could see it was with him the whole time. And I walked behind him, and my shadow was cast over him pretty near the whole way.

CHAPTER FORTY-ONE

I was sitting in the courtroom, microphone in front of me, waiting for Zogg to arrive. They'd had some trouble setting the equipment up. Charlie Rowen had forgotten a cable wire, or else one was broke and in any case, Bean had to give him a key to the hardware shop to fetch a new one; it was that, or miss several minutes of an audience with Zogg. When Charlie ambled by me, I slipped a word in his ear, to fetch that string of lights for the tree while he was at it, and he said okay. The desk was set facing towards the street, and there was a clock set above the doorjamb. The Christmas bells fixed to the door chimed as he went out. Jesse and the Lesses ran around the corner to the front hall, and I couldn't see them but every now and then.

Yellow was hovering under the clock. His gaze was flat and steady. There was a bunch of kids racing around him, waving sheets of music over their heads. A teacherish-looking lady was standing there, under the swooping, shadowy authority of the state flag. She frowned, and collared any kid that came within collaring distance, then called out to them at large to settle down, please, children, a courtroom is not a playroom. The kids was in the school choir, and they was slated to sing in a spot after Bean's.

They were running around Yellow like butterflies flitting around an abandoned icebox. Yellow stood up straighter and taller, like if they jostled him, some of him would go spilling out. One boy had a high pitched whine that had got stuck in his nose. He was a nephew of some variety of Mrs. Greenfield's, and he had a stick-on red bow tie like a prize teddy bear's at a carnival, and a cowlick that had been slicked down but kept popping back up. He run his hands down over the back of his head, his hands got greased up, so he wiped them one by one on the nearest shirt, his own, then he went back to staring open-mouthed at the sheet of music he held out, in front of his nose. A little girl with white knee socks that kept falling down followed the boy around and bleated after him, I kin carry your music for you, when we go to see the santa, I kin carry it for you, I kin.

Can't! he shouted once, and tore off down the hallway.

Then I saw E. He was in a corner by himself. He had that shiny little guitar we'd got him. It looked like it'd been glued together out of wood as thin as the soles on a cheap pair of shoes. He had it slung across his back. He stood there, dignified, oblivious, and ridiculous. The kids running around him commenced to thump on his guitar as they went by, so E tried turning his back to the wall, but a ledge got in the way, and the guitar scraped against it.

"Why'd you bring that thing with you anyhow?" the teacher lady said. She forsook the protection of the flag, and stood herself between him and a bunch of kids waiting there, a forest of hands sticking up, ready to strike. She pelted most of the waiting palms out the way.

E shrugged. I was glad to see he liked the toy so much, I guess, but of course, I was thinking mostly about Jesse. My stomach was jumpy as a green frog inside of me, and I was so preoccupied and nerved-up with what Jesse and me was about to commence that I weren't real attentive as to what was happening beside me. Only when I looked up, did I notice Zogg had slipped in beside me. His mouth

301

made a small dark smirk like a blackberry in a panful of milk, and his eyes was so black they looked almost unnatural, like they was something tattooed in place.

"You know what they say," Zogg said, by way of greeting.

"What's that?" I said. I fiddled with the microphone so as not to look at him.

" 'Young'uns is our future.' " The words came out of him sing-song and arsenic-coated, and just mouthing the vicious sentimentality put a glitter in his eye. "In which case," he went on, "I am glad to be more'an halfway home myself - of course, I ain't referring to your boy. Not many as special as that one." He jerked his chin towards the far end of the room. Jesse had backed himself into our line of vision. He looked my way a second, then he ran straight out of sight again.

I could hear Bean midway down the room. He was ferreting out details about some deal somebody had wrangled on an order of remaindered house paints. He caught Zogg's eye and grinned.

"Mind you watch your time proper, boy," Bean called out to me.

"Dr. Zogg's got another engagement lined up. He's what they call a fella in demand." Bean winked at him, and Zogg snorted, in modesty or Bean-mocking it was hard to say. Then somebody by Bean's shoulder was asking if them house paints had a bulk order discount on top, and Bean swiveled his nose around to catch the answer.

"All these here kids," Zogg said. "Jabbering about going to see Santa Claus." He smirked. "When we both know that seeing their Lord'd do 'em more good, wouldn't it, Jud."

He was looking into the side of my face. I looked forward into the depth of the room, and said nothing.

"And my own set-up'd teach them a sight more," he went on.

I could feel his eyes still upon me, watching, merry as

ever. I turned to face him. "Eyes quick and black as a robin's," I said.

He looked at me. "You know what kind of eyes you got?" he said.

"What kind?"

"Silvery-green, Jud. You got eyes the color of money." He smiled. "Whichever way it comes, in greenback, or in silver coin. Either kind can pay my wages." He smiled, as if at some secret joke of his own. He looked down straight ahead of him, into the room full of people.

Charlie Rowen was coming up through the doorway. His head was yellow and round and slicked, and faintly luminous, like a lemon pie left out in the rain. He had the rope of lights lassoed over his shoulder, and the points of the star kept folks at a distance. The bells on the door jingled after him. On the threshold, he paused a moment, lowered his head and went up to Bean. He said something in Bean's ear, at which point Bean's brow lowered and his lips went tight. He said something, close as the star's points would let him, right into Rowen's face, and waved him away.

"Two minutes, folks," Charlie Rowen said.

Soon as he said that, Jesse poked his head around the corner and looked at me. I beckoned for him to come over. The Lesses straggled along with Jesse a little ways, but then they hung back and lurked, a little knot of maladjusted brotherly flesh, beneath the state flag. Then Jesse was standing right beside me, and I turned in my chair away from Zogg to face him. Zogg winked at him.

Now don't be nervous, son, I told him; it's as easy as my talking to you right here.

"I know," he said, "I ain't a bit nervous." He did look a little white around the mouth. He took out the script he'd written for himself, and flattened it out in front of him. I could make out two main headings. His printing was scrawling and oversized, and he'd used a purple crayon.

Why Denny Colt is a Christmas hero but Halloween is better and then, farther down, *Fruit cakes is okay, and how to make it.*

"What you got there is good," I said, "I can see that. But now I got something for you that is a whole lot better."

Jesse looked at me.

"I've got here the kind of pronouncement you need to be heard saying," I said, "because then folks will begin to know who you are."

"Oh, they'll know as soon as I tell them. I got that up top, see, My name -"

I tried smiling, but Jesse weren't buying. "What I mean is," I said, "that they begin to get a sense of how special you are. When I was child I spake as a child, but when I was a man, I put childish things away. And I am giving you a chance to do that right now."

"But I am a child," Jesse howled. "And if I can't say what I done myself, like you said I could, then I ain't doing it at all."

I had him by the elbow. I didn't want folks to hear the commotion and start looking our way, so I kept my voice down. My grip tightened. "Now Jesse," I said real low, "you can maybe read that Denny stuff some other time, but this go around, it's Christmas, it's Mr. Bean's show, and you got to read what I got here."

"You promised," he said. He kept saying it, like a cry, and that cry seemed to bounce all over the room, hard and high as a wonder ball flung against the wall. "You promised, you promised, you -"

"One minute," Charlie said.

"You promised -"

"And you did, too," Reck said. He turned and faced me square. "That boy's been talking all about what he was writing up, and how you said he could tell any kind of story he wanted, till time comes I couldn't hardly stand to listen to him no more."

"You promised -"

"Son, now listen, I never actually -"

Reck snickered. "Just proves that this here radio show ain't only for goobers," he said, "it's for folks what don't keep their word as well." He shoved off from the wall he'd been leaning against, and hunched up his shoulders.

"Hey Reck, don't you want to hear Mr. Zogg?" Mirth said.

"I already heard him," Reck said, "on a national-wide kind of show, and right now, I got better things to do." His head didn't budge as his eyes shifted from Mirth to me to finally Jesse. "You coming with us or ain't you?"

Jesse looked at me, and I seen that look on somebody's face but once before, when I upped and kissed him and they laid their hands upon him and took him away. Jesse would have broke free of me, except he didn't need to because I had already dropped my grip upon him. He gave me a look of unforgettable reproach. I cast my eyes down, for determined to fulfil the Word, I had again betrayed it.

"Let's go," Reck said, from his place by the wall.

Jesse turned his back on me, and soon as he did, I was making a prayer of atonement, short as a vow, and as resolute. I held out my hands to reach for him, but he was a step too far. I turned to follow his progress, and E, leaning against a patch of wall, swung into my field of vision.

"Jesse," I called out, "I'm sor -"

At the sound of the name, E's head bobbed up. I saw him in the outskirts of my vision. His mouth opened, and he looked astonished, and momentarily out of kilter, as if he'd just been dunked into the waters of the Jordan. He stared at us.

"Thirty seconds," Charlie cut in.

They were already crowding towards the door, the Lesses and Jesse, Reck out in front and the younger ones hopelessly in each other's way. Jesse dropped back and headed out last of all. As he slipped out, the bell on the door rattled. I wanted to chase after Jesse straightaway and make it right with him, but of course I couldn't. I was tied to the power and the light, and charged with a broadcast of radio.

I saw on the clock it was drawing up towards noon. It hit me with a cold panic that I'd have to be more or less talking for the next fifteen minutes. I saw the time before me as a blank space upon the clock face, and it was a span that bizarrely widened with every second its start-point drew closer. Then Bean stepped out into the middle of the room, and his head blocked my view of the clock for a moment.

"Fifteen seconds," Charlie said.

By then, I could see the hand ticking round and the space between it and the next one getting smaller and tighter, and I faced the encroaching reality that when Zogg got up and left, I'd be left with a terrifying silence with nothing proper to fill it. A dread crept over me, quick as a fever, and attendant with my shame; for the measure of what I was to do became clear to me, and I was dazzled near sick to my stomach with the thought of my wavering voice raveling its way to a multitude of unseen folks. I rolled my eyes to get them away from the sight of the clock; and just then my eyes fell upon E. He was looking over the radio equipment like it was a counter full of candy bars, and he was taking his time. He registered modest calm, and did not say a word.

I dipped my head in his direction, then I reached out and clutched him by the elbow. I pulled him towards me, so close that I was speaking right into his ear. "Want to sing on the radio?" I said, real low. It was his eyes that gave assent. "Then wait on me, boy," I went on, "I may have need of you."

E looked at me, and he nodded. He retreated just out of my field of vision.

Charlie gave me the signal, and as required of me, I started talking, though my mouth was dry and I was plenty preoccupied. Then Zogg started talking, right after I finished what I was saying, and it went the way a conversation is supposed to. Or I guess it did, because to tell you the truth I don't remember hearing his voice or mine; what I remember is seeing his teeth bared, at one point, for a grin. The whole time, I was eating my heart up with guilt on account of I'd done wrong by the boy. I would tell him so, and I pictured me telling him, and hanging my head down, contrite, and he would forgive me, with a kiss. For even with his childish fancies and unlikely notions, Jesse had surely been about his father's business, making ready to launch his voice upon the airwaves; and all such voices dealt with breath and inspiration, were linked to the power and the light, and so were pure.

Zogg was rounding off a funny little story it looked like. His mouth made a smile just a little wider than a paper cut. He glanced at the clock, took its measure, and I did the same. Zogg went on yakking until he wound up his part of thing straight on the dot, amateurish and homespun to the last, as only a true professional knows how to be.

Bean was already waiting on him, grinning and bobbing and telling him by gestures how fine he'd done. Zogg said, loud and plain, because he didn't care if his stray voice did get picked up: well, I'd say fifty percent of the show belongs to this fella here beside me. Bean gave me a short nod, acknowledging my existence, as had been just bestowed upon me by Zogg. Then he favored Zogg with a smile like they'd been in cahoots their whole lives long. Zogg got up, and they was making their way through the crowded room. By then, I was already launched into reading Bean's sales pitch.

Bean, Bean, from cradle to grave
and all your housing needs, in between,
it's just got to be Mr. Orville Bean.

I had some trouble with the rhythm, and the jingle aspect hardly registered the way I got through it, but Bean didn't notice none. He was too busy chattering away to

Zogg. The bells on the door jangled, and Zogg and Bean went out. Just as I was coming up to the end, I heard the engine of Bean's Ford car start up, and drive off. I looked over to my left.

E was waiting there aside me. He took one step forward from the shadows. I nodded to him.

"Folks," I said, "Looks like I uh got a few minutes extry. I'm going turn it over to a young fella here, he's gonna do some singing for you I think you'll like. His name is Elvis Presley."

E was already stood in front of the mike that'd been set up for the chorus singers. I divested myself of the mechanics of the power and the light, and rose up, and made my way through the crowded room. It was warm with the sweat and breath of the crowd. Every noseful I took in was full of the smell of folks, their clothes, their breath, their colognes and whatnot; and just to inhale proper was a struggle.

At first, there was only the sound of the toy guitar. It offered up notes, one by one, most of them pinkly and flat and misplaced, and all of them tentative and sad, like the parts of something broken laid out on a cloth. Then the boy started singing. It was more a crooning, a voice getting a sense of its own color and shape and breadth. It was weak and thin and sounded like it was ready to crack and give out in more than one place, and weren't going to make it all. But it kept on going, all the while I made for the door. Yellow was standing there, motionless as wood. He was watching the show, and gave me no notice. The bells on the door rattled after me.

I lit out onto the main road, and the gravel crunched under my heels. The air was gloriously cold and empty, and I breathed in deep of it. I could feel it surge through my lungs. It was like to cleanse my sorrow, and feed my pity; and both were like a flame within me, that kept me pure and righteous.

I passed by a house that was innocent of paint but had

a stretch of tinsel across its weatherworn front rail; and all the while I was taking in the sound of that boy singing, as clear as if I was still inside the courthouse. The radio broadcast had declined to forsake my ears; and I could not mark my progress from the courthouse by the failing of the sound, for the sound failed not. Then it became clear to me, what folks in town weren't at the courthouse had their radios tuned into it. No matter how far I wandered down those streets, hunting down my boy and bound to make my peace with him, I would hear, if I chose to listen, the sound of the power and light in the valley and its environs.

*   *   *

Reck was to tell me of his wanderings that day; and his account has melded with my own recollection, and, as I have relived the day so many times in the years that followed, the two have merged as seamlessly as rain into the sea. When they'd gone trooping out of the courthouse, Reck weren't exactly sure where they were going. He stood on a patch of brown grass just beyond the courthouse steps, and rubbed his neck a moment, to help him think. Luck trundled off in one direction, not even looking back, and Reck hollered at him to stop right there, they weren't going that way at all. He led them forward, and they turned the corner by the hairdresser's shop. Mirth looked up into the window, and saw a placard balanced against it. He read it aloud: "Set and Wave." Then he waved, and was on point of doing the set part right out on the sidewalk, when Reck dragged him upwards by one arm, like a dead chicken by its drumstick, and said, I don't want no frozen butt hanging off of you that I got to take care of all day long, com'on.

While Reck still weren't clear where he was headed exactly, he was clear where he weren't. The line at Koehner's for Santa'll be around the block by now, he told them, though he knew even as he said it, it weren't true. Jesse stayed by his side, nodded, and said nothing. They kept walking straight down the road, past a couple of houses, then the butcher shop, Luck trailing behind and whining, but I want to see Santa, Reck, you promised. Reck told him they'd get to it later, when the crowd thinned out, the tail end of the afternoon most like.

Above them, a sign was posted on a shop roof, at a precarious angle. The placard was unwieldy and flapped in the wind, like a shirt collar several sizes too big:

Power and Light in the Valley

and slashed across that, in a thrilling insinuation:

> *World's First Town Xmas Tree Lighting*
> *Tupelo Park*
> *Brought to you by the TVA*
> *- and BEAN'S Hardware!*

Reck kept looking up at the sign, and he said it just weren't right that old man Bean got put in charge of the tree lighting. Luck stuck out his chin and said he was going to see it anyhow. He was still fussing about that a few yards on; and that's where Mirth confronted his third sign.

This one weren't an official posting. It was hung with a bit of butcher's string around one of the streetlights that never been actually lit, and it was so badly scrawled that Mirth had trouble making out the words. "Church of the Expedi-" there his reading faltered. He tried to sound the word out but it was too long, and even Reck, when he went nose to nose with the sign, said that word reminded him of a creepy crawly insect with too many legs awavering - and so Mirth went on to the next word, which he knew how to say - "Death." There was a short arrow scrawled under the words, pointing to the left. Reck weren't sure where it would lead, but he felt somehow the sign marked out a subject fit for his researches. He followed the sign's directive literally, as it seemed to call for, and walked straight through an overgrown hedge of forsythia. And when he emerged, he was nose to metal with the side of Zogg's van. "Whoah," he said, and gave a short sharp whistle at his own good fortune. "Looky here."

So then Jesse and Luck passed through the hedge, hand in hand like kids jumping into a swimming hole. The van glinted silver in the winter light. The back door of it was a few inches ajar, and a fat wire snaked out of it. The door was banging against it now and then in the wind.

By that time, I reckon I was nearing the hairdresser's, where I rounded the corner, same as the boys had done. And some ways down, behind the hedgeful of brambles, Reck would have been just approaching the back of the van. I picture him progressing in that moment with the stealth of one graced by awe. Mirth let out a whoop and ran towards the door, but Reck caught him around the waist, held him dangling above the ground a few seconds, spun him around and set him down facing the other direction. So it was Reck who stepped up first. The inside was dark, and when his eyes saw clear again from the circles of light that swam before them, he was directly facing the chair.

It had a seat wide enough for two folks next to each other, and a back near as tall as a grandfather clock. Reck said it took his breath away. It was like folks tried to tell him being in church would be but never was; and he felt he was in the presence of something great, and fearsome, that he couldn't figure out. It was gross and majestic, and the only thing that had near ever made him feel that way, Reck told me after, was the time he came across a possum dead on the forest floor, and slit it open, and found it was a she with seven babies, bloody and blue and velvety, stowed away dead inside of her.

He was standing stood in the van, and the hush of the

place fell upon him heavy as a shadow, and he declined to move, lest he disturb it. But Mirth and Jesse and Luck all clambered aboard, and they made a racket. Reck turned and told them not to touch a damn thing.

Mirth spied a sign wedged up against one wall, and read it out loud:

THIS WAY TO THE FRY UP

What's he frying? Luck asked. He cooking like Jud and you get up to?

Ain't that kind of fry up, Jesse said. He looked pale, Reck said, and his face glowed blue-white.

By then, I was proceeding down the side street. The wind was against me, across me, beside me. I felt my shoulders bear its weight, and they held up square. The street was lined with an overgrown and thorny hedge. The boy's voice was on the radio, wavery like something at a slant, and it was singing.

Little town of Bethlehem how still we see thee lie
Above thy deep and dreamless sleep the silent stars go by
Yet in thy dark streets shineth, the everlasting light

And the town he was singing about was like my first vision of Tupelo, its hard white radiance that illuminated the night. Since ever I landed in the valley, I had felt my wanderings had come to their origin and end point; and in that moment most of all, as I proceeded down that road with the Christmas broadcast resounding in my ears, I knew I had found my bearings. Soon as I found Jesse, and we embraced, my penitence would be at an end. And that town vista that so had struck me weren't but a prefiguring of Jesse himself, all those times I stood and watched him sleeping: for, of course, in him the hopes and fears of all the years did meet. When I caught up to him, I would hold him fast, to fate and to life both; because as soon as you exile yourself from one, you ain't but a fugitive from the other. I knew that much. The wind blew and I gripped my coat a little closer; and I stepped a little more lively, for I wanted sooner to be upon him, to comfort, and be comforted.

Meanwhile, inside the van, the Lesses was gearing up towards a set-to. "When we going to see the Santa," Luck kept asking, "we ain't never seen one in the flesh, and when we going to see the tree?" Luck ran his hand along one arm of the chair.

"I told you not to touch a damn thing," Reck said.

Luck lowered his brow, and said nothing.

"Get away from there," Reck said. He made like he was going to swat him one.

Luck took a step back, and bided his time, as it turned out.

"Where's that wire go?" Mirth asked, and immediately lost interest in the answer. He was sitting down by the fry up sign, and looking at the other ones, old traffic signs and such, that were wedged up in the corner. It was so dark, to make out their lettering, he had to draw his face up close to them. His mouth dropped open as he read them out loud, but softly.

"I expect that there wire goes to the tree," Reck said. He had thought, as soon as he'd heard about it, that it was a crime old Bean was slated to do the honors. Then he thought of something else.

"Bean won't be lighting a damn thing," Reck said. He said them words like they was wild things cooped up inside of him, and he was setting them loose, into the open air. "We'll do the lighting up ourselves." And he gave a whoop.

And his cry came down like a slash across my ears, and across the singing that was going forth upon the air: *Oh morning stars together, proclaim thy holy birth*: for at that moment, I had drawn up alongside the stretch of overgrown hedge. Before I had even turned my head to look proper into it, my eyes had caught sight, up ahead and through the hedge, of a silvery glint, a gleam of light that was fugitive and cold; and it was the kind of dead luminescence I come to associate with Zogg. I stood, and turned, and through the branches and the winter light, my eyes made out his van. I drew myself up in perfect rectitude; and I closed my coat so as to keep it contained for the moment, and directed myself forward.

Inside, Reck was picturing something to himself: Bean's face as the old skinflint arrived for the tree-lighting, his smile false and broad and crafty, and slipping off entirely when he saw the tree was already aglow. Reck went over beside the switch. He reached up and pulled it. He had to pull down on it with all his weight - and he did not see that Luck had defiantly sat himself down in the chair, and was patting all around it, the plates and the clamps, like a blind man getting a sense of a thing.

You mean I got time for another song? Oh! Uh okay -

Reck heard a hum through the van like running water. He said he smiled when he heard it because he was picturing the tree all lit up in the daylight - until the next thing he heard, which was Luck on the chair screaming, and then on the floor, as Jesse had jumped up, and thrown him clear.

I heard that scream, I was near enough alongside the van by then, and, hastening, I passed through the nettlesome hedge. My coat fell open to the wind, and I scrambled up into the open van. The radio sound squawked, and then went dead.

My eyes were just getting used to the murk of the space. I looked down the far end of the van, and stumbled across towards what I saw, and could witness, but not prevent.

Jesse was lying across the chair. He was crumpled up, and still, but for the fluttering of his eyelids. I sunk down beside him. I took his hand in mine. I think I must have called out his name; and when that sound was near finished, the radio kicked back into sound, and E's voice was abroad on the air.

And the voice was like a fall of rain gathering pace and sweeping over the land, and making the sky, the earth, and the water all as one again; and so it was the creation of the world happening in reverse.

Jesse's eyelids fluttered open. The light within his eyes receded, and slowly went out. He was gone.

This time, the song weren't one of Christmas. It belonged to Easter. It was the kind of song that made you stop what you was doing and look off into the horizon; and it made every horizon you faced turn blank and unanswering and coldish blue. And it is the song that has echoed down the corridors of my heart, and oh down these many years.

Were you there when they crucified my Lord?
Were you there when they crucified my Lord?
Oh sometimes it causes me to tremble, tremble, tremble.
Were you there when they crucified my Lord?

Not once but twice, I was. I seen the first and I seen the last.

*   *   *

That night, the Lesses came by my house, or maybe it was the next one. They stalked across the field in back of the house, unseen, and settled down somewhere beside the porch. I heard the stiff grass snap. "You okay, Jud?" Reck called out. "Anything I can get you, sir?" I was sitting in the broken-down rocking chair. The dark had gathered around me, and my heart was numb. No thank you, boy, I said. I rocked back and just as the chair began to creak, Mirth cried out, "I'm sorry!" It was as if the creak of the chair had become in that instant part of his voice. Then he and Reck and Luck started crying in the dark.

I wished I'd done this one thing, I've seen it in a movie since: I lead off singing a line from an old beloved hymn, and they each take up a line in turn, and that's how we would have grieved, tipping our sorrow onto the night air like a boat made of sound that we pieced together ourselves, and launched onto the waves of darkness, and let it disappear under them. But I guess I just weren't up to it. I kept rocking, and they were crying. After a while, they lit off. I heard them move through the dead grass, almost skimming it and barely parting it, like beetles across the surface of still water. In the morning, I found a stack of Denny Colt comic books on the bottom step. The edges was blurry with running ink on account of the morning frost gone melting.

Bean donated the coffin himself. When he was about to present it to me, there in the backroom, he fished a moonpie out of his pocket, broke it in two, and offered me half. It was the one time I remember him openly candy-fying in the shop. He stood, looking out the window a moment, manly and doleful; then he ran his hands along the soft pine, full-sized length of the thing. (A month later, while he was buying a pack of peppermint chewing gum, he let drop to Mr. Greenfield that a child-sized box weren't something anybody could rightly let go for free: they always fetched a premium price on the market.)

He looked me in the eye and told me not to think twice about it, I'd earned that coffin and then some.

"I want you to know that, boy," he said.

I told him I did. My head was hanging down low, and he looked steadily away like he thought I was crying; and then I was.

CHAPTER FORTY-TWO

Yesterday Carwitt, my office neighbor and dedicated insurance professional, installed a new clock on the outside of his office building. When I look out my side window and stretch my neck up high, I can see it pretty well. It stares out from the center of the front, like a big single eye growing out of a yellow forehead. If you listen closely enough, you can hear the sound thicken as the hour approaches, and then on the hour, the clock sounds. It begins with a slight *tsk*, and then moves into a sterner admonition already fading as it is born, sighing like the sound of something being flushed away: *if you waited until you're hearing from me, brother, you are already too late*. It's coming up to twelve. I can see the hands swooping down, and then swooping up, as high as they can go.

I know what some folks'd want to tell me. They'd say I got the whole story wrong, and got it wrong in the first instance by fixating on the wrong brother. That Jesse weren't but the shadow, and his dying proved it; and E was the one God marked out, and his talent and the devotion of the people proved that; and how the white hot heat of his fame came to melt anyone who came near him proved it all over again.

So maybe I got it wrong at that point, or maybe I got it wrong someplace else, some place little and minor and overlooked. Like, if I had kept on the radio myself the whole time when I was doing Bean's radio show, Elvis wouldn't have got his start singing to folks all over. And if I had kept my word to Jesse, about how he could proclaim what he had wrote, the boy wouldn't have fled me, to find his death. More than once I have concluded, as well as a man who wanders the earth without end can ever conclude a thing, that maybe Jesse was ordained to live as a boy, and a man, no different from the common run of men; and that his life weren't no allegory, and the Lesses weren't some figures fallen off a parable into flesh, but his own best buddies, like maybe you used to have yourself; and if I hadn't insisted on things being otherwise, we all of us would have gone on living as what we had become, the closest of all kind of families that there is: a band of outsiders.

But other times, I figure the opposite: that, though I been at this so long, I still couldn't precipitate nor pre-vent a damn thing if I tried; that I am condemned always to post-vent it, amble on up when it's too late but to watch and witness. That you can't force fate any more than you can escape it. You ain't got a thing to do with it, and you may as well try wrestling the wind right out of the sky; for the way of the Lord winds like a mighty river that rolls past all obstacles. That day, E gave his voice over to the world, and Jesse's slipped away forever. The same source, the power and the light, that announced one to the world, had sent the other to his death; and in that moment, unto E was visited the strength of two brothers, and the weakness too. I resent not E, for he weren't hardly to blame for being the instrument that he was - but the god who let me watch the boy I loved die, and witness some other one raised up in the eyes of men. And I got to figure I am the dupe all over again, and you can't wonder why I go through this life with a laugh that has festered so long inside of me it's turned as bitter as bile.

And so, there are times I get in a mood, and I reckon what I got wrong goes a whole lot deeper than just reading signs wrong, or picking the wrong brother: and I figure finally that there are no signs, and there is no fate and there is nothing but what you see right in front of your nose. Jesse was the flip side to a miracle - he was the flip side to the notion of a miracle. John got it wrong and Luke and Mark and all of them, but it don't make me any jubilant like I used to think showing them wrong would. And Carwitt, who thinks he knows it all because his thinking is based on hard numbers and statistics, and don't even realize they are as figurative as allegory, and but a new-fangled form of prophecy, and just because there's a profit attached don't make them more advanced a notion, is wrong too; and he is further wrong because there *is* such things as accidents. Matter of fact, there is only such a thing as accidents. Nothing makes no sense, stories ain't but what we tell, and not what is. Except -

Except, and this is where I feel as if somebody'd kicked me in the stomach, I ask myself, why am I here, still wandering the face of the earth, and telling my story? If it ain't one thing, it's another, Joseph used to say. Only I'd say, it ain't one thing, nor another. I've lived this time to tell my story, and Jesse's. Because Jesse and me, we was both dispossessed from the start, writ out like we never existed, consigned to oblivion, and swallowed up by it. Our brothers became the substance of the stories that men tell, and Jesse and I shadows lost upon, and then within, the page. Well, I have rescued those shadows. I have called us out by name, and given us substance; and that substance is this here story.

Of course, the flip side to my telling is that I never allowed Jesse to tell his own and that's how he got killed. The flip sides of coins, silver and otherwise, are the story of my life, ever since that time, I embraced my brother, and betrayed him. Likewise, when I did as my brother bid me, and I delivered him to death, I condemned myself to unending life on this earth. So if I get too thinking about it too long, seems like my whole life is exploding with coins that are all flipping over, like flapjacks on the griddle. And I am left here flipping the last coin I got.

Though I ain't never sown the wind, truly I have reaped the whirlwind: the wind has carried me across time and given me breath, and speech; and like I say, it was them things I denied to Jesse. And so I do believe that one part of my penance has been to expend my breath telling this story. One way or another, I've been living Jesse's death ever since it happened; and never more so than today, when the voice of his twin brother fills the air, in the season of his own demise, and outlives and outweighs any excesses of his flesh.

So I got to hand it to those Scripture boys after all, because they figured out straight away to tell a story. But I got to say one other thing: it ain't so much as John has it, that in the beginning was the word. It's that, by the end, there ain't much anything else left but.

*   *   *

Carwitt has "gone over." I ran into him in the parking lot this morning and when he told me, at first my stomach tensed up, on account I thought he was talking about finding a new way to God, but that weren't what he meant at all. He pointed to the sign hitched up over his window, and it read: AllState. You know, he says, " 'You are in good hands.' " He demonstrated by shaking his right hand to his left, and hoisting his lips up over his teeth in a grin that strived to be knowing, but gave up, and settled for self-conscious.

I reckon I ought to fix up a sign like Carwitt's outside my own workshop. Because who else do you know with hands that have done what mine can claim: took the money and tied the rope? And held the boy's hand as it went as cold and blue - cold and blue as his face the first time I ever did see him. Who better to hammer and nail your wooden vessel into eternity? I got my own all done up, simple pine, unlined, unvarnished. I store it under the house, in a canvas wrap like a boat out of season.

Sometimes I catch a noseful of bacon frying, and I get reminded me of how Jesse and me used to make supper: and the smell of grease and greens and Jesse waving the Red Rock cookbook under my nose and telling me, "It says 'brown lightly,' Jud, not 'soak in oil.'" And that memory punctures my heart, and I feel it go empty.

After what happened that Christmas, Bean called the county services on the Lesses, mostly on account of getting squizzled on the tree lighting, I am convinced, though he threw the matter of Jesse into the pot in the last instance. A few years on, I skedaddled up to Memphis, and by the next Easter, E in his thirteenth year fled there too, with his folks (*into Egypt I have called my son*). On the whole, a city of the dead seemed the right place to be. The Lesses run away from the county home, and hitched along with me. They stayed about a year before setting out again on their own. I got a postcard a few years back with a lighthouse on it, postmarked Biloxi: it bore a two word message:

Conducting research.

In the years that remained for him, Bean didn't so much mellow as turn waxen, like he was being preserved from the inside out. The year I lit on up to Memphis, they found him dead. He was behind the wheel of his car, at the main intersection of town: a heart attack at a red light. When the lights changed, the man in the car behind, a copper fittings salesman, waited a few minutes, honked and tried to look apologetic-like, as if his elbow'd just glanced the horn by accident. He finally got out of his car, walked up to the window ready to have few words. Then he saw.

A few days after doing Bean's radio show with me that

Christmas, Zogg took Yellow out hunting. He said they were going to shoot themselves the biggest turkey in the state, and roast it up for Christmas dinner. Zogg didn't come back alive. I can picture the whole set-up in my mind: the spotted, yellow woods, the yelping liver-colored hound, the pick-up truck they borrowed from Bean, with its left-side door battered in years before. Somehow, when the two was heading into the country, the truck spun off the gravel road. Both doors was flung open, and Zogg's head struck a tree. Nobody was sure who was driving, Yellow or Zogg, and they never did find out for sure.

Yellow walked away with nary a scratch, same as the hound, but when they asked Yellow what happened, he just tensed up, like he was caught in a cold and sudden private gust of wind, and he couldn't never recall a thing. Bean said to me, one day in the shop that spring, what do you expect from an idiot, he couldn't tell you the truth if he tried. Bean allowed as he felt implicated himself, since it was his truck that had been the vehicle of death. And standing by the open window in that April sunlight, the sawdust piling up in a golden litter at his feet, and outside the lilacs just in bloom, Bean seemed to feel honored by that implication, as though it brought him and Zogg closer in spirit; and he raised his nostrils up, in appreciation of camaraderie, and himself. I got the newspaper clipping of Zogg's death in my wallet. It gave his place of birth: Pontius Pilate, Missouri. I bet Reck's got the clipping too, wherever he may be.

*   *   *

If you are a white man, work a manual trade, skilled, and make it to the age of 45, there is a 89% chance you will live to the age of 72, Carwitt is telling his secretary. Carwitt spins out such statistics like an improvisation in a jazz made up of numbers. I like watching numbers that sit in a circle, and don't move, so as I can keep an eye on them.

Like I been sitting here watching that clock right now as it approaches high noon. The hands of the clock, they move like a man climbing across the desert sands, going in circles and leaving no trace. They reach the top, and then they swoop down like somebody's slipped and his neck done broke. Twelve hours, one for each of us, I guess. Noon, that's my hour of the day. The hands keep climbing up, one over the other, as high as they both can reach, till they're at the very top and they choke the numbers tight. Then the hands sweep down again and start another twelve all over again.

In another minute, I'll be hearing the clock strike, slowly, thickly through the still and blazing air, like a stack of coins falling one by one. That sound smites my ears dully, like a word from some language I knew a long while ago, and don't have much occasion to use, a language with words like "son," or "father," say, or "brother": the sound and not the substance is mine.

I look at the face ringed with numbers again. Carwitt is in the window. He sees me, and smiles with his jagged grin. With great show, like someone play-acting a victorious prizefighter, he raises his arms up over his head, and shakes his left hand with his right. I do not smile. My hands put down the hammer they've been holding, and they move to reciprocate.

AFTERWORD

If you enjoyed this book, you might be interested in *Fly By Night*.

FLY BY NIGHT
BY
E.N. MCMAHON

It's 1930s Hollywood, and Nick de Blegny is a vampire on a mission. This town just doesn't get it. Jean Racine, now he really knew how to tell a story. What the movies need is more Phèdre.

So what if the studios are giving Nick the bum's rush? He has his minion; he has his genius - and exploitation movies are crying out for a creative type who knows how to save a buck or three. Who needs actors, when this burg is chockful of stock footage, just waiting to be snapped up and put to good use?

No - the only good thing about actors is their celebrity - and Nicky D, the man who invented celebrity culture back when he was still warm - knows how to turn a pretty profit: by selling extra-special blood to the more discerning vampires.

Everything's coming up roses - so long as he can stay ahead of gangsters - both warm-blooded and vampiric - and keep from being once again rudely interrupted by the local gendarmes...

Meet Nick de Blegny: self-styled genius; acknowledged father of PR; and the greatest physician, adventurer, huckster, and vampire that 17th-century France ever produced. As he'll be the first to tell you.

ABOUT THE AUTHOR

E N McMahon has a Master's degree from the London School of Economics, and a PhD in French literature from Duke University. She has worked as a reporter, television researcher, bagel maker (briefly), and (even more briefly) in encyclopaedia sales. She divides her time between England and America.